the loving couple
his story

BY THE AUTHOR

Oh, What a Wonderful Wedding

House Party

The Loving Couple

the loving couple

his story

virginia rowans

THOMAS Y. CROWELL COMPANY · NEW YORK

Library of Congress Catalog Card No. 56-10793

Manufactured in the United States of America by the Vail-Ballou Press, Binghamton, New York

THIRD PRINTING, SEPTEMBER 1956

for J. P. M.
another dedicated book
from an undedicated author

All the characters in this book
are fictitious,
and no reference is intended
to any actual person,
living or dead.

the loving couple
his story

one

"All right, damn you," she shouted, "*leave* me! get out, get out, get *out!* Get out and don't come back!" The front door slammed with a force that shook the house. Then there was an eerie quietude like the silence that follows a major explosion. The only sound he could hear was the click of his leather heels on the flagstone walk.

It was a beautiful October morning in Riveredge, cool—but not too cool—and clear with a blue, blue sky. The elms, the maples, the copper beeches were all doing their stuff "Jack Frost's paint brush splashes exclusive Riveredge with all the glorious colors of Autumn's Palette," the real estate brochure had said. "Well, let it splash!" he muttered. "God damned prison of a showplace!"

He reached the road and turned sharply to the left. Too late he remembered that he had left the car keys on his dresser, his hat on the bedroom floor, his topcoat in the closet. "To hell with them all," he said, "I'll walk to the gate and then call a cab. I'd walk to Moscow before I went back to that house and *her*."

"What say, sir?" one of the grounds crew asked, leaning picturesquely on his wooden rake. "Didn't quite hear, sir. Lovely morning, sir."

"I said *good morning!*" he shouted and kicked viciously at the blue gravel on the road, defacing a good square foot of what the brochure called "more than three miles of glorious drives winding through beautifully landscaped terrain to be enjoyed only by members of Riveredge, their families and their guests." Member of Riveredge, eh? At the moment he'd rather be a member of the House of David—much rather. Not only had his wife set him to bleeding figuratively from every pore, but his razor had nicked him seriously in three different places so that he was bleeding literally from what were, thank God, not yet jowls. Never shave when you're shaking with rage.

At the moment he would have liked to have looked back at the house—for the last time, of course—just to see if she were gazing at him from a window. But if he *should* glance over his shoulder, and she *should* be peeping from behind a curtain, then she'd have seen him looking back and that would ruin the whole exit. Even if she tried to call him back—not that she would; that woman was so stubborn she wouldn't have called to him if the house were on fire—he'd march on to the gate and ignore her.

It did seem kind of a shame to leave a forty-thousand-dollar investment—and an investment he'd go on paying for for years—without one last look. But there *were* things that money couldn't buy and pride was one of them. "Forty thousand!" he scoffed. "More like fifty."

Yes, once Alice Marshall, his wife's power-driven sister, and her stuffy husband, Fred, had lured them into buying a piece of Riveredge; once the Membership Committee had interviewed him, bringing everything to the four meetings but thumb-screws and a lie-detector; once he had been checked and double-checked for veracity, gentility and credit, then it was his privilege to live out here with ninety-nine other prime grade, government-inspected, well-heeled young husbands and their wives and their families and their guests.

He still had the agent's brochure to remind him that Riveredge was "no ordinary *housing development*, but a proud and gracious Hudson River Estate, exquisitely converted into an exclusive community of just one hundred distinguished families—ladies and gentlemen of breeding, taste and background whom you would be proud to call your friends." In other words, a snob subdivision where everything cost twice what it should and everybody pretended they could afford it. "Yep, more like fifty thousand smackers," he said. His acre on the river had cost three thousand—"You'd think it had uranium under it instead of the lousy Hudson River," he growled.

The house, a trim little Regency pavilion, had been built by a prospective Riveredge member who had been *almost* successful in concealing from the Membership Committee the unsettling fact that his wife was part Jewish. But they had found out in the nick of time, had had three scenes and two lawsuits and had finally sold the completed house to John at thirty-five thousand—not including kitchen equipment at twenty-five hundred.

Repainting had cost another thousand, moving had run to nearly five hundred. New furniture and old antiques from Mrs. Updike's decorating establishment had come *at cost* through his wife's connections, but *cost* was just under five thousand plus fifteen hundred for carpets plus four hundred for what Mrs. Updike and her sibilant son, Gerald, called "the sheerest conceit of a chandelier, dear." Landscaping had been a thousand and John's own forays into the garden—a pastime which he detested but felt that he *ought* to like to be as one with the men of Riveredge—had been so disastrous that the man from Goldfarb's had to come back to replant two hundred dollars' worth of hardy perennials.

A car was essential in Riveredge, unless you were a cross-country runner. Most of the members had two cars—a big one and a station wagon or a jeep. But if you only had one, it had to be spiffy. His—well, like the house, it was in *her* name—was a mammoth black convertible. And that had cost plenty, although his Christmas bonus would undoubtedly cover it.

And then there were the steady, clipping assessments for the services and improvements that made Riveredge the showplace it was. He had been hit for his share of dressing rooms at the swimming pool; a boost in the life guard's salary—since the lifeguard had been popping corn with Fran Hollister all summer, he didn't know why Fran didn't reimburse him out of her considerable alimony for services above and beyond the call of duty. Then there were hospitalization and pension plans for the staff of men who guarded Riveredge's privacy at the gate and trimmed the hedges and mowed the lawns within; for the private bus that carted husbands to the station and kiddies to the school.

And the last blow had fallen at his sister-in-law's house two weeks ago when, instead of leading her monthly Discussions of Foreign Affairs panel, Alice had rapped for order and launched into her own plans for building a private school for Riveredge children. "It is not fair," Alice had said, "for the less privileged children in the town to have to compete with *our* children. You all know that I am one hundred percent for democracy and the public school system, but a method of education that holds back exceptional children and forces children beyond their . . ."

He had stopped listening right there. He knew his sister-in-law Alice, all right. She had a gift for taking the simplest statement of fact, such as "I want my children in a private school," and twisting it, coloring it, reversing it, filling it with psychiatric terms and liberal sentiments until it sounded like a declaration by Charlotte Corday. You could take a girl out of Santa Barbara, but you couldn't take Santa Barbara out of a girl. Alice was one of the most elaborate and self-effacing snobs John had ever known, and Mary—well, no, there was nothing snobbish about her. That was one thing—and just about the only thing—he could say for her. But the upshot of the whole school plan was that now everybody would be assessed five hundred dollars to turn an old stable into a very progressive and very private school. And John and Mary didn't even have any children.

Of course there might have been a child. It would have been born about now. He wondered aimlessly what the baby would have been—a boy or a girl—and what it would have looked like. The miscarriage had been a horrible, horrible thing. Heavenly Rest, the Mother Immaculate Peace maid, had called him at the office, wailing and blubbering and praying over the telephone. By the time he had got to the hospital it had been too late and there wasn't going to be any baby—at least not that time. "At least not *ever*," he said aloud.

He supposed it was all for the best. A couple splitting up was messy enough—complicated enough—even when there were just two adults unencumbered by children and livestock. No, it was better not to have kids to worry about and fight over. He knew a number of men—three, anyway—who were divorced and spent weekends and holidays with their children. The strain and the competition were terrible. Well, take Jack Hennessey, just down the road: there he was, a big, hearty loudmouth—yes, loudmouth—with a tart for a second wife, being visited every so often by his mousy little girl of twelve with braids and pink-shelled glasses who . . .

John had just come abreast of the Hennessey's house, its solid glass sides opened to let in the cool air, its fieldstone slabs of chimneys belching smoke from the four huge fireplaces. There was a big yellow Cadillac in the drive next to Hennesseys' souped-up red Jaguar—company for the weekend. The red Jaguar was just as typical of Jack and Adele Hennessey as the three stars painted on their front door, as typical as their playroom with its tipsy glasses and dribble glasses and its quarter slot machine and the gin bottle that played "How Dry I Am."

Jack and Adele were older than most of the couples in Riveredge—older and a lot richer. They kept a colored couple and served St. James's Scotch. All their furniture was custom-made and expensive and terrible. They were loud, gregarious, aggressive people, always pressing invitations on you to meet the loud, gregarious, aggressive people whom they had picked up on West Indies cruises, at the Shamrock in Houston, in the club car of the Super Chief. The Hennesseys were incapable of living in quietude. Their house contained four television sets, five radios, two record players and hi-fi piped throughout. The Hennesseys liked popular tunes delivered by Sammy Kaye and Julius la Rosa, for more serious music they leaned toward André Kostelanetz and Liberace—and they liked all of it *loud*.

As he passed the Hennessey house he could hear Arthur Godfrey, a news broadcast, Ravel's "Bolero," "All the Things You Are" and a women's commentator issuing simultaneously. He thought he could get past without being seen. He was wrong. "Howdy, neighbor!" a voice boomed. It was Jack Hennessey. Jack was given to fringed buckskin shirts, to tartan trews, Countess Mara ties and unusual footgear—purchased mostly by his wife, whose taste in men's clothes was a little worse than his own.

Today Jack was wearing a pink shirt with a black shoestring tie, black Bermuda shorts, black tasseled loafers and black and pink and white Argyles to the knee. On a younger, thinner, taller man the outfit would have inspired whistles. On Jack it drew only a stunned silence. His large pumpkin of a stomach, his two muskmelons of a bottom, his thin, slightly bowed legs, his red

Irish face just didn't *go* with so carefully contrived a costume. His wife joined him, wearing an identical get-up plus a pink hair ribbon.

"Hello, sweetie," Adele called, "how's your cute wife?" Terms like sweetie, cutie, honey, and doll came naturally to Adele. She was able to convince some people that she was only thirty-five, a few people that she was actually an ash blonde, and almost no one that she was a lady. Rumors—all of them totally unfounded—had placed Adele in a number of interesting occupations before she became Jack's second wife. She had been variously described as a model, a show girl, a manicurist, a secretary, a call girl and a gangster's mistress. As for Adele herself, she was secretive about her past, which had almost certainly been a checkered one.

Adele said things like "between you and I" and "lonjeray" and "It'ly" generously interspersed with such recently acquired elegancies as "eye-ther" and "to-mah-to" and "*entré nous.*" Well, one who *knew* simply *knew* that Adele didn't *know*. But Adele did know that, with the possible exception of Fran Hollister, she could buy and sell every well-reared young matron in Riveredge. She revelled in the knowledge.

There was considerable speculation as to just how the Hennesseys had been admitted by the Riveredge Membership Committee and there was even more considerable speculation as to what Jack had done for a living before all that Army surplus material came his way. People at Riveredge said—and with some reason—that the Hennesseys were common, pushy and ostentatious. Jack's booming openhandedness was felt to be especially vulgar and the people who owed Jack the most money—payable when convenient and without interest—were the most captious in their muttered criticism.

"Hey! C'mon in an' bend an elbow," Jack roared, flourishing an Orrefors vase filled with milk punch. "We sure hung one on at Ver-sales last night. Boy, what a head!" The Hennesseys' boxers, Scotch and Soda, bounded out, barking ecstatically.

"Yeah, come in, honey," Adele called. "I want you to meet my two favorite people—Dan an' Peggy Slattery." She indicated a small brunette in leopard slacks and a big Irishman with black hair sprouting from his ears, cheeks and nose.

"Pleased to meet you," Mrs. Slattery called. Mr. Slattery shouted something jovial, but he couldn't hear him above the barking of the dogs.

"S-sorry, I can't," he yelled, with a stab at good cheer. "I've got to get to town." If the Hennesseys had to find out about their split-up, they could find out from her. He was damned if he was going to stand in the middle of the road and announce his impending divorce like a train caller. As he disappeared behind a hedge he could hear Adele screaming something about showing the Slatterys their dreamy house—"all Regent."

Although he usually went out of his way to defend the Hennesseys in front of Fred and Alice and the Martins or a bitch like Fran Hollister—the *real* Riveredge people—he privately felt that Jack and Adele were a little cheap and more than a little tiresome. One thing about leaving Riveredge forever, he reflected, was that he'd never have to see the Hennesseys again; never again have to listen to Jack's barroom platitudes such as "first today" and "tee many martoonis"; never again be confronted by Adele's impregnable vulgarity as she described "Car-tee-air's dreamy little store on the Roo dee la Paze" or the "cute old antique voz" which she "purchased on Lye-sess-ter Square." Yes, divorce had its advantages.

There was a blast of a horn and he was nearly run down by a United Parcel truck. "Watch it, stupid," the driver yelled.

"Bastard!" he muttered.

"And good morning to you!" a hearty voice called. He stood face to face with Whitney Martin, flanked by his wife and two children.

If the residents of Riveredge had been put to a vote to select the community's ideal family, they would have unanimously elected Beth and Whitney Martin, their children Peter and Deborah, and the soon-to-be-born littlest Martin who, no matter which sex it happened to be, would be named Goodhue for Beth's family.

Both Beth and Whit came of very good stock. They had gone to excellent schools. While Beth had been coming out, Whit had been very brave in Naval Ordinance. Their wedding had been the first really big social function—for nice people, that is—

after the war and in suitable time little Peter had been born. (The story of the accouchement, with its many mix-ups, the drive through the snow from a weekend party in Bala Cynwyd, Pennsylvania to Doctors' Hospital in New York, was a familiar one in Riveredge, but Beth and Whit told it with such charm and taste—such refreshing spirit of cooperative raconteurism—that people pled to hear it again and again.)

The Martins had progressed appropriately from two rooms on Washington Square to four rooms in Gramercy Park to six rooms above East End Avenue to their present Georgian splendor at Riveredge, concurrent with Whitney's meteoric rise from junior contact man to senior vice-president in Beth's cousin's advertising agency.

And Whitney, although in advertising, was a gentleman and no huckster. Both he and Beth considered his work a mission—that of informing a woefully neglected public of the splendid new products which were appearing on the market solely to brighten their drab lives. Whitney took his calling seriously and spoke often—and at some length—of the Service which advertising performed.

And Beth took her career as a wife and mother seriously, too. In her efficient, ladylike way she endeavored to indoctrinate her children with the True Values, to bring warm, cultivated conversation and continental cooking—somewhat modified—to her heirloom Sheraton dining table, to keep abreast of current events and to read *The 100 Great Books*.

Together the Martins operated as a powerful force for culture and a better way of life. Whitney was on every committee in Riveredge, except the Mothers' Child Development Group (and Beth was co-chairman of that with Alice Marshall).

Together the Martins went all out for liberal Republicanism, subscription dances, the United Nations, free enterprise, the recognition of both Fascist Spain *and* Communist China, natural sports, private schools but not *snob* schools, casual clothes, European travel, exchange students, psychoanalysis, foreign films and the preservation of wild life.

Together they deplored reactionaries, Hollywood and Miami, bright colors, communism *and* fascism, juke boxes, slums, child labor, strong labor unions, vulgarity, social climbers, snobs, comic books, tabloids, the *Reader's Digest*, *Life* and the Book-of-the-Month Club—although they solemnly agreed that anything that instilled the reading habit among those less fortunately endowed couldn't be *entirely* bad. You could hardly wonder that everybody loved the Martins.

"Well, you're out bright and early," Whitney said, his tortoise shell glasses and splendid white teeth sparkling in the sunlight. Whitney's statement, while cordial, also managed to convey surprise, criticism and hope for reform. Both the Martins and the Marshalls had always felt—and said as much—that he and his wife did not enter enough into the abundant life which Riveredge provided. They had never, the Martins and the Marshalls thought, taken full advantage of the glories of the countryside, the Autumn colors, gardening, the Discussions of Foreign Affairs, the Sherry-and-Good-Conversation Parties so readily available to people who cared.

"I—I've got to go into town. I—there's some work I have to do." John felt himself blushing.

"Not coming over to watch the Notre Dame–Navy game this afternoon?" Whitney persisted. Although the Martins disapproved of television, they did turn it on to witness world events, major sporting attractions, discussion panels and Shakespeare. Most of the time, however, their set sat dark and deep within the bowels of their Sheraton breakfront while its neighboring high fidelity apparatus boomed Bach's Brandenburg Concerti much too loudly for cultivated conversation or comfort.

"Afraid I can't," he said, "you see, there's this work I have to . . ."

"You haven't forgotten that this is the Marshalls' anniversary?" Beth Martin said, drawing the good polo coat over her maternity blue jeans. The Martins made a big thing of blue jeans. They almost always wore them at Riveredge and said exhibitionistically that they cost less than two dollars, although Whit's socks cost ten dollars a pair.

"Oh, no indeed not," he said, blushing again. Indeed he had quite forgotten. He'd never even cared whether the Marshalls were married or not.

"Then, of course we'll be seeing you tonight." Beth made the statement in her usual quiet, assured ladylike way. All of her statements were delivered as he imagined the young Queen Victoria's pronouncements had been delivered. They put your back up.

"Uh—well, I—that is, if I finish this . . ."

"Daddy, what's that bird?" Deborah cried, showing a glittering mouthful of straightening bands.

"Debby, dear, don't interrupt," Beth said with the calm air of firm but affectionate chastisement advised by her child psychologist.

Whitney, however, was ardent about birds. "Why, Debby darling, surely you recognize that old friend. What bird is it that goes pee-weet, pee-weet? Now you . . ."

"Whit, dear," Beth said a bit grimly, "I wish that when I'm trying to teach the children common courtesy, you wouldn't undermine . . ."

"Well, so long," he said and almost ran from the Martins.

He hurried on, grateful to be alone, anxious to be away. This fatuous encounter with the fatuous Martins would be just the first of a long, long series of embarrassing meetings—meetings with people he even *cared* about. At first they would ask genially after his wife, then they would be shocked to hear that the two of them had split up. The news would get around quickly—"Have you heard . . . Can you imagine . . . Of all the people in the world to have a thing like this happen . . . Why, they were always called the Loving Couple . . . If you can't believe in a marriage like that, what *can* you believe in?" Then there would be even more embarrassing meetings; meetings when any mention of Mary would be as elaborately avoided as the mention of a social disease. People would undoubtedly take sides. There would also be a series of dinner invitations for him to meet a series of unattached females each described by his hostess as "a perfectly grand girl."

Hurrying along the gravel drive, he thought of the few times in more than five years of marriage when he had yearned briefly to be a bachelor once again; like the time he met that Italian actress at one of Lisa Randall's cocktail parties or when two men he knew at the Bacchus Club asked him to chuck everything and spend a year sailing around the world on a big sloop. Now that he was, for all intents and purposes, a bachelor once again, he felt that he never *had* been single.

Aloud, he totalled up his assets: "White, American, male. Thirty-three years old. Five feet, eleven and a half inches—practically six feet. Tonsils out, appendix in. College graduate, honorable discharge from the Army. Full head of hair, high arches, sound teeth, 20–20 vision. Said to be quite good looking. Gainfully employed as advertising manager of a major watch company. Salary in five figures. Christ, I'm practically a catch." He supposed he ought to do something fairly drastic to celebrate the severance of his marriage—set off on a binge, go to a whore house, seduce his secretary, get tattooed—but somehow he didn't feel like much of anything but escape.

A Buick station wagon filled with children passed him with a maximum of honking and waving. The Kennedys, he believed—distant cousins or close friends of the Martins. Since most of the people in Riveredge looked exactly alike to him, he could never quite be certain.

He thrust his hand into the jacket pocket of his good English suit and immediately withdrew it with a howl of pain. His hand had been badly cut and severely burned just three hours ago. That, in fact, had set off their quarrel—quarrel, hell; *World War III!*

One of those damned birds indigenous to Riveredge had awakened him on the tick of seven. He'd got out of bed with a God awful headache and a hangover. (It seemed to him, that they drank more out in the pure open spaces than they had in New York. At least the liquor bills and hangovers were about double.) He had felt just like hell but, seeing her still sound asleep in the big double bed, he had been ostentatiously considerate about not making any noise. He had put on his robe and slippers with the softest whisper of silk. He had tiptoed cautiously into the bathroom and had engineered the opening and closing of the medicine chest, the brushing of teeth and flushing of the toilet with an almost inhuman silence. He had even tried to still the Alka-Seltzer as it hissed and bubbled in his tremulous hand. All that for *her!*

And through it all he had looked forward to just one thing—that first cup of black coffee. Heavenly Rest was an indifferent maid, a negligent cleaner, an inventive transmitter of telephone messages, an abominable cook and a religious fanatic. But one thing Heavenly Rest *could* do was brew ambrosial coffee. Quivering with anticipation, he had crept unsteadily down the Regency staircase to Heavenly Rest and her strong black coffee. The house was silent.

The sun, pouring into the formal, white living room was blinding. The shafts of light darting from the mirrors, the crystal vases, the pendants and spikes of the Regency chandelier had assaulted his eyeballs mercilessly. Blindly, he had groped his way into the dim little den. Nothing had been touched there since late last night. The room had reeked acridly of snubbed out cigarettes. The ashtrays had been full to overflowing. Two glasses, gummy with fingerprints, and an empty Scotch bottle had borne testimony to a depressing evening in front of the television set.

Yes, last night he had watched *Pulse Beat*, the prestige show for which he was solely responsible. And it had been a perfect little stinker. The orchestra had flatted. The leading man not only blew his lines twice, but his fly had remained wide open after his quick change in the last scene. The star, an untalented grue from Hollywood, had appeared to be under the influence of either drugs or alcohol—possibly both. The commercials had been unendurable. And the show had run thirty seconds overtime—a cardinal sin considering that *Pulse Beat* was sponsored by one of the world's leading clockmakers. The whole show had looked more like an Elks' Frolic than a prestige program with a weekly budget of fifty G's.

The only thing on the whole show that hadn't been downright third rate had been the president's wife's daughter, a torrid brunette from Bennington whose name really *was* Besame Bessamer. Miss Bessamer had been shot onto the program through the family entrance and almost over his dead body. But her performance, while not likely to win a Peabody Award, had at least been adequate, unlike the rest of the show.

Well, he'd been so depressed by *Pulse Beat,* that he'd simply sat morosely in front of the set drinking and drinking until after the Late Late Show. All the other programs had stunk, too, but none as highly as his.

Looking around the den that morning he had shuddered. Glasses, ashes, his silver tennis cups tarnished. Heavenly Rest was slatternly beyond belief. Right after he had had some coffee, he'd speak to her about it. But the dining room had been empty and so had the kitchen. Then it had dawned on him that Heavenly Rest had been given the weekend off to attend a big Mother Immaculate Peace outing.

Grimly he had set about making his own coffee.

When they had lived in New York they had been the happy owners of a plain granite coffee pot retailing at forty cents, and producing eight cups of perfect coffee per time. Even a child could work it.

But in Riveredge no such pot remained. It had been replaced by a complex structure made up of electric hot plates, glowing coils, pyrex hour glasses, filter papers and pull-chains. There was a kind of instrument panel involving electric switches, two regulators, a red light, a yellow light, a green light, an automatic timer and a warning bell. He had had the feeling that postgraduate work at M.I.T. was essential before even turning on such a contraption. He had very little mechanical aptitude and even less confidence. Still, he was barely human without his morning coffee.

Gamely he had plugged in the infernal machine, poured water and coffee into the places he felt they should go and stood back to watch. There had been a humming and whirring. The green light had flashed. A bell had tinkled. The timer had begun clicking. He had stood back to admire his handiwork as the electric coil turned from gray to mauve to scarlet. So far so good. Then he had recalled something about a watched pot never boiling and had gone virtuously into the den to tidy up the ruins surrounding the television set.

He hadn't really meant to do quite so thorough a job on the silver trophies, but one brightened cup had led to another. The last cup had just been placed next to its radiant neighbor when he had become conscious of a strong odor. From the kitchen a bell had rung furiously. He had sniffed the air like an old bloodhound, had said "Oh oh," had grabbed up the bottle and glasses and raced out to the kitchen.

And he had arrived just in time. The bell had pealed incessantly. The red light had flashed on, off, on, off—faster and faster. The glass coffee urn had hopped and jumped hysterically on the hot plate. Inside, an insidious brew, the color and consistency of lava, had bubbled and spat furiously.

"Jesus," he had breathed and advanced cautiously toward the mechanism. At just the moment he had reached out a tentative hand to shut off the switch, the whole thing had blown up. Like a porcupine, it had shot shafts of glass across the kitchen. A tidal wave of scalding black coffee had burst over him. He had howled with surprise and anger and pain. "Goddamned, son-of-a-*bitch!*" His right arm had shot out to dash the whole contraption to the kitchen floor. He had managed to do that, all right, but not without impaling his hand on a jagged shard of glass.

In a blind fury he had crashed out of the kitchen. Burned and bleeding, he had gone Godding and damning up the stairs to where *Mary*—of all the lazy, good-for-nothing parasites ever born—lay sleeping. *Sleeping,* if you please!

The scalding coffee had seeped through his dressing gown and his pajamas and had begun trickling painfully down his chest, his stomach, his groin and down the insides of his thighs. Good God, he could have been rendered sterile! Blood flowed steadily from his right hand. But the pain was nothing to the wild fury he felt at seeing her there asleep, as soft and tawny as a leopard kitten.

"*What have you done with the coffee pot?*" he had shouted.

"Glmph, gliph?" she had muttered, shaking her tousled curls and burying her head under the pillow.

He had grabbed the pillow and flung it across the room. "*Answer* me! Where's the coffee pot?"

"In kitchen," she had groaned.

"Not that Goddamned cyclotron. *My* coffee pot. The one we had in New York."

"Gave to cleaning woman," she had moaned and pulled the sheet above her head.

"Gave it *away?* That coffee pot was priceless!"

"Oh, don't be stupid," she had gasped.

Well that had *really* set him off. "*Stupid?*" he had howled. "Stupid, hell, if you ever did anything around here except loaf and run up bills, I wouldn't have to be up making coffee!"

She had raised her head and squinted first at the bedside clock and then at him. "Honestly, darling, you're acting like a naughty child and at seven o'clock on a Saturday morning—*really!*"

"Yes, *really!* Cut and scalded and damned near killed by that lousy steam calliope down in the kitchen. Just look at my God-damned hand!" He thrust his bleeding hand out over her, as his blood poured down onto the new satin comforter.

She had stared, horror-stricken. But he had felt that her concern was for the comforter and not for him. "*Good!*" she shouted. "If you don't know how to run a simple gadget that even a half-witted religious fanatic like Heavenly Rest can work, you *deserve* it!" (True, she had never been at *her* best before coffee, either.)

Well, if she'd thought he was going to take *that* lying down, she had another think coming. He had opened up on her rotten-spoiled childhood in Santa Barbara with that nitwit of a mother. *That* had routed her out of the hay. She had got right up and poked a finger painfully into his hot, wet chest. "Just you keep a civil tongue in your head!" she had yelled. "And another thing . . ."

Well, that other thing had led to still *another* thing and *that* had brought to mind two or three further failings. They had aired their grievances loudly and extravagantly. He had been so mad that he ignored the bleeding and the scalding. They had shouted at one another for a full hour before his big opening came. Then she had said something that left her wide open and his reply—oh, but didn't he wish he could remember just how he had phrased it now—had got her right between the eyes. She had been so stunned that she just stood there in her nightgown, her mouth hanging open. Well, he always knew a good exit line. He had marched into the bathroom, locking the door behind him with a click of finality.

There he had peeled off his pajama coat. His whole chest had been red, but he had felt that skin grafting wouldn't be necessary. By now he had developed a sort of controlled fury. He had hung up his pajama coat with elaborate care. Then he had begun lathering his face with the deliberate concentration of a pastry chef decorating a wedding cake.

It had been quiet in the bathroom—an unhealthy silence broken only by the trickle of the hot water into the basin. Then the storm had broken. She had been mustering her forces on the other side of the door and suddenly the barrage began.

I'll just ignore her, he had thought, scrutinizing his soapy face in the mirror. No matter what she says, I won't answer. She had begun raving. He had begun shaving.

He had tried not to listen, to concentrate on his shaving. Let the hurricane blow herself out, he had thought. Conscientiously he had drawn the razor down over his jaw, trying not to hear her words, grimly concentrating on his reflection and the soft, rasping noise of the razor against his beard. It had worked pretty well, for a while, but her epithets had begun coming faster, louder and with a more deadly aim through the locked door.

Then she had said something that really made his blood stop running. He had caught just a glimpse of his face reflected in the mirror—it had gone so white with fury that it matched the lather. He dropped his razor with a clatter and had pulled open the bathroom door with a force that had nearly ripped off its hinges. Towering above her he had bellowed down into her face. He had been so angry that the torrent of words—the gist of which had been "Silence"—tumbled out in one great incoherent roar. The force alone had stunned her into momentary silence. It had stunned him, too. Then he had slammed the door once more and resumed his shaving, but his hand had shaken so that his face and throat were now a mass of nicks. She had regained her breath, picked up the continuity and went right on screaming, but he had been unable to listen. That one thing she had said about him had been too much. Of all the dirty, vile, bitchy, *female* accusations! And not a vestige of truth in it, either. That was what had been so grossly, villainously unfair. Nothing she could have said could ever erase those words.

He had doused his face in cold water and dabbed himself with a styptic pencil to stem the flow of blood. And then, while she had villified him through the door, he put a Band-aid awkwardly on his wounded hand, stepped out of his pajama bottoms, hung them up with great care, opened the bathroom door and stalked silent, naked and haughty into their bedroom.

She had gone right on screaming at him, but by now it had become perfectly obvious to him that he could never again live beneath the same roof, speak to her, even look at her.

In majestic silence, he had dressed—a little *too* carefully. With each garment he had grown more aloof, more dignified. By the time he had got into his London suit—with buttons on the cuffs that really undid—he had begun almost to enjoy his haughty calm.

"*Where are you going?*" she had shouted.

"Out," he had said with a frosty grandeur. What a splendid monosyllable that had been; an epigram almost—written by Oscar Wilde, delivered by Noel Coward, directed by Max Reinhardt, produced by J. Arthur Rank. He had been so pleased with his rendition of that deathless line that he had allowed himself a certain cavalier jauntiness as he clapped his new homburg onto his head. Then he had caught just the briefest glimpse of his reflection in the mirror. He'd put the damned hat on backward! All control had left him. He had torn the hat off his head and dashed it to the floor—and it had bounced; twice. "I'm *not* coming back! I'm not coming back to you or this goddamned house or this stinking little suburb, *ever!*" He said it—*roared* it—with such force that it had nearly torn his throat out.

Then he had dashed down the stairs, with her shrieking after him, and left the house. *Forever.* That had neatly—or untidily—wound up five years and ten months of marriage.

He had been so engrossed in the playback of their epic fight, that he hadn't noticed that he was already at the gates of Riveredge. Only a violent honking and a strident female voice bawling out something quite senseless made him snap to attention. He saw a dark red Jeepster disappear around a bend and realized that he had missed his last chance to see his sister-in-law Alice Marshall. That was all to the good. Alice was one of Riveredge's many features he'd be delighted never to see again.

The gates of Riveredge were large, wrought iron, impressive and firmly closed to all who had no business to be in Riveredge. Even now Murphy, the gateman, strutting like a bantam cock, was eloquently ordering away a dented old Dodge filled with faintly swarthy people. Its rusty bumper bore a spattered streamer proclaiming a visit to Howe Caverns. A pair of soiled baby shoes swung against the windshield and a sluttish kewpie doll hung in the back window. One needed less than half an eye to see that such people had no business in Riveredge.

"Figawd's sakes, we on'y wanna *look*. Is there a lore against *that?*"

"Be off with yez, now," Murphy said grandly. "Awnly the guests of *members* of Riveredge is allowed inside. On yer way, now." The car chugged off and Murphy turned around imperiously, "Writchid farriners! Oh, good marnin' sir. Lovely marnin'!" Murphy touched his cap, proving that he could also grovel.

"Good morning, Murphy," John said. "Would you please telephone the station for a taxi?"

"Not takin' yer foine big ottymobile out on a beautiful day like this, sir?"

"No. Just a taxi, please."

"Certainly, sir. Right away, sir. How's the pretty missus, sir?" Murphy disappeared into the gatekeeper's lodge. In a moment he was back. "The cab'll be here in foive minutes, sir."

Just five minutes and he'd be out of Riveredge forever. "Thank you, Murphy," he said and handed the old pirate a quarter.

two

The train pulled out of 125th Street Station, rolled with increasing speed past sordid tenements and then plunged into its dark hole—out of sight of the chill affluence of upper Park Avenue—for the last lap of its trip toward Grand Central.

Sitting grimly on a green-plush seat in the Smoking Permitted car, he thought for the hundredth time that this commuters' train was his cross, and a cross with fourteen stations, for there were just fourteen jerking, shrieking, clanging stops between Grand Central and the nondescript little town that served as a point of departure for the denizens of Riveredge.

"Only ninety-nine scenic minutes from Grand Central," had seemed almost pleasant when printed in tall Egmont type in the Riveredge brochure. Yet "ninety-nine scenic minutes" never sounded as long as the just-short-of-two-bloody-damned-jouncing-hours they actually were. For a time he had tried to read, to work, to sleep on the commuters' train.

But the men of Riveredge were a clannish group, a close-knit contingent bound together by the superiority of their names, addresses and incomes. If you lived in Riveredge, you took the Riveredge bus with the other Riveredge squires. You waited at the sooty little station in a shifting knot of Riveredge men, well apart from the lesser village males. Then you got onto the next-to-the-last car, which was unofficially recognized as Riveredge's own, and you talked to another Riveredge man—about business or Republican politics or Riveredge—or else you played a frenetic, murderous and costly bridge game on a plywood board with *three* Riveredge men. To isolate yourself in a book, a paper, or work was considered anti-social, eccentric, anarchistic. To get into another car was betrayal.

However today's was a late train and a Saturday train. It was even older, slower, dingier. There were no men from Riveredge, thank God, but there were, instead, suburban housewives piling on at every stop in shrill, overdressed throngs, bound for Schrafft's and the Helen Hayes matinee. By the time the train came to a halt at Grand Central Station, he felt that he had aged a hundred years in the gabble of the ladies.

He made his way hurriedly through the station and got into a taxi.

"Where to, Mac?" the driver asked.

Well, that question stumped him. He hadn't really thought about where he *was* going. The Algonquin, was the classic address, he supposed, for all men who have left their wives. But he was damned if he was going to be trite. Besides, he had very little money on him and he'd need to cash a check.

"I sez where to?"

"The Bacchus Club."

"The *where?*"

This was obviously a driver unaccustomed to transporting homeless husbands in the higher social and financial brackets. No use trying to explain to him that the Bacchus Club was, in its special way, as one with the Union, the Knickerbocker, the Century. He wouldn't have heard of those, either.

"Just drop me at Lexington and Thirty-eighth," he said.

It was really too easy to give the driver fifty cents and stroll ten paces into the Bacchus Club. He almost wished for a few cumbersome properties, such as a trunk, a briefcase, two or three satchels, golf clubs. They were the snowstorm and illegitimate baby in the melodrama of a male leaving home. It also occurred to him, as he strode up the club's single marble step, that a few such burdens as a toilet kit, check book and clean linen would be essential to his new way of life, unless he intended to go native.

"Well, here I am," he announced to absolutely nobody whatsoever in the dim foyer of the Bacchus Club.

The Bacchus Club was a wildly social organization which he

had been invited to join, much to his surprise, at college. In fact, he had been so surprised at being asked along with far tonier students, that he had accepted. And that had surprised him even more.

At college the Bacchus Club had not been the oldest club, and certainly not the most respectable one. But it was the club that attracted the most curiosity, the most envy, the most inexhaustibly festive membership. It was also the only club on campus which had contained enough jovial alumni so as to set up permanent postgraduate quarters in New York, where it had continued to operate at only a small deficit.

In the year he had been born, the Bacchus Club had been founded by a group of fun-loving undergraduates dedicated to high living, deep drinking and the discreet manufacture of nontoxic gin. Its John Hancock, so to speak, had been Teddy Edwards, an incorrigibly gay blade who was the contemporary and nodding acquaintance of such luminaries as Scott Fitzgerald, Connie Bennett and Red Grange.

Teddy Edwards had been so perfectly cast as the Ivy League child of the Twenties that he had never forsaken the role. Teddy had attended college from Tuesdays through Thursdays on a sort of lax Five Year Plan and a fat allowance from his grandmother. Teddy's career as permanent Undergraduate, Founder, Supreme Arbiter, President and Angel of the Bacchus Club had seemed a lifetime vocation when, on the very day Lindbergh landed in Paris, Teddy learned that he had amassed sufficient credits in snap courses like Music Appreciation and Art History to graduate. The shock had nearly killed him.

But no cloud was without its silver lining in the Twenties. The shock *had* killed Teddy's grandmother. A week after commencement Teddy was stocking Granny's cellar with "the real stuff, right off the *Cité de Paris*," to be served across the walnut bar already in Granny's back parlor. Granny's passing had brought to birth the Bacchus Club—New York branch—and assured it of a long and lusty life.

Today the silence of the Bacchus Club was as unusual as it was depressing.

John stood at the yawning fireplace in the hall, beneath the life-sized portrait of Teddy Edwards as Bacchus, and yelled up the gloomy old staircase. "Hey! Anybody here?" There was no reply.

He walked into the empty lounge and flung himself onto a rump-sprung old leather couch. The place was even shabbier than he remembered.

At some length he was greeted by the shuffling old steward. "Yassuh," the man said with less than no interest.

"Where is everybody? Where's Mr. Edwards?"

"Mist' Edwards's up in his room talkin' to the movahs."

"Oh? Is the club moving?" It dawned on him suddenly that he hadn't been here for more than a year, and that he'd visited very rarely before then.

"Club closin', suh."

"*Closing?*" It was like hearing that the U.S. Mint had decided to sell out to Tiffany's. "Why?"

"Ask Mist' Edwards, not me. He be down tereckly."

"Is—is the bar still open?"

"No, suh, it ain't. We got cookin' whiskey an' apple jack. That's all. An' it's cash, no mo' chits."

"Bring me cooking whiskey and plain water, please."

"Good thing you ask fo' branch water. Mist' Edwards finish all the seltzer las' night an' . . ."

"Okay, okay. I don't want soda. I *said* I didn't."

Still muttering, the steward shuffled off.

He had just taken the first sip of his drink—and cooking whiskey it was—when he heard Teddy's high, rather excitable voice from the head of the stairs. "But I tell you, I *can't* give you anything in advance. I don't get my own check till the fifteenth. It's *unheard* of to pay down for moving a few pieces of furniture—most of it'll go in the auction, anyway . . ."

"Not this stuff, it won't, Mr. Edwards."

". . . besides, my credit is excellent. All you have to do is ask around town and . . ."

"That's just what we done, Mr. Edwards. Now supposin' you call us up *after* you get this check and then we can talk turkey about the . . ."

"But *everybody* knows I've sold this house. It's being pulled down next month. Why, as soon as I clear away a few minor obligations, I'll have . . ."

"That's the trouble, Mr. Edwards. It's them minor obligations. Now you just wait till you get that check, then give us another ring and . . ."

"*Well,*" Teddy's voice was growing higher and higher; he spoke more and more in italics. "Just let *me* assure *you* that it'll be a frosty Tuesday in *hell* before *I* call *your* firm to move *my* . . ."

"Suit yourself, Mr. Edwards. G'bye now."

John could hear two pairs of feet on the stairs—one heavy, one light. The front door slammed. "*Thug,*" he heard Teddy mutter.

"Hey, Teddy!" he called.

"Who's *that?*" Teddy answered irritably. Then he poked his head into the lounge. "*Hey,* Chum! Long time no see!" Teddy came bustling into the room and threw himself down on the couch, which responded with a death-rattle of broken springs.

The shock of finding the club on its last legs was nothing to the shock of seeing its founding father and subsequent house mother, Teddy. He recalled an old photograph of Teddy in the Bacchus Club at college—round and pudgy, moonfaced; his dark hair parted in the center and slicked down with what was apparently Simonize. He had worn a sweater with a jazz stripe, plus-fours, hound's tooth hose and saddle shoes.

But today Teddy looked every minute of his age. His hair was plastered across his bald cranium in six wispy strands. Teddy's stomach bulged beneath his Bacchus-striped waistcoat. The cuffs of his J. Press jacket were frayed. His suntans were too tight and badly spotted. Teddy's eyes bulged and the broken blood vessels across his nose and cheeks gave his bloated moon face the appearance of raw hamburger.

"Well, Chum," Teddy cried, "come back to the fold at last." Teddy took both his hands in his own trembling ones and held them for just a moment.

"Actually, I only came in to cash a check." It struck him that he hadn't said a very tactful thing. "And of course to have a drink with you."

"A check, Chum?" Teddy said vaguely. There was a short pause and then he raced on. "Gee, that's too bad. I just made a great big deposit. Hate to have a lot of cash kicking around over a weekend."

So it was as bad as that. Poor old Teddy. He'd probably been supporting the Bacchus Club, both on campus and off, with Granny's bequest ever since the depression.

"I hear you're closing down," he began cautiously. Now, I'd better give him a break, he thought. "What's the matter? Getting sick of throwing the drunks out?"

Teddy looked at him gratefully. "That's it, Chum. Besides I've finally sold the old place. It's coming down on the first. They're going to put a big skyscraper here—all glass and air conditioning. Of course I held out for a while, but they made such a whopping offer that I really couldn't refuse. Besides . . ." he paused and looked down at his plump little hands, which were faintly dirty. "Besides, the membership here is dropping off. A lot of the real old sports—men in my class at school are dying. They aren't old, either. Hell, *I'm* only fifty-four. Guess it's all the rotgut we put away back in the good old days."

"It's a shame about the club, Teddy. A real shame." The only emotions he actually felt were pity for Teddy and remorse for himself. At college he hadn't taken the Bacchus Club at all seriously. During the war he had found it only a place to get a decent meal and a drink, a shower and a night's lodging. After the war, when he had been a struggling young writer, he couldn't really afford the club. He'd only come in rarely to order a beer and cash a check that wouldn't be quite good until another check had cleared. Knowing Teddy's laxity in matters of money, the practice had always proven safe.

When he got married, he was poorer still and he'd thought of resigning. But one way or another he'd always managed to pay his dues, even if he never set foot in the place, except to come in and thank Teddy for the standard Bacchus Club wedding present—a complicated silver bottle-opener adorned with an intricate pattern of grape leaves, as ugly as it was useless and expensive. His wife had relegated the gift of the Bacchus Club to a high shelf with his tennis trophies, well out of view, not that he had blamed her. Today, however, he felt that she had been particularly cruel and unkind about the club gift.

"No, Chum," Teddy was saying, "I don't think I've seen you for more than a year."

And indeed Teddy hadn't. On the day when fate had brought him to Mr. Popescu of the Popescu Pulse-Beat Eternal Non-Magnetic Watch, he had come to the Bacchus Club for a private little celebration—still not believing that from an obscure young script-writer with more prestige than income, he had suddenly been catapulted to a fifteen-thousand-dollar-a-year job as head man with the Popescu family. He'd got mellow that day on martinis and lobster farci and hock and told Teddy of the rich business luncheons and dinners he was going to hold in the private dining room at the Bacchus Club.

But it hadn't worked out that way. Mr. Popescu just wasn't the sort of man one took to a club. Even if Popescu had been, he was never away from Mrs. Popescu—except when he was visiting that secluded bagnio in the West Eighties—and Mrs. Popescu liked to go to places where she could dance. Dancing with Mrs. Popescu, in the Stork Club, the Persian Room, the Maisonette and a dozen other places, had been one of the major occupational hazards of the advertising manager of the Pulse-Beat watch. As for his business meals, they were always spent with the kind of people who preferred Twenty-One, the Chambord and the uptown expense-account restaurants where they could see—and be seen by—all the other people eating on expense accounts.

". . . just doesn't seem to be any club spirit nowadays," Teddy was saying. "Kids in college don't do anything but study or get drafted or get married before they graduate. Then they all move out to the country and have a lot of kids. It's the wives that are ruining all the decent drinking clubs these days. Hell, I remember when I was a gay young buck around New York—*everybody* was a bachelor—had a waiting list here for rooms. Why, Charlie Armstrong—he was '30, no, '29—kept a suite of rooms here and . . ." Teddy took another gulp of his drink and apparently forgot about bachelordom, Charlie Armstrong, and the suite of rooms. "Yep, it's the wives, Chum, they're what . . . By the way, you're married now, aren't you? How is, uh, um, your wife? Janet, that's her name, isn't it?"

"No, her name *isn't* Janet," he blurted out. "And she's just lousy, thanks. We're both lousy. We're splitting up as of today." He waited for Teddy's shocked reaction.

"That's the trouble, Chum," Teddy droned on, "no more club spirit. Can't get the guys to pay their dues. Taxes are double what they were. Been carrying the club myself for the past . . ."

My God, he thought, the poor old boy isn't even hearing me. Here I tell him that my whole life is coming to an end and all Teddy can talk about is *club spirit!* Then he thought again, a little more kindly. After all, I guess this is the end of his life, too —only he's been at it longer than I have. "It's a shame about the club, Teddy," he said inanely. He was getting awfully sick of saying it was a shame about the club. After all he was not a sentimental person given to college reunions, platoon get-togethers and the remembrance of things past. Actually he had fallen away from the Bacchus Club just as painlessly as had all its other members. He wouldn't even have thought of the club today if it hadn't been for *her*.

He had come to the club quite selfishly. He had come first to cash a check, second to take a room until he could find something more attractive, and third, to drown his sorrows—yes, that was the term—among the jovial males who traditionally frequented the Bacchus Club's bar. He had come expecting Babylon and found, instead, Philadelphia. The whole place was dusty and gloomy and old and depressing—just as dusty and gloomy and old and depressing as Teddy, himself.

These thoughts were interrupted by a low rumble and shrieking of plumbing that shook the whole building, followed by a piercing yell of pain. "Jesus!" a distant voice shouted and there was a scampering sound of bare feet on the stairs.

"Oh, the shower room again," Teddy moaned. "I told Toby to . . ."

"For Christ's sake," the voice shouted. "That Goddamned shower of yours nearly killed me!" A youngish man, very yellow of hair, very blue of eye, very, very red of skin burst into the lounge, clutching a limp towel around him.

"Toby!" he cried, getting up from the sofa. "What are *you* doing here?"

"What am I doing here?" Toby said, with a lunge toward the rye bottle. "Practically getting my ass frozen off. That's what *I'm* doing here." He collapsed onto the sofa and poured a large drink.

Two features of the Bacchus Club have always been notorious for their merry pranks. One was the Scotch needle spray shower, planned for the assuagement of hung-over members and operated by elementary hydraulics, an archaic pressure pump and sheer luck. More than one member had scampered naked and shocked to safety from its fits and starts, its eruptions and explosions. The other feature was Toby Wentworth, whose alarums and excursions, whose affairs and exploits had kept the gentlemen of the bar chortling for years. That the two should burst forth at the same time seemed an almost Olympian justice.

"Toby! You silly bastard!" he cried. "How long have you been back?"

"Couple of days," Toby grinned, drinking deeply of somebody else's drink, "and I wish to hell I was still in Ecuador."

"Teddy," he said, "why didn't you *tell* me Toby was here? For God's sake, we were *roommates*."

"Oh, Toby? Toby?" Teddy said vaguely, trying to focus his eyes. "Funny, it just slipped my mind. Golly, Chum, *isn't* that strange. Why, I was just saying to Walter Goodenough—class of '34, '33, somewhere around in there—I was just saying that if there was one guy with real club spirit, it was Toby."

"Come off the maundering you old stumblebum and get some more ice and a glass for me," Toby said, arranging the towel more modestly about himself. Still muttering, Teddy disappeared toward what had once been a well-stocked bar.

Toby Wentworth was really named something impressive like Alexander Hamilton Wentworth, 3rd. He was the second son and first remittance man of some people in Cincinnati who'd made a killing in soap. Before he was twenty Toby had cracked up six cars and two marriages—all belonging to other people. Toby had a gift for bringing out the mother in women and a genius for bringing them to bed shortly—say an hour—thereafter. During the war his adventures had been legendary. Toby had insulted General Patton, gone A.W.O.L. to Paris for six weeks, been caught in the WAC barracks, black marketed six thousand dollars' worth of gas and got away with it. Since the war he had had a couple of dozen jobs—all glamorous and all in exotic places. He had faced man-eating tigers in India, Communist guerrillas in the Philippines, a bandit king in Sicily, a revolutionary assassin in Iran, and irate fathers of wronged daughters in almost any country you might care to name. The only things Toby had not faced were reality and the fact that he was no longer eighteen.

"Toby, for God's sake," John said reminiscently. "I can't believe it's really you."

"Well, it is," Toby said. "Come on upstairs and talk to me while I get dressed."

"What about Teddy?"

"Nuts to Teddy," Toby said. "The old creep gives me the willies. We'll just skip the ice and take the bottle up with us. Teddy drinks too much, anyway."

Picking up his glass he followed Toby and the rye bottle up the stairway. The halls were dim and cobwebby and smelled faintly of mice. Toby's room adjoined Teddy's suite on the second floor. It was a dim little room, its one window overlooking the bleak and rather weedy back yard which had once been known as the club's Summer Terrace—two ailanthus trees, a dozen rattan chairs, and a noseless statue of Bacchus, but a pleasant spot withal. The room, too, would have been decent enough, given a good cleaning and a coat or two of paint. Yet Toby Wentworth always left his hallmark on any he occupied. In fact, he hardly had to set foot inside the door until a place became chaotically his own.

Toby's half-emptied trunks and suitcases yawned rudely from the corners of the room. A cascade of neckties fell from the top of the chest, swirling in bright little rivulets and eddies on the worn carpet. His toilet articles sprawled over every surface, some few of them half buried in drifts of spilled talcum powder. Toby's shirts, his suits, his trousers, his coats and dressing gowns were draped over every piece of furniture. A black sock hung like mourning crape over a James Montgomery Flagg sketch of Bacchus. A small bale of dirty laundry filled the easy chair and in the middle of the unmade bed, forming a snug little nest, were Toby's wrinkled pajamas.

"Sit down, make yourself at home," Toby said genially. Then he poured two stiff drinks from the rye bottle.

The drink was too strong to taste really good and it occurred to John, vaguely, that he'd had no breakfast and might very reasonably expect to feel a little woozy drinking on an empty stomach. Yet this was so much like old times, sitting in a messed-up room with Toby and drinking while Toby dressed and talked amiably on.

Automatically he began to pick up Toby's ties—someone always had to tidy Toby's messes—and thought back to the first time the two of them had been in a room together. It was on the first day at college, years ago. He had been a scared, green young kid away from home for the first time and beginning to doubt the rightness of his hard new salt-and-pepper tweed suit, described by the salesman at Kampus Klothiers back home as "perfect for the Ivy League." It wasn't. It wouldn't even have been right for the University of Stalingrad, pleated, padded, patch pocketed as it was. In fact it was thoroughly wrong. Forty dollars down the drain.

He had sat miserably on a hard bentwood chair that day watching the sleek Gilmore trunks—each stamped A.H.W., III —being dumped into the bleak double room which was to house him and some total stranger possessing, apparently, untotaled wealth and the initials A.H.W., III. He had looked at the splendid new luggage and felt bitterly ashamed of his own—Dad's old gladstone, Aunt Lucy's steamer trunk and Mother's scuffed black pullman case with the violet moire lining. Then he felt even more bitterly ashamed of being ashamed. But he had begun thinking that perhaps the state university back home would have been better, after all, than this expensive Eastern college when his wretched revery was interrupted by the arrival of A.H.W., III himself. It had been Toby.

"Hi!" Toby had said. That seemed to have been all that was necessary. The ice had been immediately broken and a beautiful friendship established.

At seventeen Toby had looked like a cross between Peck's Bad Boy and a Botticelli cherub. He was rich, spoiled, willful, self-confident, dishonest, childish, and utterly captivating. The apparent fountainhead of all carnal knowledge, Toby had taught him quickly how to smoke Indian fashion, how to needle beer with grain alcohol, how to tell which town girls would and which ones wouldn't.

Although smaller and younger, Toby had immediately taken him under his wing and served as guide and mentor to a world he had never known. Because of Toby, Cincinnati became Paris; the Wentworths' Norman-type house on Indian Hill Road, with its real, live, Finnish butler-chauffeur, was the Palais Royale; the Cincinnati Bachelors' Cotillion was gayer, more brilliant than any court ball and Toby's debutante sister—in sorry truth an aggressively plain girl with drooping lids and no eyelashes to speak of—reigned over it like Pompadour. Toby had more than charm. Toby had *glamor*.

John had always felt beholden to Toby—grateful when Toby had candidly pointed out that all of his clothes were impossible; obligated for the loan of a tie; eternally indebted to Toby for the Spring Vacation week he had spent under the Wentworth roof; sick with remorse when he could only spend five dollars on Toby's Christmas present; understanding when Toby gave him none in return; happy to lend Toby money, to do Toby's assignments, to make Toby's bed, to dance with Toby's dreary sister. Everyone had always done things for Toby. They felt that it was only Toby's due. And Toby agreed.

He watched now, amused and bemused, as Toby combed his wet, yellow baby hair in front of the mirror, pressing the deep, boyish wave above his forehead. He had seen Toby do just this at least a thousand times before and today in his happiness at being once again with lovable, witty, prankish old Toby, he either would not see or could not see that the yellow baby hair was thinning at the crown. Just as he would not see or could not see that Toby was getting a bit heavy beneath the arms and the jaw and that Toby's dashing clothes—like Toby's dashing face —were beginning to show signs of wear, neglect and age.

It was more than the drink and the dimness of the room. Toby to him was a symbol, a symbol of youth and gaiety and freedom and eternal—eternal what?

". . . so this dame in Calcutta came around with her old man and claimed I was the father," Toby was saying as he got into his shirt. "And I . . ."

Eternal sex appeal. That was what Toby had. He could remember the leather-framed photographs of Cincinnati girls on Toby's dresser at school—girls in riding clothes squinting into the camera at the Carmargo Club; girls in bathing suits at the Miami Boat Club; girls in their white coming-out dresses sitting bouffantly on gilt chairs at the Sinton Hotel. Compared to his own modest gallery of enchantresses—a second cousin at Mills College and a girl named Lila Lewis who was said, later, to have gone to modern dance and the dogs—Toby's collection was awesome. These were pretty girls, nice girls, rich girls, all of whom, Toby allowed to be surmised, either had or would have gone to bed with Toby. And at seventeen!

No, he reflected musingly, no woman could ever resist Toby. No woman except one—Mary! Peter Pan, *that's* what she'd called Toby! And how like her! Anything to be different! "I suppose he's nice enough," she had said. (She *supposed* Toby was nice enough—how about that!) "But he always gives me the feeling that I'm talking to the most precocious little boy in the fourth form and that the minute I've finished he'll be writing naughty words on the blackboard." A character assassin, that's what she was, talking that way about his best friend.

". . . turn 'em upside down and they're all the same!" Toby said with a flourish of his necktie.

Amen, he thought. Toby had the right idea—no strings and no connections; travel light and travel alone. That was the only way to be. And what a perfect time for Toby to turn up again. Maybe they could find some kind of furnished apartment and start in all over again, just the way they'd lived in college.

"Let's get the hell out of this hole," Toby said. "Maybe you'd like to buy me some lunch."

"Sure. Sure thing, Toby," he said. With a slight lurch he got out of his chair.

"Bottoms up," Toby said.

In silence they emptied their glasses. He was beginning to feel almost anesthetized.

"Well, let's be off," Toby said, flinging his worn old polo coat around him. In the dim light Toby looked just eighteen as he strode out of his room.

A little unsteadily, John followed Toby, stopping only long enough to pick up Toby's towel from the floor and to turn off the light.

"Hey, chums," Teddy called, from the lounge. "Hang on a second—wait for . . ."

"For God's sake let's shake *him*," Toby said in a voice that could have carried to Connecticut. "So long, Teddy. Don't wait up."

With a slam of the door they were out of the Bacchus Club and onto the street.

three

THE TAXI CREPT UP PARK AVENUE THROUGH THE USUAL NOONDAY congestion, reached Fifty-fifth Street, trickled a little to the west and stopped before the pink and black marquee of the Rococo. The meter read sixty-five cents.

"Here we are, Toby," John said, fishing into his pocket. He had exactly sixty-five cents and not a penny more. He flushed uncomfortably and said, "Uh, Tobe, do you happen to have a quarter on you for the driver? I haven't got any change and . . ." Once more, for the thousandth—the ten thousandth—time in his life, he felt inferior and beholden to Toby.

"Sure," Toby said crawling out of the cab. Toby reached into his pocket, pulled out a lackluster old rupee and flipped it to the driver.

"Thanks a lot, Toby."

"Don't mention it, pal!"

"You smart son of a . . ." the driver yelled, but by then they were out of earshot.

Rococo was the third newest of New York's twenty-five most fashionable restaurants. Like twenty of the other twenty-four most fashionable restaurants, it occupied the ground floor of an old brownstone house and an unwarranted amount of space in the gossip columns. "Oillionaire Tex Perkins and Starlet Gigi Fontanel a duo at Rococo . . . Sir Stork to visit Mario and Rita Pucci (he's men's room attendant at Rococo) in May . . . Overheard at Rococo: 'She's the kind of girl I could remarry.'"

The columnists, force-fed by hourly news bulletins from Rococo's hard-bitten public relations girl, had given the place a tremendous, though spurious, chic. They told their readers, for example, that Rococo had been decorated by a famous society woman (true—and as tastelessly as possible); that the doorman at Rococo was a Russian Grand Duke (untrue—he was an ex-wrestler named Dubinsky); that the backers of Rococo were a famous composer, a famous actor, a famous writer and a famous producer (partially true—these backers were actually fronters for a famous gangster who found it healthier to live abroad). Rococo had served as the setting for six women's magazine stories, as the background for a hundred fabulous beauties posing for fan magazines, fashion journals and beer ads. Thus Rococo became a by-word for the millions who could no more afford it than they could pronounce it. Rococo had become the standard, the goal, the Elysian Fields of the nation. Such is the power and the glory of publicity.

John didn't like Rococo very much, but his boss, Mr. Popescu, and his boss's wife adored it. They had urged him to entertain there, had given him unlimited credit there. By now he was well known at Rococo, there would be no waiting and he could cash a check for almost any amount.

His stock went up slightly as they entered. The doorman greeted him by name, so did the hatcheck girl and so did the bartender, over the heads of the people who were stacked three-deep at the bar. (Rococo had achieved such eminence as the playground of New York Society that tourists, unemployed actors, impressed nobodies and even New York Society would wait hours for tables which were occupied by dress manufacturers, out-of-town buyers, employed actors and impressive nobodies). And the Congressional Medal, the Legion d'Honneur, the Papal Blessing of Rococo was bestowed upon him when M. Josef, the headwaiter (né Giuseppe Marcantonio Maria Schifozzi) recognized him from beyond the red velvet rope, slithered under it, pushed his way rudely through the waiting customers, and did all but fall prostrate at his feet. Such a *Monsieur*-ing and *bon jour*-ing and *ça va*-ing hadn't been heard at Rococo for at least fifteen minutes.

Two-thirds of the people at the bar—roughly that segment of smart society which feels that to be known by name by a headwaiter amounts to winning the Nobel Prize—turned reverently to wonder just which noted gossip column personality this handsome young man could be. Even Toby was faintly impressed.

"Hello Josef," John said hastily. He loathed Josef. Josef had been a bootlegger, a dope pedlar and a pimp—and looked it. He meant nothing to Josef and he knew it. All that Josef cared about was the monthly tip of a hundred dollars and the annual Christmas present of a thousand which Mr. Popescu handed to Josef so that Mr. P. and ranking executives of the Pulse-Beat Eternal Non-Magnetic Watch Company might be suitably fawned upon while entertaining important people. "Could I cash a check? And then . . ."

"A-nee amount M'sieu' weesh. I mortgage my own home to geevc M'sieu' the money. M'sieu' know that. I say to my wife theess mor-nang, I say . . ."

"It's just for a hundred, Josef," he said, coloring. What a pain in the ass this phony wop could be! "And then will we have to wait very long for lunch?"

"*Wait? Sair*-tain-ly *not!* I have pair-fect table, re-sairve' zhust for M'sieu'. Theess way, please." Josef puckered up his lips and made an obscene kissing sound at which every captain, every waiter, every busboy turned and looked as though transfixed.

"Etienne," Josef called, "*Tabla Numero Deeeeess pou' M'sieu'.*"

Etienne, who was the only French French waiter employed at Rococo, bowed coolly and began to clear the table just vacated by three ravishing Hungarian whores.

He and Toby were herded swiftly through the waiting throngs.

"Hey, listen," an angry Texas voice called out, "they just come in an' we been waitin' here since . . ." The rest was lost in the clatter of china and silver.

"Jesus," Toby said, as the chair was slid gently beneath his buttocks, "it looks like a Rue Blondell cat-house."

Toby had a point. The famous society woman, who had become an even more famous decorator of public places, hadn't spared a trick to make the Rococo rococococo. There wasn't a straight, clean line in the place. The tufted magenta banquettes along the mirrored walls rose and fell in undulating swirls and waves, while the purple valance above fell in horrifying tangles of loops and swags. Great, gnarled blobs of white plaster served as candle sconces. A tortured chandelier, also in white plaster, cast a feeble, jaundiced light on the pink table cloths.

The menus, which were somewhat larger than the tables, credited the famous society woman with the decoration, as did the matchbooks, the swizzle sticks, the bar napkins, and the coasters. John had wondered idly, before this, why they hadn't gone all the way with their credits:

Paint job by Benjamin Siegel
Upholstery by M. Leighton Co.
Carpets by N. Rejeb
Electrical work by Arthur Guth
Rest Room fixtures by Crane and Co.

Well, it had only been a random thought.

"It's handy to my office, Toby," he said, almost apologetically.

A silver inkwell attributed to Thomas Germaine, and an engraved house check were placed reverently in front of him. He made out a check to cash for a hundred dollars and signed it with just a hint of a flourish. It was swept away with a far greater flourish. Then ten ten-dollar bills were laid before him on a sacrificial platter.

"Oh, My God," Toby said.

"Come on, Toby," he said, "Let's have a drink, then we'll order lunch."

He felt that the meal hadn't quite come off right. Oh, it had been very grand and very showy, but somehow he hadn't been able to talk to Toby as he had wanted to. In fact, Rococo was not conducive to serious conversation. There was a constant gabble of voices, punctuated by crashes from the pantry. Since anything you ordered—except possibly an aspirin tablet—was rolled in ceremoniously on a cart, like a patient about to undergo major surgery, the traffic problem was severe. And then Rococo had the unnerving habit of setting fire to practically every dish it served, so that in the continuous blaze you almost thought you were in hell. Nor were you ever left alone. Not only did the captain hover perpetually asking if everything was all right, but Josef always made a minimum of three short visits—if you were known to him—to ask the same question.

Customers table-hopped, called out greetings from across the room—whether you knew them or not—and the Hollywood actress who'd added so much to the debacle of last night's television show had thrown her arms dramatically around John, kissed him and asked him how her performance had been, just as he was getting around to telling Toby the true facts of his marital troubles.

And even Toby had been something of a disappointment as the sympathetic listener. He'd given an impression of detachment, disinterest and sometimes complete absence. If he'd said anything, it was always some offhand comment like "Oh, well," or "There are other dames" or "Shouldn't we have another drink? You know, kind of drown your sorrows."

He wondered now if Toby had sensed that his wife disliked him and if he disliked her in return. The pervasive feeling of animosity between Mary and Toby had always made him edgy. He had forever wanted the people he loved to love each other, too. Now he didn't love *her* at all, but he still felt a little unsporting to be discussing her with someone who seemed—if not out and out unfriendly—a little too indifferent. After all, this was a big problem and it was his. Maybe Toby was better for gay conversation while some quack like that psychoanalyst his sister-in-law was always going to might have made a better audience.

"Compliments of Josef, M'sieur," the captain said, landing two vast balloons of cognac on the table before them. The ritual of the brandy on the house was reserved exclusively for the charge account patrons, probably on the theory that the cash customers had got so used to paying and paying that it would be wrong to disrupt the habit pattern.

John hated brandy almost as much as he hated Josef. "Thank you, Etienne, and please thank Josef for me," he said.

". . . anyhow this dame in Calcutta—her father was the maharajah of something—was giving me the eye, so I played it close and pretty soon this card comes over asking me to join her party. Just like that. And I mean she was really built like a brick . . ."

It suddenly occurred to him that he wasn't listening to Toby's amatory triumphs any more than Toby had listened to his defeat.

He leaned forward politely, smiled and murmured "Mm-hmm."

". . . anyhow ten o'clock comes and she gives me one of those looks that says 'Let's go upstairs," so I said, 'Let's go upstairs.' Well . . . *Hey!* Speaking of getting the eye from a table across the room," he lowered his voice portentiously, "there's a dame over there—really a dish—who's been giving me the once-over for about the last hour. She's looking over here again."

"Where?" he said, glancing cautiously to the left and to the right. The restaurant was almost empty by now.

"No. Directly behind you. She's sitting with two other dames—real dogs. Can't you see her? She's really been giving me the . . ."

"Not having an eye in the nape of my neck, Toby, I . . ."

"Well, here, look in the mirror behind me. The other two look like a couple of typewriter jockeys out on a spree, but this little brunette job . . . And she's been staring over here like . . ."

He sat up quite straight in his chair, almost lifting himself off the seat and peered into the mirrored wall behind Toby. The first thing he saw was the thinning crown of Toby's head. The second sight to meet his gaze was that of three women sitting at the table for one, right next to the pantry door. They were all secretaries at Popescu Pulse-Beat Eternal Watch. He sat down again. "They're *all* typewriter jockeys on a spree, Toby," he said. "The 'dish' happens to be my secretary. Would you like to meet her?" Without waiting for an answer, he wheeled around in his chair. "Hi!" he called gaily, almost hysterically. "Come and have a drink with us!"

There was a pretty confusion at the opposite table—an embarrassed giggling, a bustling, a lot of whispered "Oh, we *shouldn't* . . . No, we *can't* . . . Oh, *let's* . . . Just *one* little drink." Then the three got up and advanced reticently, jostling one another delicately.

Etienne took in the situation with a practiced and impassive eye. While Rococo had little interest in the morals of its clientle off the premises, pick-ups were discouraged in the dining room, unless those involved were *very* illustrious. The classes were never encouraged to mingle. And these girlies were strictly from the wrong boroughs of Greater New York.

Etienne looked at this trio again. It was the same old story—the budget-shop dresses, the dyed fur pieces, the beady little hats clamped onto their temples. Yet *this* customer was a gentleman. Etienne had served him before—served him and the beautiful wife he obviously adored. "Hello, Miss Lacey," Etienne heard him say. "How are you Miss Schmidt, Miss Koosis?" Etienne sighed with relief. They *knew* one another. It was going to be perfectly all right. Defferentially, Etienne hurried to draw up extra chairs at the table.

"*Well*, ladies," John said with bright inanity, "sit down. I'd like you to meet my old college roommate, Toby Wentworth. Miss Lacey, Miss Schmidt, Miss Koosis, this is Mr. Wentworth."

"Well, Miss, uh, Lacey," Toby said, inching over on the banquette to make room for her, "I *hoped* we'd meet. I felt, when I saw you looking over in this direction so often, that perhaps we were destined to . . ."

"Oh, yes," Miss Lacey said, beaming at Toby, "I've been trying to catch his eye for *hours*."

Toby reddened and there was a brief, awkward pause. Then John took over.

"Well, let's see now," he roared brightly, rubbing his hands together for no reason at all, "what'll it be? Miss Lacey works for me, Toby, poor girl and . . ."

"Oh, he's the most wonderful boss a person could ever have, Mr. Wentworth!"

". . . and Miss Schmidt is really up with the top brass. She's Mr. Popescu's girl Friday. And Miss Koosis . . ."

"Pleased to meet you, I'm sure," Miss Schmidt said.

". . . Miss Koosis is in, um, in . . ."

"Pössonnel," Miss Koosis said.

"Yes, that's right, Miss Koosis does the hiring and the firing at dear old Popescu Pulse-Beat E . . ."

"Oh, brother!" Miss Koosis said.

"Maybe you've got some odd job for a guy like me, Miss Whoosis," Toby said, smiling up at her with his notorious blue-eyed boyish grin. The eyes were a trifle bloodshot by now.

"Dig *him!*" Miss Koosis screamed.

"G'wan, hire 'im, Lucille, honey," Miss Schmidt said. "He's cute!" At this there was a great burst of hilarity from the ladies.

"Honestly," Miss Lacey said, wiping her eyes, "Pearl's just a scream! She ought to be on television or something." He looked at his secretary again. He'd never noticed how very pretty she was. "What'll it be, Bernice—I mean Miss Lacey?"

"Oh, dear, I don't think I should have anything more. We had two cocktails while we were waiting to be seated and . . ."

"Oh, come on, now, Bernice," Toby said, a little slurringly. "You're among friends."

"Sure, honey," Miss Schmidt said, her rimless glasses glittering from behind her nose veil, "have a little somethingue. Mamma's along. She'll look out for you. I'll have a daakery, myself."

"One daiquiri, Etienne," John said animatedly, "and for Miss Koosis—surely you'll have a . . ."

"Well, all reet," Miss Koosis said. "Lemme have anothah Jack Rose."

Toby gagged. "And a Jack Rose, Etienne. Miss Lacey?"

"Well, maybe I'll have a brandy like you and Mr. Wentworth," she said with a shy little smile.

"And three brandies, please." Then he turned to his secretary. "Do you eat here often?"

"Oh, no! But Pearl and Lucille and I pick a famous restaurant —a kind of gourmet place—every Saturday. You know, a place like this, where all the celebrities go. Like last week we went to the Le Valois and we've been to Vwah-zan and Sardi's and the Barberry Room—oh, we always do it. It's more fun if you've got someone else with you."

"Three musketeers, eh Bernice?" Miss Schmidt said. "Oh, here's the refills!" That brought down the house.

"Isn't Pearl a panic?" Bernice asked him. "Honestly, when I first came to Popescu's I was just a green kid out of business school and I was so scared that . . ."

"Scared? You mean you were afraid of *me*?" he asked. She'd been the first secretary he'd ever hired and he had been terrified of her.

"Oh, I was scared silly. Here you were a big, important executive with a beautiful wife and always going out to places like this with big movie stars and I . . . Well, Pearl just took me under her wing—Pearl *and* Lucille. I don't know what I'd of done without them."

The thought of a pretty little thing like Bernice spending her free time with a pair of crones like Miss Schmidt and Miss Koosis depressed him.

"I always love a riss-kay story, Mr. Wentworth!" Miss Schmidt screamed.

"Wha' hoppened?" Miss Koosis said. Miss Koosis, it seemed to him, was a walking compendium of all the catch phrases of the past decade. Terms like "Hubba, hubba, hubba," and "I've got news for you" seemed to comprise her entire fund of small talk.

Miss Schmidt and Miss Koosis (he felt that he should call them Pearl and Lucille, although the very notion shocked him quite as much as that of calling his own mother by name) were well embarked upon old maidenhood. Having failed at Woman's First Function, they had triumphed at Woman's Second Function —typing and shorthand. Lacking looks, taste and intelligence, they had been more successful than they could have reasonably expected to be. Now they had reached their zenith. They had their little apartments and their fur pieces, they could eat at places like Rococo once a week, they were the queen bees of the ladies' room at the office and they could be just a trifle scornful of the girls half their age who had quit work to marry.

No, John said to himself, there's nothing of the incipient spinster about Bernice Lacey. He looked at her carefully across the table. Why had he never noticed the wonderful dark hair, the liquid dark eyes? "Um, tell me, Miss Lacey," he said, "do you live here in town?"

"Oh, no, my folks are dead . . ."

That was good.

". . . and I live with my married sister in Astoria."

That was bad.

"Nice, Astoria," he said. He had only the vaguest idea of where it was.

"It's very pretty. My brother-in-law owns his own home."

"That's nice," he said.

"But it's such a long trip on the subway, that I've been thinking about taking a place right here in New York and . . ."

He thought fleetingly of Bernice Lacey in a snug little flat, like the one he had had in the East Sixties before the move to Riveredge. It would be pink or pale blue and he would pay the rent ever so discreetly and she would be waiting there for him when he left the office and . . .

". . . and so Pearl, that's Miss Schmidt, said why don't we take a place together . . ."

The bubble burst. The picture of Bernice living with that garrulous old crow was not a pleasant one to put into focus. He shuddered at the very thought of a sweet little thing like Bernice being enmeshed in the web of Miss Schmidt—a captive, forever, to Miss Schmidt's vulgar sallies, her antique witticisms, her pig-ignorant opinions.

"I don't mind if a joke's dirty, Mr. Wentworth, as long as it's funny," Miss Schmidt was saying. John looked at her with ill-concealed distaste as she crooked her little finger, took an elegant sip of her drink and produced a soft, furtive little belch. "Like I always say to Mr. P—that's Mr. Popescu, my employer; it's a forrun name—I always say there's nothingue like a sensa yuma. Now, for eggzampul, do you watch Jackie Gleason on tee-vee?"

Oh no, Never. A sweet girl like Bernice just *couldn't* get mixed up with a common old frump like Miss Schmidt. He'd never had a mistress—couldn't afford one—but he wondered if Bernice might not do. Then he wondered just how one went about setting up such an arrangement. One just didn't say something like: "Miss Lacey, your shorthand and typing and filing are wonderful. I think you're beautiful. Will you be my mistress?"

He suddenly became conscious of the pressure of many knees beneath the table. It was pleasant, but since the table was a small one and there were ten knees under it, it was difficult to tell just whose were touching his. Then he glanced at Toby's face across the table. There were the unmistakable signs of distress, distaste and disdain as Miss Schmidt continued with her tortuous description of the long and apparently side-splitting sketch she'd seen on her television set the night before.

He felt himself getting as desperate as Toby looked and also drunker than Toby looked. Anesthesia was indicated. "Etienne," he called suddenly, "another round, please."

"Oh, please, I *can't!*" Bernice said.

"Hubba, hubba, hubba!" Miss Koosis said.

"Don't be sil, Bernice, honey," Miss Schmidt said, probing delicately at her bicuspids with her little finger. "With two gentlemen like this to see us to the subway, who minds being under the alfluence of incohol?"

"Isn't Pearl a perfect *riot!*" Bernice said, her wonderful eyes glowing with pleasure. "*Al*-fluence of *in*-cohol! Have you ever heard that before?"

"Only about ten thousand times," Toby muttered beneath his breath. Then he turned a little lurchingly toward Bernice. "Listen, beautiful . . ." Toby began.

John felt just a little apprehensive. He hoped Toby wasn't getting too potted to behave himself and he thought with a touch of irritation that even if Toby was his best friend, Bernice was still *his* secretary. It was a matter of squatter's rights.

Bernice looked across the table at him with a glance that was a trifle frightened and questioning. He wanted to leap into the conversation—break it up. Poor little kid. But Miss Schmidt had fixed him with her glassy gaze, her shark's smile.

". . . talk about double in-ten-dree, Groucho Marx comes on the other night with this couple from—I don't know where they come from, some place like East Jesus, Nebrasker, if you'll parm my being sac-ree-lidge-us. Well, anyhoo, he says to this girl—quite a cute dish—he says . . ."

A torrent of relief swept over him as he saw Etienne approaching with the tray of drinks. At least that would quiet Miss Schmidt for a blessed moment so that he could return his attentions to Bernice.

"'. . . double *beds!*' Um-majin! Right over television with milliums of people listeningue. Oh, I hope you don't mind an noff-color story, but Groucho's got such a suttle sensa yuma that . . . Eeeeeeeeeeeeeow!"

With a jungle scream, Miss Schmidt ended her anecdote and leapt to her feet, exerting such force that the table and the tray of drinks crashed to the floor. Even Etienne was almost overturned.

"Miss Schm . . ."

"Oh, my God," Toby groaned. "I got the wrong leg!"

"Wha' hoppened?" Miss Koosis said.

And then Miss Schmidt was confronting John like a wounded

panther, her spectacles blazing. "Of all the dirty, low-down mashers I ever seen in my *life!*" she screamed.

"Miss Schmidt," he said, "*I* didn't . . ."

"Don't tell *me* what chew did. *I* oughta know. An' don't think I ain't goingue to report this to Mr. Popescu. You an' yer . . ."

"But, Miss Schm . . ."

"Donchew Miss Schmidt *me.* I seen *your* kind before, don't think I haven't. You men all think that if you buy a party a cocktail you got the right to . . ."

"Miss Schmidt, I didn't lay a hand on . . ."

"Oh, pipe down, Grandma . . ." Toby began.

"Toby, please . . ."

"An' you, too," Miss Schmidt bellowed, wheeling on Toby. "Yer all alike." As Miss Schmidt's diatribe increased in volume and scope, he noticed an interested audience gathering. Even if the place was practically deserted by now, it was amazing what a sizable crowd could be summoned by the outrage of a virgin of nearly fifty.

"*Please,* madame," Etienne said, approaching her with a flourish of his napkin.

"Take yer hands offa me, you lousy . . ." She raised her purse menacingly at Etienne. The purse flew open, its contents thumping and clattering every which way.

"Oh!" Bernice cried. "*Oh!*" And then she burst into tears.

At that moment Josef arrived. "*Out!*" he said. "Get out and *stay* out!"

"Listen, Josef," John said. "I can explain everything. There was just a . . ."

"I run a decent place, M'sieu', I don't want . . ."

"You run a decent *place,*" Toby roared. "Why, you lousy dago racketeer, all you run is a . . ."

"Toby!" he shouted.

Bernice stood up, tears streaming down her face. "I've—I've never been so insulted in my life! Here I thought you were a gentleman and . . ." She broke down briefly. "Well, just let me t-tell *you,* I won't be in Monday or *ever.* Poor *Pearl!* Come on Pearl," she said, stepping over the upset table. "Lucille, come on. We'll take Pearl home."

"But, Bernice . . . I mean, Miss Lacey . . ." It was too late. They had marched out to the street. A second later John and Toby found themselves propelled also to the street.

"I've been thrown out of better places than this, you stinking wop bandit," Toby yelled back toward the door. Toby was laughing. Toby was having the time of his life. But wasn't Toby getting just a little, well, *elderly* for college-boy larks like this?

four

In his embarrassment, his confusion and his drunkenness, he lurched out into the street almost in the nick of time to be knocked flat by New York's most outstandingly vulgar automobile.

There was an ear-splitting screech of brakes and he was jerked out of the path of the monster by Toby just as a shrill feminine voice screamed "Well, of all people!"

"Oh, my God," he groaned, "out of a million cars in New York, I have to pick my boss's!"

Like everything Mr. and Mrs. Manfred Popescu owned, the car was expensive. Like everything Mr. and Mrs. Manfred Popescu owned, the car was unique. And like everything Mr. and Mrs. Manfred Popescu owned, there was little fear that anyone else would want to copy it.

The Popescu vehicle was a brand new, custom-built Cadillac town car, one foot lower and two feet longer than any other Cadillac in America. It was pitch black with gold trim instead of chromium. The interior was upholstered in black persian lamb and fitted with a bar, writing desk, radio, telephone, television (color) and a solid gold Popescu Pulse-Beat Eternal Chronometer which gave the time in the major capitals of the world, the date, the phases of the moon and tolled every quarter of an hour in either Westminster or Whittington chimes. The controls were manned by a chauffeur *and* a footman who wore white linen dusters in the summer and black livery with persian lamb collars in the winter. Mrs. Popescu thought it was divine.

The electrically operated rear door flew open and out flew Manfred Popescu himself, followed by Mrs. Popescu. Before John could speak he had been embraced, kissed on both cheeks, and felt for broken bones. Then he and Toby had been thrust into the rear of the Popescus' town car while Mr. Popescu began to berate his chauffeur in the unintelligible melange of languages he had learned in the many years between his birth in a Balkan goatherd's hovel and his contemporary eminence as a Swiss watch manufacturer.

"*Porca madonn!*" Popescu began temperately in his Neapolitan Italian. "Of all the bloody, stupid, mucking asses," he continued in what was almost Oxonian English. "*Psiakrew cholera!*" he added quietly in heavily accented Polish. "Almost you are killing my how-you say *direktor für die reklamen* . . ."

"Advertising manager, honey," Mrs. Popescu translated.

"*Ja, exactement!* Advertising manager! Ruin my car! Ruin my business! Ruin my *directeur de publicité*—advertising! *Stupido! Idiot! Idž do djabla!*"

"Yass, Excellency," the chauffeur said. He was a Harlem boy upon whom any languages other than basic English and advanced Bebop were wasted.

"*Oi veh!*" Popescu moaned, slapping his brow. He took a deep breath and launched into Hungarian. "*A büdös anyád avval kérkedett hogy kupleráјosné pedig valójában orgazda volt! Lófassz a segedbe, te szarházi!* Lazy black fool! *Merde de merde! Va donc te faire foûtre vieux con!*"

"Really, Manfred," John said, "it wasn't the driver's fault. I just didn't look where I was going."

"Don't interrupt," Popescu said quietly.

"Manny, honey, we're holding up traffic! You boys jus' come along with Manfred and I," Mrs. Popescu said in her motherly fashion. "Tell 'im to drive us back to the apottment, Manny."

"*A la maison!*" Mr. Popescu screamed through the window that separated him from his luckless chauffeur.

"Home, Fabian," Mrs. Popescu translated.

"Yass, Excellency," the chauffeur said.

Then Mrs. Popescu pushed a button. The electric door closed and the town car rolled majestically toward Central Park South.

By the time John had been deposited on the white velvet sofa in the Popescus' duplex penthouse, he had more or less recovered from the many shocks of the afternoon. Mr. Popescu had exhausted most of his dozen languages and Mrs. Popescu was becoming excessively cosy with Toby.

Looking around this hideous room, which Mary had done her level best to *un*-decorate, it was impossible to believe that he had been admitted to the room and to the august presence of Manfred Popescu only a year ago. Yet it was just twelve months ago that his wife, under the banner of Mrs. Manley Updike, Inc., Interiors, had been called in to tone down Lillian Popescu's flamboyant taste. Just a year ago that Manfred Popescu had come roaring home in a polylingual rage after having fired his advertising manager, his advertising agency and having cleaned house, down to the last pitch pipe, of the all-girl orchestra that had for years brought schmalz, corn and semi-classical airs to an ecstatic, if undemanding, radio audience on the Popescu Pulse-Beat Eternal Non-Magnetic Swiss Watch *Hour of Refinement*. Just a year ago that his wife had put in a whispered call on the gold telephone in the adjoining room urging him to hustle right over to the Popescu penthouse and sell the old brigand on a big new television show.

It had worked. After five straight hours of being understanding, after five straight days and five straight nights at his typewriter he had brought forth five of the best television scripts ever written. A week later he had been appointed the advertising manager of the Popescu Pulse-Beat Eternal Non-Magnetic Swiss Watch Company of Geneva, London, Paris and New York, Ltd., at fifteen thousand dollars a year with all the comforts of home. He had had no experience, no references, no pull. Only charm, talent and luck —and the fact that Manfred Popescu was of a mercurial nature— had got him the job.

Until that day he had been a struggling writer, albeit a good one. He and she had lived in decorative but genuine uncertainty in one handsome room in the East Sixties. They had lived on charm and hope, on her salary from an interior decorating firm and on his all-too-occasional sales of stories and revue sketches and television scripts, on the proceeds of his play that had been produced on a shoestring off Broadway and succeeded and advance royalties paid on this same play that had later been produced rather lavishly on Broadway and failed. Lillian and Manfred Popescu had changed all of that overnight and put him not only on Easy Street, but in Riveredge.

He supposed that he should be eternally grateful to the Popescus. Instead he detested them.

A year ago he had been moderately awed and extravagantly amused by Mr. and Mrs. Popescu and the *opéra bouffe* grandeur of their way of life. He had accorded them the good natured forebearance usually reserved for the antics of the Indian who strikes oil on the reservation, the factory girl who becomes Mrs. Manville, the colored laundress who invents a successful hair-straightener. He had been pleasantly tolerant of their childish squandering—this penthouse, the Palm Beach villa, the castle on the Thames, the château on the Loire, the schloss on the Rhine, the Popescu suites and flats and houses and lodges and numerous *pied à terre* that peppered the globe like buckshot. He had been hugely entertained by the Popescu fleet of outlandish cars, by the diesel-powered *Lilliman* bobbing serenely out in the yacht basin, by the dizzying profusion of furs and jewels and clothes and parties and restaurants and servants. The fabulous expenditures of the Popescus had given him a witty glimpse of life á la Bemelmans.

In the Popescus he had seen that never-never land of Newport in the Nineties, Hollywood in the Twenties, Houston in the Fifties rolled into one year. The Popescus had been just a couple of babes in Toyland and he had loved and admired them for their uninhibited enjoyment of all the bad taste they could afford.

A year ago Manfred Popescu had seemed to him a lovable old gypsy—a jolly European soldier of fortune, gay and relaxed with a zest for living his rags-to-riches life to the hilt. He had idealized Manfred into a kind of real-life *Laughing Cavalier*, as passionately interested in a good meal, a good wine, a beautiful picture or a beautiful woman as he was in winning a battle, besting a rival or ruling his peasantry.

And he had romanticized Lillian Schneider Bessamer Popescu into a fun-loving grande cocotte of nineteenth-century Paris. In his mind's eye she had become a Nana, a Zaza, a Sapho—a plump, fortyish widow, frivolous, frolicsome and fey, with no thought in her hennaed head other than pleasing her rich, new catch, his fine friends from the Jockey Club and his business associates from the Bourse with succulent suppers, cheerful chitchat and womanly wiles.

Together, the Popescus had inundated him and his wife with warmth, with love, with food, with liquor, with money, with gifts and with their endless invitations. There had been invitations to lunch, to cocktails, to dinner; invitations for a dozen weekends; invitations to cruise down to the Villa Manfrillian aboard the *Lilliman;* a standing invitation to pass all of next summer *with* the Popescus in the various Popescu properties abroad. The prodigal generosity of the Popescus had prompted him and his wife to refer to Manfred and Lillian as Mr. and Mrs. Santa Claus.

It had taken him just shy of a month to realize that if Santa Claus, with his constant, obese, ho-ho-ho-ing high spirits actually existed on earth at any place except a toy department at any time except the weeks between Thanksgiving and Christmas, he would most certainly be shot, his passing as little mourned as that of Adolf Hitler.

It had taken him just as long, too, to realize that Mr. Popescu was Santa Claus only to those associates whose society or whose talent Popescu desired and/or envied. To all others, Manfred Popescu was the spawn of some Central European bogeyman like Dracula thrust upon this country with the knowledge of only such archaic American business pleasantries as "The Public be damned" and "I won't sue you, I'll *ruin* you." As Popescu's Favorite, a position held in considerable scorn by the Popescu men who had once been or who never would be Popescu's Favorite, he had been both shocked and wounded to discover that his mentor—his Santa Claus—was something less than mortal. But it was true.

He had seen Popescu break executives of twenty years' standing on whim and whim alone. He had watched Popescu, the watch manufacturer, remove his greatest holdings for "tax reasons" from the three governments that had been the most responsible for keeping Popescu, the man, out of the gas chamber. He had heard Popescu urge the employment of the blind, not to give a boost to the disabled, but because the men and their dogs would work better and longer and quieter and cheaper in dark windowless rooms, hermetically sealed, as it were, from the distractions of light, air and labor unions.

And by the time he had worked for Popescu just a little *too* long to turn back—when his wife was pregnant, when the house in Riveredge had been financed, furnished and warmed, when he and she had become accustomed to smart, expensive clothes in smart, expensive settings—then he discovered that *he* had not created *Pulse Beat*, America's prestige television show, but that Manfred Popescu had. And around that time he also learned the lowly arts of blandishment.

As advertising manager of the Popescu Eternal Non-Magnetic Swiss Watch Company, Ltd., he had been forced to use blandishment not only on the ignorant melogomaniac above him by telling ingratiating lies ("Listen, Manfred, you know much more about advertising than I do") when it came to producing his own television program, but also to use blandishment on the capable specialists beneath him by telling the honest truth ("Listen, you guys, you know much more about advertising than I do") when it came to preparing the millions of dollars worth of magazine pages, bill boards, display pieces and car cards essential to promoting Popescu watches. He suspected that he was despised from both above and below and he couldn't honestly blame either faction for hating him. He thoroughly hated himself.

So the job that was to have given him financial security and creative freedom wasn't really a job at all. It was a position. And an ulcerous, uneasy, overpaid position it was, too, his time and effort devoted mainly to smoothing rumpled feathers while he played courtier and while his unfinished play and his unfinished novel grew dated and stale in the center drawer of his olive wood desk.

Nor had *Mrs.* Santa Claus turned out to be an unqualified delight. Lillian Schneider Bessamer Popescu was vain, vulgar, and vituperative, constantly demanding to be danced with, flattered, courted. If Lillian wore a new dress, a new hat, a new jewel—which was almost always—it had to be noticed and raved about. But if he made the mistake of raving about anything a second time, she would sulk, complain about the obsolescence of the article, accuse him of being unobservant, or, worse, indifferent. And Lillian was not as wrapped up in Manfred Popescu as she originally seemed to have been. Lillian was wrapped up in Lillian. Lillian didn't give a damn about Manfred except for the garish pleasures Manfred's money could buy for Lillian.

This would have been perfectly understandable had Lillian been half as old and twice as attractive. But Lillian had made a career of being a legalized courtesan and she knew the pitfalls. As a plump, young typist in Milwaukee, Lillian had been sufficiently seductive and cagey to become the adored second bride of a rich brewer, the mother of his only child and the complete mistress of all she surveyed—*in* Milwaukee *in* 1930. But Lillian's first victim, Mr. Bessamer, had been small beer, so to speak, as compared to Popescu. Today, Mrs. Santa Claus had good reason to believe that Mr. Santa Claus had good reason to be tempted by younger, tenderer cuts of beef.

The sight of Lillian's colorless, slightly bloodshot eyes darting beneath their stubby, mascaraed lashes as they fastened upon Manfred's beady black eyes fastening upon trim ankles and slim waists was a disquieting one. It made good sense—*dollars* and cents to be quite crass about it—for Lillian to see that Manfred was surrounded by attractive entertaining young people who would be too well bred to try any of the tricks Lillian herself would have tried in the days she hooked Mr. Bessamer and Mr. Popescu.

And so the invitations continued to parties and dinners and dances and luncheons and nightclubs and races and weekends. The wine flowed, the waiters bowed, the *Lilliman* tooted up and down the coast and Lillian continued watching Manfred watching. But the invitations were commands when issued to those employed by the Popescu enterprises. Whatever moments Manfred did not claim in the realm of industry, Lillian claimed in the half-world of pleasure. And there was no time-and-a-half for overtime. Manfred's chaste popularity and Lillian's peace of mind were bought and paid for by Popescu Pulse-Beat Eternal Non-Magnetic Swiss Watches, Ltd.—all tax-deductible.

Mr. and Mrs. Santa Claus may have been as roly-poly and as jolly as all get-out, but they were a despotic pair of patron saints—as likely to leave you at Christmas with a lump of coal and a stout stick as an electric train. There it was. And here he was, on what was to have been his day off, sitting on a white velvet sofa in his own semi-private North Pole.

He was startled from his unhappy introspection by the voice of Mr. Popescu. "But Sonny-boy," Manfred said, crossing the room to the fireplace wall, "you must let me give you something for killing you God-forbid on the street today, *hein?* A little—how you say—*cadeau* . . ."

"Present, honey," Lillian translated.

"Exactly, present." Mr. Popescu swung a large Matisse painting, chosen more because of its price than the Popescus' taste, back on its hinged frame and started twiddling the dial of a wall safe.

"Please, Manfred," he said. "No." Endearments such as Sonny-boy from Manfred were the order as long as one remained Popescu's Favorite. After a certain subtle change took place, former Favorites called him *Mister* Popescu and he called them Smith or Jones.

"Nonsense, Sonny-boy!" Popescu said jovially, closing the safe with a thump. "Here it should pay for your suit." He airily proferred a one thousand dollar bill.

"Manfred! Don't be silly. My suit isn't torn. It isn't even wrinkled." He heard Toby give a long, long whistle. "Your car didn't hit me and even if it had, I was to blame for being so . . ."

"G'wan, dearie, *take* it!" Lillian cried. "Why, you could of sued Manny for . . ."

"Take it, for Christ's sake," Toby muttered.

Suddenly, for the first time in a year, something inside him rebelled. He realized now that if the Popescu town car had struck him, mangled him, left him a basket case and public ward, he could not touch that money. He needed a thousand dollars just as badly as anyone else, but not *this* thousand. "No, Manfred," he said quietly. "I won't take it."

There was a long, fetid silence.

Then Popescu chuckled. "So! So, you don't *want* it? You're a good boy!" With that Popescu stepped forward and tousled his hair affectionately. He could feel the very walls of the room breathe a sigh of relief. Like many people who are prepared to buy their way through life, Manfred Popescu was not prepared to have his largesse refused, for denying the tyrant's grace was denying the tyrant's power. But today Popescu had accepted graciously what had been intended and delivered as a slap in the face.

"Ha ha ha!" Popescu chuckled in his bearlike fashion, "He's a good boy, Tony . . ."

"Toby," Toby said.

"Yes, exactly, Toby. He's a good boy. He's a smart advertising manager. Best I ever had. You ever look at my program, *Pulse Beat?*"

"Never," Toby said.

Good old Toby, John thought gratefully. You can still spot a gent and this is one who would just as soon spit in Caesar's eye as not.

"You should, Toby-boy," Popescu continued blandly. "Sonny-boy here produces it. He's one man who's a good listener. He comes to me. I give him my ideas. Next week there it is in the television set—black and white *and* the color. We win all the awards, don't we, Sonny-boy. Ha ha ha ha ha! Ring for some drinks, Lillian. These boys must be, uh, how-you-say *avoir sois?*"

"Thirsty, honey," Lillian said, pressing the button at her side.

John went scarlet with discomfort and embarrassment. If there is anything more unsettling than offering one's gift and having it refused, it is offering one's enmity and having it ignored. Popescu was now sitting between him and Toby, shaking with jolly chuckles and slapping his knee rather too often and too hard for comfort. "Yes, he's a good one, my Sonny-boy. Beautiful production on the television last night, Tony, beautiful. Lillian's little girl was in it. Lovely show. One of our best," Popescu went on with his maddening habit of repeating and repeating and repeating everything he said when he was in a good humor.

Thoroughly defeated by the man, he made a half-hearted attempt at good humor and good manners. "It had a lot of faults, Manfred. For example . . ."

"Nonsense, Sonny-boy. Beautiful show. You must come around some day, Tony, I'll show you the—how you say *cinematograph?*"

"Kinescope, honey."

"Exactly. And, Tony?"

"Toby."

"Just so, Toby. Here you take this thousand dollars. Buy Sonny-boy something nice for old Popescu."

Toby paused. "Well, gee, Mr. Grotescu . . ."

"Popescu."

"Roger! *Popescu*. Well, gee, Mr. Popescu . . ."

"Here! Take it! It's nothing. You save my Sonny-boy's life. You get the, um, uh, Lillian, how you say . . ."

"Reward, Manny?"

"Exactly! Reward."

"Well, gee . . ." Toby faltered.

"*Pleeeess!*" Popescu urged.

"Well, as long as you feel *that* way about it," Toby said, folding the bill.

"Toby!" John couldn't have been more shocked if Toby had accepted the Stalin Prize. Yet there Toby sat, confident and boyish, tucking Popescu's bribery into his wallet.

"You're cute, that's what you are, Toby," Lillian said, giving Toby's cheek a little pat.

"Toby," John breathed. "*You* can't . . ."

"So now we all happy friends!" Popescu boomed. "And here come the drink, so we all celebrate together! *Non, non, non, non, non, non, non! Ici, ici, ici!*" He boomed at the butler, tapping the porphyry slab of a coffee table in front of him.

"Yes, Excellency," the butler said. He put down an immense silver tray all but covered with Waterford decanters and Steuben glasses. Then he turned and left the room, his well-tailored back quivering with hatred.

In his shock and disillusionment, in the noise and confusion, he was barely conscious of having said "Scotch" when the cumbersome, icy glass was thrust into his hand. Then Mr. Popescu was making all kinds of jolly—and probably indecent—toasts and in all kinds of jolly languages. Lillian was getting a good deal shriller and a good deal giddier. (Although Manfred disapproved of women who drank too much, Lillian displayed an ever-increasing tendency to leave the room "for just a sec, honey" only to return a trifle more unsteadily, a trifle more noisely, a trifle more slurringly, but indescribably refreshed.) And of course Toby's legendary social gift was rising to the fore. Well, it ought to, he thought, very few people are paid a thousand dollars for nothing except sitting around and being charming for ten minutes.

He could hear Toby complimenting Lillian Popescu on the hideous red, white and blue knit dress she was wearing—"every stitch by hand, honey, done by these two French women that have a shop up on Madison, but strictly custom work, honey"—and on her fake-looking genuine ruby, diamond and sapphire bracelet with a Popescu Pulse-Beat watch concealed among the cabochons. Toby's tone was a bantering one—one of mocking insincerity. It suddenly occurred to him that Toby was trying the same line on Lillian as he had on the unattractive, unpopular girls whom he had chosen to thrill for five or ten minutes at dances or house parties back in college. In those days everyone had been in on the joke except the poor girls who were being treated to Toby's charm. Oh, Toby'd been a riot then. But Toby wasn't being quite such a riot today. Somehow the barbed and smiling ease of Toby's delivery that had made him so adult and witty as a college boy now made him seem immature and cruel as a man. John felt almost sorry for Lillian—so dumb and vain and befuddled—being patronized by this cunning, boyish Machiavelli whose patron, to the tune of a thousand dollars, she should have been.

". . . just can't get over it," Lillian was screeching. "Here Manny goes an' offers him this money and he don't even take it. Why, Manny thinks the world of 'im."

"Well, he always was pretty much of the good little Boy Scout," Toby said, grinning at him. He didn't return the smile. In this room, at this moment, the Boy Scout movement, with its homely Christian credo looked pretty good.

"Ya know, Toby, he's just like my little girl Besame," Lillian said. "Why, Besame won't take a thing from Manfred and I and she . . ."

"Who's just like Besame?" a cool, crisp voice sounded from the doorway.

John looked up and there stood Besame Bessamer, cool and detached and beautiful.

He had seen Besame Bessamer only a few times before: first a week ago when she read for a part on *Pulse Beat* (as though Popescu's stepdaughter would have been turned down, even if she had a harelip and two heads); then at dress rehearsals; and then last night on the program.

And he had to admit that his first impression of Besame had been mixed. When she came in to be interviewed—ordinarily he didn't bother to hear the stammered readings of inexperienced performers, but Popescu had *naturally* set up an appointment—she had been on time. That surprised him. Little else had. Besame Bessamer had looked like almost every other aspiring young actress—hair too long and too black; face too cold and too white; mouth too large and too red. They were all making up that way this year. Still she was dressed a good bit differently and a whole lot better than the other TV girlies in a go-to-hell tweed suit and a perfect menagerie of sable skins. Well, what the hell, he had thought, she *ought* to be better dressed than the rest of those poor, starving television tramps. Her outfit had been perfect—for, say, a Junior League committee meeting—and that had irritated him. Any other young actress would have had to do two half-hour shows a week and still sleep around all year to afford an outfit like that.

He'd been politely civil to her, as he *had* to be, considering his hangover, and she had been more than politely civil to him, which was damned nice of her considering that she would undoubtedly get the job no matter how badly she read.

The part she tried out for was a large one and a hard one in a perfect clinker of a story. The script had been a mishmash of cloak and dagger didoes concerning a gorgeous American actress (the alcoholic old movie star) and a dashing British agent (a broken-down matinee idol) harried by red spies in a mythical principality on the very hem of the Iron Curtain. Also involved were a top-secret bomb hidden in a hat box, a cocker spaniel, two dialect comedians, some torture, and the lovely young princess of the mythical country who gave her life to save the bomb recipe for the West. Besame was reading for the role of the princess.

Since it was a foregone conclusion that Miss Bessamer would be hired, he turned right to the princess' longest speech in the script to hear the worst.

It went something like: "*Mon dieu!*" (The script writer had tucked in scraps of easy French to give the mythical nation sufficient foreign flavor.) "How can it be that since all the people in the world are taught to love one another in the" . . . pause . . . "church, still they wish to kill their brother-men with the secret bombs . . ." Well, it went on in that vein.

He had seen enough inexperienced actresses to dread any kind of attempt at a foreign accent. Either they went all out in the best Irene Bordoni tradition—"Moan dooo! 'ow can eet be zat seence oll zee-peep-hole een zee wore-old lairn to loaf wan annozer een zee cherche . . ." or, in the case of the rich-bitch Besame Bessamer type, they played it like a Foxcroft girl ordering lunch at the Tour d'Argent—"Maw dyerr! Haow con it be thot sinnss ull the pöple in the wöld lön to love one anothah in the chöch . . ."

But Besame had given that dreary line neither the Gay Paree nor the hot potato delivery. Instead she had read with an engaging ingenuous dignity, pausing occasionally as if actually groping for the right words for the right thoughts. In fact, her reading of the princess lifted the less-than-mediocre story up to the level of the scripts *he* had first written for *Pulse Beat*.

When she had finished she looked up at him.

"Turn the page and go on," he had said calmly. "I'll read the part of Eric. Now. Down at the middle of the page where Eric says, 'But we of the Free World are fighting for peace and liberty . . .'"

In the end, she read the entire part, standing calmly in his office while he fed cues and stage directions to her.

"Well?" she said, shutting the script.

"Well, you were swell. Perfectly swell. The part is yours—needless to say."

She looked up at him sharply. "You're not just doing this because my mother is married to the boss? If you are, you can forget . . ."

"Believe me, I'm not," he said. "I was asked to hear you, not to hire you. If you hadn't been good I'd have thrown you right out." This hadn't been entirely true. His instructions were to find something for Lillian's little girl; even if it was only a walk-on. Well, he'd done his duty and, luckily enough, the girl had talent.

"You're not kidding?"

"Of course I'm not. Take it easy now or you'll talk yourself right out of a part." Then he smiled at her, not that he either liked or approved of her as a person. Bosses' daughters and step-daughters just rubbed him the wrong way. "Tell me, what have you done before?"

"Nothing."

"Nothing?"

"Well, nothing really professional. At Bennington there was *Antigone* . . ."

"In modern dress?"

"In modern dress. And *The Doll's House* and *Saint Joan*—the usual stuff. Then two seasons of summer stock . . ."

"I get the picture—*Sabrina Fair* and *Autumn Crocus* and *Spring-time for Henry?*"

"Exactly. And *Private Lives* and *Blithe Spirit*. Terribly sophisticated stuff and at least one guest star per week—two for the Fourth of July and Labor Day."

He supposed that he would have got to like kidding with Miss Bessamer if she hadn't been who she was. Instead, he cut the interview short by scratching a note to the director and shooing her off to rehearsals.

Since then he'd been of many minds concerning Besame Bessamer. He'd disapproved of her for taking advantage of her position to get a job. On the other hand, he'd approved of her as an actress. But then he'd doubted her frankness—phony, he felt to this minute—in saying that she had to be hired on merit alone, when she knew damned well that . . . Then again, she'd been the best thing at the dress rehearsal and the only member of the cast to have memorized any lines. Still, he'd suspected her of *noblesse oblige* when she demurely and good naturedly allowed her part to be cut because the star complained that the ingenue and the cocker spaniel were stealing great gobs of scenes. (A simple word from her would be enough to send the falling star back to another season of unemployment in Hollywood.)

But neither Besame nor the cocker spaniel had growled about having their parts slashed to the bone and that made him uncomfortable and distrustful. And, after all, the newcomer Besame Bessamer *had* been the only capable performer on the show.

The noise and general commotion surged up once again as Besame strode smartly into the hideous living room. He was conscious of standing up and grinning vacuously while Lillian kissed her daughter and introduced Toby. Then he was somewhat more aware of Manfred pawing and embracing his stepdaughter like a grizzly bear in mating season. He also sensed, rather than saw, the shudder that passed through the young actress as she broke away from Popescu.

Well, who could blame the girl for that? Manfred's greeting had been one of those wet, hairy, groping lurches more appropriate to the Dirty Old Man than to the indifferent Stepfather.

When his turn came, he took her long, firm hand in his and smiled at her. "Hello," he said. "You were great last night. I really mean it. You were the only decent thing on the show."

She looked at him long and hard with her fine, dark eyes. Then she decided that he meant what he said and answered, "Thank you. Thank you very much. But I'm glad to say that the competition wasn't very stiff."

"You're right," he said. "It was a real rout."

"Oh, it was a beauty-full program!" Lillian screamed. "The best one ever! Manny an' I hustled back from the Plaza—we always have dinner in the Rondyvoo Room on Fridays so's we can come back to our little home an' watch *Pulse Beat*—an' we saw it on color TV. Oh, it's gorgeous in color!"

"I'll *bet* she is," Toby said, giving Besame his famous old blue-eye treatment.

"Honestagod, Toby," Lillian said, drinking deeply, "I jus' sat in the Fun Room an' cried. There was my own little baby right there in fronta my eyes an' so real that I thought fer a minute she *was* a forrun princess being murdered by the Commyunusts. Oh, I tell yuh, I was so duppressed that poor Manny had to take me right back to the Plaza. Dinchew, Manny honey?"

"And what does my little Sarah Bernhardt want to drink, *hein?*" Mr. Popescu said, giving Besame's arm a pinch.

"Nothing, thank you," she said coldly. "I just stopped in to return Mother's furs. Thanks for letting me borrow them," she added, unwinding the great scarf of nine perfect sables and holding it out toward Lillian.

"Oh, Besame!" Lillian cackled. "*You* don't have to bring them pussycats back—I always call my fur pieces pussycats, Toby, Manny gets such a laugh out of it. I *told* you you could have them. I got some lovely new ones anyways. They're mutation—almost blue and very shick. You can have these old . . ."

"No thank you, Mother. They're just a bit too grand for a working girl."

"Tcha! Now isn't that the silliest thing you ever hear of, Toby? Just like I been telling you, John and Besame are igzackly alike. They won't take anything! Why, Toby, I remember back in Milwaukee when I was married to Mr. Bessamer an' Besame was just a little girl, I yoosta take her down to the Boston Store and . . . Say, I bet I never told you how I happenda call her Besame, did I?"

"Please, Mother," Besame said.

"No. Now that you mention it, I don't think you did," Toby said maliciously.

"Well, it's kine of a cute story. When I had her—an' oh what a time I had with her. It was a breech delivery an' I nearly yelled the roof off of the hospital. Anyways, when I saw my precious little baby girl, I wanted to name her after the two most precious people in the whole wide world: my mom, who was named Bessie an' my little sister Mae. Poor little Mae. She always had terrible trouble with her ovaries. It killed her. Cancer, *I* said, but do you think I could get that dumb doctor ta bulieve me?" Mrs. Popescu's eyes filled with tears. She took another enormous swallow of her drink and plunged bravely on. "But anyways, the two names Bessie an' Mae seemed so kind of old fashion' that I put 'em together and called her Besame. That means 'Kiss me' in Spanish, you know."

"Does it now," Toby said. "Well, I'd be delighted."

"And I've been stuck with the name ever since," Besame murmured.

"Hahahaha! Arnchew *cute!* But, like I was saying. Here Besame is an' she won't take anything from Manfred and I. All she's got is a couple of acting jobs every now an' then and what her uncle—Mr. Bessamer's late brother—left her. She could be living here with us but instead she lives in a slum way over on the East Side . . ."

"Mother," Besame said a bit tensely, "I don't think Sutton

Place is exactly a slum area, or that—even if it is—Mr. Wentworth cares."

"Oh, but I do care," Toby said lightly. "In fact, I can't imagine a man alive who wouldn't care about your exact name, age, address, telephone number and availability this evening."

"Hahahahaha! Isn't he cute!" Lillian shrieked. "I'll betchera devil with all we poor girls! Here, Manny, get Toby an' I another lil drinkie."

"He's simply adorable," Besame said coolly. "Well, thanks for lending me your furs, Mother, I think I'll be running along."

There was a great clamor for her to stay and have just one drink. Toby even managed to be louder in his demands than Mr. and Mrs. Popescu.

Besame cast a helpless look toward John.

He heard himself saying "Please don't go just yet. Stay and talk to me about doing more work on the show." If he hadn't quite liked Besame at first, he certainly did now. He felt that she was a goddess descended into a sty filled with swine—himself included.

"Very well," she said and sank to the sofa beside him. "Scotch and plain water, please, Manfred."

The sky was lavender over Central Park when he and Besame finally slipped away from the Popescu penthouse.

"I hope I wasn't rude to your friend," Besame said in the elevator.

"He isn't my friend," he said calmly and the speech shocked him so much that he was unable to speak another word all the way down. Either something had happened to Toby or something had happened to him, but whatever it was, this afternoon spent in the company of his oldest and dearest comrade—*and* with Mr. and Mrs. Santa Claus—had been a nightmare. In fact the whole day had been cataclysmic. In less than twelve hours he had seen the crack-up of his marriage; the disintegration of those symbols of gilded and eternal youth, Teddy Edwards and the Bacchus Club; the disillusionment and humiliation of his secretary; the true, mean, shoddiness of Toby, his idol and—most unsettling of all himself.

This was a new self, far different from the hundred selves he saw passing through the mirrored reception room on the Executive's Floor of the Popescu Building. That self had been a talented, vital young man, slim and trim in well-cut clothes. It was a man on the way to the top because of his God-given gift as a writer and an administrator. Today the self was just an English suit with a genius for toadying to a fat, ignorant pig of a man and his fat, ignorant slut of a wife. If he had ever had talent, if he had ever been able to write he had exchanged it all for twenty-five thousand a year, plus bonuses, plus tips, plus free food and liquor as the official sycophant and court jester of Manfred and Lillian.

The quiet afternoon in the penthouse had decayed rapidly into one of the smaller, but noisier Popescu bacchanales. After her second public—and third private—drink, Lillian had become her old kittenish self and moved the party into what was misnamed the Fun Room, a chamber of horrors decked out in brass and leopard, teakwood and vinyl tile, a pseudo Dali, two double-image paintings, alleged to be terribly naughty if one stood close enough, and lots of photographs of Manfred and Lillian grinning cheek by jowl with whatever second-rate celebrities they had been able to lure into their web.

"Mamma loves mambo!" Lillian had screeched. With that, she had set into action a machine that looked like Univac, but actually played records, and began lurching across the floor with Toby, her great breasts jouncing obscenely, the blubbery buttocks gyrating, the abundant flesh of her thighs quivering beneath the tautness of her knit dress.

Toby was a good dancer, a clever dancer, with a bloodhound's sense of direction when it came to manipulating his partner round the floor. That afternoon he had diabolically gone out of his way to make the most of Lillian's awkwardness, her drunkenness, her rotundness. Accompanied by sly smiles, he had done everything possible to make Lillian even more ludicrous than ever.

Toby had spun her, swung her out, encouraged her to perform. Lillian may have thought that she was the belle of the ball, but this afternoon she had looked like nothing quite so much as the pathetic, fat, old, drunken slattern she was, cavorting about with a partner who may have thought that he was the college cut-up, but who looked like nothing quite so much as the cruel, seedy, middle-aged, drunken adventurer he was. Neither made a very inspiring sight.

Then there had been a rather taxing scene while Lillian had gone off to revive her sagging face and lagging spirits. Toby had sprung to Besame's side, grabbed her wrist in that boisterous, boyish fashion that had set so many young girls' hearts to beating faster, and begged her to dance.

"No thank you, Mr. Wentworth," Besame had said.

Toby had been dumbfounded. He seemed not to have heard, had taken a pull of his drink, stared at her glassily and said: "Oh, come on, Bessie. Get up and dance."

"I said no thank you."

"Well, maybe my little girl dance with Pappa, *hein?*" Manfred had offered jovially.

"No thank you, Manfred. I said I didn't want to dance. In fact, I think I'll be going."

"Going?" Toby had said brightly. "Going where?"

"No place. Just going." Besame had risen to her feet.

"Well, baby, in that case, you come out with us. We all go someplace get a *big* dinner," Manfred had cried, beaming at her from the leopard couch at the side. "Then we go someplace to dance—maybe you like El Morocco? Here Sonny-boy, telephone the little lady tell her come in town and join us, *hein?* We all make big party."

"I—I'm sorry, Manfred," John had stammered, "but my wife . . . that is I . . . *we* rather . . ."

"What Sonny-boy means, Manny," Toby had roared, splashing liquor into his glass, "is that he and that beautiful, frigid, hunk of ice he married have . . ."

"*Toby!*"

"Na, na, na, Tony-boy. Mustn't talk like that! A very beautiful sweet little lady, that girl. I like her. She bring me Sonny-boy and . . ." Popescu's loyal little speech had been interrupted by Toby's lurching off in search of a bathroom.

"Look," Besame had said, "I'm sorry. I've got to go."

"Wait," he had said, without quite knowing why, "I'm coming with you."

Of course there had been quite an altercation in the Popescus'

Moroccan-style foyer. Lillian had emerged, amazing in gold lamé, and pled with them to go dancing. She had become teary and accused her little girl of no longer loving her; then she had accused him of indifference. Toby, back from the bathroom, had joined in. Finally the elevator door had slid open and they were mercifully alone and away.

Before he could adjust his brain to thinking again, they were standing in the ornate lobby of the building. "Well, goodbye," Besame said, holding out her hand. "I wish I could say it's been a lovely afternoon. Unfortunately, it hasn't been—not through any fault of yours."

"Listen," he said abruptly, "please don't go. Come out and have a drink with me."

"No thank you. Going out with other women's husbands isn't exactly in my line."

"I didn't mean that kind of going out. I asked you to have a drink with me. I want to talk to you about your work."

"Oh come now. I may be only twenty-two, but I've heard *that* line . . ."

"Damn it, don't be so smart and cute! I'm hardly dumb enough to try to seduce my boss's daughter . . ."

"Stepdaughter, please," she said.

"Stepdaughter, then. Besides, my wife and I are separated."

"Oh? Well in that case . . ."

"Will you come, Besame? I mean, Miss Bessamer?"

"In that case, I will. But just one question."

"What's that?" he asked.

"Just what would you do if the boss's daughter tried to seduce *you?*"

five

He had no idea how he and Besame happened to end up at Chandelier, except that Chandelier was next door to the little restaurant where they had dined and he'd told her all about his new play.

Now he wished that they'd gone on to some other place. Chandelier had very definite memories for him. It was the first New York nightclub he had ever been in. That was fifteen years ago and the place had been firmly established even then. "Chandelier" was practically the password of the Bacchus Club and an evening there with a dreamy-eyed blonde had been the aim of every kid at college, rich and poor alike—and he had been among the poorest. It had been strictly formal in those prewar days; certainly black tie and preferably white. Prices were stiff then—a two-fifty cover charge on Saturday nights; bar whiskey at eighty cents a shot; beer at fifty cents a bottle and Coca-cola at seventy-five. (Everything was now exactly double, except Coca-cola which had rigidly maintained its same old, reasonable depression price, but was still discouraged by the Chandelier waiters.)

He had always been afraid that he wouldn't be allowed in or that his money would run out and he'd be humiliated in front of his date and have to call the Bacchus Club for bail. Chandelier was that impressive. It had had the wholesome chic of the St. Regis Roof or the Rainbow Room and you could take nice young girls there because their mothers simply felt that they wouldn't get into any trouble—as long as they got home by one, *and no later*—what with its nightly Big Apple, its contests for singing debutantes, its conga chain. No dormitory room in the East was considered complete without its Chandelier matchbooks and swizzle sticks and ashtrays and menus.

He had been equally awed by the prices; the luster of the patrons; the names of the diseuses (late lamented charmers like Helen Morgan and Elsie Houston); and the daring, old world conservatism of the decor (dark blue walls, red divans and, hanging above the circular dance floor, the overpowering chandelier that gave the place not only its sole illumination, but its name).

Chandelier had changed hands a dozen times in its twenty-five years, but nothing else had changed. Today it looked old and dusty and shabbily pretentious. Just as old and dusty and shabbily pretentious as John himself felt. The place was threadbare and absolutely dirty, yet it was still thronged with people who were impressed, just as he had once been, by its elderly style, and by others who still felt a sentimental attachment to the place, as though it were an old tweed coat, worn out but too good to throw away.

Nothing had changed. The grizzled, ill-natured old bartender was still on duty in the outside room, still snarling and snapping at customers, still padding the checks, still being called Charlie with great affection by those who hadn't been to Chandelier often enough to loathe him.

There was still the bronze easel on which was mounted an elaborately retouched photograph of the current entertainer, and the following message in flowing script:

Chandelier
presents with great pride
the American debut
of
MLLE. CHOU-CHOU LA GRUE
The Sensation of Paris
Singing Twice Nightly

Yes, the French imports, more often than not unheard-of in their native land, were all the rage now. And they were cheaper to hire, as well.

He could hear the thump-thump-thump of the orchestra from the inner sanctum and he knew it was the same old bunch that had been playing there when he was in college and, indeed, playing the same old show tunes that were the standard standbys of the so-called "society" band.

But there was a difference. The same old headwaiter, who had terrified him in his poor days, now gave him and Besame a quick scrutiny, bowed much lower then necessary and started issuing instructions to have a table set up next to the dance floor.

"Oh, please no," Besame said.

"No. Look," he said to the headwaiter, "thanks, but no thanks. We really don't want a ringside table—just something small back in a corner and out of the line of fire."

The headwaiter looked hurt. Perhaps it was because his kind-hearted gesture had been spurned. Perhaps it was because he liked to have the frugal East Side gentry prominently displayed to the expense-account customers, who were paying, after all, to see Society at play. Or perhaps it was because the unfortunate term "line of fire" reminded him of the fatal shooting here twenty years ago, of a gangland celebrity who was certainly no gentleman, before the place had achieved its reputation as a kind of finishing school for the daughters of the genteel. Cursing silently in Greek, he escorted them to a divan table between a party from Lubbock, Texas, and a costume jewelry buyer from Akron who kept telling her costume jewelry manufacturer escort that Chandelier was much more refined than the Latin Quarter.

How funny, John thought, that back in the days when Chandelier spelled glamor, opulence and the high life, he would have given his right arm if the staff had set up a special table for him. But the staff wouldn't have done it if he'd surrendered both arms. While today, when they were willing to do anything for him and asked only his continued patronage and a small tip, he really wanted to sit back at the kind of dim corner table to which he had been relegated as a kid.

"A penny for your thoughts," Besame said quietly.

"Dirt cheap," he said lamely and he was pleased that this un-witticism hadn't brought forth a tinkling cascade of stagey laughter. He liked Besame and he was delighted that he had pegged her all wrong when first they met. She had even come, gradually, to *look* like a different, individual girl instead of the run-of-the-mill aspiring actress.

The waiter put their drinks deferentially onto the table now and left. Left them flat, he felt. After the business of pouring Scotch and mixing the drinks, after the lifted glass, the customary "Cheers!" and after the first sip, the conversation seemed to die of a long, wasting illness.

Peering through the gloom of Chandelier, he saw all the familiar Saturday night sights and wondered again how it had ever been possible for him to like this place. There was the inevitable family-reunion table—a dozen uncomfortable looking people ranging in age from seven to seventy and all trying desperately to be very, very gay; to have their host's money's worth. A little girl of seven, quite plain in her ruffled pink tulle party dress and modified harlequin glasses, was performing an off-beat one-step with a gnarled old man who was not only old enough to be her grandfather, but who *was* her grandfather.

"Show Gramps how to do the cha-cha, Darlene," voices called from the anniversary table. Darlene, unmindful of the fact that the orchestra was playing a waltz, happily obliged, throwing Gramps into a quandary. The table roared with laughter, browning gardenia corsages heaving on the bosoms of the women. A good time was being had by all—nearly as much fun as they could have had in the living room back home in Jackson Heights.

There was a birthday table. It was *always* somebody's birthday at Chandelier. If the party was sufficiently august, the orchestra would even sing and play "Happy Birthday to You." This party was not. They looked like the kind of people who read confession magazines. The women had all too obviously spent the later afternoon at inexpensive establishments called things like Bea's Salon de Beauté or Al and Irma's Vanitee Shoppe. Their hair clung to their skulls in rigidly lacquered waves and ringlets, their set faces proclaimed the Complimentary Hollywood Glamour Makeup thrown in free with each shampoo and wave. Girdled, cinched, laced and padded beneath bright acetate dresses known as "Cocktail Gowns," they were like iridescent May flies, freed for a brief moment from the diaper pails, pressure cookers and easy time payments of the vast New Jersey housing development that formed their common chrysalis.

But the world into which they had flown with high spirits and higher hopes had proved to be a cold and terrifying place, expensive, austere and disappointing. Sitting sedately around the ruins of a cake—most of its message, "Happy Birthday Marge from The Gang at Hemlock Park" could still be deciphered—the lady May flies, overdressed, overfed, overawed, smiled cautiously and uncomfortably and wished that their six hours of worldly life might soon end.

As for the May flies' husbands, they were mystified and a little terrified by their unexpectedly decorous and decorative mates; just as mystified and terrified as they were by Chandelier, its trappings, staff and clientele. None of the men at the birthday table had shone quite as brilliantly as he was accustomed to shining back in the modest purlieus of Hemlock Park. The Aggressive Go-Getter—fearless in the face of school board, police force and zoning laws of Northern New Jersey—had been too cowed by the headwaiter to protest the inferior table. The Perfect Scream—always the life of every party back across the Hudson—had yet to tell a joke, propose a side-splitting toast or do his locally famous impersonation of Liberace. The Sophisticate—a college graduate who had been stationed in Paris for nearly a year and, who subscribed to *Esquire*—had been so undone by the *sommelier* and the wine list as to stammer and slur tragically when ordering the "pretentious little Alsatian *vin blanc*" to accompany the sweetbreads and capon *sous cloche*. The resultant 1931 red burgundy had been vile and almost opaque with sedimentation, but at least it had been *old*. Too mortified to protest, the Sophisticate had pronounced it *merveilleux, trés bon, magnifique* and not even the Aggressive Go-Getter had had the spirit to remark that the wine was neither Alsatian nor *blanc*. Stoically they drank of the cup.

Now the husbands were bolstering themselves with hard liquor—rye and gingerale for all but the Sophisticate, who had recovered sufficiently to insist on Scotch and Perrier Water (fifty cents extra the Aggressive Go-Getter noted silently). It would be a vast relief for all concerned to listen to this French singer—acclaimed as *merveilleux, trés bon* and *magnifique* by the Sophisticate, who felt that he ought to have heard of her—pay their ransom and return to their baby-sitters in Hemlock Park, New Jersey.

Two young people, obviously just married, sat at a table recently cleared of everything except an overflowing ashtray. Embarrassed, uncomfortable, over-spent and drained of small talk, they wanted to go but knew that they should stay, if only to tell the folks back in Scranton that they had dined at Chandelier and heard the famous Chou-Chou la Grue on their New York honeymoon.

A pair of college kids remained doggedly on the dance floor, casting surreptitious glances back toward their tiny divan table where a furious waiter *and* a check were impatiently waiting. The kids had coasted since eight on two beers and a Tom Collins. Now they hoped to glide through the ten o'clock show. The waiter shared no such hope. Bigger spenders were already waiting for tables and at Chandelier turnover was *everything.*

Suddenly John called the waiter.

"Yes, sir?"

"You see those two kids on the edge of the dance floor?" he asked.

"Yes, sir?" the waiter said with a somewhat puzzled air, but ready to pounce.

"Send two more of whatever they've been drinking to their table and put it on my bill, please," he said.

"Yes, *sir!*" the waiter said, all smiles and beams, and darted away. The college kids had been recalled from exile. With any luck, they could nurse their drinks right through the midnight show.

All of these people—and dozens more like them scattered around the room—were the ones who *didn't* belong at Chandelier; the ones who would come this one time and be too humiliated ever to return again, although they wouldn't admit it under torture.

His glance fell now upon the people who *did* belong at Chandelier. They made, if anything, an even less inspiring sight.

A number of tables were occupied by May-and-December couplings. There were fun-loving old gentlemen in their sixties boyishly cavorting with chemical blondes who could easily have been their daughters. The girls with their soft curves and hard eyes all looked enough alike to be sisters and they were of a genre usually described by the tabloids as Starlets or Models. They dressed almost identically. They walked with their bosoms and bottoms thrust out too far and as though their shoes were too tight, which they were. They were capable of just three facial expressions apiece: sympathetic interest ("Ethel is a fine woman but she just don't understand me . . ."); hysterical glee (". . . and then this travelling salesman says—I hope you don't mind a slightly off-colored story, baby . . ."); and, when unobserved, stupid, stony sullenness.

The gentlemen could look back on this evening, through coronary thromboses, slight strokes and hardening of the arteries, as one last, wonderful fling with that cute trick in New York. Their girls could look forward from this evening to one or two thousand evenings just like it, then to wrinkles and crow's feet, a visit to the gynecologist or a visit from the vice squad. But there were better things to look forward to for the moment: Hollywood; a rich marriage; the green satin strapless at the Wilma Shop; a kindly old partner for the night—"Lookee here, baby, I gotta little girl just your age. Here's Betty Lou's photo, but it don't really do her justice. She's kinda squinting in the sun . . ."—who would be normal and dull and gentle and grateful and generous to a fault. Yes, tonight would be all right. "Oh, honey, lemme write down that killing joke about the hunter and the bear. I never *can* remember a joke."

There were far fewer older women with young men, but they, too, were at Chandelier this evening, grateful for the concealment of flesh and hair in the dim light, eager—but not too obviously so—to return to their rose-lit parlors for ". . . one last little drink and a bit of mood music . . ." with their polite, resigned and rather bored youthful escorts. ("You're so lean and muscular, Jimmy, I'd love to paint you sometime.") Haughty with nice old cab drivers and doormen, vicious to their maids, these women were like aspic in the long, lean hands of the handsome boys who offered their services in exchange for a tailor-made suit, a silk brocade robe, half a dozen ghastly ties or, possibly, a two-week trip to the warmer climes before the Big Scene—the tears, the accusations, the renunciation or denunciation—took place.

And then there were the really social people. At a table on the edge of the floor, for example, there was . . .

"Aren't you *listening* to me?" Besame said.

"Uh, what? I beg your pardon." Now he was flustered and suspected that he had been very rude.

"I said, Did you know that young couple you sent the drinks to?"

"Oh. No. Never saw them before in my life."

"But then . . . then *why* did you want to send drinks to their table?"

"Well, I guess because . . . Well, to tell you the truth, I really don't know. I just felt like sending the poor kids a drink, that's all."

"You're very sweet."

"What?"

"I said, you're very sweet."

"Oh, come off it, Besame."

"You might even be sweet enough to ask me to dance. Mother tells me you're wonderful."

"Why . . . well, sure," he blurted. "I didn't think you liked to dance. This afternoon you said . . ."

"I'd like to dance—with *you*," Besame said.

They made their way through the closely packed tables to the even more closely packed dance floor. He stood a little tensely, a little ridiculously, at first, making himself too tall, too erect, as though he were facing a prospective employer.

"My, but aren't you towering?" Besame murmured and slid into his arms.

Then he relaxed, fell in with the music—a waltz by Rodgers and Hart called "Lover," which he dimly connected with an early talking picture starring Maurice Chevalier and Jeannette MacDonald. He danced well. Besame's mother had all too often assured him of that. Tonight, with a partner who was thirty years younger and thirty pounds lighter and thirty drinks soberer than Mrs. Popescu, he danced even better.

The pianist and guiding spirit of the doughty Chandelier band

—a middle-aged roué affectionately known as Sonny—began singing in his hesitant, husky tenor, his toupee glistening in the rose spotlight.

"Luv-verr when nime ne-err yew
An' die he-err yew
Speak my name
Soffly in my year yew
Breathe a flame . . ."

"Ouch!" Besame said.

"What's the matter?"

"It sounds so painful. Having a flame breathed into your ear, I mean."

"I never thought of it quite that way," John said and began to laugh.

"But, Fred," a strident voice came ringing from the sidelines, "he's here, *too*. Just look at him, if you please, out with another woman!"

The laughter died on John's lips. The voice could only be that of Alice Marshall, his wife's sister. He stared unbelievingly in the direction of the voice. Sure enough, there was Alice looking like an outraged mother eagle in her feathered hat, clutching at her reluctant husband with one claw and groping for her spectacles with the other. "Fred, aren't you going to *stop him?*" Alice cawed.

"Please, dear," Mr. Marshall begged.

Aghast, John danced Besame, somewhat out of step, into the thick of the crowd. It was in this state of shock that he remembered dimly that today marked the fifteenth year of poor Fred Marshall's bondage to Alice. Naturally they were out celebrating.

"What's your hurry?" Besame asked.

His flight across the dance floor was stopped only by one of the ringside tables. He hit the table hard, bruising his thigh badly.

"I—I'm awfully sorry," he blurted, "I lost my balance and . . ."

"Hello, sweetie," a brassy voice said. It was Adele Hennessey.

"Why, why Adele . . ."

"Howdy, neighbor!" Jack Hennessey said in his club car baritone. "C'mown over an' bring the missus. Bring yer whole party—the whole fam damily!" he added, eying Besame appreciatively.

"Oh, please do, honey," Adele said. "I want for you an' your wife—an' yer other friends, too, of course—to meet my two favorite people, Dan an' Peggy Slattery. Maybe you could join our table, doll."

"Well, thanks," he began, "but I'm afraid that my wife isn't . . ."

Undaunted, Adele Hennessey plunged on. "Peg, these are our best neighbors. She's just a living doll an' their house is the one you saw. We tried to give you a ring this aft, but there wasn't any answer."

"Here, I'll get her," Jack Hennessey said, rising from the crowded table. "Just you show me where's your table an' I'll . . ."

"Gee, I'm—I'm sorry, but I seem to be holding up traffic," John said in a sweat of anguish. "So long." With Besame in his arms he stumbled away just as he heard Adele saying to one of her favorite people, "She's very small an' kinda put-teet an' they have this darling house that's all done in Regent . . ."

Glancing across the dance floor he could see his sister-in-law Alice plainly—just as plainly as she could see him. She had her glasses on now and while he couldn't hear what she was saying to her long-suffering husband, he could easily imagine both its content and volume.

He was only half aware of the baleful, doelike brown stare of Beth Martin as she danced by, cumbersome in her brown maternity dress, and of the slightly horrified look in the flash of Whitney Martin's tortoiseshell glasses as he piloted Beth across the floor.

"Good evening," Whitney said in a tone which, while pleasant, implied that it was addressed to a cad, a bounder, a card sharp, a receiver of stolen goods and someone who was certainly no gentleman.

"You certainly are popular," Besame said with an ill-concealed air of amusement.

"*Popular?* I'm being plagued—*pursued!*"

The orchestra now began another elderly waltz, something about a Foolish Heart which John associated somehow dimly with his lieutenant's uniform and Mary Martin and a show that was almost as hard to get into as *Oklahoma.* Pursued, that's it.

Yes. Either all of Riveredge was spying on him or else he was becoming a first class paranoiac. His hands were soaked with perspiration and he whirled like a dervish with Besame in his arms.

But there was no place to whirl *to*. On one side of the floor sat the Hennesseys with their guests, ready to pounce. On the opposite side of the floor was Alice Marshall, ready to spring. He could even catch snatches of Alice's conversation as it rose in both pitch and dudgeon. "What kind of a man do you . . . break my baby sister's heart . . . cast aside like an old shoe . . . basic sense of insecurity . . . Don Juan complex . . ."

The room went unpleasantly around and around, the chandelier above his head swirling at crazy angles. He had to get out of this place if he could only find a means of egress that wouldn't involve meeting the whole Riveredge Grounds Committee.

"You're making me terribly dizzy," Besame said a little miserably.

He kept right on spinning.

"I said," Besame repeated, "that you're making me *quite dizzy.*"

"Wh-what?"

"I said *Stop!*"

"Oh!"

Gradually his speed slackened until he and Besame were at a standstill. His head reeled so badly that he had to close his eyes for a moment.

"Really!" Besame said, "I thought you were trying to kill me."

"What?" he said. Then he opened his eyes and stared directly into the horrified face of his wife.

six

FLABBERGASTED, HE ALMOST FELL HEADLONG DOWN THE STEEP FLIGHT of steps leading to the Men's Room. He hoped, but without much conviction, that through some automatic sense of decorum he had managed to lead Besame off the dance floor and back to their table; that he had summoned up sufficient words or gestures to excuse himself for a moment; and that he hadn't trampled any women or children to death while getting out.

The Men's Room—its door was erroneously marked "Gentlemen"—was dankly contained in the rumbling bowels of Chandelier, along with the inadequate ventilating system, the ice machine, the serving pantry, the food checker, the dishwashing apparatus, the dirty linen, the waiters' locker room, the garbage and a small but costly cache of narcotics available to only the very best customers. That part of the basement which the male patrons saw *looked* sanitary enough, but the more intuitive could sense rather than see and hear the fetid dripping of pipes, the scratching of rats, the scurrying of vermin through the catacombs beyond. Try as they would, neither the management nor the Creco Deodorizing Air Purifiers could quite dispel the vague hint of sewer gas, festering food and soiled underclothing that hung pervasively on the stale air of this unlovely quarter.

Chandelier aimed for class, but like those less pretentious establishments that labelled their rest room doors Ladies-Gents; Pointers-Setters; Little Boys-Little Girls, Chandelier also suffered a lapse of taste when it came to being able to divorce humor from elimination. True, there were no obscenities, telephone numbers or improbable drawings hastily pencilled on the Men's Room walls—well, at least the porter scoured them off every morning.

Instead, Chandelier imported its naughtiness from Eighteenth-Century France in the form of four hand-tinted engravings in which plump peasant girls and powdered court gentlemen of astonishing proportions were engaged in—and presumably enjoying—various amorous exercises of a most contortionistic nature. Extravagantly framed and matted and bolted into the walls (petty thievery was not entirely unknown at Chandelier), one pornographic engraving hung over each urinal. Also above each urinal was a carefully focussed magnifying mirror. Apparently the mirrors and the curiosa formed an unbeatable combination, for no evening went by without at least ten newcomers to Chandelier wiping tears of mirth from their eyes and chortling: "Say, that *is* clever!"

The large chunk of ice in the bottom of each urinal, merely in the interests of fresher air, also brought on a couple of dozen on-the-rocks witticisms every night.

Oh, it was a laugh riot down there!

Otherwise the room was tricked out in whatever Crane and Company, the color consultant and the management felt were essential to masculine comfort. Crane and Company had supplied the four urinals, two toilets and four wash basins. The color consultant had supplied a grimy shade of gray-blue for the walls—"It's restful. Men like it."—and a deep navy for the ceiling—"It's masculine. It'll cover those ugly pipes." Unfortunately the wall color was not restful nor did men like it; the navy paint was not masculine nor did it conceal the Gordian knots of pipes and valves that meandered tortuously across the ceiling.

But no one ever went there to admire the decor, anyhow. The management supplied the four pictures, the mirrors, some disinfectant, a few combs and hair brushes which no one in his right mind would think of using, various brands of aspirin, antacids, mouthwashes, stomachics, laxatives and hair tonics and a little gnome of a toilet attendant to dispense them. The management further supplied a battered chair for the attendant to sit on. The attendant supplied a whisk broom and a shoe cloth as well as selective line of more personal manly requirements for sale at three times the going drug-store price.

But John had come down here for none of these things. He wanted privacy. There wasn't much privacy here in the Men's

Room, but it was considerably quieter than upstairs and there was almost no chance of running head-on into his wife again.

In a corner two college punks, dressed more for the campus than a New York supper club, were uneasily adding up the contents of their combined wallets.

A big butter-and-egg man, too convulsed to be quite able to do up his fly, kept saying through paroxysms of laughter, "Say, Ed, that *is* clever! I gotta tell the boys back at the Athulletic Club about this place."

His friend, Ed, a bigger butter-and-egg man, casually pushing back his cuticles with a towel, said with just a hint of world weariness, "Oh, yeah, I come here pracktuckly every time I hit Noo York."

An unseen reveller was having a bad time of it in one of the toilets.

"Don't talk to me about no rupture," the attendant said belligerantly while, on tiptoe, he swept imaginary lint from a customer's shoulders. "Sixteen, going on semteen years now I had this rupture. A double one. A real beaut. Yuh know what I fin'y done about it? I sent off to this-here place in Kansas City specializes in ruptures. They don't do nothing else, see, just ruptures. They gimme this brace, see, an' right away I think . . ."

John supported himself weakly against one of the wash basins and looked grimly at his face reflected above the unused bottles of Kreml and Brylcreem, Vitalis and Lucky Tiger. He was a little disappointed to notice that his hair had not suddenly turned white, that his face—though somewhat flushed—didn't look any older than it had that morning. He realized that these reactions were corny in fiction and if they ever happened in real life they were newsworthy enough to hit the front pages. But still he had the dramatist's feeling for the dramatic and felt that it was regrettable that he couldn't have changed into a haggard and broken old man during one moment of shock.

So this was how it was, the innocent Wellesley virgin whom he'd carried off from the decorating department of B. Altman's, had turned out to be about as virtuous as, say, Fran Hollister. The naive young lady of good background whom he had taught the facts of life and love—taught her every blessed thing he had learned from a dozen or so more or less successful encounters and two careful readings of *Ideal Marriage: Its Physiology and Technique*—had learned her lessons all too well.

And to think that on the very night of the break-up of their marriage she would be indifferent enough, wanton enough, *brazen* enough to be out in public with another man and dancing! He didn't know exactly what he had expected her to be doing or where he had expected her to be, but *not* waltzing at Chandelier.

Well, it certainly hadn't taken her long to get over the blow. Just about twelve hours ago she'd been screaming at him like a fishwife, ordering him out of the house and out of her life forever. Now here she was, as sweet as pie, her eyes closed blissfully in the arms of another man. Good God, she'd probably been seeing him on the sly since—well, since who knows when. Had she lain warm and fragrant in her lover's bed whispering and giggling, confiding her husband's inadequacies to this other man? Had she rigged the whole fight this morning just to be shut of her husband and free to go straight to the arms of her lover?

It was shocking, that's what it was. Disgusting!

What a sap he had been! This was the girl whose chastity he had respected; the girl to whom he had paid the highest compliment of all, that of making her his wife; the girl for whose creature comfort he had hammered out stories and plays and sketches and scripts. (Well, to do her justice, she'd kept on working, first at Altman's and then at Mrs. Updike's, right up until the baby was evident.) This was the girl for whom he'd traded his happy, catch-as-catch-can way of life for the edgy security of a big job with Popescu just so that she could have a fancy house in Riveredge, a car, a maid, a yellow nursery and grass and trees for the baby's well being. How would he even be sure now that the baby was his? Well, it's a wise father.

Thinking back a bit more rationally, he decided that the baby undoubtedly had been his unless she had managed a wild, sweet coupling with Gerald Updike atop a pile of chintz samples. No, such a picture taxed even his fertile imagination.

Ah, he saw it all clearly now. Of course she had been faithful to him when she had *had* to be; when money was scarce, when she was busy working, when he had been around the apartment every day battering away at his typewriter. Yes, she had almost certainly been faithful then. But when they had moved out to Riveredge, when she was free of her job and of financial worries, *then* she had taken a lover or many lovers. A small, distinct voice of reason now told him that it was quite difficult to play the seductress when six months pregnant. He dropped that theory.

No, it was *after* she lost the baby that she had turned from him. It was then, when bored and idle and comparatively rich, that she had given him her goodbye Judas kiss each morning and prepared herself and his bed for the arrival of her stealthy swain. But who? Who could the man—or men—be? Only a legal holiday or a severe hangover kept any of the male population of Riveredge off the commuters' train from Monday through Friday and not even the most casual of the Riveredge husbands got into his office a minute later than ten-fifteen. So it couldn't be a neighbor who had turned him into a cuckold.

He wondered now, incredulously, if she could possibly be like those lonely, frustrated matrons one occasionally heard about—the delivery boys' delight. A quick kiss for the postman, a tussle with the television-repair man, a grope for the grocer boy. The Fran Hollister sort of thing where any interested passing male was fair game. Maybe she'd even shared Speed, the Riveredge lifeguard, with Mrs. Hollister.

He tried hard to envision his wife writhing and panting in the arms of any of the local tradespeople. It was an improbable picture at best. He had seen the postman on his rounds almost every day, a kindly, garrulous old codger always anxious to talk about his sinuses and to show snapshots of his grandchildren, but unwilling to get out of his Chevrolet even for a registered letter, let alone mere adultery. The television man was a crabbed misogynist with four teeth missing in front and a breath like the Cloaca Maxima, so surly to the housewives of Riveredge that half of them refused to deal with him. Of course that could just be a pose. *No.* It was *not* the TV man. As for the grocery boy, he was fifteen, backward and ravaged with acne. Nor did it seem likely, even if she had found one of these improbable seducers attractive, that she could have managed much of an assignation, what with a religious fanatic like Heavenly Rest under foot with her constant psalm singing and predictions of the Armageddon.

Speed, the lifeguard, was a vague possibility. At least he was handsome in a grunt-and-groan muscle magazine sort of way, but too stupid to do much more than swim the length of the Riveredge pool underwater, and just barely bright enough to come up for air. Besides, he was Fran Hollister's—or so rumor had it—and anyhow, Speed had drained the pool, packed up his barbells and diaper bathing trunks and departed on Labor Day.

No, the man she was with tonight was no errand boy; not in a place like this wearing a suit like that. Nonetheless, a lover there was.

"It isn't that I give a damn," he whispered to his angry face in the mirror. "It's her life. Let her lead it or mislead it anyway she wants to. But the idea of showing up in a public place with some guy on the very day she . . ."

The Men's Room door opened behind him and he found himself staring at the well-tailored reflection of The Other Man.

Hypnotized, he stood motionless at the mirror and gazed at The Other Man. He had a pictorial mind, heightened further by work in television. He had seen this man only for a second on the dim dance floor upstairs, but he had formed a picture of him that time would never erase. Of course this was The Other Man. He could have picked him out of a room of thousands of men. Now in the brightly lighted Men's Room, he could see him even better.

The Other Man was damned good looking. There was no getting around that. But they were the good looks of a gentleman and not those of a model or an actor. For a brief moment he was almost relieved that she had chosen a man who was respectable and presentable instead of a racetrack tout or a garage mechanic or one of these grimy quasi-bohemians living in the artists' colony up the Hudson from Riveredge. He wondered quickly whether this was vanity for himself, of affection for her. Then he let the whole thing drop.

No, The Other Man seemed a gent, all right. About his own age, possibly a year or two younger, better looking and far better preserved. The Other Man acted a little tense, as well he might in a situation like this. He wondered whether she'd managed to tell The Other Man that her husband was also among the merrymakers at Chandelier that evening. Probably not. She had seemed pretty stunned, too.

He stood there leaning on the wash basin staring at The Other Man in the mirror. Then The Other Man also looked into the mirror and flashed him a brilliant, beautiful smile. That undid him. His hands slipped on the porcelain and his forehead came into into sharp contact with the mirror.

In a fever of activity, he ran both hot and cold water into the basin and began scrubbing his hands furiously. The Other Man shrugged slightly and strode over to one of the urinals.

He saw that The Other Man ignored the bawdy engravings hanging above the urinals. It indicated to him that The Other Man was an old hand at Chandelier. The word "Playboy" rose to his lips. Seething, he scrubbed his hands harder and harder.

Now The Other Man zipped up his trousers and headed straight for him. He cast his eyes away in a hot flush of embarrassment. The next thing he knew, The Other Man was at his side, running water into the neighboring wash basin.

The Other Man filled the bowl, removed a small gold signet ring from the little finger of his left hand and placed it on the glass shelf with a little clink. He watched him hoist up the sleeves of his jacket —a very good jacket, he noticed; not in its first youth, perhaps, but very good all the same—revealing the cuffs of an excellent broadcloth shirt and large gold cuff links monogrammed R. C. L. The term "Fop" came to mind, but he dismissed it as both inaccurate and subjective. While the cuff links were large, they were tasteful and not ostentatious. Had she given them to him, he wondered. The signet ring, he could see, had a look of heirloom to it. The cuffs of the shirt, he noticed, were just the least bit frayed. The genteel but casual type, eh?

So she's gone and got herself a real gentleman of the old school, he thought. Then he wondered with mounting anger, mystification and hurt what crass, boorish things he had done to drive her to The Other Man. Had he picked his teeth at the table, broken wind loudly in his sleep, humiliated and disgusted her unknowingly in some way so repellent that she hadn't been able to stand him for another day?

As The Other Man bent down to give full attention to his splendid hands, he looked anxiously into the mirror, hoping to see signs of thinning hair. No such luck. The reddish hair grew thick and glossy—brilliantine?—with just the slightest tendency to curl. He'd heard legends of the potency of redheaded men and now he was almost inclined to believe them.

He was still staring into the mirror when The Other Man's face appeared, right next to his. The Other Man smiled charmingly.

"Could I please trouble you for the nail brush?" he said with an ingratiating grin.

John was so startled that he jumped. "Oh! Oh, why, certainly," he said, trying to regain his composure. With a trembling, soapy hand he grasped the wet brush. He was shaking so badly that he had to cling to the brush as though it were a life line. But he clung too hard. The brush shot out of his hand, rose into the air and fell with a wet plop into The Other Man's basin, bringing forth a resultant splash that inundated The Other Man's tie with sudsy water.

"I-I'm so sorry!" he stammered, reaching for a towel just as the attendant came charging over with a handful of them.

"That's perfectly all right," The Other Man said genially, unbuttoning his jacket to survey the full devastation. "It's an old tie, anyway—University of Virginia."

"Gee, I'm awfully . . ." The speech faded away as he thought how incredible all this was. Here he and The Other Man were passing soap and towels back and forth making polite civilized conversation when what he actually should have done was to drown The Other Man headfirst in the toilet and then flush it.

"You see," The Other Man said, tossing the towel into a basket of soiled linen, "it doesn't show at all. No harm done." There was another dazzling smile and then The Other Man was busy putting on his ring while the attendant swept away at his shoulders with the whisk broom. "Please don't bother," The Other Man said to the attendant in his elegant English-Southern accent.

A sudden crafty burst of inspiration struck him. "I'm awfully sorry about ruining your tie," he said with a forced smile. "If you'd let me have your name and address, I'd be glad to buy another one just like it and have it sent to you."

But if he was being cagey, The Other Man was being cagier.

"That's mighty nice of you, but I wouldn't dream of putting you out. It's an old tie I was about to throw away. Goodnight." Another winning smile and he was gone.

"Cheap bastard," the attendant grumbled. The Other Man had neglected to tip him.

John took the towel the attendant proffered and not-quite dried his trembling hands. His head swam and he was just barely aware of the attendant scraping away at his shoulders with the whisk broom.

"Here," he said, thrusting a crumpled dollar bill into the old pirate's hand, "it's for both of us."

He was just about to dash out of the Men's Room when the door swung open and there stood his neighbor, Jack Hennessey, with the black Irishman who had been with him this morning.

"Hi there, neighbor!" Jack roared. "Long time no see. You an' the missus tripping the light fantastic tonight?"

The sight of Jack Hennessey was always unsettling. Tonight it was even more so. Mr. Hennessey was wearing a black silk dinner jacket, a red-polka-dot ruffled shirt, red glass—or possibly even ruby—studs, a red moire cummerbund with matching bow tie and black suede loafers, the fruit of another of his wife's pillages into haberdashery.

The only people who ever dressed at Chandelier were those who didn't know any better or an occasional couple who had broken from a dull dinner party in time to catch Chandelier's even duller floor show. Adele Hennessey, however, loved to "go faw-mull" and she always dressed her husband to match. Tonight he looked like a river-boat gambler.

"Oh, hello there," John said nervously. "Nice to see you. As a matter of fact, I was just leaving."

"Goin' awready? It's the shank of the evening. The night is young. Yuh better stay an' get a load of that French singer. You know what they say about those French dames." Jack gave him a playful nudge. "Here, I wantcha ta meet my friend Dan Slattery.

Dan, here, is in auta-motive parts. He and his missus are bein' transferred here from Detroit."

Mr. Slattery, dressed in a perfectly plain dinner jacket, stretched out a hairy black hand. "Pleasure's all mine," he said, quite accurately. "We looked in at your home this aft. That's some place! Peg—that's my little woman—was nuts about it. That's some little community, Riveredge. Beats Grosse Point all hollow. Course I don't presume you'd ever wanta sell a lovely home like that—a real showplace, really—to Peg an' I, but if you should ever . . ."

"Well, Dan," Jack Hennessey said largely, "I'd have no trouble gettin' you inta Riveredge if only there was a place ta buy. But I don't think the loving couple here—that's what they call he and his missus out around Riveredge—would ever . . ."

"Well, well I'm glad you liked it," John said, withdrawing his hand from Mr. Slattery's death grip. "I've got to be getting out of here. See you soon, Jack."

He darted out of the door just as Hennessey was saying, "Come over here an' take a look at these French 'art studies,' Dan."

"Sssssay," Mr. Slattery was saying, "that *is* clever." The Men's Room door swung closed and John bounded up the stairs, two at a time, desperate to escape this place.

seven

Besame returned from the powder room and sat alone at their empty table. She was grateful that the table was empty, that he was still downstairs powdering his nose or doing whatever men were supposed to do when they excused themselves. Besame was grateful, too, for the intense gloom of Chandelier and, feeling confident that no one could see her plainly, she allowed the perfect mask of her face to relax—even to slump—from its habitual expression of bemused serenity into something not quite so lovely.

In repose her face felt a lot better than it looked. With her perfect circumflex brows lowered temporarily from their usual half-mast position of elegant questioning, Besame's lids became heavier—almost pudgy—and her glorious dark eyes had just the slightest tendency to droop. As her eyes drooped, so did her cheeks, the corners of her mouth and, lastly, her chin. Fat—to be overweight like her mother—had always put the fear of God into Besame and all her life she had fought it; fought fat with citrus juices and Scandanavian crackers, fought it with starvation and strenuous exercise, with massage and modern dancing, with pills and potions and proteins and poultices. But just now her face looked heavy and unhappy and much, much older than it should have.

And Besame didn't even care. Alone at this moment, Besame welcomed the opportunity to let her face fall, to be without an audience and—if only for just a little while—to stop acting.

Besame Bessamer was an actress and a good actress. All of her life she had had to be. As a rich Milwaukee brewer's adored only child—a tangle of ebony curls and eyes like sloes gazing liquidly through incredible lashes—Besame had been told that she was a fairy princess. She saw no reason to doubt this bit of information and played the role to perfection from the time she was housebroken until the day when she was led off to a private kindergarten —run, it seemed, exclusively for the daughters of rich brewers—dressed in a profusion of tucks and frills. Too many tucks and frills, the other Milwaukee mothers said.

The kindergarten had been Besame's first unsettling experience and marked the first occasion she had ever heard the word Vulgar. "*My* mother says that *your* mother is very vul-gar," one of her classmates had said with the endearing candor of a five-year-old. The word meant nothing to Besame, but she lost little time in learning its definition. It came as a nasty shock.

So did the fact that little Besame Bessamer was not invited to the birthday parties of her school friends and the fact that, while they were invited to *her* parties—always big elaborate affairs; *vulgar* affairs you might almost say—their mothers always sent polite but firm refusals. At least the *nice* ones stayed away.

Besame's father had committed the unpardonable sin among Milwaukee brewers. He had divorced his first wife—a thin, shy, barren woman to be true, but a Schulz with von Seidlitz, Niemeyer and Frumke connections—to marry Besame's mother. Had Mr. Bessamer forsaken his first wife for a Schlitz, a Pabst, a Blatz, even for a non-Milwaukee brand like Ballantine, Feigenspan or Ruppert, the sudsy society in which he moved would have been sadly understanding. Incompatibility is, after all, incompatibility.

But to leave a Schulz with von Seidlitz, Niemeyer and Frumke quarters for a common slut like Lillian was beyond the pale. The beer baronesses came to call on Lillian *once*, but that was all. The sight of her dyed hair, her chaise longue, her movie magazines, her liqueur chocolates had confirmed their every suspicion. The second Mrs. Bessamer was simply *not* the sort to be included in the *kaffee klatsches*, the Junior League, the matinee excursions to Chicago, the ponderous dinner parties in the Rhenish mansions built by fathers-in-law and grandfathers-in-law.

Besame's mother was, to be sure, *de classée* in Milwaukee and the arrival of a fairy princess daughter, just eight months after her nuptials were solemnized, did nothing to further Lillian's social position.

So Besame had grown up a lonely, only child, with her mother's dogs, two pekes named Charlie Chan and Fu Manchu for playmates and with her mother and the servants to keep reminding her that she was a fairy princess. The legend grew. Preening in silks and satins, the most opulent that her father's fat fortune and her mother's tiny taste could buy, the child Besame lived in a world of storybook fantasy. It was almost too easy. The little ermine coat, the chinchilla hat and muff, the blue velvet with real sable collar and cuffs —were these not the trappings of a true princess? And how perfect the setting—the Bessamer's Frankenstein Castle of a house with its stained glass, its antlers, its grotesque carvings, the fake Louis IV furniture which her mother had installed here and there among the established General Grant, Art Nouveau and Mission pieces of the Bessamer family—for a little princess.

Thus the first five years of Besame's life were spent toeing daintily among the monstrosities of the Milwaukee *schloss,* dressed in incredible clothes and being alternately imperious and cuddlesome with the servants, her mother and her father, all of whom assured her every half hour that she was the most beautiful, most intelligent, most gifted, most adorable little fairy princess in the whole, wide world.

Nor did rejection at kindergarten do anything immediately to shatter the grand illusion. Even at five, Besame had been too tactful, too regal, to take the subject up with her mother. But she had mentioned it to her nurse, who mentioned it to the cook, who confided in the parlor maid, who whispered to the tweeny, who could never keep anything from the chauffeur, who was the gardener's cousin and they all came up with the same verdict: "Those girls are just jealous of Baby Besame because she's a real fairy princess." That had seemed enough for the time being, and even though Besame had been hurt and mystified that her classmates had not immediately become her courtiers, she was satisfied to believe that envy was all that kept them away.

Meanwhile she worked hard at being the prettiest, brightest, most talented pupil in the class and her teacher thought that little Besame was enchanting, in spite of that unfortunate mother to whom she penned a carefully worded note suggesting that serviceable serge might be better adapted to the sandbox and the finger paints than pleated taffeta.

Besame's mother was not a bad mother; neither was she a good one. Being as lazy as she was sentimental, she was as neglectful of her child as she was overindulgent, but in fits and starts. She bore no rancor toward the frosty brewers' wives who had refused to accept her into their dismal milieu. They had bored Lillian after two minutes and she was delighted not to be one of them. Lillian had achieved what she had set out to achieve—a rich husband and an heir to cinch the will.

She was perfectly happy to loll on her gilded chaise longue and have lengthy telephone conversations with Ruby and Belle and Tootsie—all friends from humbler days. And once or twice a week, she was even happier to dress herself to the teeth and be driven to the wrong side of town to exhibit to her old pals the spoils of matrimony—the limousine, the mink coat, the new jewelry and Besame. A good time was had by all.

But when Lillian first sensed that her child was not being asked to nice birthday parties, and that no nice children were coming to Besame's parties, she laid aside the *Photoplay* and the *True Romances* long enough to do what any mother *ought* to do—to establish her ewe lamb socially.

This was the final disaster.

Besame, an oversweet confection in tulle and ribbons and rosebuds, was packed off with the nurse and the chauffeur to pass long and squalid afternoons with the uncouth offspring of Ruby and Belle and Tootsie in their sordid flats and bungalows. The twain did not meet. The children of Ruby and Belle and Tootsie were either awed speechless by the splendor of little Besame or violently resentful. The servants, being servants, were horrified that their fairy princess should be forced to profane so much as a patent-leather slipper on the domestic Oriental rugs of Lillian's friends and they took no trouble to disguise their indignation from Besame; first the nurse, then the cook, then the parlor maid, then the tweeny, then the chauffeur, then the gardener. Thus the child found no niche other than the one in fairyland and she set about portraying her role even more ardently.

But Besame was nobody's fool, and although she went on acting the fairy princess part for herself and her contemporaries, she began to get the impression that while she was divine, her mother had feet of clay right up to the waist. Little snatches of conversation overheard at the dentist's, at dancing school, at the riding academy, at the class play in which Besame had starred, naturally, as the fairy princess made everything fairly clear. "Such an enchanting-looking child! If only her mother weren't so common!" "Of course her father is a Bessamer, but the *mother!*" "A darling little girl, but with that mother I really wouldn't want Gretchen to play with her." And from casual eavesdropping upon the grumblings and mutterings of the Bessamer servants—the tone of which was what-can-you-expect-from-a-woman-of-that-class—Besame got the breezes.

If Besame was hurt or shocked—and, in fact, she was—the hurt and the shock were only in terms of herself and neither lasted long. As a fairy princess, Besame found it irritating to be morganatic, but in no way her own fault. Lillian, she decided, was just one of the cares that wait upon a crown. And since Besame loved no one, it was quite easy for her to look at her mother objectively and to profit from her mother's myriad mistakes.

From that day forward, Besame went systematically about being as different from her mother as possible. To be as brunette as Lillian was blonde, to be as willowy as Lillian was plump, to be as dulcet as Lillian was shrill, to be as conservative as Lillian was flamboyant, these were the goals of the fairy princess. Besame even hated beer; not because it was the bread and butter of the Bessamer family, but because her mother's bathroom was piped for hot, cold and lager, and Lillian turned on the lager more often than the water.

And so until she was ten, Besame lived her solitary royal fantasy, hating her mother for being what she was; hating her father for having married her mother; and hating the rest of rich Milwaukee for hating her. It was only Uncle Norbert who proved to Besame that life was more than beer and idyls.

Mr. Norbert Bessamer was Besame's father's older brother and the crown prince of the brewery. But Uncle Norbert had abdicated in favor of his younger brother years before. Uncle Norbert did not like Milwaukee, nor did Milwaukee care for Uncle Norbert. Uncle Norbert referred to himself as esthetic, Milwaukee called him la-di-da. Milwaukee thought of itself as vigorous, Uncle Norbert spoke of it as barbarous. Their final separation, hastened by Uncle

Norbert's ill-advised seduction of a bellhop in the Schrader Hotel, came to everyone's mutual satisfaction.

Uncle Norbert was far happier in places like New York and Paris and Capri, where he toyed with his collections of Fabergé, Bach and boys, with all the benefits and none of the worries of owning a large brewery. Only a matter of the most pressing importance could lure him back to Milwaukee and Besame had reached the age of ten before such a matter had called Uncle Norbert back to a full-dress Bessamer board meeting.

Reluctantly Mr. Norbert Bessamer returned. Even more reluctantly he put up at the hideous home of his youth. As Uncle Norbert had always hated Milwaukee for being boisterous and krautish and totally lacking in chic, so did he hate the Bessamer house and his brother Rupert. One look at Lillian had sent him scuttling to his room with a sick headache. Lillian was just what Rupert and the house deserved, Uncle Norbert decided. And the midday meal with a pitcher of Bessamer's Best at each place put Uncle Norbert quite out of sorts. It was only the sight of young Besame, curtseying fairylike to him in her drab school uniform that restored Uncle Norbert to anything like geniality.

For both uncle and niece the meeting was epic. Save for his mother and an old terrier bitch named Frieda, Uncle Norbert had never experienced the slightest vestige of affection for anything female until he caught sight of this gravely exquisite little creature standing before him. Nor had the child ever seen anything quite like Uncle Norbert with his slight lisp, his fluttering white hands, his big chalcedony ring (said once to have belonged to Queen Christina), his foreign airs and graces. Besame listened to her uncle in wonderment as they foregathered in the ponderous dining room at six for a heavy, bready, beery dinner. Uncle Norbert announced that *he* never dined before eight—bedtime in Besame's world. Uncle Norbert spoke of the stunning creations of Fabergé. Lillian said she didn't like those French dressmakers nearly as well as the Hollywood designers who ran up clothes for movie stars. Uncle Norbert's eyes shot to the ceiling and right back down again, as the ceiling was decorated with a frieze of nymphs, cherubs, satyrs, grapes and hops. He had forgotten that detail.

Then more hopefully Uncle Norbert switched the subject to

Bach. Lillian said that she felt it was too dark and heavy. Uncle Norbert raised his suspiciously symmetrical brows and said, "Dark and heavy, my dear? *Bach?*" Lillian said "Yer darn tootin'. Give me Bessamer's Pale Lager any time." Rupert agreed. Uncle Norbert asked to be excused. Enchanted, Besame followed him from the table.

For the rest of the visit—and a visit which, to everyone's surprise, was extended to a full week—Uncle Norbert and Besame were inseparable. To Besame, Uncle Norbert was a debonair and cultivated man of the world, a perfect court chamberlain to the fairy princess. She prayed for him to take her away from her horrid mother, this dreadful town and into a life of chic urbanity. And to Uncle Norbert, Besame was an elegant and adorable fairy princess, a perfect subject for a worldly Pygmalion. He prayed to take her away from her horrid mother, this dreadful town and into a life of chic urbanity.

But Uncle Norbert bided his time and played his cards carefully. From a handful of old Milwaukee acquaintances—two gentlemen who sold antiques and a talented young man who kept a rather expensive hat shop—Uncle Norbert learned exactly how the land lay. It was just as he had expected. Because of Lillian, Besame was spurned by the local Society. Still Uncle Norbert was smart enough not to pounce immediately. An old hand at the seduction of the innocent, he knew the difference between courtship and rape. Casually he took to sending pretty presents to pretty little Besame from pretty little shops in Paris and Rome. He began remembering his brother's birthday, his name day, his anniversary. He found garish gifts for Lillian, which delighted her even though Norbert did talk like her hairdresser. Uncle Norbert resumed an interest, in absentia, in the brewery and indulged in a cordial correspondence with Rupert. Even Rupert had to concede that Norbert wasn't *all* bad.

Gradually Norbert moved a bit closer infield. How nice for little Besame to have a cultural weekend of Shakespeare, Chopin and Marshall Field's when Uncle Norbert "just happened to be" in Chicago. How nice for little Besame to get away from the slush and sleet of Milwaukee for a week on the sands of St. Simon's with Uncle Norbert, what with the child so thin and so pale and travel so broadening. How nice for little Besame to spend a fortnight in California with Uncle Norbert when he was there "on business"—maybe even meet some of the stars.

Little by little Uncle Norbert had them all in the palm of his hand. He took his time. He was discreet. Never once did he let the girl see his flicker of interest in the fair young man who sold them Besame's little amethyst locket, in the slim waiter who served them inflammable food at the Pump Room, in the muscular male dancers at the ballet. By the time Besame was twelve, Uncle Norbert was choosing her meals, her clothes and her reading. At thirteen, her room in Milwaukee was done over with furniture and plans sent from Italy by Uncle Norbert. When Besame was fourteen, Uncle Norbert knew that it was time to strike.

Norbert was very much the older brother in his letter, six times rewritten, to Rupert—friendly, firm and forthright. Lillian was a dear with a heart of gold, Norbert wrote, and undoubtedly a sterling mother etc. etc. But Rupert must realize that Milwaukee would never accept Lillian or grant Besame her rightful place etc. etc. And surely Rupert also saw that Besame was a girl of exceptional beauty, talent, intelligence etc. etc. Wouldn't Rupert consider sending Besame off to a really first rate New England boarding school where the girl would have a chance to meet other girls of etc. etc. As ever, your affectionate etc. etc. etc.

Rupert spent a troubled night. The next morning he looked at his daughter who was almost a total stranger to him and who was very, very beautiful. Then he looked at his wife who had become far too familiar to him and who was not. Reluctantly he decided that Norbert was right. The following fall Besame was entered in Miss Spaulding's School, well up in Connecticut, but not too far for Uncle Norbert to keep an eye on her.

With his Galatea close at hand for most of each year, Uncle Norbert was in a ferment of joy, but again the situation had to be handled with care. No one knew better than Uncle Norbert the double cross that had to be borne at a smart Eastern school when one had both Milwaukee *and* beer as background. He was Machiavellian about preventing Lillian's projected visit to the campus. He bought Besame's way into Miss Spaulding's School with blandishments, stealth, and cold cash, starting with Miss Spaulding herself, who was also mad about Bach and enthralled to receive an original Bach score and an old harpsichord to play it on with the compliments of Mr. Norbert P. (for Pilsner) Bessamer.

He made surprise raids in a hired limousine to take Besame and her classmates off for treats at the local inn. And how could Miss Spaulding object? Such a lovely man, Mr. Bessamer! He planned edifying weekends in New York for Besame and two or three of her little friends, intellectual with trips to the Met and the Frick, but fun, too, with an evening of virtuous musical comedy, a pale lipstick and a crème de menthe apiece to make the girls feel grown up and terribly sophisticated.

It all worked like a charm. Uncle Norbert was delighted to see Besame become the most popular girl in her class. Uncle Norbert was delighted to see Besame receive invitations to visit in Aiken and Tuxedo and Southampton and Watch Hill with four of the very nicest girls from Miss Spaulding's. He purred with pleasure.

But there was just one thing that Uncle Norbert did not see—could not have seen, considering his own ambiguous nature. Besame liked boys and boys liked Besame. Of course Uncle Norbert liked boys, too, but he would *not* have been delighted to see Besame in the woods at Aiken, in the canoe at Tuxedo, on the beach at Southampton or in the guest room at Watch Hill with the very nice older brothers of the very nicest girls from Miss Spaulding's. Standing serene in her appropriate pumps, young Besame was as soigneé a subdebutante as only Uncle Norbert could have produced, but lying down, young Besame was as sensual a slut as only Lillian could have produced.

And what of the fairy princess herself? At sixteen Besame was a belle and a beauty; a creature of smouldering moods, given to carefully concealed hatreds and dark introspection of what she believed to be her true personality—that of a passionate goddess surrounded by fools and clods.

Alone in her dormitory bed, Besame tried occasionally to list in alphabetical order all the people she hated. The task was too great for her. She hated the girls at Miss Spaulding's because they were such asses—almost as asinine as Miss Spaulding herself. It amused Besame to see how easily they could all be bamboozled, how endearing she could make herself to them, how they mistook her play-acting for "qualities of true leadership." There wasn't a one of them she couldn't twist around her little finger and the easier they twisted, the more Besame loathed them.

She had been cautiously sleeping around for almost two years and she detested the boys whom she had allowed to seduce her. *Seduce?* That was a laugh! It was Besame's policy to lead them on, to tease them until they were in a lather of doggish desire before she submitted—*if* she submitted. She rarely enjoyed the act of love, but she adored the sense of power it gave her. When the whole thing was finished, when the boy lay gasping beside her, then Besame would drive her final thrust into the young man's most vulnerable spot. If he had been callow and inept, Besame would analyze his shortcomings with a cool candor that could drive him to tears. If he had been anywhere adequate, Besame would insist that he repeat his gala performance instantly and then villify him when he mumbled that he could not.

Nor did her sadism end with the postlude. When the boys wrote love letters to her afterwards—and all but one of them did—Besame saved them carefully and sold them back just after each swain had announced more honorable intentions with some far nicer girl. For the one who was a poor correspondent, Besame had an even more diabolical torture. She drove him to penury, pawnshops and potential suicide by announcing that he was the sire of a totally fictitious foetus and that she had to have five hundred dollars immediately.

Besame had little use for the piddling amounts of money she wrung out of her youthful lovers. It was just the sense of power and principle of the thing that seemed important, plus the fact that once Besame had finished with them, she felt positive that her lovers were too defeated ever to mention her name in polite or impolite society and that her flawless reputation was still secure. The very paradox entertained her hugely and gave her even more pleasure in hating.

And away from home, among America's elite, Besame discovered that she hated her mother even more for being a tawdry tart, her father for being a bourgeois brewer and Uncle Norbert for being the biggest fool, *the* consummate ass in the world. And still she kept on charming, twisting them all around her finger. The more they worshipped her, the more she despised them.

Now Uncle Norbert, in his pursuit of Besame, had by no means abandoned his original interests. And for some time his abnormal appetites, meager as they were, had been more than satisfied by the presence of a young man from Virginia whom Uncle Norbert referred to variously as "my companion" or "my secretary" or "honeybunch," depending on the company. To Mr. Norbert Bessamer, Besame was a real live doll whom he could dress and give tea and carry about and show off, nothing more. The young man filled a more pressing need. With these two exquisite young people, beautifully clothed, groomed, tutored and kept well apart, Mr. Bessamer was in seventh heaven.

But the temptation to show off his two creations at once was too strong. When Besame was sixteen and when Mr. Bessamer's companion was twenty, Mr. Bessamer arranged a week's holiday in New York. No coupling since that of Adam and Eve was ever more cataclysmic.

Randolph Carter Lee, as the young man called himself, had all the lazy, handsome charm of the Virginia gentleman he was not. He found serving Mr. Bessamer something of a bore, but far preferable to working in the bath house whence Mr. Bessamer had lured him. Randy's life as companion was secure, comfortable and not too onerous and he had always found opportunities for a quick roll with whichever waitress or chambermaid was available during Mr. Bessamer's absences from the apartment. But the arrival of Miss Besame Bessamer for the week of spring vacation put Randy in a turmoil. If Randy had ever spotted a sure thing—and Randy had spotted many—Besame was it.

And Besame scented something unusual about Randy. Of course she had suspected for some time that all was not strictly kosher with Uncle Norbert, but she'd never discovered who the other man —or men—happened to be. This domestic set-up intrigued her and she gave her bottomless capacity for destruction full sway by flirting outrageously with Uncle Norbert's young man.

As for Mr. Bessamer, he was in ecstasy. Here were his two adorable, beautiful darlings; his *achievements,* for all the world to see.

Quivering with pride, he showed them all over New York. It was just too delicious having people stare at his stunning young couple as they entered restaurants, smoked during intermissions at theatres, danced together at smart nightclubs. Mr. Bessamer's ecstasy lasted for almost the whole week until the night he simply had to attend a meeting. Leaving the two people he loved the most decorously playing backgammon among his collection of Fabergé Easter eggs and cigarette cases, he bid them a gay farewell and announced that he'd be home early.

No sooner had she heard the elevator door close behind Uncle Norbert than Besame gave Randy a burning dark gaze. What fun, she thought, to play with this one. Lead him on. Maybe even get him to make a pass, if such a thing was possible with that kind of man, and then tell Uncle Norbert. Maybe she could even . . .

Besame had no more time to think. A second later she felt Randy's mouth crushing down on hers, felt his hand surely and steadily pulling down the zipper at the back of her dress; felt the hand warm against her tingling flesh as he expertly loosened her brassiere. Before Besame could collect her wits sufficiently to speak, she found herself on Uncle Norbert's bed—not *in* it, if you please, but *on* it—with Randy's hands, his lips, his teeth exploring her whole trembling body. Nothing like this had ever happened to her before in all of her carefully calculated life. She was oblivious of time, of sound, of light—and only vaguely, hungrily conscious of Randy's body pressing against, and into, hers.

Unfortunately she was soon made eternally aware of light, sound and time. There was a brilliant flash of Mr. Bessamer's Murano chandelier. Then she heard a gasp, a shriek, a scream, a thud and a ghastly gurgling. The coroner established the time as nine-thirty-one. Mr. Norbert P. Bessamer had died of natural causes—a heart attack.

Everything that happened after that was a nightmare—the feverish dressing, lugging the still-warm body up to the soiled bed, Randy's calm call to Uncle Norbert's physician and then, on the following morning, the arrival of Besame's father.

Rupert Bessamer was, as Besame had always thought, a bourgeois kraut with no sensitivity, hammy hands and a roll of fat over his collar. But Besame had never reckoned with the brain pan above the roll of fat. Her father took one look at Uncle Norbert's corpse, one look at Uncle Norbert's apartment, one look at Uncle Norbert's Randy and one look at Besame. Within ten minutes Besame had an ugly red welt across one cheek and her father had the whole, unabridged story. The following day Randy had decamped to parts unknown and Besame, chaperoned by a warty old German woman, was on her way to a prison of a school in Switzerland. Bessamer Beer could get through red tape faster than it could get through the human system.

Naturally Besame won out in the end, for that is the fate of any fairy princess. Save for a paltry five thousand dollars for "my faithful companion, Randolph Carter Lee," the whole of Uncle Norbert's estate went to "my beloved niece, Besame Bessamer of Milwaukee, Wisconsin." Her father, much to Besame's delight, died immediately afterwards, leaving, much to Besame's chagrin, everything to Lillian. A year later Besame was free of her Swiss school, but saddled with her mother, grotesque in jets and black chiffon, smoking black-tipped cigarettes and talking incessantly about "my husband, the late Mr. Bessamer," while flirting with Manfred Popescu, a man rich enough to make Besame's father look like a pauper. Of course Besame could have had Mr. Popescu herself, but she was too snobbish and too dispirited to make the effort. That awful night with Randolph Carter Lee had blighted her whole schedule. Besame, utterly shattered, stood through Lillian's marriage to Mr. Popescu without being able to think of anything more than what the bulk of their two estates might amount to.

Now, more decorous than ever before, her own boss with her own money, Besame was quietly at it again, venting her hatred on all comers. There had been no one sensational; a young actor or two, a script writer, the assistant cameraman on the *Pulse Beat* show, her osteopath, a sculptor with a beard, the husband of her roommate from Miss Spaulding's—nothing to write home about. But at least she was out destroying people. She had almost forgotten the incident with Randy Lee—six years back, as it was. As far as Besame was concerned, *everybody* who knew *anything* about that night was dead; dead and buried.

But tonight, not ten minutes ago, she had come face to face with the magnificent mug of Randolph Carter Lee. Besame could have died—almost as willingly as she could have murdered Randolph Carter Lee.

She thought that she'd seen Randy on the dance floor. Besame wasn't quite sure—she had a fleeting impression of Randy dancing with a terribly pretty young woman who was wearing a beautiful hat and a beautiful dress and probably keeping Randy. Besame hadn't been *certain* that it was Randy she saw. (Besame never liked to concede that any man she had tangled with could possibly still be going about to the better places, well dressed and well fed. A slow, lingering death or an ignominious end in the Foreign Legion fitted in better with Besame's malign fantasies.) But then, no sooner had they sat down at the table, no sooner had the man she was with excused himself than there was old Randy, as close to her at *that*. True, Randy had seemed just as surprised as Besame had, but Besame knew Randy too well even to hope that he wasn't up to some deviltry. Hadn't he tried to blackmail the Bessamer family when Uncle Norbert died? And now that Besame was on her way to becoming an established actress—possibly even a star—how like Randy to come back and make trouble.

Besame had gone up to the Powder Room to arrange her face and collect her wits and it was there that she became positive that Randy had been talking. For, staring at Besame in the mirror was the pretty little thing who had been dancing with Randy. So he'd told all. No question about it. Randolph Carter Lee, Virginia gentleman, catamite and seducer, had just been waiting until Besame grew into something big enough to be worth fleecing.

Well, Besame would see about *that!* She'd use her own money, Popescu's money, a gun if necessary, but she'd get Randy out of the way and fast. However, all Besame wanted to do now was to get out of this place. She'd plead a sick headache or . . .

"I'm back," John said, pulling his chair out from the table.

Instantly Besame's face resumed its masklike loveliness. The eyebrows rose to their inverted V's, the great dark eyes glowed with warm bemusement, the full lips took on their Gioconda smile. "I thought you were never coming," she said in her carefully cultivated husky voice. "But if you don't mind, could we . . ."

"If you don't mind," he was saying, "could we get out of here?"

"Two minds with but a single thought," Besame said lightly. "Yes, let's do go. It's awfully . . ."

"Waiter!" he called. "The check, please."

Just then Chandelier was plunged into complete darkness. There was a roll of the drums and an impressive fanfaronade from the orchestra. The dance floor was flooded with light and the orchestra leader stepped forward to announce the appearance of "that singing sensation of Paris and the Côte d'Azur, Mlle. Chou-Chou la Grue." There was thunderous applause from all those who had never heard of Mlle. la Grue.

"Waiter!" he called louder. "The check!"

"Shhhhhhhhhhh," someone said from a neighboring table.

John lowered his voice. "Waiter!"

The orchestra was now blaring Mlle. la Grue's entrance music—something about Paris.

"Waiter!" he called louder. "The check!"

"I'm sorry, sir," the waiter said. "No service while Mlle. la Grue sings."

"For Christ's sake," he said, "who do you think she is, Mary Garden?"

"Sorry, sir," the waiter mumbled.

The ovation was tumultuous as Mlle. la Grue appeared in an evening gown composed of the pelts of six white foxes, eighteen pounds of rhinestones, thirty yards of satin and best described as Modess Regal. The press had made much of Mlle. la Grue's wardrobe, which seemed kinder to describe than her voice.

"Listen, waiter," John said, "we've got to get out of here."

A voice from the darkness said, "If you can't appreciate a great chan-tooce, kindly allow others to do so."

"Oh, shut up!" he said. "Waiter!"

Chou-Chou la Grue stood in the exact center of the floor, her heavy arms upraised, her tremendous bosom heaving, her stays creaking. Eventually the applause died down. "My faires nome-Bair is an old French song about a midinette *de* Paris who loves an American how-you-say *Zhee-Eye*—soldier—and every night she sleep away from her 'ouse to meet heem undair zee Pont Neuf—a famous bridge across the Reevair Seine."

The light dimmed to blue. There was a shivering run from the harp, a majestic chord from the orchestra, a sputter of static from the public address system and Mlle. la Grue was off; "*Minuit! Les étoiles de Paris. Une pauvre fille mélancolique* . . ."

"Isn't she superb!" someone breathed.

"Waiter!" John snapped.

"Shhhhhhhhhhhh!"

". . . *la Seine est claire comme le crystal, la lune* . . ."

"I'm very sorry, sir, no service while . . ."

"So *here* you are!" a familiar voice cut through the reverent hush of the room. It was his sister-in-law Alice. He looked up unbelieving. It was all true. Alice Marshall towered above their table, her feathered hat flapping, her electric-blue maternity blouse and her spectacles glittering ominously in the reflected glory of the spotlight.

"Please, Alice . . ." he started.

"Don't you 'Please, Alice' me, you Lothario! I'll teach you to . . ."

"Who *is* this madwoman?" Besame breathed.

"Believe me, I never saw her before in my life," he groaned. "Waiter! Check!"

"Take my sister and turn her into something as low and vicious as yourself and then . . ."

". . . *c'est le printemps, les feuilles sont tendres* . . ." Mlle. la Grue shrieked gamely.

"Shhhhh! Shhhhhhh! Honestly, the class of people who have money to spend in nice places nowadays!" an indignant music lover hissed through the darkness.

"Well, let me tell you one thing, young man," Alice went on loudly, either oblivious to or enjoying the commotion she was creating, "if Fred and I have to fight you through every court in the country, you're going to . . ."

"Sir, madame," the waiter said. "I must ask you to leave. Mlle. la Grue . . ."

"Leave?" John shouted. "I've been trying to get out of this dump ever since . . ."

". . . and another thing," Alice raged, "when I . . ."

". . . *romance sous le Pont Neuf* . . ." Mlle. la Grue continued a little louder.

"*Out!*" the headwaiter said, flanked by two captains.

"Come on, Besame," John said, grasping her hand.

They made a run for the exit, dodging chairs, tables and enraptured customers. At the door the headwaiter said, "Your check, sir."

He didn't wait to look at the check. Instead, he reached into his pocket, pulled out all the currency he had—eighty-some dollars—and flung it into the man's face.

"Now get out and stay out!" the headwaiter snapped.

"You bet your life!" he said.

As he and Besame whirled through the revolving door it occurred to him that it was the second time in his life—and the second time today—that he had been thrown out of a restaurant.

eight

"I TOLD YOU IT WASN'T VERY FAR," BESAME SAID, DRAWING A SMALL ring of keys out of her purse and handing it to him.

Besame lived in a building described by its rental agency as in the "Sutton Place Area." That is to say that it was neither *in* nor *of* Sutton Place, but that it was a swanked-up old tenement house which had had the good fortune to be situated where it was some fifty years before Sutton Place ceased being a slum and became a fashionable cul-de-sac. The façade had been treated to a coat of black paint (doesn't show the dirt), with white trim (shows the dirt, but oh the contrast), and a vivid red door (chic). The rambling railroad flats had been gutted and divided in two with such added refinements as yellow plumbing and artificial tile, although little had been done to the sagging floors and rotting woodwork. In the interest of public safety, the rat-gnawed old wooden stairway had been replaced by one of steel and terrazzo that clanged with every step. The names on the bellboard had changed from O'Shaunessy and Palucci and Przybilski to Baroness von Plotnich and Reginald Honeywell Kirby, IV and Mrs. Bullock Bleek.

But even though Baroness von Plotnich and Reginald Honeywell Kirby, IV and Mrs. Bullock Bleek would not have known the O'Shaunessys and the Paluccis and the Przybilskis socially; even though they did not lean out of their windows by day or sit on the stoop by night; even though they were too refined to engage in very loud family brawls; even though their names were occasionally mentioned on the Society page and, in one or two cases, the Police Blotter; even though their rents were a thousand percent higher than those of the former tenants—if they bothered to pay them—they were hardly more substantial people than the O'Shaunessys and the Paluccis and the Przybilskis had been.

The people who lived in Besame's building constituted a new social phenomenon, a new ethnic group called Almost Society. They lived as near to the rich as possible with all of the trimmings but none of the responsibilities of money. Their pasts, their presents and their futures were largely matters of conjecture. Usually personable and often entertaining, they had enormous circles of alphabetically listed acquaintances, but no friends. They were invited out a good deal and usually repaid every five invitations to dinner with one for cocktails. They lived rather stylishly on loans, commissions, handouts, credit and their wits. Some of them had alimonies or settlements or tiny trust funds from more prudent forebears. These sums were always given glamor, mystery and an extra digit or so by being described deprecatingly as "a little money of my own." Those who worked didn't have real jobs but glorified hobbies—doing table arrangements, designing coats for poodles, writing an occasional piece on wine or food or an unspoiled island —that took them into the milieu of the Very Rich. Their god was Fashion, their paradise was the Social Register and if they could not quite get into heaven, at least they could worship from the front pew.

"It's quite a hike up," Besame said, looking back over her shoulder as she began climbing the stairs.

The halls were painted battleship gray (doesn't show the dirt) punctuated by scarlet doors (chic) and they smelled vaguely of broiled lamb chops, brioche, Siamese cats, cigarette smoke, Air Wick and Chanel Number Five. One of the doors was open and John could hear the last murmurs and chuckles and tinklings of ice from a cocktail party that hadn't quite ended when scheduled. Little garbage cans sat outside a few of the red doors, but the cans were painted unusual colors and piled high with wilted roses, wine bottles and empty boxes from Bergdorf Goodman waiting to be collected. It was very *fashionable* garbage. A telephone was ringing on the third floor and through one of the doors John could hear a voice saying petulantly, "But, darling, *nobody* goes to Miami anymore."

"Just one more flight," Besame panted.

John took a deep breath, grasped the handrail and plunged onward and upward.

"Here we are," she said. "Seventh Heaven."

He unlocked her front door and swung it open. Besame reached around the door jamb and switched on the lights. "Make yourself at home," she said. "Sit down and I'll get us a couple of drinks. I have *some* Scotch and a lot of rye." She disappeared beyond the foyer and he could hear water running and the rattle and bang of an ice tray.

The living room was overheated and there was the hiss of steam in the archaic pipes. It felt good. The night had turned chilly enough for him to regret marching out that morning with neither hat nor coat. Like a cat in a strange house, he was unable to settle. He strode over to one of the windows and looked out. He could see the letters si Co of the red neon Pepsi Cola sign across the East River. The rest of the sign was obliterated by two large buildings on Sutton Place.

"Have you admired my view?" Besame called from the kitchenette.

"I was just looking at it," he answered. Then he let the heavy curtains fall back into place and wandered idly about the room.

The room was as sleek and impersonal as Besame herself. Decorated in black and white and gray, it was starkly modern, its principal feature being a tremendous sofa upholstered in black. The only color was lent by a large painting by Joan Miro and some faintly menacing-looking green plants. It was an expensive room, a smart room, but it was utterly devoid of personality. No photographs, no books, no magazines existed to give even a hint of what the occupant was like.

John had met a lot of actresses in his time, ranging from the almost-unknown who had taken the lead in his off-Broadway success and the fast-fading star of his Broadway flop to the glossy Hollywood queens who appeared weekly on *Pulse Beat*. Their living quarters were almost identical—highly personalized places crammed with flowers, with photographs, with scrapbooks, with pets and friends and hangers-on. They were all alike and even the most sterile hotel suite, leased for a week, was soon deep in a clutter of memorabilia that fairly shouted "Lovely me, wonderful me, popular me, famous me!" If it was only to the chambermaid, an actress made her presence known. But Besame's apartment was as clean as a barracks on inspection day, offering no clues—not even a hint.

Besame was certainly different, he decided, nothing actressey or stagey about her at all. And except for her considerable physical charms there wasn't even anything particularly female about her. Talking to Besame was almost like talking to another man—no artifice, no coquetry at all. He supposed that it was because Besame, in spite of her hideous mother, had been born with all the creature comforts—the security, the food, the social background, the medical care, the education—that money could provide, and that there had been no reason for her to pretend that she was anything she was actually not. He felt that Besame was a gentleman among women. He felt that Besame was . . .

The telephone at his side began to ring.

"Shall I get it?" he called.

"No!" Besame called back, almost sharply. He could hear her hurrying from the kitchen. Then she said with a little more control, "I'll answer. It's probably only Mother."

Besame answered on the third ring. "Hello?" The voice was cool, crisp, remote and not quite hers. "I'm sorry," she said in a still stranger voice, "but I'm afraid you have the wrong number." She hung up rather briskly and marched back to the kitchen. In a moment she returned with two drinks—his quite dark, hers very pale.

"Now," she said with a warm smile, "let's sit down and talk about your play. Do you think there's anything in it that *I* could do?" She sat down quite close to him on the sofa. Almost too close. He could feel the warm pressure of her thigh against his and smell the mixed fragrances of her perfume and her tobacco. The combination of odors proved to be a little less pleasant than he had anticipated.

True, he had halfway anticipated some sort of intimacy with Besame, even though his boss did happen to be her stepfather. But he had rather planned to take whatever sexual initiative that was to be taken all by himself.

Besame laid a long, tapered hand on his knee. He almost jumped. "Of course," she said, "I don't think I'm ready for a starring role . . ."

Well, he liked that! Here she'd done a summer in stock and one television part and now she was talking about being a star.

"But I *am* a good actress."

"Yes-s," he said hesitantly, "you are a good actress—a *very* good actress." This was certainly true. But he just wished that now she'd spare him one or two of his illusions; that she'd take her hand off his knee and let him make any passes that were going to be made.

"And, of course," Besame continued almost too matter-of-factly, "there'd be no trouble getting backers. I have some money; Mother has even more; and Popescu has all the dough in Deauville—even if he did steal every penny of it."

"*What?*" John said with a start. He was not fond of Manfred Popescu. He found him vulgar, overbearing, crafty and certainly not above sharp practices. But he had a respect for the man's business acumen and a certain streak of puritanism which would never have permitted him to work for a man or a firm whose dealings were open to question.

"Surely," Besame said, smiling into his face, "you couldn't be so naive as to think that Popescu is honest or that he makes his *real* money out of those wretched watches. Please don't joke with me." Her tone was that of someone discussing the weather or a current bestseller, but the casual off-handedness of it merely served to double his shock.

"Listen, Besame," he said, "I only do the advertising on *Pulse Beat*. I don't know anything about your step-father's financial set-up—and I don't want to."

"Go on!" Besame said with a chuckle that could hardly be called pleasant. "You mean to tell me you don't know about Dr. Schwartz in Bern or Mr. Gomez down in Rio or that interesting Mohamed Maloof in Cairo? Don't make me laugh!"

"I swear to you, I never heard of any of them," he said.

"Good heavens, I believe you're telling the *truth*," she said, treating him to a quizzical smile. "Well, if you want to have some fun with the old crook, just mention them to him. Why, I know enough about Popescu to hang him. That's why I'm certain that we won't have any trouble raising money to get your play on the stage."

"Listen, Besame," he said, "the next time I get a play produced it'll be like the last two times—because enough people like it to invest in it. My God, the play isn't even finished yet. I haven't had a chance to fix the last act for a year."

The doorbell rang. Besame made no move. It rang again.

"Aren't you going to answer that?" he asked.

"No," she said coldly. "I am not. He'll give up after a while." The bell rang another time. "Now, as I see it," Besame continued calmly, "you'll have plenty of time to finish the play while you're sitting out your divorce . . ."

"Hey, wait a minute!" The bell pealed once more.

"I'll get Popescu to give you a leave of absence long enough for your divorce and then to get the play on the stage . . ." The doorbell rang again loud and long. "Persistent, isn't he?"

"Hey, listen," John said, "not so fast! You haven't even read this play. You might hate it." The bell rang again and he raised his voice. "There isn't much of a part in it for you—only a kind of poor relation with hardly any lines at all . . ."

"Well, you could always build the part up a bit," Besame said calmly over the din of the bell. "The play could probably be tailored to fit me. You know how much plays are changed before . . ."

"And as for the divorce," he shouted above the clangor, "that would be up to my wife. We haven't discussed it . . . God, I wish whoever that is would go away. Is it Halloween or something?"

"It's just this crackpot who keeps pursuing me."

"You mean a *maniac?* You ought to call the police," he said. "It's dangerous for a woman living alone to . . ." The bell pealed again. "Here," he said, reaching for the telephone, "I can put an end to this in five minutes."

"*No!*" Besame said, snatching the telephone away from him. Then more calmly she said, "I don't want to get involved and have my name dragged through the tabloids. I know who it is and . . ."

"I thought you said you *didn't* know who it was," he said. The bell rang again.

"Well," Besame said in pretty confusion, "I meant that I don't know him *personally*. It's just this harmless old anarchist who lives here in the neighborhood. All he wants to do is pass out tracts and talk about Sacco and Vanzetti. Crazy, of course, but not dangerous and I wouldn't want to be the one who was instrumental in getting him locked up. He's probably given up already. The bell hasn't rung for at least ten seconds. Now, to get back to this play of ours . . ."

"Ours?"

"Well, you know what I mean," Besame said stroking his cheek. "You can help me and I can help you. I can give you ideas and inspiration and all the financial backing in the world. We might even let Popescu think he's producing the play. He'd like that. 'Manfred Popescu—from procurer to producer in ten easy lessons!' "

"*What?*"

"Oh, surely you knew that he used to be a pimp in Bucharest before he got sidetracked into smuggling and money-changing and . . ."

"No," John said, "I did not."

"Well, leave Popescu to me. That's *one* of the places where I can help you. And here is where *you* can help *me*: You know that I'm a damned capable performer, don't you? *Don't* you?"

"Y-yes," he said slowly, "you are." And it was true that she was, but he would have preferred that she not make the announcement herself.

"And you also know that I acted rings around that old bag from the West Coast last night, *don't* you? In fact I acted rings around the whole bunch of them in that creaking melodrama. I stood by and let them cut my part down to the bone when a word to Popescu could have had every last one of them—yes, and you, too —kicked out. But I still walked away with the whole show. *Didn't* I?"

"You did," he said quietly. He realized that every word she was saying was correct, but he couldn't help wishing that she weren't saying them, and saying them as calmly as anyone else would be reciting the alphabet. There was something eerie about her total self-assurance.

"But you don't realize the obstacles that stand in the way of a genuinely talented actress," Besame continued in her businesslike fashion. "I mean an actress like me who has background and an education and a certain amount of money and who isn't willing to sleep around with every shoestring producer in town just to get a walk-on in some turkey that may never open."

"I have heard of similar cases," he said.

"But you can't know what it's like to be a—well, to be a *lady*, if you'll forgive so archaic a term, with taste and intelligence and have to . . ."

"It must be very difficult," he said uncomfortably. He almost never had bursts of intuition and usually ignored his hunches. But tonight, right now, he had an uneasy feeling about Besame that had been building up ever since he set foot into her apartment. It was something he couldn't quite label. He still found her attractive and he still *thought* that he found her likeable. And if she was acting right now, she certainly was turning in an offbeat performance, because he'd never heard another actress go after a part in a play she hadn't read in quite this manner.

"Of course I knew the minute I met you that you and I were going to amount to something—to something *big*."

"Oh, really?" he said.

"Yes. *Really*. I went straight to the Drama Collection and read your first two plays, and Popescu let me see the kinescope of your first *Pulse Beat* shows. They were good—all of them; *especially* the plays. I could see right then and there that you were the kind of writer I needed. That you and I could . . ."

It just occurred to him that the question was usually: "What kind of *actress* does the *writer* need?" and not "What kind of *writer* does the *actress* need?" but he was too spellbound to comment. He felt absolutely flattened beneath the steamroller of her logic, her confidence, her personality and her power.

Besame gave him an astute glance and decided that now was the time. "And you know as well as I do," she continued, "that you'd far rather be a successful playwright than simply a cog in Popescu's machine, which could collapse at a moment's notice."

"Sure, sure. Who wouldn't?" he said groggily.

"Very well then. Listen to me and you can really go places without taking any risk at all. You can use Popescu while he's using you. First this play, with a decent part in it for me; a part where I can really command some attention from the critics—where they can see how I look and how I can act. With the notices I'll get, I'll be ready to star in your next play. Agreed?"

"Well, I . . ."

Besame realized perfectly well that she had him where she wanted him. She had made it abundantly clear to him that she could get him backing, plenty of free time to work and a first-class production of any suitable play he might turn out. And right now struck her as a good time to tie him up emotionally.

"Good," she said quietly. "This is one step you're never going to regret. How shall we seal the bargain? Would you like to kiss me?"

It suddenly struck him that he *didn't* want to kiss her; that he was being completely and utterly trapped; that if he had ever wanted to have an affair, it would be with a nice cuddly little thing like his secretary and not with a powerhouse like this—attractive as she was. However, a gentleman could hardly refuse.

Before he could answer, Besame was in his arms, eyes closed, lips parted. It was something more than a kiss of business partners. His reason began to quaver. Maybe I was wrong, he thought, as she stirred voluptuously in his arms. Maybe this girl really does like me. Maybe . . .

"Mmmmmmmmmm," Besame moaned, running her hands under his jacket.

Good God, he thought, maybe this girl . . .

The air was rent by a crash that sounded like the end of the world.

Besame thrust herself away from him, her face white, her eyes bulbous with fear.

"My God!" he said, "what was that?"

Besame didn't bother to answer. She bounded to her feet and raced across the apartment in the direction of what he supposed was her bedroom. He could think of very little to do but follow.

He saw a light flash on and heard Besame scream. Dashing into the bedroom behind her, he was aware, in his vast confusion, of an overpowering odor; of an open window and fluttering curtains; and of a man in dinner clothes.

"Besame," the man wailed brokenly, "you've *got* to give them to me!"

"My God," John said, "*Whitney Martin!*"

The bedroom was tiny, just large enough for a double bed and a small mirrored dressing table. The dressing table had been overturned and Whitney Martin stood in the middle, broken bottles of perfume and cologne up to the tops of his pumps.

"How did *you* get in here?" Besame screamed.

"The fire escape, Besame," Whitney moaned. "You wouldn't talk to me. You wouldn't let me in. All I want is my letters. I . . ."

"Whitney Martin," John said. "What are *you* doing here? How the . . ."

Besame turned to him. "This is the one I told you about. This is the maniac who goes around ringing doorbells and talking Communism all the time and breaking into lone women's apartments and terrorizing . . ."

"Correct me if I'm wrong, Besame," John said, "but I believe you told me that this was a local crackpot, perfectly harmless and an anarchist. Elderly was my impression."

"Yes," Besame said wildly. "That's the one!"

"Well, he *has* been deluding you," John said. "Actually, his name is Whitney Martin. He is my age. He lives in Riveredge. He's Chairman of the Membership Committee, as a matter of fact. And I suspect that he wears an old Landon button on his B.V.D.'s."

"Besame," Whitney bleated, stepping forward through the debris, "if you'll just give me my letters, I swear to you that you'll never hear from me again. Please, John," he begged, "*reason* with her. She's driving me out of my . . ."

In spite of his astigmatism and his consequent tortoiseshell glasses, Whitney Martin had always been considered a very handsome man, patterned, more or less, along the lines of those gentlemanly models who pose for higher-priced ready-to-wear suits. Probably no one had ever seen Whit's face in repose, because it was such a *busy* face—its lips always winding up to pitch a brilliant smile upon meeting someone important; its brows always prepared to pucker becomingly and sympathetically upon hearing of an Eastern plague, a social injustice or a Yale defeat; its nostrils set to quiver exquisitely upon hearing the name of T. S. Eliot or the more profound strains of Couperin. From sheer force of habit, the face strove for animation as Whit began to smile and to say,

"John, this is all a terrible mistake. I must have been delirious or . . ." But tonight the lips gave up their grin before showing even the bicuspids. The smile that orthodontists love withered and died. The face was just too tired to go on.

Besame turned to John beseechingly, her face also haggard and ashen and far from its public self. "John," she said, clutching at his jacket, "I was wrong. This isn't the one. The light fooled me for a moment. I swear to you on the grave of my father that I've never lain eyes on this man before."

John hadn't liked Whitney Martin from the moment of his first interview with the Riveredge Membership Committee. But he had never quite summoned the energy to despise him. He and his wife had tagged Whitney as a completely empty being, inflated to the bursting point with glib, readymade virtues such as Civic Responsibility, Good Fatherhood, Love of Nature, the Fellowship of Intellect, the Obligations of Aristocracy—all splendid qualities when genuine, but ludicrous if fashioned from shoddy and worn without alterations. Yet he felt reasonably certain that Whitney was too successful, too snobbish, too faint of heart and just a little too bright to supplement his income as a house-breaker or a rapist.

Looking at the two of them, he was as moved to laughter as to pity. He had no idea what there could be between them, but he was certain that the answer would be as amusing as it would be amazing.

"This is obviously a matter for the police," he said, turning on his heel. "I'm going to telephone right now."

"John! Please don't!" Whitney groaned.

"No!" Besame cried, harshly, shrewishly. She clutched his arm and held on tight. "*Don't* call! Just get this sneak thief out of here. That's all I want. Get him out and no trouble."

"Nonsense, Besame," he said. "How could I do that? Here he is a fifth-story worker and dangerously insane, as you point out. He must have wrecked a couple of hundred dollars' worth of your stuff. He's a total stranger. He's a local crank. You're an innocent maiden living alone. He's a proselytizing anarchist and/or Communist. It might even be a case for the F.B.I. My duty as a citizen . . ."

"John," Whitney blubbered. "For the love of God don't call the police. If our friendship means nothing to you, think of Beth. Think of my children. Think of Riveredge! I only want my letters. When I saw you two at Chandelier, I thought I could just slip over and get them and then get right back. I thought she'd still be out. Nobody answered the bell. I . . ." he broke down completely, shaking with sobs, his lenses steaming with passion.

"He's lying," Besame said levelly.

"Why don't you give the poor chump his letters?" John said. "They're undoubtedly as dull as hell anyhow. Now, Whitney, if you'll explain just once more how you happen to be here . . ."

"Very well," Whitney said brokenly. "It all started last summer when Beth and the children were up at Mother Goodhue's in Maine. I ran into her on Madison Avenue. We had drinks together. I got to telling her about this play I've been working on. You didn't know I was writing a play did you?" Whit asked hopefully.

"So many of us are," he said.

"And it was a stinker!" Besame hissed.

"And before I knew it, I started getting involved. Well, you know," Whit said in a lacklustre man-to-man intimacy, "a man gets lonely all by himself and what with Beth—um—*enceinte,* you know . . ."

"Oh, yes," Besame said. "*You* know. But how was *I* to know that he was married and had children? He's one of those typical men who lead a girl on without telling her that . . ."

Shattered, Whit said, "Besame was my wife's roommate at Miss Spaulding's. She was a bridesmaid at our wedding. She wore yellow."

"How very pretty," John said. "And I suppose your fan mail is all tied up in a yellow ribbon."

"I've done everything she's told me to do," Whit said. "I've given her money. I've arranged auditions at the agency. I've made appointments with producers. I've . . ."

John looked squarely at Besame and he didn't like what he saw. "Give him back his letters, Besame," he said.

"No," she said. "I don't have them. I threw them away. I don't even know where they are."

"They're right there in the drawer of that dressing table," Whitney said.

"Go on, Besame," John said. "Do something decent for a change. Give him his letters." He still didn't like Whitney, but he had a feeling for the underdog, for the fly in the spider's web.

"I won't," she said.

"Then I guess the only thing to do is to call the police," John turned toward the door and again Besame restrained him.

"Listen," she said earnestly, "you can't! Think of my career. Think of how it would look—an actress living alone and . . ."

"Please don't!" Whitney bleated. "I'll do anything you say. I've got a wife and a family to think of. I have a position in . . ."

"You certainly spent all summer thinking of them, too, didn't you Shakespeare?" John said. "Now get this straight. I don't give a good God damn about either of your reputations. You both deserve anything you get: you, Whit, for being such a smug snob slob, with literary pretensions when you're actually too stupid to write anything more than some hot mash notes to a scheming, blackmailing little bitch like . . ."

Besame's hand swung wildly out and caught him across the face.

Very calmly, John turned, took aim and gave her a slap that sent her sprawling across the bed. She was too surprised even to cry out. Then he moved to the overturned dressing table and gave its drawer a vicious kick. The drawer flew open and a dozen letters tumbled out. He picked them up. "Are these yours, Whitney?"

"Yes. Yes, they are," Whitney gasped, grasping for them.

He glanced at the letters. "*Whitney!* Written on Yale Club paper! I'm *ashamed!* And now," he said looking scornfully around the room, "I think I'll get the hell out of here. Going back to round out your gay evening with the Marshalls, Whitney?"

"Y-yes. Yes. I'll have to get back right away. Beth will be wondering."

"I shouldn't be at all surprised. Goodnight, Miss Bessamer," John said. "Watch out for all this glass. I'd hate to think of your cutting an artery—or anything as painless as that. Coming, Don Juan?"

"Yes, wait for me," Whitney said, crunching and tinkling out of the shattered scent bottles.

They were at the head of the stairs when Besame appeared at the door looking like a witch and screaming like a banshee.

"Get out of here! Both of you! As for you, you'll never work for Popescu another day. You'll . . ."

"You bet your boots I won't, Miss B. Goodbye."

As he and Whitney started down the stairs, Besame's door slammed with the report of a cannon. In silence they descended to the street. An empty cab was making a U-turn in the middle of the block. Whitney whistled for it and it pulled up smartly at the curb.

Whitney had regained a bit of his usual composure. The facial muscles had resumed their old fight and John could see Whit's glasses and teeth gleaming through the night. Whitney held out a muscular hand. "Naturally I can never thank you for this, so it's silly even to try."

"It is."

"And I know that, as a gentleman, you'll never repeat a word of . . ."

"Goodnight, Whitney," he said.

"Oh, but here, old man," Whitney said, "can't I drop you?"

"I'm dropping *you,* Whitney—and I'm walking."

"Make up yer mind, rose bud," the cab driver said, sniffing eloquently.

John heard the door slam and cab drive off as he strode down the empty street toward First Avenue.

nine

THERE HAD BEEN ONLY ONE REASON FOR HIM TO RETURN TO THE Bacchus Club. He was broke. He had thrown something like eighty dollars in the face of the Chandelier waiter. It had seemed worth every penny at the time, just to get out of the place. But he had begun to regret his imprudence when he discovered that he had just fifteen cents in his pocket, enough for a one-way trip on a jouncing, nearly-empty Lexington Avenue bus.

It was just midnight when he got to the Bacchus Club. There were lights in every room. The front doors stood wide open and so did every window. A policeman on the club's marble doorstep was hawking and spitting noisily.

As he made for the front door the officer straightened up and barred the way with his night stick. "Can't go in there, buddy," he rasped and went into another violent fit of coughing.

"I'm a member," John said. The statement sounded pompous and foolish beyond belief.

"Don't matter. Nobody's allowed in. Guy tried to bump himself off. Gas."

"Who?"

"Can't tell yuh, buddy. City ambulance took him off fifteen-twenty minutes ago."

There was a tremendous rumbling from within the hall and he could see Toby's luggage cascading down the stairway in glorious disorder. Toby followed jauntily behind.

"Hey, Toby!" he called. "What's happened? Who . . ."

"Sonny-boy!" Toby said gaily. "No room at the inn. *Autres temps, autres moeurs,* and all that sort of thing. Officer," he said to the policeman, "would you just hail a taxi for me?"

"Huh?" the cop said.

"I said, 'Would you just hail a taxi for me?' "

"Oh, sure. Sure thing, sir!" Still coughing, he bustled to the corner and began tooting his whistle.

"But, Toby, what *happened?*" he said.

"Oh, nothing. Teddy tried to 'do 'way with himself,' as they say. The dinge who works here came home and found the silly bastard with his fat head in the oven."

"Is Teddy dead?"

"Only from the ears up. Teddy goofed—*natch.* Never could do anything right."

"But where is he now?"

"Bellevue or some such place. How should I know? I was upstairs packing when they carted him off. Thank God I'm going. Place smells like a crematorium."

"But if Teddy . . ."

"To hell with Teddy," Toby said. "He'd be better off dead. Got a cigarette on you, kid? Careful with the match."

"Sure, Toby. Here. But who's looking after . . ."

"Here's your taxi, sir," the policeman said with a smart salute.

"Oh, thanks. Now would you mind giving me a hand with my bags? Here," Toby said, settling himself into the back of the taxicab, "give the poor flatfoot an assist. New York's finest, you know."

Silently, John and the policeman piled Toby's scarred kit into the front seat with the driver.

"Much obliged," Toby called to the policeman. "Now, get in, kid. I'll take you to wherever you want to go. Besides, I've got news for you."

"B-But somebody ought to be with poor old Teddy," he said getting into the cab.

"Oh, forget about Teddy. This is *important.* Where to? Grand Central and thence to squalid suburbia?"

"No. I can't go home. I don't really know where I . . ."

"Well, you can ride along with me while I tell you the big news. The Plaza, driver," Toby said.

"Listen, Toby . . ."

"For Christ's sake stop yammering all the time. I'm trying to tell you something. Guess where I'm going to be working at ten or eleven or whenever I happen to feel like getting up on Monday?"

"I give up, Toby. Where?"

"Right in your office. Just Sonny-boy and Toby-boy and Papa Grotescu. I'm your new *assistant,* kid! Think of the boffs we'll have."

"What are you talking about?"

"What do you mean what am I talking about? Popescu and Lillian took me out for dinner and after I steered that tub of guts around the dance floor for a few miles and shot a line of bull to the old pirate, he ups and offers me a job as your assistant. Public Relations in Charge of Entertaining. That's me. Of course I had to tell him that you and I collaborated on all the college shows and that I gave you the original idea for *Heart Beat*—or whatever it's called. I knew you wouldn't mind. He wants us to work very close together, which I think is all to the good so you can teach me the lingo and . . ."

"Listen, Toby," John said quietly. "Do you mean to tell me that you actually talked yourself into a job that you know nothing about? A big job?"

"Well, I don't know how big it is. It only pays twelve thou. per annum, but that's better than a kick in the ass. Besides, what's there to learn? You can show me the ropes and . . ."

"Toby, do you think that what you did was entirely honest or even . . ."

"What's honesty got to do with it, stupid? I need the dough. Anyhow I knew you wouldn't care, since you seem to have the old man's daughter sewn up."

John felt the last prop falling away from his life—not with a crash but with a gradual crumbling, as though termites were finishing the final course of a long, heavy meal. I'll try one more time with Toby, he thought, just to make absolutely certain. As the cab turned north on Fifth Avenue he moistened his lips and said tentatively, "Moving into the Plaza, Toby?"

"Hell, yes," Toby said. "The Bacchus Club was giving me the creeps—lousy service and Teddy always whining around for his money. I . . ."

"Toby, if you could get a double room I wonder if . . ."

"Well, actually it's a small suite. You know, now that I'm the dashing boy executive I have to live in a style commensurate with my . . ."

"Toby, I happen to be flat broke at the moment and I haven't got anyplace to stay tonight. I wonder if you could put me up—just for tonight until I can get a check cashed and . . ."

"Gee, kid, that's a shame. You know I'd like to, but this dame I know—she's a hat-check girl at Chandelier—is coming up after work and . . . Well, you know: 'Two's Company . . .' All that sort of thing. I tell you what, though, why don't you give me a ring tomorrow and we can get together in the evening. Then you can coach me in this watch works thing and just give me the general line of patter. You know I can talk myself into anything if I just . . ."

Now the disaffection was complete. In the dimness of the cab he saw for the first time the petulant baby face, the selfish mouth, the cruel little wrinkles around the eyes as Toby squinted in a cloud of cigarette smoke. He cleared his throat. "Sure, I understand Toby. I won't be able to see you tomorrow and I'm not coming into the office on Monday, but I can give you a couple of pointers right now."

"Good. Shoot!"

"Well, if you *really* want to make an impression on Popescu, go right into his office and be sure you close the door—he hates drafts—and ask him about Dr. Schwartz in Bern and Mr. Gomez in Rio and Mohammed Maloof in Cairo."

"Well, what'll I say about them?" Toby said, all interest.

"You don't have to say anything about them. Popescu will do all the talking. *You* just kind of start the conversational ball rolling. Say something like: 'Say, Manfred, I bet you could tell me a lot of fascinating things about Dr. Schwartz in Bern and Mr. Gomez in . . .' "

"Gee, that's swell," Toby said effusively. "Show him I'm really interested in his business. Wait'll I just jot those names down." He took out a pencil and began writing on the back of an envelope. "Dr. Schwartz, Bern; Gomez, Rio; Mohammed Aloof . . ."

"*Maloof*, Toby."

"Oh, sure, *Maloof*, Cairo. Gosh, thanks a million. I'll really bowl the old boy over."

"You really will, Toby."

"Well, here we are," Toby said as the cab drew up to the blazing marquee. "Sorry I can't offer you the sofa tonight, but you know how it is. Oh, by the way, can you take care of the cab? All I seem to have is this thousand dollar bill of Popescu's and . . ."

"Afraid not, Toby," he said as he got out of the cab. "But I'm sure the doorman can change it for you—in nickels and dimes. Thanks for the ride, though. It's been one of the big events of my life."

"Well, maybe I do have a couple of singles. I . . ."

"So long, Toby," he said and walked away in the darkness.

ten

HE WALKED RAPIDLY AWAY FROM THE BRILLIANCE OF THE PLAZA, crossed Fifth Avenue and wandered into a dim side street. He had no place to go and plenty of time to get there. Broke—stony, flat, penniless broke—he had nothing to do all night but to walk.

This had been his first full day of independence and he hadn't made much of it. Or had he? In a negative way he had accomplished quite a lot. He had shed himself of a humiliating job; of a hollow idol; of the Bacchus Club; of a scheming adventuress; of all of his cash; and of a wife. Just now, he only regretted the cash. Although he was certainly curious about the wife. On Monday morning he could start out from scratch and begin an entirely different life with none of the same mistakes. For the present, well, he could walk; walk the night away.

He pounded his way across Fifty-ninth Street to Third Avenue. Third seemed so big and broad and wide and naked with the elevated gone. He paused hesitatingly on the corner for a moment and then turned north. The wind swirled down the avenue, sending up little whirlpools and eddies of paper and grit. He pulled up the collar of his suit coat and hoped that he wouldn't look too much like a vagrant. How perfect, he thought grimly, the young executive, cut off from everything, walking along Third Avenue with the collar of a London suit turned up and not a penny in his pockets. Camera pan out. It's like the kind of TV script I always rejected for *Pulse Beat*.

He kept on walking, thinking about everything and about nothing, not even paying any attention to where he was going, passing bars and antique shops, delicatessens and truss dealers. He was snapped out of his revery only by a fearful clanging of gongs and wailing of sirens. He stopped and realized that he had walked all the way up to Sixty-seventh Street, where the fire department was rushing out on an emergency call.

This was his old neighborhood, the neighborhood where they had spent their poor years together before the big move to Riveredge. There wasn't a shop on either side of the avenue that he didn't know. He walked on more slowly, conscious of the fact that he could go into Oscar's or Shannon's, where they knew him well, and cash a check to see him through the night. He wondered if he shouldn't and then thought better of it.

He looked in through the plate glass windows at the Irish hunched over the bar in Shannon's Cafe. It would be so easy to go in and get ten or twenty dollars. Instead, he decided to suffer the night out as a kind of self-punishment. He came to the Playhouse and then sauntered west on Sixty-eighth Street. Their old apartment was only a block farther on. He had no idea why he was going to see it. The building looked like any of a hundred other converted townhouses in New York. But he told himself that he had nothing better to do and all night to do it in and kept on going.

He felt his heart bound as he crossed Lexington Avenue. There, on the other side of the street stood the row of elaborate old houses—Georgian, Palladian and baroque—each one eighteen feet wide; each as tall as the law would allow; and each as overornamented as its architect could permit. They were the sorts of houses that Mary Petty's people still inhabited, put up by the rich when taxes were nothing and servants were cheap. Each had changed hands more than once and each had been converted into apartments.

He stopped under a plane tree across from Number 123 and stared across at it. The place hadn't changed since they had lived there on the parlor-floor front. Mrs. Larson on the floor above theirs—that would have been the master bedroom in the first youth of the house—was still growing ivy in her window boxes. The Condons, who lived in what would have been the old nursery, were still addicted to late parties. The commercial artist who lived above and behind the ornamental cornice was undoubtedly still trying to teach her parakeet to talk. It was odd how he knew exactly what would be going on in the house at exactly what hour. Only the big windows of their old apartment were dark. There was a sign in one of the windows. He squinted in the darkness trying to read it from across the street. APARTMENT TO LET —at least that's what he *thought* it said. He was about to go across to make sure when a taxicab came along, stopped at the door of Number 123, and a woman got out.

I'll just wait until she goes in, he thought, and then I'll cross over and see.

But the woman didn't go in. She looked flustered and confused at first. Then, like a damned fool, she just stood back at the curbstone and gazed and gazed and gazed up at the old house.

"My God," he growled, "isn't she *ever* going in?" He reached impatiently into his pocket for a cigarette. He hadn't any. Toby had kept the whole pack.

Just then the woman turned and stared in his direction. There was a pause and then he heard a loud, rather scared voice say, "Sir, are you following me?"

Well, who did she think *she* was, Helen of Troy?

"No, madam," he said loudly and angrily, "I am not!"

"Oh, it's you," she said from across the street.

Stunned, he recognized that it was his wife.

Slowly, he crossed the street. She might just be in trouble.

"What are you doing out on the streets alone at night?" he asked.

"I don't see that it's any concern of yours. Certainly not after this morning."

"Believe me," he said coldly, "it's none of my affair *where* you go. But I shouldn't like to see *any* woman mugged or raped."

"How thoughtful. I had no idea you cared so *very* deeply." Oh she could be a bitch!

Well, he wasn't going to take that lying down. "I thought that you were probably safe at home until I saw you *cavorting* around Chandelier tonight."

"Oh," she said, "I could tell that you were thinking about me every minute. I suppose that brunette snake was your marriage counselor."

"She happened to be Popescu's stepdaughter," he said quickly. "So don't try to make anything out of that."

"Who cares who she is or what she means to you. I simply remarked that you didn't seem to be holed up in the exclusive male society of the Bacchus Club or some wholesome Y.M.C.A."

"The Bacchus Club no longer exists," he said.

"What a loss!" she said with heavy sarcasm.

Well, just how one-sided could this interrogation get? "And you seem to have picked up a prize package in Uncle Tom, or whoever that big economy-size helping of corn pone was."

"He's some friend of Fran Hollister's," she said quickly. "I don't even remember his name."

"Oh, Fran Hollister, eh? You *are* running with a smart set!"

"After all," she said stuffily, "Fran and I were schoolmates at Baldwin and . . . Oh, lay off, please. Go away and leave me alone. I've spent the day with such awful people that I . . ."

"So have I," he said quietly.

"*What?*" she said with elaborate bitchiness. "With charming people like the Popescus and their gifted daughter? I should think you'd call it furthering your career. Don't worry, *you'll* get ahead!"

"Maybe. But not with Popescu. I'm quitting my job."

"*Quitting?*" That shook her. "Don't kid, please," she said irritably.

"If you're still that interested," he said, "just try to call my office on Monday. You'll only get Toby."

"Toby? Toby W*entworth?*" she said. "What does little Huckleberry Finn know about running a television show?"

"Nothing. But he knows enough about Popescu to hang him. Or at least he will. It should be interesting to watch—like a fight to the finish between a ferret and a rat."

"What on earth are you talking about?" she asked.

"I thought you didn't care."

"I don't," she said. "Really. Not in the least. I just love standing out in the middle of the street in the middle of the night making idiotic conversation with my ex-husband. Aren't you cold?"

"No, I am *not,*" he said. He was almost frozen solid. "Furthermore, I am not your *ex*-husband."

"You might as well be," she said with a touch of bitterness.

"I suppose you're right," he agreed.

"However, there's no reason why we can't act like civilized people. I hope you'll be very happy. I just never want to see you again, that's all."

"That suits me fine," he said. He hoped that it sounded sufficiently casual. "I would like to say, though, that I'm sorry about the coffee pot this morning. That seemed to bring the whole thing to a . . ." Well, he didn't know what the incident had brought anything to, except a quick and violent grand finale.

"Oh, don't worry about that. It made lousy coffee, anyhow. But of course you're right. It takes more than a broken coffee pot to ruin a marriage." A little less guardedly she said, "It takes things like a husband who suddenly ends up married to his job and a Manfred Popescu pinching your rear and a year or so isolated in a stagnant backwater like Riveredge and . . ."

"Well! This *is* interesting," he said grandly. "After you nearly drove me to bankruptcy moving out there with your sister Alice and a pack of snobs and squares to face on the commuters' train twice a day . . ."

"Don't blame *me* for Riveredge," she said quickly. "I hate it. I always have."

"That's a pity. The house is in your name."

"Well, it won't be for long," she said. "I'll sell it."

"Good. That'll give you a settlement of some forty or fifty thousand dollars, provided you can find anyone who's a big enough fool to buy the place."

"Thank you," she said. "But I happen to be an independent, educated woman quite able to earn my own living without alimony *or* a settlement. And you may quote me in court. But in case you should be interested, I do know a couple of prize customers."

"Who?" he asked. Of course she was lying. Just getting fancy with him.

"They're two of the Hennesseys' favorite people—Dan and Peggy Slattery from Dee-troit. The only trouble is that you could never get them past the Membership Committee. That's too bad —for *you*."

Was she kidding? "Do you *really* know someone who might want that house?"

"Yes, indeed. Mrs. Slattery peeked through the windows and pronounced it de-vine. They want to buy it lock, stock and barrel. But as I say, they're even worse than the Hennesseys. That snobbish Membership Committee would never . . ."

"I think the Membership Committee could be handled," he said. "A word or two with Whitney Martin and your friends will be in like Flynn." Just a *glance* at Whitney Martin and he could move the whole Jukes family into Riveredge.

"That's your worry. Not mine," she said. "You bought the house. You sell it. *I'm* going to try to get back into our old place."

"Here?" he said.

"You see it's for rent."

"Oh, really?" He was on his guard now. "I just happened to be strolling past and kind of thought of moving back myself."

"Well, you'll undoubtedly get it. You have all the money."

"That's a hot one!" he said.

"What?"

"Nothing," he said.

A querulous voice called down from above: "Would you two mind not standing directly below my window and talking at the tops of your lungs? It's one o'clock in the morning!"

"Sorry," he called, looking up.

"My God," Mary said with a nervous laugh, "that's old Mrs. Larson who used to live above us and grow all the ivy."

"I suppose she still bangs on the pipes every time the Condons pour a martini." John was almost beginning to enjoy himself with Mary. It was like old times.

"Yes," she said, "those were awfully funny years living here at one-two-three. Well, Mrs. Larson *does* have a point. I've got to be going anyhow."

"Where?" he asked. He hated to think of her walking away into the night, of being left all alone here.

"I can't see how that's any of your business. But as long as you ask, either back to the garage and then to Riveredge, or else to some hotel. I haven't decided which."

"You really oughtn't to be running around alone at night," he said. Damn it, he *was* concerned about her. You couldn't just go and wipe a whole person out of your life as easily as that. "No woman in her right mind would . . ."

"Thank you for your vote of confidence," she said icily. "But we're better off going our separate ways. I think you made that *quite* clear this morning."

Could it possibly be that those were tears he saw in her eyes?

"I've m-managed beautifully by myself all day," she continued. "So beautifully, in fact, that I'm just . . ." her speech faltered. "That I'm just *miserable!*" With that she broke down and wept like a child. "Oh, darling," she cried, "I've been so lonely and frightened and unhappy. I've—I've . . . Have you a hankie?"

"Here," he said, fighting the wave of tenderness that swept over him.

She blew her nose. Then she straightened up and managed to get control of herself. "Thank you," she said. "I'll have it laundered and send it back."

"Don't bother," he said largely. "I have dozens." All at once his pride collapsed in a heap. "Listen," he said tensely, "you think *you've* suffered. I've never spent such a day in all my life. I'd rather work all year in that Goddamned garden than spend another minute like the minutes I've put in today!"

She looked up at him through misty eyes. "Do you honestly mean that the Other Woman—I mean the Bessamer girl—is nothing to you? That she isn't your mistress? That you only walked out this morning because of . . ."

He thought for a moment. This was no time to tell a lie. Nor was it the time to tell the complete truth. In fact at *no* time would he tell the whole truth about having been made a fool of by Besame. Slowly he said, "I swear that I've seen her just four times in my life: first when she read for a part, again at dress rehearsal; last night over TV; and today for the last time. She means *less* than nothing to me. With both of us it was purely business." What answer could have been truer?

She looked at him solemnly. "You're telling the truth?"

"I'm telling the truth," he sighed. He felt purified. "But Uncle

Tom?" he asked. As long as the mass confession was going on out here in the cold, he might just as well tax her with some of her escapades. "This *friend* of Fran's?"

"Who," she said, "Randy?"

Aha! "I thought you didn't even know his name!" he said sharply.

"I don't," she said quite simply. "Randy's all I recall. He's just someone I met with Fran five or six hours ago. He's not a bit nice. None of Fran's friends could be called nice. Neither could Fran, in fact."

Oddly enough, he believed her.

"God, but I'm sick of terrible people," he said. "After today, I . . ."

"So am I," she said. "And I'm so afraid that we've been turning into terrible people ourselves. Vicious, grasping, scheming, mean, withered people—just like the ones I've been with all afternoon and all night. And we're on our way, you know. I've even *admired* some of them. But their terrible-ness rubs off. I can *feel* it on me."

Was this the time? He hoped so. He was going to take the wild chance anyway. "Well," he said, "it won't any longer. That is, it *wouldn't* any longer, if only we could get our feet back on the ground."

"You mean *off* the ground," she said. "Off the hallowed soil of exclusive Riveredge."

"And off the sandy soil of the Villa Manfrillian and off the dance floor of El Morocco and off . . ." he said excitedly.

"We're too old for that sort of life, darling," she said. "I'm nearly thirty and . . . Well, I mean we should be grown up and . . ."

"And forget all this nonsense about who has the smartest house and the biggest car and the most progressive children . . ."

"*Could* we, darling?" she cried. "Should we just chuck the whole thing and start right back here where we were before? *Right here?*" She gestured toward their empty apartment.

"*Will* you?" he shouted. "Remember," he added with an air of caution, "I'm off the payroll. There won't be any Mr. Santa Claus with a fat check every week . . ."

"And no fat hand on my thigh every night. Of *course* you'll quit," she said. "You never should have gone there. It was all my fault. You should have refused. You should have finished your play. You've wasted a whole year with Popescu."

"Not wasted," he said. "I've learned a lot. I've met a lot of people who *know* I can write."

"You'll finish it, then? We'll sell the house and come back here. I'll get another job . . ."

"And a baby?" he asked excitedly.

"Certainly a baby," she said. "Several perhaps. But we'll worry about that when the time comes. And when that time *does* come, there won't be any overpriced little housing development, no interfering sister, no Dr. Needles. We'll raise our children where we're happy. Then they'll be happy."

"In one room?" he asked dubiously.

"Perhaps in two—or three. But only when the time comes and then not in Riveredge. I don't even want to go back there tonight."

"Where do you want to go?" he asked.

"Let's go to a hotel. They'll think we're lovers—no luggage, no reservation, no nightie . . ."

"No money," he said gloomily. "It's a beautiful idea, but I'm flat."

"I have some," she said. "We'll go nearby. The Margate's said to be sinful. Then we can get up first thing in the morning and beard the superintendent here. I know he'll let us come back. You tipped him when we left, didn't you?"

"I gave him millions, my beloved."

"Then come, darling," she said. "Come before some horrible thing or some terrible person happens along to ruin everything again."

"Where to? The Margate?"

"*Any* place. Just so we get there soon enough to save our lives—our *life*."

A car turned slowly into East Sixty-eighth Street from Park Avenue. They were bathed momentarily in its lights.

"Stop the car, Fred!" a voice called. "*There* they are!"

Mary looked at John in panic.

"Wait, you two," the clarion voice shouted. "I want a word with you!"

"My God," he groaned, "it's *Alice!*"

"Run for it!" she cried. "It's our only chance!"

He grabbed her hand and they started pounding along the pavement.

"Turn the car around, Fred," he heard Alice call. "Follow them!"

"I'm afraid I can't, dear," Fred said. "It's a one-way street."

Laughing and running down the sidewalk with her hand secure in his, he couldn't for the life of him remember just what their quarrel had been about.

the loving couple
her story

BY THE AUTHOR

Oh, What a Wonderful Wedding

House Party

The Loving Couple

the loving couple

---

her story

virginia rowans

THOMAS Y. CROWELL COMPANY · NEW YORK

Library of Congress Catalog Card No. 56-10793

Manufactured in the United States of America by the Vail-Ballou Press, Binghamton, New York

THIRD PRINTING, SEPTEMBER 1956

for D. E. B.
half a book is better than none

the loving couple
her story

one

"ALL RIGHT, DAMN YOU," SHE SHOUTED, "*leave* ME! GET OUT, GET out, get *out!* Get out and don't come back!" The front door slammed with a force that shook the house. Then there was an eerie quietude like the silence that follows a major explosion. The only sound she could hear was the click of his leather heels on the flagstone walk.

"How *dare* he?" she asked the empty reception hall. "How dare John talk to me that way after the things I've had to put up with —the sacrifices I've . . ." She stopped talking. In the first place it was perfectly ridiculous to be staring into a convex eagle mirror and conversing with her own distorted balloon face. In the second place, to be fair—and she always tried to be eminently fair—she couldn't actually think of any real sacrifices she had ever made. Oh, there were little things like putting up with his old tennis cups in the den and not having chartreuse in their bathroom because *he* didn't like chartreuse. She had compromised on those. And there was a big thing, too, giving up her job and that snug little apartment in New York to move out here, like her sister Alice. It was a thing she said she'd never do and yet she'd done it. "For *him,*" she said aloud. But that wasn't quite true either, she thought. I would have had to quit my job with the baby coming anyhow, and since the apartment wasn't really big enough for a baby we'd have had to move. No, there hadn't been any real sacrifices—"Just five, going on six, years of my *life,*" she snapped. She kicked the train of her housecoat and strode into the living room.

The living room was two steps down, an architectural conceit that had cost an extra five hundred dollars and also the baby's life before the baby even had a life. She'd fallen into the living room when she was six months pregnant just after the last ashtray had

been placed, the last picture had been hung in the new house. The baby had been taken from her at the hospital that night. Now she made her way down the two shallow steps very slowly, very carefully, almost painfully. It made her feel like an old lady—eighty-two instead of twenty-eight—but she had learned to hate and fear those steps.

"He was kind about, about the baby," she said to the empty living room. "Bringing me flowers and perfume and a fur scarf as a consolation prize and all that. But he blames me for it. I know he does. And ever since I lost it—ever since we came out here—he's hated me. No man could talk to his wife that way unless he really loathed her." She thought of the baby again and wondered what it would have been like. Then she shrugged her shoulders. "Probably just as well the poor little thing never *was* born. It can't be very pleasant to live with a mother who has to work to support you and . . ." She was getting dramatic now. She realized it and she stopped.

She took a cigarette from a crystal urn and lighted it. It tasted stale and terrible—God only knew how long it had been sitting there. She made a face and put the cigarette out. She rarely smoked anyway and never when she was alone. "Well, I guess I'll be alone for a good long time," she sighed. She glanced at the formal and rather austere perfection of the living room and decided she hated it. Everything in it was pure Regency, genuine and expensive. When they had bought this house and moved out here she had decided that *her* living room wasn't going to be like any of the other living rooms at Riveredge. That precluded Modern, Early American, Eighteenth Century, French Provincial and Williamsburg Restoration. She and Lisa and Gerald and Ronny and Mrs. Updike and several other friends who were only too happy to give her advice had finally settled on Regency. Gerald had said the room was delicious. Ronny had photographed it in color. Lisa planned to do one quite like it next fall. Mrs. Updike took full credit for it and even brought a client up to see it. But today Mary hated it.

She wandered angrily to the window and gazed out at the well-groomed grounds of Riveredge. Down on the road the grounds crew was raking leaves. Through the autumnal trees she could see

the glass and fieldstone expanse of the Hennesseys' house. Smoke was curling up from the chimney and there was a big, vulgar, yellow Cadillac convertible standing in the drive next to the Hennesseys' big, vulgar, red Jaguar convertible. That meant that Jack and Adele Hennessey were entertaining guests for the weekend and that soon they would all come clamoring noisily over to look at the living room and cadge from two to five drinks apiece. A United Parcel delivery truck moaned up the road and disappeared, narrowly avoiding collision with a Buick station wagon full of children. She looked at her Pulse-Beat wristwatch. It was just ten. Ten o'clock on a Saturday morning at Riveredge. A happy family unit came trudging up the road on foot. She knew that they were the Martins. Mr. Martin was in advertising, Mrs. Martin had been a Goodhue and they lived in a white colonial house that *didn't* look out on the river but *did* have heirloom furniture, including a Copley portrait of an early Goodhue and a Sheraton breakfront whose grilled doors concealed television and high fidelity. Mr. Martin was wearing an imported chamois shooting jacket and blue jeans. The two children were wearing corrective dental braces and blue jeans. Mrs. Martin was wearing a vicuña polo coat and maternity blue jeans. There was a good deal of calling back and forth to the family in the station wagon—something about being due any moment now, something about storing tulip bulbs and something about watching the Notre Dame-Navy game together that afternoon. The Martins epitomized Riveredge dwellers and she hated them.

She turned unhappily from the window. "Pretentious little suburban housing development!" she muttered.

In five words she had described Riveredge with deadly accuracy. It was pretentious, it was little, it was suburban and it was a housing development. But there were hard and fast lines drawn at Riveredge that made it stand head and shoulders above the usual housing development, to make it the Versailles of the suburbs. To begin with, Riveredge was a Good Address. It had once been the Hudson River estate of a very rich family who, in the face of rising taxes and falling dividends, had been delighted to sell out to a smart real-estate operator. So Riveredge was no arid expanse of barren soil with a few pathetic shrubs and saplings struggling for

existence. Every tree and bush and flower had been a tradition for generations, only the houses and the people in them were new. New, but by no means *nouveau*, with the possible exception of the Hennesseys. You didn't just buy a little plot and put up a little house at Riveredge, you *joined* Riveredge. And you joined Riveredge only after the board of governors had put you to a number of soul-searching questions as to the education, occupation, race, religion, political affiliations, financial and social standings of you and your spouse, your parents and their parents. This was also followed up by private investigation and all references were carefully checked.

Once you had been admitted to the charmed circle of Riveredge, there were other restrictions as well. No plot could be smaller than an acre and no house less expensive than thirty thousand dollars. If you commanded a view of the Hudson, the land cost more. No two houses were alike and they were so far apart that you saw your neighbors only through binoculars—a popular pastime at Riveredge.

You also signed a sort of Loyalty Oath at Riveredge. You agreed—and the agreement was notarized—to keep your lawn and shrubbery trimmed, your house painted, your windows washed, your dog muzzled and your language clean. You agreed not to drive faster than twenty in the grounds of Riveredge, not to keep explosives or wild animals, not to appear at the swimming pool indecently clad, and not, under any circumstances, to sell to someone whom the board of governors did not approve.

Finally there were fairly stiff annual assessments for the man at the gate who kept out those who had no business in Riveredge, for the lifeguard at the pool, for the bus that took the young bankers and brokers of Riveredge to the station each morning and met them each night, for the grounds crew that trimmed and snipped and clipped all summer and raked and shoveled and graveled all winter. Not everybody could live at Riveredge—just a hundred lucky families. But it was *so* worth it. Just as the ads said in the days when they still had to *sell* Riveredge, it had "the convenience of the city, the charm of the suburbs, the peace of the country."

She moved to the long windows on the opposite side of the room and stared down at the Hudson sparkling below. It was one of

those perfect October days—warm in the sun, chilly in the shade. It was a day without a cloud in the sky; a day that made you think of football and chrysanthemums and new fall suits; a day when you could drive with the top down and be glad you were alive. Well, she wasn't a bit glad she was alive. She wished she were dead and *he* were dead and that they were buried in different cemeteries. She wished that it were cold and foggy and bleak—just as cold and foggy and bleak as she felt.

She picked up another elderly cigarette. Lit it. Made a face and went slowly to the kitchen. The kitchen usually rang with the ungolden voice of Heavenly Rest singing along with an endless program of hep gospel choristers emanating from a mysterious two-watt station in Harlem. The airways between Riveredge and Harlem never carried the hymns smoothly. The plastic kitchen radio snapped and crackled with static and Heavenly Rest had what amounted to a genius for tuning in a program so that it sounded as though it were being transmitted by dental floss between two tin cans. But today the hymns, the static, the gospel singers and Heavenly Rest would all have been very, very welcome. Actually, she reasoned, it's really all Heavenly Rest's fault. If I hadn't given her the weekend off to go to that Mother Immaculate Peace outing, then *she* would have made the coffee and *he* wouldn't have got up and broken that expensive glass coffee maker and *I* wouldn't have called him stupid and *he* wouldn't have . . . She felt herself growing a little wistful. But bending down to pick up the shards of what had been guaranteed to be an automatic, never-fail, unbreakable, pyrex, electric coffee maker, she felt that old rage returning and flooding into her cheeks stronger and hotter than ever.

It wasn't that he had broken the damned coffee pot. That wasn't important. But then *he* had come storming up to their bedroom, yelling and cursing, and awakened her out of a sound sleep. So *she* had said he was stupid and *he* had said: "Stupid, hell, if you ever did anything around here except loaf and run up bills, *I* wouldn't have to be up making the coffee!" Then *she* had said that he was acting like a naughty child and at seven o'clock on a Saturday morning—*really!* Then *he* had said he was cut and scalded, thrusting out a bleeding hand above the bed,

thus ruining the new satin comforter. Then *she* had said: "*Good!* If you don't know how to run a simple gadget that even a half-witted religious fanatic like Heavenly Rest can work, you *deserve* it!" Then *he* had said that if she had been properly brought up and not rotten-spoiled by that old imbecile of a mother out in Santa Barbara, he wouldn't *have* to get up and make his own coffee. Then *she* had said: "Just you keep a civil tongue in your head and . . ."

Well, one thing had led to another. Nobody had *ever* talked to her that way. And there'd been the time, around eight-fifteen, when he had got off a particularly good one; at least *he* must have thought it was good. And a biting, cruel, twisted, completely unfair and untrue statement it had been. Then he had slammed off to the bathroom and locked the door. But that hadn't quite silenced *her*. Oh, no indeed! *She* had gone right to the bathroom door and delivered a few home truths about some of *his* less endearing traits until the door had burst open to reveal him trembling in his pajama bottoms, his face covered with rage and shaving soap. Well, he'd absolutely *screamed* at her and then slammed the door in her face when *she* screamed at him.

And so it had gone. After he'd finished shaving, he'd changed his tactics. Instead of bellowing like a mandrill, he'd gone in for silent dignity and stalked naked into the room with thin lips and raised eyebrows while she let him have it good and proper. Well, she reflected, there were two schools of thought as to just how dignified you could be when your costume consisted of a wristwatch and a Band-aid, but as he began adding clothes his eyebrows went higher and his lips grew thinner. His comments were restricted to cold expletives such as Really? Indeed? How interesting.

While she railed at him he had dressed rather grandly in one of his new English suits which were usually reserved for such vital business functions as Board Meetings, the President's Cocktail Party and Lunch at Twenty-One with the Advertising Agency. And he had dressed with an elaborate calm that infuriated her. It had only been when his hand shook so badly as he picked up his change from the dresser that she knew how terribly angry and upset he really was.

"*Where are you going?*" she had shouted. Then she was furious with herself for having shown any curiosity about him at all.

"Out," he said, clapping the homburg onto his head.

"When are you coming back?" she had yelled. Once more she could have bitten her tongue off. As if she *cared!*

"I'm not," he had said rather too elegantly. Then he had seen in the mirror that his hat was on backward. All his reserve failed him. He had ripped the hat off his head and thrown it to the bedroom floor. "I'm *not* coming back!" he had roared. "I'm not coming back to you or this goddamned house or this stinking little suburb, *ever!*" Then he had pounded down the curving stairway, with her hot on his tail, shouting at him and damning him, and slammed out of the house. It had been, for all practical purposes, the end of the marriage.

"Five years thrown away on the wrong man," she said, dropping the remains of the coffee maker into the garbage can with a crash. Still angry, she stomped up the stairs to their bedroom. There was his hat on the floor. She stepped on it very carefully and then kicked it across the carpet. The silent disorder of their bedroom depressed her. She tripped over one of his slippers as she crossed the room. "Slob!" she said, picking up the slipper and hurling it into his closet. It struck the door jamb and bounced back into the room. Furiously, she began making the bed, setting the room to rights. When she saw the drops of his blood on the yellow satin comforter she said aloud: "I wish he'd cut his *throat!*"

She went to the bathroom to brush her teeth again—that always calmed her—and to take a couple of aspirin. There she saw his pajamas. They had actually been hanging very neatly in exactly the place where they were always hung, but today the sight of them enraged her. "Men!" she muttered, "dirty, untidy, inconsiderate . . ." She tore them off the hook with a loud sound of ripping. She had bought them for him herself last Christmas. They were made of shantung and monogrammed by hand and they'd been very expensive. Now she wanted to slash them with a knife. Instead, she rolled them into an untidy ball and crammed

them into the laundry hamper. Then she stalked back into the bedroom and sat fuming at her desk.

She was a tidy and systematic young woman. She had always *had* to be tidy and systematic. The dour Scotswoman who had raised her and her sister, Alice, had taught her to be. Life with Mother, in a series of hotel suites, after Daddy died and Alice married, had given her practice, what with picking up Mother's underwear and finding her purse and her pearls and her traveler's checks and packing and tagging her luggage when they moved on to still another hotel suite. And working for Mrs. Updike's decorating firm, with samples of chintz and wallpaper cluttering up the squalid little offices behind the elegant showrooms and Mrs. Updike and Gerald having perpetual *crises de nerfs* over lost invoices, had shown how well tidiness and system could pay.

"Now," she said, "what are the things a woman does when she leaves her husband?"

She got out a pad of scratch paper and a pencil and began to write tidily and systematically:

1. *Go Home to Mother.*

Well, that was out. In the first place, Mother was more an old Tools than a mother. In the second place, Home was whatever hotel in whatever country Mother happened to be visiting at the moment. Home was now the Royal Danieli in Venice. Next week it would be the Albergo Something in Genoa. Then the Negresco in Nice until the thirtieth, when Home would be Care of Morgan and Company, Paris, *Ier.* And Mother could drive you madder faster than any brute of a husband, what with her vacillating from Methodism to Swedenborg to Christian Science to the fruit and nut diet to deep massage to henna packs to the Hay diet. Hadn't she sent Daddy to the grave before he was sixty? No, Mother made a better pen pal than a wailing wall.

2. *Call Alice.*

That was *absolutely* out. Alice was her older sister. Alice lived about two thousand yards down the road in a severely modern house. Alice had got her to move out here in the first place. Alice would tell her that Alice had told her so. Alice would give her the complete psychiatric reasoning behind every word and gesture

that had occurred. Alice was very interested in psychoanalysis and knew everything about it. In fact, Alice knew everything about everything and had never once in her life been wrong about anything. No, Alice just wouldn't do; not quite yet.

3. *Get a job.*

The job wouldn't be so hard. She could return to Mrs. Manley Updike, Inc., Interiors. Hadn't Mrs. Updike and young Gerald Updike both wept when she said she was leaving to have a baby? Hadn't they offered her a hundred and twenty a week to come back the minute the baby was born? Hadn't they sent her off with a non-expense account luncheon and a fitted alligator bag and a pint of *My Sin* and a carriage robe trimmed with *point de venise* lace? If the Updikes wouldn't take her back, a dozen other decorators would leap at the chance to get her.

4. *Get an apartment.*

She'd look at the *Times* tomorrow and call an agent on Monday.

5. *Get a lawyer to get a divorce or at least a legal separation.*

Yes, a lawyer would be essential—a lawyer to do the talking to John. *She* wouldn't say another word to him if her life depended on it. She knew a lot of people who had been divorced, but she didn't know much about the details. She supposed she could get alimony, but she didn't want any. The house and car were in her name, but she didn't want those, either. All she asked were the few knick-knacks she had brought to the marriage and her freedom. As for him, well he could . . .

The doorbell rang.

If a bomb had fallen in the middle of the bedroom she couldn't have been more startled. She glanced wildly around the room and saw the car keys on his dresser. If he had forgotten the car keys, of course he had forgotten his house keys, too.

"So, he's back," she said aloud.

The bell rang again.

She caught a harried glance at her reflection and flew to her dressing table. Dabbing on lipstick and running a comb through her hair, she squinted out through the glass curtains. There was no car, no delivery truck. It could only be he.

The bell rang again, louder and louder.

"The gall of him! Storming the house as though this were an MVD raid."

She hurried to the stairs and started down them. Then wisdom overtook her. She straightened her back and slowed her pace. She became rigid with cold hauteur. Whatever it was he wanted, he could have—his clothes, his tennis rackets, his trophies, the silver, the car, the deed to the house. He could have anything except her forgiveness. Fortified, she marched to the door and swung it wide. "Yes," she said icily.

"*Well!* I thought you were dead." It was her sister, Alice.

"Oh," she said. "Alice. It's *you.*"

"Certainly it is." Alice swept into the hall. "I've always hated this hall of yours, Sis—these Regency affectations, this harking back to a dead past. Not appropriate to contemporary living. And certainly not appropriate for the country."

"I'm so sorry, Alice."

Alice stalked along the hall, her tweed cloak billowing out behind her. She leaned her alpinstock against the white wall, leaving a mark. Alice looked like a caricature of a country squire. She was wearing a pork pie hat, a three-piece tweed suit, gaiters and a tattersall waistcoat. She felt that this costume was appropriate for the country. Alice had a good deal to say about what was and what was not appropriate and few people ever saw fit to disagree with her.

Alice clomped down into the living room, reached the exact center of the floor, spun about with a great flourish of her cape and stood there arms akimbo. "I passed that husband of yours this morning as I was driving back from the supermarket. I waved, but naturally he preferred not to see me. If you ask me, he has dangerous hostilities. I do think a talk with Dr. Needles would do him good. Why, the doctor released most of Fred's tensions in three sessions and said there was no need for him to come back."

"How nice for Fred," she said. Really, she thought, how very much the big sister Alice seems today. And Alice *was* the big sister. Not only was she seven years older, but she was bigger, taller, heavier, bonier. Alice had inherited neither their mother's beauty

nor their father's gentleness, but she made up for looks and tact with size and force.

"Not dressed?" Alice asked with a note of disapproval.

"Certainly, I'm dressed, Alice," she said. Let me get through this session just as quickly and lightly as possible, she thought, I just can't take too much of Alice today. "I'm wearing a rose brocade ballgown and a feather fan and an emerald tiara. I thought surely you'd remark about its inappropriateness, Alice."

The older woman thought over her sister's reply carefully, realized that she was not wearing any such thing, and continued with her mission. "What I actually came for was to deliver an invitation. Today's our fifteenth anniversary. I suppose you've forgotten . . ."

"I haven't forgotten at all, Alice. In fact I went into town last week and ordered something—nothing very grand—for you and Fred. It should have been delivered by now."

"Perhaps it has been," Alice said curtly. "There are a lot of things at home I haven't troubled to open yet. Everybody keeps sending me things."

Everybody damned well *has* to, Mary thought.

"Anyhow," Alice continued, "Fred thought it would be nice if we drove into town for dinner and then go on to some sort of night club—just the Martins and us and, of course, the two of you, if you can come. I'm sorry this is such short notice. I meant to call earlier, but I've been so busy addressing notices to the League of Women Voters, and then there was the meeting about the school last night—I didn't see *you* there, by the way—and Timmy's stomach has been upset and I haven't been feeling any too well myself with this new one on the way and . . ."

Alice's incessant talking always gave one time to think of a splendid excuse and today she was grateful to wait out the calendar of events in her sister's busy life. "Alice, I'm *so* sorry. We—I just *can't*."

"Why?" Alice was never satisfied with a simple yes or no. Being versed in psychoanalysis, she often took her interrogation through the conscious, the subconscious and the Id for the true facts.

"Well, Lisa's having one of her big dos and she's invited . . ."

"Really, Sis, why you waste your time with that foolish Lisa Randall, I'll *never* know. She's schizoid, empty-headed, lives in a pure fantasy world and there are decided signs of the worst infantalism—just as there are in you. Well, it doesn't matter, I suppose. Come afterwards. You can leave Lisa's by seven."

"I'm so sorry, Alice, but we just can't. Thank you so much for. . ."

"I don't see why not, you can leave Lisa's and get uptown in plenty of time to . . ." Alice's eyes narrowed. "Unless," she said, slowly, "unless you still feel an animosity toward me because of the father relationship. Well I can tell you that fifteen minutes with Dr. Needles would . . ."

"Alice, I don't feel anything. I—that is, we—just can't make it and it was sweet of you to . . ." She saw Alice stand a little straighter, arch her back, lift her head and take a deep breath. Oh, please God, don't let her start play-acting now.

Before the war effort, marriage, child bearing, psychology, suburbia, the League of Women Voters, the Parent-Teachers Association, the Committee for Political Awareness, the American Association of University Women and Planned Parenthood captured so much of her time, Alice had a passion for the stage. As a school girl in Santa Barbara, she had thrilled the whole community with her performances of Shakespeare. Alice had been a stern Portia, a brisk Ophelia, a business-like Juliet. Only German measles had prevented her ultimate triumph as Goneril in *King Lear*. But although Alice had cast aside the Bard for bigger things, her dramatic background was still evident.

"Listen, Sis," Alice began, "the behavior pattern you and John have been following has given me great concern. I went to a lot of trouble—and so did Fred—to get you out of New York and accepted here among well-adjusted, oriented people, totally unlike the neurotic milieu you ran with in town. But ever since you had that miscarriage—and both Dr. Needles and I feel that some inner compulsion toward self-destruction forced you to throw yourself down the stairs—you and he have . . ."

"Alice!" Mary cried. "Alice, he's gone. He's gone and left me. He . . ." she buried her head in her arms and burst noisily into tears.

Alice stopped with a gulp. She was of many minds about this scene. First of all, Alice did not like being interrupted by anyone at any time for any reason. Secondly, she detested signs of weakness in people because the mature, adjusted person could arrange life to suit himself and face it on his own terms. Thirdly, Alice had always had a sneaking suspicion that her young brother-in-law found her, in some inexplicable way, *comical*. The feeling jolted Alice's firm security and she had to admit—if only to herself and Dr. Needles—to disliking him and wishing that he were out of the way. Fourthly, Alice saw in her weeping sister the beginning of what might be a very interesting case—a kind of guinea pig or charity patient psyche—which she might plumb, examine, dissect, discuss and then turn over to the better-worn couch of Dr. Needles. Alice was a zealous missionary for her analyst. On a commission basis, she would have been a very rich woman. Fifthly, Alice saw herself in the role of the understanding older sister, experienced with the peccadillos of the human emotions. It was a part she had never been invited to play and she was anxious to get her teeth into it.

"Sis," Alice said briskly, "you're allowing yourself to sink into the quicksands of emotionalism and . . ."

"Shut up, Alice, p-please." The sobbing continued. She hadn't cried so hard since the day Daddy died.

Alice was stunned. She had always talked to her children this way, analyzing away the pain of skinned knees and the dentist's drill and it had always worked with them. *Eventually* they stopped screaming.

"Sis, um, *dear*," Alice said uneasily. "Sis, dear, please don't cry so—so terribly. It isn't the end of the world and . . ."

"It f-feels like it," Mary sobbed.

"He was all wrong for you, anyway. *I* thought so, *Fred* thought so and Dr. Needles *said* so. Besides, you're young. You have years ahead of you. And you always have Fred and me." Alice couldn't have sworn to it, but she thought she saw her sister almost *shudder*. "You've made a mistake—a serious mistake—but it isn't irreparable. The best thing to do is to admit it. Have a little talk with Dr. Needles. Cut your losses and start over again with a new slant and a new outlook and a new personality."

In spite of her determinedly motherly rendition, the old matter-of-factness was creeping back into Alice's voice. She had once been very active in the Camp Fire Girls.

"Now the thing for you to do, Sis, is to get a good grip on yourself. We all go through the emotional traumas and the best way out is . . ."

There's one thing about Alice, Mary thought through her sobs, nothing's ever so bad that Alice can't make it seem worse. Visions of her divorce raced through her head as Alice droned on. There might be the collusive New York divorce with embarrassed, stammering witnesses perjurously testifying as to the "unknown blonde" in a West Side hotel room. She could already feel the vulgarity of the dude ranch outside Reno, the humidity of the hotel in the Virgin Islands, the loneliness of six weeks in Idaho. She thought of all the dreary places where weary women waited to shed their men.

". . . thing to do is to get out of this atmosphere," Alice was saying. "Now just go upstairs and pack a little overnight bag and you can come right home with me. It'll do you good to be around a wholesome household full of well-adjusted people. We'll all go out tonight, just as though nothing had ever happened, and on Monday I'll run you into town for a good talk with Dr. Needles while I'm getting my check-up . . ."

"No!" Mary said. Then she was afraid that she had sounded rude. "Alice, thanks, but I can't. I'd rather stay here alone, thank you just the same. I. . . ."

"He'll only come back and you'll have to undergo . . ."

"He won't be back. He'll more than likely be staying at that club of his. I guess he'll arrange to come and get his clothes sometime when I'm out. Or maybe I'll go and he can keep the place. I don't want it."

"You mean he's moved into the Bacchus Club? Well, if *that* isn't a sure sign of immaturity! Talk about returning to the womb! Why . . ."

"I didn't discuss housing with him, Alice. Now, if you'll excuse me for just a minute, I'd like to go upstairs and get a hankie." With a resonant sniffle, she left the room.

two

"GOODBYE, ALICE," SHE SAID FOR THE TENTH TIME. "AND THANKS again. Thanks for just everything. Yes, I'll telephone this afternoon. Really I will. Now *don't* let me keep you any longer, dear. *Goodbye!*" She closed the front door behind her sister and leaned limply against it.

Even the ruse of going upstairs for a handkerchief had failed. She hadn't been alone for five minutes before she'd heard the stealthy clump of Alice's Space Shoes on the stairs. Like a zealous Saint Bernard, Alice had found her, pushed her down on the bed and dabbed cologne on her temples, pouring a lot of it into her hair and a good deal more onto the bedspread. Then, Alice had sat down beside her and treated her to a brief psychoanalysis.

Alice had selected her own school, or *schools*, of psychology as a venturesome tourist chooses dinner in a smorgasbord restaurant. Alice had begun with a big gob of Freud—perhaps too much?—and a salty helping of Jung. There had been a dab of Adler, a smidgin of Karen Horney, a generous portion of Flanders Dunbar, equal amounts of Reich and Reik, an indigestible mixture of Krafft-Ebing and Stekel and a final dollop of Harry Stack Sullivan. Piled high on a very small plate, it made for a confusing meal, but Alice always had the satisfaction of knowing that she had devoured something very, very rich.

When Alice had finished psychoanalyzing her sister, she psychoanalyzed the bedroom—its frivolities and conceits. Then Alice had launched into a singularly unflattering capsule diagnosis of her brother-in-law's failings, which Alice had felt to be legion and insurmountable.

Lying there in the fumes of cologne, hopelessly besieged by

Alice, Mary had grown a little irritated—just why, she didn't know—at hearing Alice run John down that way. It was all right for *her* to call him a cad and a louse and a heel and a brute and a beast. A, because he *was* a cad and a louse and a heel and a brute and a beast; and B, because he was *her* husband—or had been until this morning. But she hadn't liked to hear Alice pulverizing him in clinical small talk. And *another* thing that had burned her up was Alice's constant trotting off to that old quack Dr. Needles to spend the whole appointment—and the whole twenty-five-dollar fee—dishing over *her* husband. Let Alice and Dr. Needles worry about *Alice's* psyche and stop gossiping about *him*. Conversely, it had always made her furious when *he* had referred to her sister Alice as a common scold. Albeit true.

"I suppose I'm just difficult," she murmured.

"What?"

"I said, Alice, you've been a perfect darling—selflessness itself—to come and solve all my problems, but I can't have you wearing yourself out when you're in this condition. It's so close to your time and you're not as young as you were with the other two. Now, why don't you let me drive you home and you can take a nice nap and . . ."

"*Nonsense!*" Alice had boomed indignantly. "Both Dr. Needles and my gynecologist say they've never seen a fitter mother—physically and emotionally. Besides, the baby isn't due for four more months and just let me tell you . . ."

Well, the trick had worked—partially. Alice had become neither silent nor absent, but at least she had started talking about something else. Alice was active in Planned Parenthood. Born a couple of decades earlier, Alice would most certainly have been jailed for passing out contraceptives on the cathedral steps. Today she took a more moderate, but no less ardent, stand. Alice believed that those who could afford children should have all the children they could afford and *when* they could afford them. Alice always said that it was the *duty* of superior people to bring forth superior offspring. So far Alice and Fred had produced two—a boy of seven, given to chronic nausea and bedwetting, and a girl of five with nineteen distinct allergies. Alice and Fred felt that they could now afford to treat mankind to yet another superior being, and its

birth had been as carefully plotted as the Invasion of Normandy.

Alice could—and *would*—tell you a full year in advance just when, where, why and how her next baby would be born. The present incumbent was due on the sixteenth of February, after the Stock Exchange closing. It would be brought into the world via Natural Childbirth. "Strengthens the bond of motherhood," Alice had explained.

"Alice," Mary had interrupted determinedly, "it's not fair for me to keep you *one minute* longer, what with your anniversary and the baby coming and Timmy's bowels . . ."

"His stomach."

"Yes, of course, his stomach. Well, I'm not going to monopolize any more of your time." She had begun propelling Alice toward the stairs.

Even so, it had taken a good fifteen minutes to buck the various tides and breakers and undertows of Alice's Sargasso Sea of theories. But now, thank God, Alice was *out*. The silence was beautiful.

She walked cautiously down into the living room, circled it aimlessly, not really looking at it, and then trailed into the study. She was surprised—and a little annoyed—to see how tidy the study was. She had fully expected to find it a shambles, after last night, just as the kitchen had been this morning. Instead it was spick and span. There was no trace of ashes or cigarette butts—and he must have smoked more than a pack, sitting there morosely staring into the television set. The glasses and Scotch and ice bucket had disappeared. Even his wretched tennis cups seemed to be freshly polished.

For some reason the cleanliness of this room angered her. She had been planning to put it in order herself as a sort of final masochistic act of marital bondage, gently cursing him as she did so. Now she was deprived of these last rites, so to speak, of her life with him. She felt even more resentment than she would have if, say, the study had been strewn with broken glasses and bottles, if furniture had been overturned, if she had found a big, smoldering burn in one of the new leather chairs and possibly a strange, slightly soiled black brassiere in a disgustingly large size. That

would have added fuel to her hatred of him—not that it really *needed* any more fuel.

Last night she'd felt sorry for him as she sat there nursing her drink and watching him watching the terrible debacle of his television show, *Pulse Beat.* The show had been a real turkey, a turkey for which he was solely responsible. Now she was glad it had been such a little stinker. She loathed television anyhow and having to sit in the study every Friday night to watch "America's *Prestige* TV Show" had been fairly onerous, especially since he took every blown-up line, every wiggle of the scenery as a personal affront.

Yes, she knew it now, she had always hated the *Pulse Beat* program. She hated the Popescu Pulse-Beat Eternal Non-Magnetic Swiss Watch of Geneva, London, Paris and New York, Ltd. She hated Pulse Beat's president, Manfred Popescu, that walking League of Nations, hand holder, knee patter and bottom pincher. She hated his dizzy menopausal American wife whose every diamond and emerald gewgaw had a Pulse-Beat watch concealed in it somewhere. She expected that she'd hate Mr. Popescu's wife's daughter by her first marriage—a ravishing brunette with the incredible name of Besame Bessamer. She'd never met the creature, but she had seen Besame's debut as an actress on *Pulse Beat* last night and Besame was just the kind of woman other women despise.

She supposed that she was being silly to bite the hand that fed her—or, rather, *had* fed her up until this morning. Besides she was out of it all now. *He* could stay here, right in this very room in Riveredge and watch *Pulse Beat* on Friday nights.

This morning she chose to forget that just a year ago she had considered Mrs. Popescu an exquisitely rough diamond and Mr. Popescu a lovable old rascal. In fact, it had been all her fault—through a series of accidents—that Mr. Popescu had swept her John to wealth and fame and John had swept her out here to this glossy little jewel of a Regency pavilion.

Until her meeting with Lillian Schneider Bessamer Popescu, she and her husband had lived blissfully on the brink of financial disaster in one charming room in the East Sixties which looked as though it cost a good deal more than it actually did. She had had her job. He had had one play produced successfully off Broad-

way; one produced unsuccessfully on Broadway; and a far better one that was going the rounds of producers' offices. He had sold a story to *The New Yorker*, four to less exalted publications, a number of radio and television scripts and had two very funny sketches in a revue that ran through a whole winter. He had had one-third of a novel in the works, too. Naturally it all sounded great, but average it out, the lean periods with the fat ones and it came to about eighty bucks a week, plus what he felt he could take from the tiny estate that was left after his father's sixty-odd years of high living.

But even with dubious checks handed out to the landlord and the telephone company, even with two solid weeks of Kraft's Macaroni Dinner after splurging on a very grand supper party in honor of a producer who later tried to touch them for fifty dollars. Even with all kinds of desperate little economies, they still had had fun. They were young and decorative and gay and popular and very, very happy.

Mr. and Mrs. Santa Claus had appeared in the personages of that Swiss fondue of mixed nationalities, Manfred Popescu and his unlovely bride, Lillian Schneider Bessamer Popescu. Having acquired a fearfully opulent penthouse on Central Park South, Mrs. Popescu next acquired the professional services of Mrs. Manley Updike, Inc., Interiors to give her "a few cute ideas, dearie." Mrs. Updike had taken one look, murmured something vague about disabusing Mrs. Popescu of *all* cute ideas and fluttered off to Santa Fe with the vapors. Still, a commission was a commission, so Lillian Popescu and the penthouse ended up in *her* lap.

It was while she was trying to dissuade Mrs. Popescu from hanging her picture window in cloth of gold that the program *Pulse Beat* was conceived. Mr. Popescu had come storming home from the watchworks muttering a most impressive rondelet of steaming Balkan curses. It seemed, Lillian had explained, that Mr. Popescu had just witnessed the television debut of the long famous Pulse-Beat Eternal Non-Magnetic Swiss Watch radio hour. It was an all-girl orchestra apparently dedicated to such inspirational numbers as "I Believe" and "My Rosary." For some years the program had been a standing favorite of people who spoke the praises of Pulse Beat's refined-type program while setting their

own dollar Mickey Mouse wrist watches to the famous Pulse-Beat beep—every hour on the hour.

However, a trombone played by a lady *sounded* a lot better than it looked. In spite of diets, permanents and fluffy tulle dresses, the Pulse-Beat all-girl orchestra, as it flickered onto the television screen, gave more the impression of a pony chorus at Camp Yaphank than one of feminine pulchritude. Manfred Popescu had a diabolical eye for a pretty female and the first sight of his famous all-girl company—hairy arms raised in ecstasy as they roared into an *a capella* rendition of "Mighty Like a Rose"—had prompted him to cancel his contract, dismiss the advertising agency and send his troupe of muscular houris back to whatever side shows and wrestling rings had spawned them. He had always been a man of quixotic moods, Mr. Popescu.

Well, one thing had led to another, and while she and Lillian were calming Mr. Popescu, she had just happened to mention that her husband was a young writer who had had *ever* so many things produced on television. The next thing she knew, the Popescus and *she* and *he* were all at Voisin discussing over Steak *Chateaubriand* a most marvellous television program called *Pulse Beat*. A week after that, five air-shaking dramatic scripts had been written for *Pulse Beat* and the Popescus and *she* and *he* were all at the Stork Club celebrating *his* appointment as advertising manager, starting immediately at twenty-five thousand a year with raises, bonuses, vacations and sick benefits commensurate with his ability.

She had been so happy that night that she quite forgave Manfred Popescu's little pinch under the table while her husband was dancing a rhumba with Mrs. Popescu. Well, Lillian could shake her can off and hang her Moorish living room in glazed chintz as far as *she* had been concerned. The important thing had been herself and John. The job, the prestige, the security had meant that she could quit working, find a bigger place, have a baby. It had been the beginning of their life.

It had been the beginning, all right. It had been the beginning of endless evenings in endless restaurants and night clubs, with Lillian's big bottom, swathed in knit suits, shimmering satin, and

spangled peplums, swinging like a Pulse-Beat pendulum to the shicka-shicka-shicka of the rhumba band. It had been the beginning of Manfred's small, furry paws groping for her under the table as whispered endearments in Rumanian, Hungarian, Bohemian, Turkish, Greek, German, Polish, French, Russian, Italian and English travelled moistly into her ear on the wings of his faintly sour breath.

A Swiss by financial, political and personal choice, Mr. Popescu had been born of capriciously mixed parentage in one of those obscure Balkan countries which is always appearing, disappearing, being taken over by this or that power, set free by another, divided, subdivided, established and disestablished at the whim of tripartite conferences, and then snuffing itself out in ensuing revolutions led by the Popular Front, the Legitimist Restoration or the Conservative Socialist faction. Between the womb and Lillian he had mastered so many tongues that he was equally at home in any, but equally incomprehensible and repulsive in each.

Well, that's how it had all started. The rest was history.

It seemed to her that today they had less money than they had had in their one-room-in-town days. They had been careful, at first; even managed to save money. But there had been invisible expenses of some magnitude—new suits to replace his shiny old serge and the threadbare flannel; smart new things for her to wear while entertaining the *Pulse Beat* movie-star-a-week at expense account luncheons; lavish floral tributes for Lillian; Countess Mara ties for Manfred.

The Popescus, who were, understandably, not very popular, had demanded a great deal of their time, and even though it shouldn't have, that had cost quite a lot of money. She and John had moved 'way out here quite as much to avoid evenings with Lillian and Manfred as to have room enough for a baby. Now the marriage was all untidily wrapped up and finished.

She moved on through the smart oval dining room—so warm and gala during candlelit dinners for *Pulse Beat* bigwigs, but cold and austere in its northlit emptiness today—and went into the kitchen. There were still dim traces of the wreckage of their forty-dollar coffee maker scattered in the corners. Stooping to clean up

what remained of the mess, she realized that she was quite hungry, that she'd had nothing to eat since dinner last night. She wondered vaguely what there was in the house to eat.

During their poor days in New York, she had been a resourceful and talented cook, the flushed author of many a towering soufflé and succulent *bourguignon.* As though by magic, little gourmet meals—equally pleasing to eye, palate and pocketbook—would appear from behind the stylish screen that concealed a grumbling, waist-high ice box, a dripping sink and a two-burner stove whose oven had a mind of its own. The whole kitchen there had been smaller than a cupboard here and yet she had made it produce miracles.

This kitchen, with its expanses of plastic and steel, its ovens and broilers and warmers and spits, its ranks of copper and spice jars, its desk and telephone and special surfaces of marble and maple, was to have been her own domain. Today she hardly knew where to find a saucepan. Since Heavenly Rest had arrived, she rarely came into this room except to create something very special, such as a lobster mousse or brioche or a sauce bearnaise for Mr. Popescu's filet. Now it seemed that she and John ate out a great deal of the time. When they were at home, guests were usually there, too, and they subsisted on party food—hot house delicacies and the grander cuts of meat. Meals that were rich, expensive and dull, ordered, cooked, served and washed up by Heavenly Rest.

It mystified her to think that in New York she had been able to manage a job, cooking, cleaning, mending and entertaining. Out here, where domesticity was a career, a vocation, a religion, she scarcely found time to make her own bed.

Her stomach rumbled ominously and turning to the cabinet where she thought the coffee might be stored she opened it. Heavenly Rest had Scotch-taped some fearful religious chromos to the inside of the cabinet door. There was a gaudy view of the Boy Jesus talking to the elders in the temple. With flaxen curls and cornflower eyes, Christ was the image of Mary Pickford, while the elders put one in mind of Fagin, Shylock, Leopold and Loeb. A garishly hand-tinted "Last Supper"—*not* Leonardo's—reminded her of a drag party. There was also a life-sized sepia photograph of Mother Immaculate Peace looking like a caramel cupid.

Curiously, she lifted a stack of religious tracts and gave a little gasp as a skittish parade of ants dashed out from under it and raced pell-mell out of the cabinet. Really, she'd have to speak to Heavenly Rest about . . . "Well, actually, I won't have to speak to her at all," she said to herself. "In a week's time it won't matter to me if a tarantula runs out of the cabinet." There was no coffee there, anyhow. She slammed the cabinet door and opened the big, yellow refrigerator.

The telephone, yellow like the rest of the kitchen, jangled sharply, shattering the silence of the house and shattering her, too. *He* was calling! It could *only* be he, probably with more abuse, or maybe trying to make up—fat chance of *that*—or possibly ordering her to pack up and get out of his house. The telephone rang again. Of course it could be Alice or, even worse, Lillian or Manfred Popescu screaming about last night's program, or . . . The telephone rang again. She might imitate Heavenly Rest's rich Mississippi accent until she found out who it was and then . . . No, he'd see through that. He was the one who'd so magnanimously given Heavenly Rest the weekend off in the first place. The telephone rang again. Or she could just let it ring. Never! Her curiosity wouldn't permit it. Her hand stretched tentatively out as the telephone began ringing for the fifth time.

"H-hello?"

"Thank God you're in. This is Fran."

"F-Fran?"

"Fran Hollister. Listen, you've got to help me. That tramp, Adele Hennessey, just called to invite herself and her shanty-Irish husband and a couple of other micks over—can you *imagine*—and I made up the first excuse that came into my head."

"Which was?"

"Which was that you two were taking me out for lunch and that we were going into town to that fool party of Lisa Randall's. I *suppose* Lisa asked you. She's asked everybody else in the world."

"Y-yes."

"Well, listen," Fran continued brusquely, "if you'll back me up in this, *I'll* take you both to lunch—anywhere you say, just so I don't have to put up with those Hennessey climbers. And you ought to be grateful. She'll be inviting herself over to your place

next. So, what do you say to lunch—that is, if your old man doesn't mind having two women hanging onto him. There's this guy I'm going to meet at Lisa's anyway and . . ."

A perfect ragout of emotions surged over her. The call could have come from him, from Alice, from Adele Hennessey, from the Popescus, from Mrs. Updike or Gerald or Gerald's Ronny. It might have been a call from Lisa or a cousin in Greenwich or Beth Martin or the dry cleaner. But Fran Hollister *never* telephoned you—if you were a woman. Even odder, Fran invited her to lunch and Fran never invited you to *anything*—if you were a woman. She'd known Fran both briefly and vaguely over many years and to her Fran embodied worldliness, glamour and mystery. She was as flattered and perplexed by the call as she was confused and upset. She didn't feel like seeing anyone today, especially not anyone as, well, *hard* as Fran. Today was a day for being alone with herself.

"Listen, Fran," she began unsteadily, "I'm terribly sorry but we . . ." Suddenly this house, the kitchen, the ants, the broken coffee maker crowded in on her. She wanted to get away from the place and from him and from Alice's imminent intrusion. She wanted to think about something new, to talk to somebody who knew something about striking out alone. Fran Hollister had shed husbands by every known means short of mariticide. Fran was exciting and experienced and, she felt, very, very wicked. Fran liked her—Fran was even *pursuing* her. Why not spend the afternoon looking at a smashed-up marriage through the hardened eyes of Riveredge's reigning menace? She'd play the whole thing gaily and she'd play it with Fran.

"I'm terribly sorry," she repeated, "but we're not, um, available in pairs any longer. He's . . . that is, *I've left him.*"

There was a sound of ulp at the end of the line. Then a pause. "You've *what?*"

"I've left him. Getting Reno-vated"—that was clever, light, brittle, *Fran*—"or some such arrangement. We haven't worked out the incidental details."

"I . . . can't . . . believe it," Fran said levelly. "Of all the people in the world. My God, The Loving Couple!"

"Well, don't look for him under *my* bed," she said with a hys-

terical little laugh. Fran laughed too, in her deep throaty bellow. That made Mary a little uneasy. She just wondered whether Fran had ever given him the glad-eye, or vice-versa. Not that she actually *cared*. Not any more.

"Well, come right over, little girl and drown your sorrows. I know a marvellous lawyer who . . . Or can I pick you up, if you're stranded in the house."

"Oh, no. No, I seem to have custody of the car." She drew a deep breath. "Listen, Fran, just let me get dressed. I don't think I'll be going in to Lisa's party, but I *would* like to have lunch with you. I'll be over just as soon as I can throw something on." No use giving Fran a chance to back out. "And Fran, let's make it dutch."

"Wonderful," Fran said.

three

Fran hollister hung up the telephone, fell back onto her unmade bed and emitted a long, low whistle. "What do you know," she said aloud. "*What* do you know!" Another woman would have telephoned a friend immediately to spread the bad news. Not Fran. Fran had no friends. Fran's acquaintances were divided, by Fran, into three general categories: Men; Climbers; and Enemies. In addition, Fran had a very small sort of Honor Roll of Individuals labeled Good Guys. The Honor Roll was populated by a highly nomadic few. You could get on and off Fran's Honor Roll within the space of an hour, depending on Fran's mood. This preferred list usually consisted of whichever man Fran planned to take as her next lover; anyone who was as rich as Fran was and hadn't done anything to warrant classification among Enemies; a couple of people she didn't know personally, but admired for some reason or other (this could be a night club comedian or an axe killer or a delivery boy or a cop); and sometimes one other woman.

Fran reached out for her cigarette and her drink. So another redskin had bitten the dust! She thought—only very tentatively—of him, now that he was unencumbered, so to speak. Only a month ago John had caught her eye at the Riveredge swimming pool. She'd never seen him without clothes on before and she was not unimpressed, to this very day, by the well muscled back, the curve of his chest, his lean hips in the tartan trunks. It was a nice body and it was a *gentleman's* body. She'd seen him at the very moment when she was so sick of Speed, the Riveredge lifeguard, that she could spit. Speed. He was well named! Well, Speed had been okay for a summer's romp. But he was gone now.

He'd taken his fuzzy yellow crew cut and his forty-eight chest and his twenty-eight waist and his eighteen I.Q. down to some third rate hotel in Florida where he could thrill all the career girls on winter vacations. And Fran had had the devil's own time getting rid of Speed, at that. You couldn't just tick off someone of Speed's class the way you could a gentleman. No, Speed had to blubber and weep and talk about love and honor and marriage and all that. Married to *Speed!* Imagine!

So old tartan trunks was coming onto the open market at last! Fran moistened her lips and took a sip of her drink. Well, Fran wouldn't think about it just now. Besides, his wife—who was on Fran's Good Guy list—was going to have lunch with her at any moment. Fran would hear all about *it*—and all about *him*—soon enough.

Fran got off the bed and stretched. It was quite a stretch. Fran stood just six feet tall in her heels. She picked up a hairbrush and ran it through her long red bob. Then she went into the bathroom.

Fran Hollister had been born at Riveredge and she still lived there. Riveredge had been her family's estate. When Fran sold the place off to turn into a fashionable club-development, she had retained the guest cottage as her own—her own and Mr. Hollister's. Fran had divorced Mr. Hollister six months ago and she was very firm about the regularity of his alimony payments to her. In her own name Fran possessed what the tabloids estimated to be somewhere between twelve and forty million dollars. (In truth, it was only eleven million.)

Fran was thirty years old, and for exactly half her life she had been awesomely regarded as sex, sin and seduction on the hoof.

Before then she had been a gangling, gawky, ill-tempered child with freckles, bristling brows and carrot red head. She had been dragged snarling and spitting to dancing classes, kicking out at her governess, the teacher and her unwilling partners with bare, bony, bruised legs. She was equally unpopular with boys and girls, accepted only because her family was so very, very rich. But at fifteen something had happened. Fran had turned into a man trap—tall and fierce and exotic looking. She had been amazed at first by the change in her and in the boys she met at junior dances, but she had soon taken their adulation as her due. Possessed of

enormous wealth, impeccable social connections and an undying hatred of people, Fran had set out to live life on her own terms.

Fran had been married three times with plenty of amatory activity before, after and during. First she had eloped, at seventeen, with a West Point cadet. The marriage was annulled, but not without great expense, greater publicity, the cadet's expulsion from the Academy and the certification of Fran's none-too-stable mother. Her next venture was also patriotic. That husband had been an Air Force flyer of such humble origins that Fran never forgot it. Nor could Fran forget the blessed wave of relief she felt when a Naval ensign of her acquaintance crept out of Fran's bed to receive the telegram announcing that her second husband had been shot down over Berlin. Lastly she had married Hollister, a man of such superior lineage that Fran never forgave it. He had endured Fran for four years, until the third time he discovered her under a willow tree with a man—always the same tree; never the same man—and permitted her to divorce him on grounds of extreme mental cruelty.

Fran wandered back to her bedroom humming a tune she connected vaguely with an old Rodgers and Hart show. She was thoroughly tone deaf. She let her grease-spotted dressing gown fall to the floor, and walked across it. At the closet door she stared at the full-length reflection of her naked body with indifferent approval. It was a large body and there were twenty pounds more of it than there had been fifteen years ago at Fran's first blossoming. She might also have profited from a shampoo and a bit of conscientious deforestation under her arms. None of this worried Fran. She had perfect confidence in everything concerned with herself. She opened the closet and took out the first dress her hand touched.

Changing styles meant nothing to Fran. She had always worn the Glamour Girl uniform of the year she came out. She had fewer than a dozen dresses and they all looked alike—black and tight and cut as low as the law would allow. They were seldom, if ever, cleaned and when one wore out she got another as much like it as possible. Her hair hung to her shoulder blades in a thick, coarse auburn mane. It was cut annually. Every so often,

Fran would begin feeling conscientious, go off to Rubinstein's for the works, but most of the time she felt perfectly satisfied with the way she looked.

She wriggled into her black dress and pulled up the zipper. It was too tight and she was conscious of a split seam under one arm, but she was sure no one would notice. There was a spot on the bosom—a drink, she supposed. She rubbed at it ineffectually. The dress was wool and Fran was conscious of its itching, so she stepped into a pair of pants which were conveniently lying on the floor. Then she thrust her large, bare feet into a pair of black suede pumps.

She trudged over to her dressing table, dabbed on brown lipstick, splashed herself with *Shalimar*, put on her pearls and three diamond bracelets. Then she picked up her shiny old suede purse, dragged her mink coat across the rug and clomped down the stairs.

Never quite in fashion and never quite out, Fran really didn't give much of a damn. Her dirty, thirty-dollar dresses, her slightly hirsute legs, so freckled that stockings were—or so Fran thought—unnecessary, her run-over suede pumps were quite good enough when set off with forty-thousand dollars' worth of ice and a ten-grand mink coat. And, to do her justice, Fran was not without a kind of raffish high style if you took only a quick glance.

Fran flung her mink coat over the newel post and surveyed her jiggery-pokery living room complacently. It was just as she'd left it last night, the empty glasses, the dying pom-poms, the oddly assorted bits of old family furniture in wrinkled new Sears Roebuck slipcovers. There was a rattling at the front door and the sound of a key being inserted. Then there was a succession of chilling noises. It was the cleaning woman. Fran nodded coolly in her direction and pointed to the ice bucket. The woman made another noise and shuffled off toward the kitchen.

Fran kept no servants. She had hired a procession of maids after her divorce but it hadn't worked. The first three had walked out, outraged beyond words by Fran's way of life. The last had tried to blackmail her. Now Fran had the ideal set-up. A feebleminded deaf mute came from the village every day—well after the time when any overnight guest had taken his leave—to clean

the house and change Fran's bed. Fran paid her fifty cents an hour and the woman was gurglingly grateful for this, the only employment opportunity open to her. The arrangment worked out splendidly for both of them.

There was a thump and clatter of ice cubes from the kitchen and the woman scuttled back, put the ice bucket on the bar, bobbed and nodded and shot off to the kitchen once more. Fran mixed herself another drink and sat down on the sofa to await her guest while aimlessly drawing a round little face in the thin film of dust on the coffee table.

Mary had never been so nervous in her life. She was actually trembling when she stopped the car in front of Fran's house. She glanced quickly at her face in the rearview mirror and was thankful that it hadn't changed for the worse since she looked at it five minutes ago. "Throw something on" indeed! She had bathed and dressed with all the care of a mannequin at a Paris opening. She had new everything on underneath and all of it real silk—no synthetics. Then she had put on the new little wool of a color that was so subtle it defied description—so soft and simple and elegant that it whispered one million dollars. It was a dress which she had bought to save for some really *special* occasion. Well, what could be more special than the occasion of shucking off a husband and having lunch with a creature as fabulous as Fran Hollister?

She had known Fran, only slightly, when she was in boarding school. She had been just fourteen, Fran sixteen. To her Fran had been the epitome of the Older Woman. Two years' difference had meant a lot then and still did. She would always think of Fran as perfect centuries older. Besides, Fran was worldly even then. Fran had already been kicked out of Foxcroft, St. Timothy's and Miss Walker's—all far grander establishments than the Baldwin School, where she and Alice had been sent. Fran's tenure at Baldwin had been short (she was expelled for smoking, sneaking out and having rum in her room) but so sensational as to have made a lasting impression.

Naturally Mary had never tried to use boarding school as a wedge into Fran's really exclusive circle. In fact, she'd hardly done

more than say hello to Fran at the swimming pool and at parties. She'd always been too afraid of her to say much more.

She readjusted the new furs. Mary had been a little doubtful about putting them on. They reminded her of the baby and of *him*. But they were perfect with this dress and she had decided to wear them just this once and then leave them behind when she moved out. She gave the furs a tender little pat, drew her doeskin gloves on a trifle tighter and marched briskly up the flagstone walk to drink in the splendors of Fran and Fran's house.

"Welcome to the fold," Fran said, giving a quick approving glance to her guest, the dress, the furs, the glistening car beyond. There must be money there somewhere, Fran thought. His? Hers? People without money made Fran uneasy. She always felt that they were after hers.

"Th-thank you," she said to Fran. "It's nice to be here."

"Come in and we'll have a drink," Fran said, leading the way into her living room. She'd better go easy at first, Fran thought. A lot of these girls take divorce so *seriously*. God, when she thought of all that weeping and wailing down in St. Thomas . . . "Sit down. What'll it be, Scotch, bourbon, rye?"

"Bourbon, I think, please."

"How?" Fran asked, gulping down the rest of the drink she had just mixed for herself.

"Why . . . on the rocks, please."

Fran sauntered over to the bar and mixed two strong drinks. Fran always bought case lots of unheard-of whiskies—there was a rye that tasted of wet straw, a Scotch labelled Loch Grymm which reminded one of creosote, and a bourbon that was pure mange cure. Blends all, and inexpensive. These were for the very few guests she chose to entertain. Fran always mixed her own drink with Haig and Haig Pinchbottle. "Here's how," Fran said. "To hell with all men!"

"To hell with all men," she echoed after Fran. The mixture in the squat ten cent store glass she held was the color of Coca-Cola and it tasted like nothing in this world.

"Well," Fran said, fixing her with a dark glitter, "now tell Mother all about it." Fran had no curiosity about other women

and so many of her own attachments had broken up that she wasn't much interested in the whys and wherefores of other romantic disasters. Yet, from what she'd seen of *him,* he didn't seem to be the sort Fran would kick out of the hay without very good reasons. Fran wanted to know what they were well in advance—just in case.

"There isn't anything to tell," Mary said with a brave little smile in Fran's general direction. "It's just finished."

Fran was a little disappointed and yet she was pleased. She hated women who blubbered about their troubles. Yes, Fran thought, she's a pretty good guy at that. "Just get sick of him?" Fran asked tenatively. If there was anything wrong with him like bad breath or impotency or a penchant for the boys Fran might as well find it out before wasting a second. You could never tell by looking. Speed had been overpoweringly handsome, and what a washout *he'd* been.

Mary stared at Fran. "Sick of him?" she wondered. Could you ever get sick of the little private jokes, the secret language, the telepathic response you'd built up with someone for more than five years? No you couldn't just get *sick* of something like that. But when the person you'd loved and trusted and shared your life and your bed with shattered all of those good things by turning into a raging, vile-mouthed, insulting brute, well . . .

She took a little gulp of her drink and felt it burning and sizzling all the way down to her stomach. It gave her a kind of Dutch courage. "Incompatibility is the term, I believe . . . darling." There, now she was back to the worldly routine that was right for Fran. It made her more comfortable. "For about a year now we haven't been exactly like Darby and Joan. Nothing you can put your finger on—if that's the sort of thing you *want* to put your finger on. Hahaha! But . . ." Her voice trailed off and she took another sip of her drink. No, there hadn't been anything definite during the past year; just a sort of growing apart, a general malaise in their marriage. "It's just that I find him a perfect beast!" There, now she'd said it. That was everything in a nutshell. She took another gulp from the glass and discovered it tasted a good deal better.

"Do tell?" Fran murmured. Fran liked perfect beasts of men. She'd known several perfect beasts—or alleged perfect beasts—and she'd never failed to trim one down to size yet. "He always struck me as one of those real Gentlemen of the Old School. Of course I've only barely met him," she added hastily.

"Gentleman! Ha!" Mary snorted bitterly. "How would *you* like it if . . . Oh, well, skip it. I won't bore you with my problems. We probably ought to be getting on to lunch anyhow."

Fran had the notion that she wouldn't be bored one bit and that she'd simply *love* it if . . . "No hurry for lunch. Here, let me sweeten your cup." She masterfully took the half-filled glass and poured cheap bourbon into it right up to the brim. "You need a little something to steady your nerves." She saw that her guest looked perfectly aghast at the drink she'd poured. Quickly Fran modified her tone. "Oh, don't tell me about these men. Hollister practically ruined my life, what with his morbid drinking, his fancy women, his incessant demands on me to . . ."

"*Your* husband—I mean, your ex-husband? Why, I simply can't *believe* it. I . . ." Mary had heard some rather perplexing stories about the dog's life which Fran had made Mr. Hollister lead; stories that had not been without a certain salacious value. But then a lot of women who didn't really know Fran well had been only too eager to gossip about her when she was going through a crisis. "I mean he seemed such a kind, gentle sort of . . ."

Well, Fran had to admit that perhaps she had gone too far. She turned her back and almost sniggered as she poured a healthy jolt of Haig and Haig into her own glass. The picture of Mr. Hollister as the surly drunkard, the chaser, the sadistic satyr was a rare one! Poor, feckless Hollister with his stuffy relatives, his interest in Henry James, his always urging her to stay home, to read, to have children. "Those gentle types are always the worst," Fran said darkly. "You know what they say about still water running deep—*and* dirty. Now, just get it off your chest. Unburden yourself. My, how *I* would have liked to have had an old friend to talk to *me* when I was going through . . ." She was interrupted by the ringing of the telephone. Cursing silently Fran marched upstairs to take the call there. Fran didn't like to

talk on the telephone in front of an audience. You never knew who or what it might be.

Left alone in Fran's living room, Mary looked cautiously around the place. Somehow she had expected it to be a bit neater, a bit smarter, a bit grander. She preferred rooms with a casual, lived-in look to the severe Model Home style of decoration, but there was something about Fran's living room that was a little too lived-in—wallowed-in you might even say. It seemed casual to the point of downright uncleanliness. She felt disappointed and then she immediately felt disloyal at feeling disappointed in her old friend—well, new friend, really.

Mary's years with Mrs. Manley Updike, Inc., Interiors had given her a quick, sure eye for style and quality. She could pick real Chippendale from Best Grand Rapids in the middle of an eclipse. The real stuff was here, all right. There was a perfect fortune in antique furniture, but why was it somehow all wrong? Why, for example, were those superb Adam elbow chairs covered in that sleazy rayon with the stripes running crooked? Why had whoever arranged this room—and presumably *someone* had—put a ten-cent paper shade on a two-hundred dollar bronze lamp and a solid gold inkwell on a borax "modernistic" desk.

She took another sip of her drink and almost gagged. She wondered if she might not just take the tiniest advantage of her hostess' absence, pour a bit of her drink into that alabaster urn of wilting chrysanthemums and dilute the evil potion Fran had mixed for her. The flowers were beyond harming and had already begun to smell like an old aquarium.

She got up slyly and tiptoed toward the vase. Then she stopped dead in her tracks. No. Surely those draperies *couldn't* be made of that plastic stuff you thumb-tacked up. Not at Fran Hollister's! She reached out gingerly to feel the curtains that hung limply at the dining-room doorway and then her hand struck something warm and almost furry. There was a deafening screech and she jumped back spilling a good deal of her drink on the dirty Aubusson rug.

The idiotic face of Fran's cleaning woman leered around the curtain and mouthed a series of animal grunts and wails and

giggles. While the facial expression was one of friendly warmth, the experience had the effect of chilling the very marrow of her bones.

Mouthing carefully and with the slow, loud voice she would generally reserve for making a long distance call to a very old relative in, say, Nome, Alaska, she said "Miss-iss Holl-iss-terr is *up*-sstairss." She pointed nervously to the ceiling.

The deafmute put her finger in her mouth, giggled. Circled the dining table. Looked back at her. Giggled again. And then shot out through the kitchen door.

Totally shaken, Mary decided not to dilute her drink, after all —rather, to strengthen it. She slopped some more bourbon into her glass and went unsteadily back to the uncomfortable old sofa to await Fran. Now she buried her nose into the glass and took a colossal swallow, grateful for the warmth she felt from the drink.

Fran stomped down the stairs in a cold fury. Here she'd been on the very verge of finding out a few fascinating facts about this fascinating man when—wouldn't you *know*—that blasted telephone had rung. And had it been anything interesting, anything important? No! Only some wretch of a salesman offering her a turn-in price of fifty dollars on her old vacuum cleaner if she'd order a new Tank-type Kleenzall. She didn't even *have* a vacuum cleaner to turn in—at least she didn't think so.

Well, the spell had been broken, all right, Fran thought angrily. Now her guest was prattling away—and rather nervously—about all manner of things that had nothing to do with anything: Baldwin School, fall hats, Adele Hennessey, Lisa Randall's party . . . Well, it was maddening. Now Fran would have to bide her time and get her around to Topic A at the lunch table.

Fran finally interrupted the floodtide of small talk. "Here, let's have one for the Load and then shove off."

"Oh, no more for me, Fran, please." What with no breakfast and the drinks and the shock she had just received, her head was spinning.

"Well, if you don't mind watching *me* . . ." Fran made for the Haig and Haig bottle.

"Oh, not at all, Fran." Really, how sweet Fran was underneath

her hard exterior, she thought a little maudlinly. This dirty house, the poor deafmute Fran had befriended, the split seam and the spot on Fran's dress—they all made her a little more human, a little more endearing. Like a little girl, really. "No, I just *can't* have another drink." Then she thought wickedly for a moment. "At least not until lunch."

four

"There," she sighed as she eased the glossy big convertible into a parking space and switched off the ignition. She had made it without killing either Fran or herself and she was amazedly, prayerfully thankful. This enormous new car—the first they had ever owned—with its gadgets and levers and buttons and dials, always threw the fear of God into her. Even if the car was in *her* name, it was his, and this would hardly be the propitious day to end up in jail on a drunken driving rap. But here they were at the shopping center, safe and sound.

There were two shopping centers handy to Riveredge. One was a mammoth affair that served the people in the town. It had a Woolworth and an A & P and a Macy's and a Rexall and a Howard Johnson's. Pork stores and cheap dress shops and cut-rate cleaners abounded and there were ten acres of supervised free parking. It was considered fine for the villagers, but infra-dig for the residents of Riveredge, except in the direst emergencies. Once a Riveredge matron had survived so dire an emergency, her adventure always made for a deliciously witty, self-deprecating and slightly patronizing anecdote over cocktails—"Well, *today* I *had* to go to the *shopping center;* the *big* one. Well, you know *me* and my sense of direction . . ."

But *this* shopping center was different. You could tell immediately by looking at the cars—either much smaller or much larger and in more subdued colors. It was called the Village Green and it was terribly genteel. It was planned and planted on more or less quainty-dainty colonial lines with bowed windows, fanlights, carriage lamps, venerable elms and air conditioning throughout. The prices ranged from high to outrageous and you had to be

fairly erudite to find whatever kind of store you were looking for.

The Mad Hatter, for example, implied millinery. You went to the Apothecary Jar for vitamin pills and bathing caps, to Frou Frou House for underwear (ladies'), and to Man-About-Town for ditto (gents')—also a distinguished collection of shirtings, waistcoats, imported ties, walking shorts and cashmere hose. *Le Cave* sold liquor and occasionally wine. The Gift Horse trafficked in bric-a-brac. It took some discernment upon meeting Margot Carpenter Austin Leach, who looked like a madam but was actually in the Social Register, to understand that the scarlet door which bore her name—or names—led to nothing more exciting than expensive dresses in misses' sizes. Heir Unapparent sold maternity clothes exclusively.

A shop called Oddments, Unlimited, dealt in such essentials as antique umbrella handles, sequined sweaters, lederhosen, monogrammed shoe trees and beads. Et Cetera, three doors north carried roughly the same merchandise. As You Like It was not a bordello but a hairdressing establishment—shampoo and set, $4.00. And *Le Chien Blanc*—despite a runny-eyed poodle wandering morosely among the customers and glowing obscenely pink beneath his dirty white fur—was not a pet shop, but a moderately-priced restaurant, featuring lunch at $1.50.

"Well, hop out," Fran said in her booming contralto, "here we are at the dog house." Fran gave the padded leather door an appraising pat and wondered whether his money or hers had paid for this perfect yacht of a car. (In truth, it hadn't been paid for at all.)

"Oh, the *Chien Blanc?*" Mary said. She hoped that she hadn't sounded as disappointed as she was. *Le Chien Blanc* was worse than a bad restaurant, it was a nondescript restaurant, except for the poodle and a certain unfortunate cuteness in its decor. John and Mary had eaten there almost nightly when they were first settling into the new house in Riveredge and they had since taken to dining at *Le Chien Blanc* on Heavenly Rest's Thursdays and alternate Sundays, if they had nowhere better to go. She had expected Fran to chose someplace terribly smart and possibly a little sinister. Just coming to *Le Chien Blanc,* with its eternal *omelette fines herbs,* Salisbury steak *au champignons* and chef's

salad bowl, was like sipping from a champagne glass only to find it filled with gingerale.

"Come on," Fran said, "don't bother to lock the car it's . . . Oh, my God!"

"Wh-what's the matter?" Mary asked.

"*Look!*" Fran breathed, pointing with a long, chipped, red fingernail. "It's Adele Hennessey! Come in here, quick!" Grabbing her by the wrist, Fran dragged her into the nearest door. It belonged to the Mad Hatter.

Mary had got just a quick glimpse of Mrs. Hennessey—a woman of uncertain years, doubtful blondness and dubious antecedents—strolling along the sidewalk in black Bermuda shorts and nutria jacket bleached the same blond as Mrs. Hennessey herself. With her was a small, dark woman wearing leopard slacks and a green suede coat. Riveredge approved of slacks and it approved of shorts, but *never* outside the gates of Riveredge. As for the Hennesseys, Riveredge disapproved of them on either side of the gates. Jack Hennessey was loud, vulgar, *nouveau* and disgustingly rich. His wife, Adele, was, if not downright C-O-double-M-O-N, certainly not out of the top drawer.

"Jesus," Fran gasped. "That's the second time in a week that Hennessey tramp has almost caught me red-handed."

"May I show you something, Mrs. Hollister?" the saleswoman asked. Fran wouldn't own a hat, but still, her name and fortune cut a lot of ice at the Village Green.

"No thanks," Fran said. "We're just hiding out till Mrs. Hennessey gets past."

"Oh, *certainly!*" the woman said, with a mournful roll of the eyes which made it perfectly clear that she, a forty-dollar-a-week clerk, and a rich nymphomaniac like Fran were sisters under the skin—rarefied, untouchable, and above all, *ladies*—at the approach of Adele Hennessey. "I *quite* understand."

If the Hennesseys were unpopular with the gentry of Riveredge, many of whom owed Jack amounts ranging from fifty to three thousand dollars, they were anathema to the tradespeople of the Village Green. This was undoubtedly because the Hennesseys spent so freely and paid so promptly that one just *sensed* that they weren't, well, Quite Nice.

Mr. Passepartout of *Le Cave* fairly snickered at Jack's pronunciation of the French wines and champagnes which he ordered in magnums and jeroboams and methuselahs and case lots. The two Lesbians who ran Oddments, Unlimited, made it a point *never* to show Adele their nicest imports—unless Adele *insisted*—and always to pad her bill by ten bucks a month. And Margot Carpenter Austin Leach's impersonation of Adele asking for "a creation by *Balenciago,* or one of the other Eye-talian designers" was an immortal favorite among women who never bought anything from Mrs. Leach unless it was marked down below cost and then rarely paid her before ninety days.

At that point Adele Hennessey and her raffish companion had drawn up to the window of the Mad Hatter. "Peggy!" they could hear Adele cry. "Just *look* at that hat. It's de-*vine!* Gee, honey, you'd be a living doll in that!"

"It *is* nice," her friend said. "I'll think about it. But hadn't we better latch onto Jack and Dan before they get so sozzled that . . ."

"Oh, migawd!" Adele shrieked. "They promised to buy you and I a drink at Lee Sheen Blank at one and it's already ha' past. Come on! We can come back later. You'll love Lee Sheen Blank, sweetie, it's so . . ." Mrs. Hennessey's words were lost as she propelled her friend along the street.

"Saved!" Fran gasped as she stepped out from the wall against which she had flattened herself.

"Oh, *poor* Mrs. Hollister!" the saleswoman cooed. "I know just what it's like to be absolutely *purseued* by one who could never hope to have anything in common with . . ." Here her syntax broke down and, rather than parse the sentence out and start all over again, she just changed the subject. "That beautiful hat in the window! I'd almost rather *not* sell it than to have someone of—well—of that *class* wearing it. It just came in this morning and it's . . . Too bad *you* never wear hats, Mrs. Hollister. Hahahahaha!" (If Mrs. Hollister *had* worn hats she would have bought them at a fire sale, and all the merchants knew it.) "But it would be ex-*quiz*-it on your friend. The color is . . ." With a neat motion, she scooped the hat out of the window. "Just look. Perfect with your skin, my dear, and that gorgeous dress."

"It's lovely!" Mary agreed. Before she knew it, she was sitting before the mirror trying on the hat. Tiresome as the saleswoman was, the hat *did* do something for her.

"Not bad," Fran said, lighting a cigarette and dropping the match on the Mad Hatter's pale blue carpet.

"Here's an ashtray, Mrs. Hollister," the saleswoman said.

"Don't bother," Fran said.

"It's perfectly beautiful," Mary said aloud to the saleswoman.

"I *knew* it was right for you, my dear," the saleswoman said, becoming all motherly. "The minute you come—*came*—into here with Mrs. Hollister I said to myself, 'Now there's one lady in a million can wear that lovely big chapeau in the window.' It's almost like Fate . . ."

Yes, Mary thought a little drunkenly, Fate and her husband and Fran and Adele Hennessey really had conspired to make her ransom herself out of this place with this wonder of a hat. She'd been told that she was pretty so often that she very nearly believed it. But this hat, casting its delicate shadow over her face, made her almost beautiful. An expensive new hat—wasn't that one of the classic antidotes for a woman whose man has left her? "I'll take it," she said suddenly. "How much is it?"

"Sixty, my dear."

"Jesus!" Fran muttered.

"And I'll wear it, so you needn't put it in a box." She thought just a little wistfully that a year ago she would have gone down to the wholesale millinery district and done herself very nearly as proudly with five dollars and a needle and thread. Still, she considered as she signed her name to a check, this was one hell of a hat . . . and Fate, as the woman said.

"You're sure you wouldn't like to open an account, my dear? Any friend of Mrs. Hollister's is . . ."

"No thanks," she said. "I won't be here long enough to need an account."

"That hat's o-*kay*," Fran said, flicking her ashes onto the rug. That was high praise indeed, coming from Fran.

"And where shall I send the old one, my dear?" the woman chirped as she discreetly glanced at the label—Saks.

"Why, why, just throw it away, I guess." My God, Mary

thought, I *must* be mad. It's a perfectly good hat in a mousey way.

"Why don't you sell it to Adele Hennessey," Fran growled.

"Oh, Mrs. Hollister!" the woman shrieked. "Hahahahaha! I'll *have* to tell that to Mrs. Leach next door. Oh, you *are* terrible! Sell it to . . . Hahahahaha!"

"Goodbye, and thank you," Mary said.

Amid peals of laughter, they left the Mad Hatter, the new hat more glorious than ever in the brilliant sunlight.

"Christ but I hate that bitch!" Fran said.

"Well," Mary said, settling back into the car, "I guess we can't go to the *Chien Blanc*—the dog house, that is—after all. Not unless you want to run head-on into both Hennesseys and their friends." She was really a little pleased at the outcome of their thwarted trip to the dreary restaurant in the shopping center. Then she caught a fresh glimpse of herself in the rearview mirror and almost gasped with pleasure. Really, this hat was a masterpiece! Too good for *Chien Blanc*.

"Wouldn't you know, damn it," Fran snarled. "Well, where do you suggest?"

"There's Tradition House," Mary said tentatively.

"We-ell," Fran said, "if you have any money on you. It's kind of expensive."

"I—I have about thirty dollars in my purse," she said.

Fran's income hovered at just about a thousand dollars a day. She lived rent-free and ate almost nothing. Her only expenses were clothes, which came to a negligible amount; liquor, which was somewhat higher; small amounts of hush-money; and an occasional new mink coat to replace whichever one which she had just lost in the woods or a taxicab or a tourist cabin. (Not even the insurance company Fran *owned* would insure Fran's fur coats any longer.) Yet with the income taxes, the blackmail, and the new mink coats, Fran came out fairly well at the end of each year. But she was perennially without cash and the quarters and dollars and fives which she had borrowed from her relatively poor acquaintances—and never repaid—came to a small fortune.

The car shot backwards from its parking place. There was a grinding of gears and they were off.

Tradition House was typical of the hundreds of expensive little inns that spring up over the countryside, like dandelions, when times are good, only to go to seed and blow away when Sunday trippers reluctantly decide that the hamburger platter at Johnnie's Drive-In is the more prudent choice in the face of increasing unemployment and decreasing dividends. Like the hundreds of other smart little country restaurants, Tradition House had been doing a land office business for the last fifteen years. Spurred on by small snobbish ads in *The New Yorker* and *Gourmet* and *Cue*, by yards of purple prose written by restaurant editors, and by queues of other suckers waiting for tables on weekends, the public had continued to drive up the Hudson, dressed in its best, to swoon in ecstasy over Tradition House's low ceilings, medium food and high prices. It had become an institution, a symbol of the American Way of Life. No upper-middle-class kitchen was complete without its *Compleat Tradition House Cook Book*, its jars of Tradition House Herb Salad Dressing, India Relish, Sauce Diable, and Formula 12—"Available at fine stores everywhere."

Actually, it was a fair restaurant.

And because this was a sunny Saturday, Tradition House was jammed today. Six hired limousines stood in the driveway and the parking area was thronged with cars, some bearing license plates from as far away as Arizona—a mute testament to the genius of Tradition House's allure.

A soignée, although somewhat high-rumped, hostess greeted them in the hall with her traditional welcome, delivered in a cordial, school-of-the-drama voice: "Gud ahftah-nyoon." Pause. Breathe. Size up clothes. "I'm afraid there will be a shawt wait for tables." Smile. Pause. Breathe. "But if you'd like to wait in the Abigail Adams Parloor, or see our unique collection of oh-thentic Rrrev-o-lyutioneddy min-ee-a-tyuahs in the John Jay Ryoom . . ."

"Where's the bar?" Fran said flatly.

The hostess was a little startled. She usually liked to work up through the delights of the Molly Pitcher Gift Shoppe and the Priscilla Mullins Terrace before she got to the hard core of

Tradition House's sensational profits; alcohol. And she considered herself sufficiently awesome—not without some reason—for guests to wait politely until she had finished her pitch.

"The Hessian Top Ryoom is to yaw left, but *waon't* you sign our guest book *first?* We have maw than hoff a million signatyuahs, representing guests from all fawty-eight states and ovah fifty foreign countries, including thrrree behind the I-ron Curtain and . . ."

"Sure," Fran snapped, "give me the pen." In her large, sprawling hand she hastily scrawled "Elsie Dinsmore" and jammed the foot-long quill back into the inkwell.

"And waon't *yew* sign, tew?" the hostess said with a horrid smile.

"I've been here before and signed before," Mary said, indicating the morocco-bound guest book with a nod. "Wouldn't that rather throw your records off?"

The hostess knew when she was licked. She really only enjoyed her work when she could patronize the patrons good and proper. Nothing made her happier than to get a couple of little Bronx *hausfraus,* out for a lark, and pulverize them with her own grandeur. She had all kinds of cute tricks she could play on them, things like picking up one of their fabric gloves from the floor, holding it at arm's length like a dead rat and saying, "Did you drop *this,* um, ma-*damn?*" Or she would pretend that *she* owned the place, instead of Mr. Pulakos. Or she might just leave them twiddling their thumbs in the Abigail Adams Parlor for as long as an hour while flossier guests were seated immediately.

However, these two bitches were solid class. The *minor* bitch, for example, looked like a lady—with expensive clothes, a magnificent hat and genuine alligator pumps and bag. That meant a lot. The *major* bitch may have looked like a tart, but the hostess hadn't seen such a mink coat since the late Gertrude Lawrence lunched at Tradition House and if those rocks weren't real, she'd eat them. No, these babies could cool off in the bar for the space of one drink. Then they'd have another drink at the table, a tab that would come to about fourteen bucks and maybe a pair of stingers afterward. Oh, *certainly* stingers.

"Step this way, pleeze," she said and sashayed elegantly to the Hessian Tap Room.

"Makes you want to goose her with a lightning rod," Fran bellowed in a sententious whisper.

Because of the lateness of the hour, there were plenty of vacant tables in the Hessian Tap Room, but Fran headed straight for the bar.

"Shouldn't we take a table, Fran?" Mary asked. She still had a kind of repression about unaccompanied women sitting at bars. Yet, Fran had certainly been around. Just look at the way she'd fixed that poor, pretentious hostess.

"Don't be a chump. Why should we make this nice bartender walk all the way across the room?" The barkeep, a towering young Irishman, had caught Fran's eye the second she entered the room. He certainly was a looker, although a number of disappointing experiences had made Fran quite certain that the nocturnal companionship of Italians and Greeks was far more stimulating. There was something so *repressed* about the Irish. "You don't mind if we sit here at the bar, do you, Mickey?" Fran asked, reading the name embroidered on the front of his jacket.

"Not at all, miss," the man blushed, "what'll it be?"

"A double Haig and Haig on the rocks for me," Fran boomed. "What about you?"

The thought of another drink actually frightened Mary. Here it was almost two o'clock and she still hadn't had a mouthful of food all day. Well, she might as well taper off with an old fashioned. At least she could eat the fruit. That would be *something*. "An old fashioned, I guess, Fran."

"Yes, Mickey, and a double bourbon old fashioned. And leave out the garbage."

As though by magic, their table was ready at the exact moment she emptied her drink. She had purposely dawdled with it, giving Fran time to have two doubles and a rather too-intimate conversation with the bartender, whose responses were little more than polite. This last drink had decidedly put her over the edge. The Toby jugs, the pewter mugs, the prints and muskets that

adorned the room spun about her head in the dim glow of artificial candle light. She was a little pleased—and even more surprised—to find herself walking in a straight line, but she didn't really care. She was also surprised to see Fran giving her card to the bartender. In her haze she felt that this was an example of democracy at work and it pleased her. Good old Fran!

Tradition House had a number of irritating traditions of its own. For example, its pre-Revolutionary War fireplace and its post-Korean War air conditioning system were both kept going full blast, thus giving the customers the charm of an open fire without roasting them to death. There were no menus. Instead, a snowy-haired old Negro in knee britches came around with a gigantic slate and read aloud what you might or might not care to eat. Muffins, cornbread and popovers were served by a lovable old mammy wearing a bandana and such a benign smile that nobody, except the rest of the staff, could possibly realize that for the past twenty years she had been County Secretary of the American Communist Party.

"This is kitchy dump, isn't it," Fran said, lighting a cigarette.

"De s'rimp jambolaya bery good, ma'm," the headwaiter was crooning. "Oh maybe you ladies rodda hab ouah famous Tradition House Philadelphia scrapple, oh de Maine lobstah . . ."

"Bring up two steak sandwiches—rare—a double old fashioned and a double Haig and Haig over ice," Fran snapped.

The colorful old servitor gave her a scathing look, wondered about chuckling endearingly, thought better of it, and shuffled off. Like the hostess, he was accustomed to having his big soliloquy reverently attended and enthusiastically applauded. But also like the hostess, he knew when he was being upstaged by a great star.

"Fran! I *can't* have another drink. I haven't even had *breakfast!*" Actually Mary had rather had her taste buds set for a plate of scrapple. It seemed to her now that since her husband had achieved his exalted new station she had eaten nothing but heroic cuts of raw beef in expensive restaurants with expensive people. Still, she was mutely grateful for any hope of food.

"Who eats *breakfast?*" Fran asked, grinding out her cigarette in a pat of Tradition House Old Style Home Churned Sweet

Creamery Butter. It made an oleaginous little hiss. "Ah, here come the reinforcements. Thank God!"

A harried-looking waitress scuttled in with their drinks. The word had got around the pantry of Tradition House that a couple of tough customers were at Table Number One in the Nancy Hanks Room. Service would be fast, efficient and totally devoid of any of the quaint nuances which had endeared Tradition House to hordes of weekend gourmets.

"Well," Fran said, lifting her glass with a practiced hand, "here's to hell with that cheap, social-climbing, two-bit whore, Adele Hennessey. The tramp!" She threw her head back and emptied half the glass.

To Fran, being the grand-daughter of a man who had amassed millions through the most questionable business practices gave her free license to live as amorally as she pleased. Born in a feudal age, Fran would have been wanton in a *big* way, fearing only pregnancy and banishment by the monarch. (But of course *Fran* would have been the monarch's mistress.)

Even in the Twentieth Century, Fran had a feudal mind and a feudal soul. Fran didn't recognize the Double Standard; she rather favored a *triple* standard—separate codes of behavior for men, for women and for Fran herself. Therefore, Fran kept a close watch on the mores and morals of those women she considered her inferiors, and that encompassed all of womankind. Fran could snatch a busboy, a brigadier and a broker simultaneously into the bushes and it was to be considered—if, indeed, it was to be considered at all—a kind of *droit de seigneur*, because Fran, after all, was Fran. But let some young housewife drink an extra cocktail or dance twice with the same partner, let some woman show her too much or—worse—not enough deference, and Fran became Carrie Nation, Cotton Mather and Savonarola rolled into one. "Tramp" was her favorite epithet.

Mary thought, a little desperately, since she could hardly think at all, that Fran was being patently unfair to poor Mrs. Hennessey. Actually, *she* didn't like Adele Hennessey. Adele was vulgar and garrulous and pretentious and practically illiterate. Adele was a social climber. And yet brassy as she was, Adele was a good sort at heart. Mary'd defended Adele and defended Adele without even

caring whether Adele lived or died. (Oh, but her head was spinning!) And now *Fran* had to start in on poor, dumb, common Adele. She really *must* say something decent about Adele. No. She was tired of defending Adele. In fact, she was tired of everything that smacked of Riveredge. "To hell with Adele," she said and she giggled at the poetry of her toast. She took a rather large peg of her drink and a feeling of perfect euphoria swept over her. Good old Fran, she thought.

"Now, suppose you tell Mother all about you and that beast," Fran said hypnotically.

"Fran, I'll tell you what . . ."

"*What?*"

"Let's not talk about him or Adele Hennessey or about anything that has anything to do with Riverish—I mean Liver-edge." She looked up and saw that food was on its way. Relief was in sight.

"Then what *will* we talk about?" Fran asked, a little irritably.

"Let's talk about . . . Life."

five

She turned the big car off the West Side Highway with consummate skill and steered painlessly through the tortuous streets of Greenwich Village. She felt fine and she'd never driven better—not a bit nervous.

Lunch had sobered her. She had eaten a great deal, just as she always did. She could never understand those poor women who had to diet. *She* could sit down and eat like a stevedore, with lots of sauces and bread and butter and potatoes and gooey desserts and never gain an ounce. In fact her figure hadn't varied a millimeter—except when she was expecting the baby—since the day she graduated from Baldwin. Whereas Fran, who had hardly *touched* her lunch . . . Oh, there she went again, having a long Think all by herself. It was almost as rude as reading when you were with somebody else. She often had one of her self-analyzing Thinks when she'd had a bit too much to drink.

"Too many drinks,
Too many Thinks,"

she thought and giggled.

"What the hell's so funny?" Fran asked crossly.

"Nothing, Fran, except that I believe we're lost."

"Well, I don't wonder in this lousy Greenwich Village place. How anybody in his right mind could live down here is beyond me."

"But, Fran, where else *would* Lisa live and who ever said she was in her right mind?" She stopped the car. "Now let's see. Here's Eighth Avenue and there's Jane Street. If Jane comes, can Jennifer be far behind?" My, but wasn't she being witty!

"Only a little behind Horatio and Minetta Lane and McDougal Alley and Washington Mews and all the rest of these lousy gussied-up cowpaths down here. Look out! Bank Street is one-way!"

Mary backed up and then headed into Fourth Street. One thing that made her uneasy about the Village was the inconsiderate way Fourth Street had of crossing both Tenth and Eleventh streets. What did it think it was, an *avenue?*

Actually, she hadn't meant to come to Lisa's party at all, but Fran had almost kidnapped her—and in her *own* car, or *his* own car in *her* own name.

She'd been a little startled when she'd had to pay the whole luncheon check, but then Fran had steered her into the bar and insisted on buying her not one, but *two* stingers. And they had had a sobering effect. They tasted so clean.

She'd had a wonderful talk with Fran, too. It was amazing the way you could always be so frightened of—well, not exactly *frightened of,* but *awed by*—someone and then have that someone turn out to be the most lovable, most understanding, most sympathetic old pal. And she'd been *perfectly fair* in everything she had said about him.

Fran *had* asked a lot of funny questions about sex and that sort of thing. That had made her a little nervous. She didn't really know very much about sex or even think about it. Sex was just something that two people who loved each other shared naturally together. She always hated to talk about it because it seemed as natural—and as boring a subject of conversation—as respiration or digestion or elimination.

But Fran had asked different questions and Fran had seemed so pleased by her answers that she had felt rather proud and happy—like a tongue-tied Ph.D. candidate who has just passed a tough session of Orals. Yet Fran had been married more than once, so Fran undoubtedly had more grounds for comparison.

And Fran had also given her a wonderful piece of advice: When she'd told Fran that she didn't think she'd drive into New York for Lisa's party, Fran looked her square in the eye and said, "Don't be such a chump, you chump. Show him you can lead a life of your own. Besides we're practically half-way to New York now."

True-blue old Fran! Fran wasn't going to let her sit home alone feeling sorry for herself.

"Oh, dear," she said, stopping to squint at the signs at a place where three streets converged and came out as five streets.

"My God," Fran snarled, scraping her cigarette out into the dashboard ashtray with a fine shower of glowing coals, "We've been around this dreary block a thousand times. Are we lost *again?*"

"I'm awfully afraid we are, Fran. As long as I've lived in New York I've never been able to find my way around the Village—not even the nice, straightforward Streets like Eighth and Bleecker. And when it comes to hunting out a place like Jennifer Street all by myself, I can't . . ."

"*Lisa!* Lisa *and* Brad! What a perfect brace of jerks. If they want to hide away down in this hell hole like a couple of hermits, why don't they *act* like hermits and not drag everybody and his brother down here to their silly parties? If I hadn't told Fletch to meet me here, I'd say to hell with Brad and Lisa and . . . Whoa! This is it, I think—that secret passage between the opium den and the knocking shop."

Jennifer Street was a twisting, gaslit cul-de-sac lined with houses said to date back to the Revolution. It had been painstakingly restored, at vast expense, by a group of arty residents who called themselves the Jennifer Street Alliance and who were allied in nothing except the feeling that Jennifer Street must be kept picturesque, recherché and invisible.

Groups of matronly sightseers who happened, quite by accident, into the labyrinth of Jennifer Street invariably shrieked "Cute . . . sweet . . . darling . . . adorable" upon glimpsing the tiny houses, the gas lights, the doors painted fuchsia, turquoise and lemon. The hitching posts, the window boxes, the antique knockers always got them.

But it wasn't long before the cobblestones began to hurt their feet, before the flickering gaslight began to hurt their eyes. They were shocked at the curses of cab drivers and delivery men who backed and filled in the narrow courtyard, crumpling their fenders on mounting blocks and hitching posts. Soot from the neighboring plastic novelties factory rained down into Jennifer Street, as did

cigarette butts from the modern apartment house to the north and garbage from the old law tenement to the south.

If the lady sightseers got out of Jennifer Street unscathed, unsullied and uninsulted they were damned lucky and they rapidly began to agree among themselves that while the *idea* of Jennifer Street was cute, sweet, darling and adorable, it was perhaps just a little *too* cute, sweet, darling and adorable to be quite suited to contemporary metropolitan living.

"Arty-farty little dump, isn't it?" Fran asked, struggling out of the parked car. "Who'd Lisa say this shindig was for?"

"P-Pericles Insofaras," Mary said a little nervously.

"What's *that*, a social disease?"

"No, it's a Greek tenor—or maybe a baritone. Brad and Lisa met him on the boat coming back from Europe."

"Well, come on," Fran said, picking her way across the cobblestones. "We might as well get it over with."

For a moment Mary hung back. This was the first time she'd gone to a party alone since—well since the night she had met John, and that had been right here at Lisa's house in Jennifer Street. Now instead of feeling gay and reckless and independent, she felt frightened and insecure. What if he should *be* here and . . .

"Come *on*," Fran began, "I told Fletch to meet me at five-thirty sharp."

She looked up at Fran, striding toward Lisa's magenta door and took heart. Good old Fran with her diamonds and her magnificent mink coat and her sort of coltish style. Fran would protect her.

Fran stumbled on the doorstep, said a coarse word and then thumped at the Randalls' antique brass knocker.

The door was opened by the hostess herself, an overweight young woman in her late twenties. "Darling!" Lisa screamed, embracing her.

"My God, what are you got up as *this* time?" Fran moaned.

It was a good question. Lisa was dressed in a gay peasant skirt, so full that it made her bottom look as big as a washtub. She wore a white muslin blouse—jingling with florins and riotous with peasant embroidery—that exposed her plump shoulders as

well as a safety pin and a strap of the slip she was wearing. Her fat little feet were thrust into thong sandals and her fairish hair caught up in a fillet. The costume was completed by a clattering array of beaten silver bracelets, a pair of dangling silver earrings so heavy that they pulled Lisa's earlobes down to her jawline, and a huge silver Greek Orthodox cross, encrusted with semi-precious stones, which swung like a hangèd man from an ornate silver chain around Lisa's neck.

"Fran, dear!" Lisa shrieked, embracing her as well. "Isn't this divine! I bought every stitch of it in Rhodes when Brad and I were there this summer. We *adored* Greece and . . ."

"It makes you look like the Colossus of Rhodes," Fran said. "Fletch get here yet?"

"Oh, Fran! You're just *awful!*" Lisa giggled. "Yes, he's in there somewhere," she gestured vaguely toward a mass of human bodies, "talking to the most *interesting* girl from the U.N. He . . ."

"Thanks," Fran said. "Where'll I leave my coat—someplace where it won't get swiped."

"*Fran!*" Lisa burst into peals of giggles. "You're *so* original!"

Mary had known Lisa Randall ever since the day they had both entered college and never for a moment in the ensuing ten years had she doubted that Lisa was the damnedest fool ever to walk on God's green earth.

Born plain Elizabeth Dempster to an oldish insurance executive and his fading wife in Evanston, Illinois, Lisa had passed a placid girlhood tagging along happily with Mummy to the St. Luke's Guild, *Le Cercle Français* and the Thursday Series at Orchestra Hall. Mummy's friends all agreed that Lisa was a lovely girl—but then change-of-life babies always *are* exceptional. Docile and sunny by nature, Lisa accepted life among the *haute bourgeoisie* without question or complaint, and she never once paused to consider that Evanston might possibly not be The World. Never, that is, until the day Mummy said, "Harvey, I think an *Eastern* college for Elizabeth."

Lisa's dormant genius for experimentation burst into full flower in the Massachusetts air. Mary had watched her alter her name from Elizabeth to Bette, to Bettye, to B.T., to Liz, to Lizette, to Lisa. Her penmanship changed often and radically.

Her infrequent letters home, written as they were in white ink on black paper, green ink on red paper, gold ink on silver paper, quite terrified Mummy—what Mummy could read of them. (Daddy's eyesight had all but given out.) Mummy had been so worried, in fact, that she conspired with a distant Boston cousin to sound out Lisa/Elizabeth over tea and send back a *frank* report.

A week later the cousin had written—in blue ink on white paper—to say that she had found Lisa to be rather eccentric and somewhat affected, but in no wise *dangerous*. The cousin had felt it kinder to omit mention of Lisa's blue nail enamel, her abstract jewelry, her harlequin britches and the faintly pinko Indonesian exchange student whom Lisa had brought, uninvited and totally unexpected, along with Mary to the Boston tea party.

Mummy had told Mary, though, that summers in the staid bosom of the family would disabuse Lisa of her fancies. But Mummy hadn't reckoned with Lisa's *own* summer plans. Her college summers were spent as exotically and as far away from Evanston as possible, culminating in Lisa's leadership of an interracial student's hiking trip across the Scandinavian peninsula, where the boys and girls not only serenaded Sibelius, but got bugs in a Finnish bath house.

Nor did the college boys whom Mummy dispatched help. Nice young men from nice old families, they preferred Mary, finding Lisa to be just too extraordinary, while Lisa found them just too ordinary. Lisa's taste in college beaux ran to Eastern philosophy majors, poets, atonal musicians, foreign students—preferably equipped with native costumes and folk songs—and anyone who had suffered intensely. Mary could never understand it.

Her junior year in Paris finished what Massachusetts had only begun to do for Lisa. Briefly back in Evanston for Daddy's funeral, she stunned *Le Cercle Français* with her command of Left Bank slang, her existentialist philosophy and her apache costumes. It was some months before Lisa was able to understand English once again and she moaned a good deal more about the loss of *mon Paris* than *mon père*.

And at commencement, when Mummy, still in semi-mourning, came all the way East just to drive Lisa back to Evanston, did

Lisa choose to make a comfortable home with Mummy? Indeed she did not! She went straight to a horrid cold-water flat in Greenwich Village to live as exotically as possible on the salary she received from a gallery that sold mobiles.

Mummy had told Mary all along that if Lisa were at least a brilliant student or a talented artist there might have been some excuse for her, well, *oddness*. But Lisa had little capacity for study and even less for art. All of her boundless energies were directed straight toward the unique. Mummy was sick about it and she only rallied when it looked, at last, as though Lisa had come to her senses.

Lisa got married with Mary as her sole attendant. She got married not to a sculptor or a radical or an atheist or a foreigner. She got married to Bradford Randall, a young man of good New York family who had inherited a lot of money and would come into still more. Lisa's mother smiled benignly. *Le Cercle Français* smiled benignly. The St. Luke's Guild smiled benignly. They were even able to forgive the bronze lamé sari which Lisa had chosen as a wedding dress—and at *St. Lukes!* But they all smiled too benignly and too soon. They had neglected to notice just one thing: Brad was twice as inane as Lisa.

After a brief honeymoon in Provincetown, Lisa was back in Greenwich Village, raring to discover the new, the exotic—and with Brad on hand to help her. Mummy passed on, sadly and quietly, just three months before Lisa's only child, little Sebastian, was born.

"Run into the living room, Mary darling," Lisa said, giving her a sisterly little squeeze. "It's absolutely teeming with tons and tons of the most divine new people—and you'll love the way Brad and I have done it over. Nothing like it in New York."

The statement covered a good deal—it took care of Lisa's entire way of life. Lisa was a born collector. She collected hobbies, causes, costumes, art, literature, music, furniture, people—*anything* that was new and different. Beards and sandals were the norm at Lisa's; far more common than business suits and striped ties. Artists who never painted (or painted very badly), writers who never wrote (or, at least, who had never been read), were

a constant source of joy to Lisa, just as long as they were sufficiently dirty, quarrelsome, unbalanced or dull to make something of a splash among her old, conservative friends. And, loyal as she was, Lisa simply could not endure normal people—*except* at her parties.

When Lisa entertained she needed an audience, for herself as well as for her mammoth cast of performers. And it was then that a hard core of prosaic but broadminded uptown friends became essential. These were the people to whom Lisa could turn, with the air of ringmaster, gamesmistress and impressario and say: "I know you'll adore meeting Nadja. She's broken away from the Graham group and she's now working on a very symbolical ballet based on the writings of Donald Webster Cory. Completely revolutionary, darling." Nadja would then be produced, sullen and brooding, wearing a soiled surplice of her own design and some heavy modern jewelry, ditto.

And it would more than likely be the only time Nadja ever *was* produced. A lack of funds, dissension among the dancers, a row with the composer or the attempted suicide of Nadja's colored lover's Japanese wife would postpone indefinitely the birth of the completely revolutionary ballet.

But Lisa didn't care, just as long as she had enough new Interesting People to fill up her freshly redecorated living room and stun her conservative friends whenever she chose to throw a party. As a matter of fact, when Lisa gave a party, it was not so much an entertainment as it was a *vernissage*. Her cocktail parties had but one express purpose: they were planned to show off a new collection—a newer and more outlandish Lisa in a newer and more outlandish setting, surrounded by newer and more outlandish people.

All Lisa really had to do was decide on her own latest personality, get the house finished—in six years of marriage Lisa's living room had gone through twelve distinct periods—send out cards to four or five hundred Interesting People, call the turbaned Goanese bartender she'd located through the Personals Columns in the *Saturday Review* and let fly.

As Lisa propelled her into the hot, thronged room—this time decorated in the Venetian manner with a *trompe l'oeil* mural of

the Grand Canal painted on a wall which had recently been stark, white brick—she thought how very right Fran was about Lisa. Both Lisa *and* Brad. They were silly and precious and pretentious; difficult to get to and rarely worth the trip. So were their parties. Mary realized, quite calmly, that she should feel nothing but irritation, indignation or indifference for anyone as fraudulent as Lisa. But in spite of Lisa's self-conscous posing and play-acting, she had never lost her one, basic, endearing quality; Lisa was, today, the same warm, foolish, goodnatured *cow* she had been on the day she left Evanston. Somehow Mary couldn't help loving her for it.

"Now, darling," Lisa said, gesticulating toward several hundred massed bodies, "I think you know everyone."

She didn't and she felt again that cold, clutching feeling in her stomach of being lost and alone at a party.

"But you *haven't* met our guest of honor, Pericles Insofaras. He's the most divine tenor *in the world*. He's going to be singing—*in Greek*—with an experimental opera group I'm interested in. We've taken an old carriage house—or carbarn, I guess you'd call it—over on Third Avenue and we're doing it up in amphitheatre fashion. Of course, Pericles *wants* to sing at the Met. Met, Met, Met! That's all the English he *knows*. Here, darling, do let me introduce you to him and *do* be sweet to him. He *lit*-rully doesn't speak a *word* of English."

"But if he doesn't know any English, Lisa . . ." she began wretchedly.

"Here he is, darling!" Lisa dragged her to a corner of the room where a strange man stood in miserable loneliness. He was short, slight and dark. His eyebrows marched militantly across his forehead, joined forces at the bridge of his nose and went single file half the way down it. In his hairy hand he held a hot martini which he obviously detested.

"Pericles!" Lisa cried.

He beamed at her enthusiastically, displaying fifteen enormous white teeth and a much larger gold one.

"Pericles," Lisa trilled. Θέλω νὰ σᾶς συστήσω σε μιὰ παλιὰ καλὴ μου φίλη καὶ how-you-say room mate at Wellesley, κολλέγιο. Oh, and let me get you another martini, Pericles. I mean, ἀφησὲ με νὰ σου δώσω

ἄλλο ἑνα ποτηράκι, poor boy. *Τό* cocktail *σου θὰ ἔχη ζεσταθῇ.* Isn't it divine the way Brad and I've mastered Greek? We just had six lessons at the Berlitz school and I was absolutely *at home* with all the natives when we were there," Lisa said in an elaborate aside. "Now do be sweet to him. Pericles! As I was saying, *'εδῶ ἡ καλὴ μου φιλη* from Wellesley, Mass-a-chew-setts, Mrs. . . ."

She was interrupted by her breathless husband, got-up apparently as a Rhodian brigand. (Lisa had a good deal of influence over Brad's wardrobe.)

"Lisa," Brad panted, "the Lipsky-Gottschalks are here. I've been looking everywhere for you. They can't stay a minute. They're flying back to Majorca tonight." He took a deep breath. "Ah, Pereicles, *πῶς τὰ περνᾶς καλέ μου φίλε,* I'll be back in just a minute. Um . . . *ζὰ γυρίσω 'αμέσως*" With that he dashed away.

"Oh, darling, I've *got* to rush and see the Lipsky-Gottschalks. He's the wire sculptor, you know. We went across Lesbos together on burros. *Do* take good care of Pericles!" *Ah! ça va, mes amis!*" Lisa shrieked in the direction of a soiled looking couple and waddled away through the crowd.

Mary had once read the Illiad or the Odyssey—she couldn't remember quite which—in translation, but it had done little to prepare her for cocktail conversation with a Greek tenor who spoke no English. "Uh, you like Me-tro-po-li-tan Op-purr-ah?" she said tentatively.

Ορίστε! Mr. Insofaras said.

"What?"

Ο'ρίστε!

"Oh, dear."

Just then, Suzette, Lisa's treasure of a maid from Martinique, passed between them, bearing a tray of canapes on her woolly head. Seizing this golden opportunity, she turned and fled into a knot of people.

"Honey bunch!"

She was immediately the unwilling recipient of a delicate embrace and a chaste kiss on both cheeks. It was Gerald Updike.

"Oh, *Gerry!*" she gasped. "It's you!"

"Darling, where have you *been!*" Gerald cried. "Ronny! Mother! Would you just come see what *I've* found—little Miss Mary Miles

Minter fresh in from suburbia! And don't you look a lamb, pet! Heavenly hat! Whose? Walter Florell?"

"No, Gerry, just a hat shop out near Riveredge," she stammered. "It *is* new. And it's awfully good to see you again. Is your mother here? And Ronny?"

"Of course, darling. Did you think we'd dream of missing one of Lisa's unveilings? *We* didn't do this room—*ça va sans dire*—and we all begged that silly bitch of a Lisa *not* to plaster the Grand Canal all over one wall, especially when we've still got thirty running feet of the most heavenly old French paper at the shop. I said, 'Lisa-belle, listen to Uncle Gerald and . . .' "

"Darling!" Mrs. Updike boomed, and embraced her. Mrs. Updike and her son, Gerald, were dressed almost identically—both had narrow black suits and gray crewcuts, tinged ever so slightly with blue. With Mrs. Updike was Ronny, Gerald's close friend for more than a year now. Except that his hair was a bit longer and a bit blonder than seemed absolutely necessary, he was dressed to match. The three of them also displayed an impressive collection of large and unusual rings.

"Hello there, funnyface," Ronny said with a feline little smile. He didn't kiss her. For some time Ronny had suffered under the hallucination that she and Gerald Updike were—or had been—emotionally involved and his jealousy of her was boundless. The whole idea somewhat amused her. Ronny was such a creepy little boy.

"Well, let's take a look at you, darling," Mrs. Updike roared in her rich contralto. Mrs. Updike grasped her by the shoulders and held her out at arms' length. She was quite farsighted. "*Sweet* hat!"

"Just what I *said* to her, Mother," Gerald said.

"Darling, we were all *sick* to hear about the baby," Mrs. Updike said. Then Mrs. Updike kept her spell-bound audience waiting while she fished into her big black purse, withdrew a gold cigarette case, withdrew a Parliament from that, fitted the Parliament into a holder and put the holder in her mouth. Simultaneously, two gold lighters—one reading "Gerald from Ronny," the other "Ronny from Gerald"—flared up to light Mrs. Updike's cigarette. Mrs. Updike inhaled deeply, went into a spasm of coughing, and had to be thumped on the back by her son.

"Thanks, Maude," Mary said after order was restored, "but it was really all for the best."

"Oh, *everything* is, darling, I . . . What do you mean, dear?"

"I mean that we're separated and we'll more than likely be getting a divorce."

"*No!*" Gerald gasped, his hands fluttering helplessly to his tie. "*When?*"

"Just today, in fact. I may even be hitting you for my old job back."

"Oh, really?" Ronny said coolly. Ronny had replaced her at Mrs. Manley Updike, Inc., Interiors. He was not terribly efficient at his work and was tolerated largely because his presence kept Gerald in the shop. Still, it was a better job than the display department at Lord and Taylor and he had no intention of giving it up without a scene, if not a struggle.

"Darling!" Mrs. Updike bellowed, "how *wonderful!* Well, I don't mean it's wonderful, exactly, but of *course* you could come back tomorrow if you wanted to."

"Tomorrow's a Sunday," Ronny hissed a bit petulantly.

"Be *still,*" Gerald whispered.

"Oh, my dear," Mrs. Updike went on elaborately. "I *promise* you, we're simply up to our *eyeballs* in work—turning *down* commissions, in fact—and I haven't been able to find so much as a swatch of sailcloth since the day you left us." She paused, cast Ronny an eloquent look and continued. "My dear," Mrs. Updike added with a portentious lowering of her voice, "don't think that *I* don't know the hell you're going thrrrough. When that no-good, drunken Updike left me . . . Oh, there I was down in Baltimore, hardly more than a *girl,* Gerry just a little baby—*and* collicky! When I think of the yeahs of struggle just to get Gerry through St. Swithin's and the Parsons School! All I had left—*everything*—was the house on Biddle Street (and that mortgaged to the hilt), my jewelry and some old family furniture—*my* family's furniture, mind you; Manley pieces, not Updike stuff. But I had courage and I had talent—yes, talent . . ."

Mary had heard the saga of Mrs. Manley Updike's rise in the decorating business so often that she could repeat it word for word. Its full recital gave her just time to bum a cigarette and a light

from Gerald, snag a martini from a passing tray, take a healthy gulp, swallow, moisten her lips and be waiting in the wings for her cue. The performance was running exactly on schedule.

"Imagine!" she said. She had always said Imagine at exactly this point in the Updike Soliloquy. It gave Mrs. Updike a chance to take a puff of her own cigarette and sip of her own drink.

"They're all alike, men. All except my darling Gerry. *He's* stuck by *his mother* and *his mother has stuck by him.*" Again she gave Ronny the fisheye. (Mrs. Updike was a worldly woman with no delusions about Gerald and Ronny. On the whole, she liked Ronny very little more than she had that tough Italian weightlifter of two years ago, but even Ronny was preferable to a daughter-in-law.) "Oh, that husband was wrong for you, darling, wrong, wrong, wrong! Gerry said so. *I* said so. Even *Ronny* said so."

"Well, he . . ." Mary began.

"Oh, yes, dear," Gerald said. "He was so awfully . . ."

"So awfully *what?*" Mary asked. She found herself growing a bit annoyed at this crew for running John down—not that they'd actually *said* anything—and more annoyed with herself for being annoyed with them.

"Well, he was so awfully sort of insensitive to beautiful things and making all that money from those horrid Popescus . . ." Gerald began.

"Whom he met through *you,*" she said rather too sharply.

"They were *clients,* dear," Mrs. Updike interjected. "No one in our *social* milieu."

"Well, you know, darling," Ronny smiled, "rather a Babbitt."

"If there is one thing John was *not*—and *is* not," Mary said hotly, "it's a Babbitt. He happens to be one of the cleverest writers in . . ."

"Darling," Mrs. Updike said, summoning forth her famous Baltimorean charm and tact. "The boys don't mean to upset you. Now stop it, *both* of you! (I'm ashamed of you, Gerry! *You've* certainly been raised better!) Now listen, dear, your problems are *your* business, and we've no in-*ten*tion of meddling. But I *do* want you to know that we're *all* standing *behind* you—and *I* advise immediate action. Any help you want, we're willing to give you. I know a marvellous lawyer who can handle the whole divorce for you. You

can go away for it, if you want, or he might be able to arrange it right here in New York. I'm sure he can get you a splendid settlement. And remember, dear, your old place is always waiting for you . . ."

She listened to Mrs. Updike rattling on and it struck her that Mrs. Updike was treating her just as she did her clients. *Now, listen, my dear, this is* your *apartment and we have* no intention *of dictating. But I* do *want you to know that Updike is always available for consultation and advice—and* we *advise avocado walls. Any help you want we're willing to give you. I have a marvellous writing table that would fill that corner perfectly. You could put it at right angles, if you want, or it might be nice flat against the wall. I'm sure it'll give a lovely effect. And remember, my dear, Updike is always . . .* She wondered if Mrs. Manley Updike was capable of any sort of sincerity at all, or if her entire mental and emotional equipment consisted of nothing more than the catchwords and fashionable endearments of East Fifty-seventh Street, which Mrs. Updike could apply just as glibly to a ruined marriage as she could to a set of slipcovers.

". . . all have dinner and then *you* could go off to the Blue Angel or someplace like that with Gerald and Ronny," Mrs. Updike was saying. "*I* have to play bridge with some old hags of about *my* age, but there's no reason why you young people don't all go out and have fun. Besides, Gerald and Ronny *like* to take girls out."

Mary almost said Yes before she caught herself. She had once known a girl named Sis Something—one of those big, good natured girls, born to be wives and mothers—who had attained the age of thirty-five before she discovered that not one of the giddy young men who asked her out with monotonous regularity was ever going to do more than kiss her forehead at the apartment door. By the time Sis Whateverhernamewas had realized that her function had been as a sort of rhino bird—to guide her pairs of courtiers into the smarter restaurants and night clubs, where unescorted men were unwelcome—it had been too late to catch that stolid, steady, sturdy stud who might have filled her and a station wagon with his babies. Now Sis was making a career, so to speak, of being the pansies' pal, the good sport of a girl who "made everything *look*

all right" in public and who wept lonely tears on trousseau linen in the unwelcome privacy of her big, cold bed.

"No!" Mary said aloud, quite without meaning to. It occurred to her that if now she had to fend for herself without her man, to find a new man or a set of men, she was going to look in a more likely place than Updike, Inc., Interiors.

"What's that, my dear?" Mrs. Updike said, somewhat startled.

"I'm so sorry that I can't, Maude," she said, "but I already have a date."

"So *soon*, my dear?" Mrs. Updike said.

"Who *is* he, darling?" Gerald asked cosily.

"Uh, it's that one," she said in a panic. "It's that one standing over there next to Fran Hollister."

"*My dear!*" Mrs. Updike gasped with a gurgle of appreciation.

"*Sssssay*, isn't he something!" Gerald whispered.

Then Fran caught her eye and beckoned wildly.

"Who *is* he?" Gerald said. "He's awfully attractive. What's his *name?*"

"I-I must go," she stammered. "Fran seems to be signaling me. Maude, thanks so much. I-I'll let you know what my plans are—just as soon as I know them myself." She almost stumbled over Ronny in her haste to be away.

Crossing the room, she realized that she would have to go back to work but that she could never, never, *never* return to the steaminess, the phoniness, the bitchiness of Maude and Gerald and Ronny at Mrs. Manley Updike, Inc., Interiors.

She pushed her way past a knot of people wearing turbans and fezzes and saris and badly made French suits, all talking at once in five different languages—Lisa was eternally grateful that the U.N. had chosen a site just fifteen minutes away from her parties—and struggled to Fran's side.

"My God," Fran bellowed, "who were those female-impersonators you got stuck with? Never saw such a pack of four-letter men in my life. You know Fletch, don't you?"

She did. "How do you do?" she said. "It's nice to see you again."

Actually it wasn't. Fletcher Mackenzie was a large, florrid man with a big nose, dark circles under his eyes and a superabundance of straight, black hair which grew too low on his forehead. He was

morbidly vain of this hair. It was one of his six topics of conversation. The other five were: 1.) Alcohol and how much of it he had consumed in the last twenty-four hours; 2.) Politics and as far to the right as possible; 3.) Money, of which he had an awesome amount; 4.) Places—clubs, hotels, restaurants, resorts—which he would never again visit; and this led to 5.) Jews. Fletch was probably anti-Semitic because he looked so very Semitic. This caused him to explain immediately to anyone he met—often to Semites who did *not* look Semitic—that he was really an Aryan. Since very few people were sufficiently drawn to Fletch to care whether he were an Aryan or a Melanesian, his impassioned and impromptu genealogical forays always had exactly the opposite effect to that which Fletch had intended and his unwilling audience began unconsciously associating Mackenzie with Mankiewitz while nodding dumbly and politely during Fletch's discourse.

Fletcher Mackenzie was so dissolute, dissipated, dispeptic, disreputable, disagreeable and disgustingly rich, that everyone said he was perfect for Fran. Happily, Fletch and Fran agreed. Their appetites for and interest in sex and alcohol were almost equal. So were their fortunes. It gave each the secure feeling that the other wasn't trying to get away with anything funny.

"And this is Randolph Lee," Fran was shouting. The stranger took Mary's hand and her knees absolutely buckled. Between the noise of her heart beating and the noise of the party she could barely hear his name. He was just about the best looking man she had ever seen in her life. He looked down on her with reddish brown eyes that almost burned. He smiled—oh, *too* beautifully. And then he spoke to her in a voice that was as hot and embracing as it was cool and polite.

"How do you do." That's all he had to say. Just How do you do. At that moment she found it the most eloquent, the most seductive, the most alarming speech ever made. She wondered very romantically and very briefly if there could be anything *to* this moth-flying-to-its-mate business. Then a little more sensibly she wondered if she felt so drawn to this beautiful Lee man because he was simply the first attractive male to have come her way since her husband walked out. Then she thought, with cold reason, that she

was probably just drunk. She took a large sip from her glass, finishing off the drink. She choked a little.

Then he was smiling down on her again with those wonderful animal eyes and saying something she couldn't possibly hear, but wanted to very much. "I-I'm sorry, but I didn't quite catch what . . ." she was absolutely shouting over the pounding she felt in her heart and her brain.

"For God's sake," Fran bellowed, "you can't hear yourself *think* in the joint. Let's all go up to Fletch's, where the liquor's better and it's quiet."

"Well, I, uh . . ." she started. Of course this would be the end of it. She would naturally have to tag along with Fran and Fletch, like a fifth wheel, while this magnificent man would smile enchantingly again, look at his watch and say Thanks so very much, but he had a date and was already late. Or he would have come with a party of people with plans for dining with them afterward. Or, the fate worse than death, he'd drag up a shrill, dowdy little wife—probably pregnant—introduce her, and then go into a long saga about getting back to Bedford Village or Coldspring Harbor . . . the babysitter . . . yes, a boy and a girl and this one due in May . . . yes, the commuting was a grind but having the kids in the country made it all worth it. No, she knew that this was too good to be true. Meetings like this one were for a women's magazine.

Then he spoke. "Frankly," Mr. Lee said, "I'd love to. I don't really know anyone here—except the hostess. If you're sure I wouldn't be . . ."

"That's the spirit," Fran boomed, downing her drink in a single gulp. "Let's drink up and get out."

Of course I'm either turning into an alcoholic or losing my mind, Mary thought. Just who do I think I am running out with the first man who comes along? What do I know about him? *Fran* doesn't even know him. Here I meet a man at a huge, silly party and the next thing that happens, I'm off to a patent medicine heir's apartment for more to drink. I simply . . . "Here, Mr. Lee," she said, handing the car keys to the stranger, "perhaps you'd like to drive."

six

"WELL," FRAN SAID, PUSHING BACK FROM THE ROOM SERVICE TABLE with a delicate belch, "I guess I'll live a little longer. Pour me a brandy, Fletch. I've got to go to the can." Then Fran got up and padded across the carpet in her dirty bare feet, casually kicking a scuffed suede pump under the sofa.

Obviously, Mary thought, Fran's been here a lot before. Yes, from the way Fran knew her way around Fletcher's suite—she didn't have to ask directions to telephones, bathrooms or ice cubes —yes she'd undoubtedly been up here many times. In fact, it occurred to Mary that Fran might even be having an affair with their host.

Fletcher Mackenzie made his home in a tiny hotel in the Fifties that was so small that almost no one had ever noticed it, and so exclusive that even fewer had ever heard of it. In fact, it had a number rather than a name. Its façade looked like a Sicilian wedding cake, its interior like a Roman mausoleum. The lobby, the halls, the birdcage elevator all smelled of rice powder, *violette du parme*, mothballs, dust and age. Fletch, at forty-seven was the youngest and the newest of the tenants. He had lived there for twelve years. The balance of the tenantry—fifty inmates in all—was made up of people patiently waiting to die: venerable grande dames and their companions; two antique actresses grown respectable through superannuation; a male recluse last seen in 1931; and a sprinkling of Czarist nobles who sallied forth in tiaras and tight uniforms on Russian Easter and New Year and spent the balance of the year quarreling hoarsely in French on the sofas of the lounge. Only the building and its staff were older than the guests.

Yet once inside the suites—there were no rooms; only suites—

one could see that the little hotel had or had once had true distinction. Despite the threadbare rugs, the spotted windows and the grimy curtains, the place still retained its air of great expense and elegance.

The meal had been excellent—steak done rare. In fact, the chef in the hotel's tiny kitchen cooked only special diets and steak. Yes, it had been steak, salad, wine and cheese—the standard meal of the rich restaurant milieu; the meal she had been eating for a year.

While Fletch opened his safe to remove a bottle of cognac, the beautiful Virginia gentleman smiled across the table at her. "It's nice here, isn't it? It's like down home."

This man, she felt was going to be different. He was romantic looking and, though every inch the Southern gentleman, romantic acting. And there was just something about this Mr. Lee—not the way he looked, nothing he had said, but something she rather sensed—that told her that he might be a very important man in her life. She could feel a nervous little throb in her throat and then another in the pit of her stomach every time he spoke to her.

An archaic waiter in shiny livery came in to remove the table. This gave Mr. Lee a splendid opportunity to get out of the waiter's way and join her on the sofa. "Mind if I sit here?" he said.

"N-no. Not at all," she said. My! She was absolutely trembling.

". . . find the Goddamned brandy anyplace . . ." Fletch was muttering.

"P-please do sit down," Mary said as Mr. Lee plopped gracefully onto the other end of the sofa.

". . . swear I had a bottle of Courvoisier in here . . ." Fletch said aloud to no one other than himself.

"That's a beautiful dress," Mr. Lee told Mary with an engaging shyness. "If you don't mind my saying so."

Mind! What woman had ever minded being complimented on her dress?

"And a beautiful hat, too."

"W-why, thank you."

There. She liked that. She liked men who noticed what women were wearing and said nice things. Well, not men like Gerald and Ronnie, who noticed nothing else, except possibly what *other* men were or were not wearing. Now take John, he never said a word

about her new clothes. Well, to be absolutely *fair*, her husband *had* once noticed her clothes, back in their poor New York days. Those had been the times when she'd been able to cull out a real bargain from the ten-dollar rack at Klein's, snip off the cheap trimmings, alter it a bit, dress it down and let her figure do the rest of the work. In those far distant days, she used to emerge from their tiny bath-and-dressing room worth twenty dollars on the hoof and looking like a million. "Well!" had been all he'd ever said, but his eyes had delivered a far more eloquent appraisal. But *now*, now that she could afford to splurge on some really good clothes, all he ever seemed to be thinking about was *Pulse Beat* and his wretched job with the watch works. At least he never seemed to notice how she looked—not even when the effect was *particularly* ravishing.

". . . keep everything under lock and key," Fletch said from the safe, withdrawing his large head and a brandy bottle. "Damned maids in this place'll rob you blind."

"Say, that's some wristwatch," Mr. Lee said, his eyes popping at the Pulse-Beat watch encrusted with diamonds on Mary's wrist.

"Oh, *this* . . ." she said. It sounded terribly arch, but she really meant it. The watch was a new model called the Lady Lillian which Mr. Popescu had tossed to her across the table at the Embassy Club a couple of weeks ago. The thing kept lousy time but the diamonds were startling—too startling, perhaps. She wouldn't have worn it at all, except it was the only watch she owned.

"Y-you're divorced?" he asked hesitantly.

"W-well, Mr. Lee . . ."

"Please call me Randy."

"Well, Randy," how nicely that name rolled off her tongue. "Well, yes and no. I suppose you might say *about* to be divorced."

"A legal separation?"

"An illegal one. But a very definite separation nonetheless."

"Brandy?" Fletch asked her.

"N-no thank you, Fletch," she said. Fletcher looked relieved. Then she thought again. After all, why not? She'd never had so much to drink in all her life, but she felt fine. Perfectly fine. "Well, as a matter of fact, Fletch, perhaps I will." Fletch looked annoyed.

"What about you, Lee?" Fletch said uncivilly. This evening for

four with drinks, dinner, and now more drinks all on him struck Fletcher as a damned useless extravagance. Since Fran rarely ate, he had planned to bring her back here—or possibly drive out to her place—throw a couple of Scotches into her and take her to bed. Yet here he was, fully dressed, and squandering his hard-probated money on all these people.

"Please," Mr. Lee said.

Oh, how Mary loved the way he said that—so polite and urbane and self-assured.

"Hey," Fran called, thumping back into the room, "I know what let's do tonight. Let's all finish our drinks and go over to that night club on East Fifty-fifth . . . what the hell's the name of it?"

"Chandelier?" Mr. Lee suggested. Everybody knew about Chandelier.

"Yeah, that's it. And see that new French dame . . . what the hell's her name?"

"Chou-Chou la Grue?" Mr. Lee prompted.

"Yeah, that's her. How about it?"

"Oh, for God's sake," Fletch grumbled, "who wants to go out on Saturday night—amateur night—and drink a lot of green liquor in some clip joint? Besides, it's late. These people must want to get to bed."

"Get to *bed?*" Fran roared. "My God, it's only nine o'clock. And who wants to sit around this morgue all night? Come on, Great Heart, you might just as well spend a little of it before the government takes it all."

Fletch writhed in his chair. Knowing how tight he was, he hated to have this defect pointed out by others *before* others. He also knew that Fran was every bit as tight, but Fran had a gift of *appearing* to be downright profligate. "Oh, all right," Fletch groaned.

"And where's my brandy?" Fran said loudly.

"Just a minute, just a minute." Fletch wondered quickly what it would be like to have a different kind of girl; a young pretty thing who wasn't used to much and wouldn't be at all demanding. She'd be a soft, cuddly working girl—a job in a store or an office, say—who'd just love to have a table d'hote dinner at Schrafft's, then possibly take in a double feature and so to bed. No, he reasoned, she'd find out about all his money and probably get even bigger

ideas than Fran had. At least Fran wasn't after his money—or not much of it—Fran loved him for himself alone.

"Uh, pardon me," Mr. Lee said, rising, "but could I, uh . . ."

"Sure!" Fran said. "It's past that door I just came through. First a right, then a left, then a right again. And look out for that seat."

"Th-thank you," Mr. Lee said, coloring slightly. "Um, excuse me."

How sweet and sort of boyish, Mary thought. Naturally a Southerner like Randy Lee would be embarrassed by the kind of language Fran used. Fran, of course, was a dear, but sometimes her conversation did get a little rough. She smiled in the direction of his high-held head as he left the room.

Fran smiled, too, but not at Mr. Lee's head. She wondered how he'd be in the hay and decided that he'd be just great. Then a flicker of intuition came over her. She had observed that real aristocrats were rarely aristocratic looking. Take the Bourbons, take the Hanovers, take Fran herself—if three generations of money could be said to constitute aristocracy. There was something about Mr. Lee that reminded her of that aristocratic looking Spaniard who'd tiptoed out of a West Side hotel room one night with her fourth mink coat, her purse and a gold charm bracelet. Yet, she thought fondly, that Spik had damned near been worth it.

Then Fran cast sentiment aside and began reviewing, quickly and practically, the advantages and disadvantages of bagging Mr. Lee for the night.

First of all, she thought, Mary was still a Good Guy and even if Fran *had* spotted this Randy Lee first, he was more or less the kid's property. Fran *had* gone to Lisa's with Fletch and it was tacitly understood that Fran and Fletch would end up in either his bed or hers at the end of an evening. They'd been doing it for years.

Second, even if Fran did get Lee away from her, it would mean taking the milk train home, then a taxi and then inspection by the Riveredge gate keeper, who would undoubtedly blab. Fran feared gossip and sincerely believed that she misconducted herself so discreetly that no one ever thought or said anything true about her.

Third, Fran continued thinking, if she did stay in town with Fletch tonight, and if tomorrow should be fair, then Fran could probably get Fletch to drive out to that fashionable mental institu-

tion on Long Island to visit Mamma. Fran disliked her mother and vice versa. The latter to a point where she had ceased recognizing Fran. But Fran hadn't been out to Mamma's looney bin since Easter and the family trustees kept sternly reminding her of a Daughter's Duty. So maybe she should finesse Dixieland tonight, but get his telephone number for another evening.

Fourth, Fran thought, what the hell, Fletch—though dull—wasn't so bad and at least she knew who his people were. Yes, I'll sleep with Fletch tonight and go see Mamma tomorrow, Fran concluded. Fran recognized Duty and bowed before it.

"Well, *here*," Fletcher said irritably, "don't you *want* it?"

"Oh! The brandy!" Then Fran was galvanized into action. "For God's sake, Fletch, do you expect me to drink it out of that eyecup? Get me a decent sized glass, for God's sake."

Fletch's face was a study of hurt pride and wounded bankroll.

"Oh, wait, I'll come out and get a glass with you." There. Fran could always soften Fletch up in the pantry.

Randolph Carter Lee did a rather remarkable thing. He went into Fletch's big, old-fashioned marble bathroom, locked the door, stripped off every shred of his clothing and observed his naked reflection in the full length mirror carefully and objectively.

Standing at attention before the faintly clouded glass, he began, as always, examining his long, neat toes and worked up, past the firm thighs, the lean loins, the clean-shaven chest, the broad shoulders and well-muscled arms. Then he turned around and glanced over his shoulder to make sure that the buttocks were still firm, the back still strongly moulded, the skin clear. He turned again and examined the side view. His stomach was tending to bulge just a little, but that was the least of his worries. If he didn't land something soon, it would be concave.

There was no vanity, no narcissism—a word which he wouldn't even have understood—in Mr. Lee's action. His face and his body and his pleasant manners were the only tangible assets which he possessed and he inventoried them with the detached air of a banker reviewing his holdings.

Mr. Lee had moved sufficiently in wealthy circles to grasp the rudiments of barter and exchange, supply and demand. And he

was just bright enough and just honest enough to realize that the supply of fine young bodies somewhat exceeded the supply of fine old fortunes in this day of surtaxes.

Ten years ago he had been equally unconcerned with his body and rich people. But he had aged faster than most in a decade. He had learned enough of the foibles of the very rich now to be most critically conscious of his own resources for as long as they remained resources and not deficits. This evening, however, he was calmly satisfied with his physical balance sheet. His assets, current and fixed, were still there.

It took Mr. Lee exactly ninety seconds to slip back into his clothes—rather good clothes, too, but showing signs of wear. He had had enough practice to dress and disrobe with the speed of a quick-change artist. He felt carefully into the secret pocket to make sure that his money was still there. It was; all sixteen dollars, plus a dollar-fifty in silver in his trousers pocket for tips and taxis and things. Then he sat down on the toilet seat and carefully replaced his darned cashmere socks and his new shoes. The shoes rather distressed him. They looked expensive, but they didn't feel expensive. Having become accustomed to spending forty dollars on a pair at Abercrombie & Fitch, he had been almost shocked last week when Grace gave him a ten dollar bill and directed him to Thom McAn's. But he had chosen well with his almost-innate good taste and there had even been enough left over for a good haircut—and a miserable tip—at Prince Gourielli's.

He stood up now and gave his face a minute inspection in the mirror above the basin. It was an excellent face—strong, firm and symmetrical. It was even better than it had been ten years ago, when he had first capitalized on it. It was better boned, better fleshed, better groomed. It was a face that placed Mr. Lee at somewhere between thirty and thirty-six. Actually, he was just twenty-six, and rather ashamed of it.

Then he turned on both taps and, with the water running loud enough to drown out any sound, opened Fletch's medicine chest. Experience had taught him that a medicine chest revealed more information than an F.B.I. report. Fletch's was no exception.

From the array of pills, potions, laxatives and suppositories, he deduced that Fletch was a hypochondriac and a constipated one

—like so many rich people. He spotted sinus trouble and a bygone bout of athlete's foot. Cremalin, Anacin, Empirin, Bufferin and aspirin, both Alka- and Bromo-seltzer proclaimed that Fletch drank heavily and suffered accordingly. There were two kinds of body powder, four toothbrushes—an unusual number. (Randolph Carter Lee's bathroom explorations had led him to expect one, two, seven or, in rare cases, fourteen toothbrushes). He noticed some green dental cream, and a manfully packaged spray deodorant. There was a forty-nine cent razor, a dollar brush and a special-offer-sale tube of shaving soap. Behind a suspiciously large and suspiciously empty looking soap box, placed on its side, he found the evidence of an active sex life and also the evidence of considerable apprehension following it. He smiled understandingly. Well, that could happen to anyone.

As he replaced the soap box, something unsoaplike rattled inside. He opened it carefully. There he found a half-emptied bottle of gooey dark nail enamel, four bobby pins, and a gold lipstick. That gave him pause. He wondered if Fletch could be queer? No. A.C.-D.C.? Unlikely. One of those twisted types who are manly all day and can't wait to get home and change to a frothy negligee? Possibly. Then he examined the lipstick. It was monogrammed F. van A. H. Fran Hollister. So that was the set-up.

He put everything back exactly as it had been, shut the cabinet and turned off the water. Like Rodin's *Thinker,* he sat down again on the toilet seat, a stunning study in despondency.

Mr. Lee had gone to Lisa's party only because it was a free evening, because Grace was visiting a cousin in New Jersey for the weekend, and because he smelled money. (Lisa had met him once at an actor's cocktail party where Grace had taken him. She'd found him attractive—as who did not—and invited him for this evening.) Since Lisa was interested in intellect, not sex, he'd seen no future there, but running into Fran Hollister had been a God-send.

He'd heard enough about Fran to know exactly the sort of girl she was and almost exactly how much she had in the way of income. He also knew that Fran had the disposition of a mink—with all that it implied—and a pretty parsimonious mink, at that. Still, he had enough self-confidence in himself to feel that

he might interest her long enough to bank a little something or at least to live out in that posh Riveredge Club in some degree of comfort until a new prospect turned up. But this more or less uxorious arrangement with Fletcher MacKenzie dashed his hopes. Mr. Lee had few qualms about other men's wives, but other men's mistresses could make for a most untidy relationship.

He looked at his face in the mirror again, sighed, and wondered just how he had got into this situation in only ten years.

Dressed or naked, Randolph Carter Lee was every inch the aristocratic Virginia gentleman. He was tall, well built, conservatively tailored, languid and spoke with an accent that was not quite Southern, not quite British. If pressed, he would recount for you how life was lived at Greenwood House, the gracious plantation of the Lee family. Unfortunately, he had never lived at Greenwood House, he was not an aristocrat, certainly not a gentleman and his real name was not Randolph Carter Lee. He did, however, come from Virginia.

Randy Lee had been born Randolph Leroy Skaggs to a poor, ignorant farm woman. He never knew who his father was, except that his mother had once described him as a fine, handsome gentleman. That had been enough for Randy. From that day forward he set about to become the finest, handsomest gentleman possible, like his unknown father. In this he had not failed. He was exactly the sort of man his real father had been.

To support herself and her son, Miss Skaggs had done washing. She had washed all day until her hands were worn and cracked and she had ironed until after midnight. On Mondays Miss Skaggs did for the judge's wife; on Tuesdays for the doctor's family; on Wednesdays for the Calhoun sisters; and the rest of the week for the Lee family who lived at Greenwood House.

It had been Randy's duty to pick up the dirty laundry and deliver the clean. He had hated this, hated the lowliness of the work, hated to hear the Negroes in the kitchens laugh their soft, suggestive laugh and refer to him as "Miz Skaggs's love chile." Only when Randy had gone to Greenwood House to deliver the linen had he experienced anything like pleasure.

Sometimes, standing in the kitchen while the housekeeper counted the laundry, he would see the pantry door swing open

to reveal the elegant oval dining room with its silver, its gleaming furniture, its damask hangings. Almost always he would see the cook at work on some undreamed-of-delicacy—a rosy roast of beef, a pink ham, a golden turkey or an unbelievable flower garden of a cake. Another time he found the butler polishing all the household silver. Randy had been almost blinded by the array of candlesticks and platters and hairbrushes and inkpots that were made of solid silver.

Once during a damp spell the Lees' laundry had refused to dry and it was evening when Randy delivered it. "Boy, Ah thought you never *would* come," the housekeeper had screamed at him. "We got twenty people here an' all they dawgs an' hosses an' I doan know what-all. Ah need all the sheets Ah kin git!"

"Twenty people stayin' *here?*" Randy had gasped.

The pantry door swung open and Randy could see the candlelight, hear the gentle laughter from the dining room beyond. Once out of the kitchen, he tiptoed around the wide verandah and peered through the dining room window. There were the fine ladies and gentlemen seated around the big table. He stood shivering in the cold dampness for hours, watching the Lees and their guests. It was after midnight when he got home.

"Son where've uh *bin?*" his mother cried. "I bin worrit haff ta death, son. I bin prayin' for yuh, son!"

"Leave me alone," Randy had sobbed. "I *hate* it here!"

From that day on, Randy couldn't see enough of Greenwood House or its occupants. Every free moment was spent spying the place out. When Miss Sally made her debut Randy was a vicarious guest, invisible in the shrubbery. In the same capacity he attended two dances, three hunt balls and Miss Sally's wedding. In his world of fantasy, he was Randy Lee, just like the real Randy Lee who was off at a rich man's school in the North. Greenwood House was his house and the Lees' elegant guests were his guests.

When he was eleven a great stroke of luck came his way. He was delivering the wash on a torrid Saturday afternoon when he heard a woman's voice say: "My stars, who is that beautiful child?"

"That's the laundress's boy, Ah believe," another woman said.

"But he's, he's perfectly gorgeous. I want to talk to him. May I? I mean you won't mind or anything, will you?"

"Why of course not, Elizabeth. Wait, I'll call him. Boy!" she shouted. "You, boy! Come up here a minute, would you?"

Randy knew it was Mrs. Lee, herself. With the shy smile that was later to stir so many hearts, he slowly mounted the verandah steps. "Yes, Miz Lee, ma'm?"

In his presence Mrs. Lee's guest had made it amply clear that he was beautiful, that his manners were quite charming, that she'd like to take him back up North with her, and that he looked like a regular little prince. "Even in those rags and tatters," she added. Randy blushed angrily.

"Elizabeth, please," Mrs. Lee had said. Then she smiled warmly at Randy and said: "Ah have a boy named Randy, too. Randolph Carter Lee. He's a few years older than you, but I wonder, maybe you'd like to take some of his clothes home with you so your mother could fix them over. He's outgrown them and it's silly letting perfectly good things go to waste. If you could use them . . ."

Randy had never come into such a windfall. There were things from Thalhimer's in Richmond, Woodward and Lothrop in Washington, Brooks Brothers in New York. The sweaters all said "Made in England" or "Made in Scotland" and they were of a softness that Randy never believed possible. In each garment was a Cash's Woven Name Tape with "Randolph Carter Lee" stitched on it in red.

It had been a big day in Randy's life. He had learned for the first time from intelligent people—rich people—that he was good looking. He had learned that he was a little gentleman, almost a prince. And he had acquired enough clothes to make him look the part. From then on many of his hours were spent in front of the cracked, dim mirror in the shanty Miss Skaggs chose to call her house.

His mother had spelled out a pathetic note of thanks to Mrs. Lee and sent it around with the washing to Mrs. Lee at Greenwood House. Randy dressed himself carefully for this visit in

his Lee clothing. It was too hot, really, to wear one of the beautiful foreign sweaters, he simply tied it around his neck, as he had seen the Lee boy do. He was terrified at having to go in through the big front door and deliver the note to Mrs. Lee, but he needn't have been. Mrs. Lee and her garrulous house guest were on the lawn surrounded by hounds and Miss Sally's babies.

"Hello, theah, boy!" Mrs. Lee called, as he approached with the wagonload of laundry. "My how spruce you look. So they did fit?"

"Yes, ma'm. Thank you, ma'm. My mother sent you this." Almost with repugnance he thrust the flyblown envelope toward Mrs. Lee.

"Oh, but doesn't he look divine!" the northern woman cried. "Just like a little English boy off the, the playing fields of Eton or something. I simply *must* have a picture of him. Son, if I give you twenty-five cents will you let me take your snapshot?"

For once in his life, Randy's vanity overruled venality. "Ah don't want no money, ma'm," he said politely. "Ah'll be happy to let you take mah picture, ma'm."

"The darling!" the woman shrilled. "Just you wait, now, till I run up and get the Kodak."

He still had the photograph—Randy in the foreground, the west portico of Greenwood House and a rakish Rolls-Royce in the background—it served as proof that he really was Randolph Carter Lee.

And indeed, he became Randolph Carter Lee at the age of sixteen. Like his father before him, Randy got a girl in trouble—a girl with three big brothers whose sense of virtue was matched only by their viciousness. Immediate departure was essential and two hours after the girl had whimpered her gynecological information to him, Randy and a cardboard carton filled with Randolph Carter Lee's cast-off clothing were bound for parts unknown.

The milk truck that carried Randy away from a severe beating and/or matrimony set him down a hundred miles away in a Virginia resort town famous for its medicinal baths and it was in a fashionable spa where Randy spent the only two days of

his life in gainful employment. The sign Boy Wanted in front of the Roman Baths—Men Only—We Never Close—started Randy on his present career.

Scared and starving, Randolph Leroy Skaggs was employed as a bath attendant under the name of Randolph Carter Lee, a pseudonym that made the proprietor of the Roman Baths whistle in amazement. The work was as simple as it was dull, which was fortunate because Randy was lazy. The salary was commensurate, but that didn't matter because Randy didn't stay at the Roman Baths long enough to collect his first week's pay envelope.

Clad in a breech clout, it was Randy's duty to pass out cold towels and hot mineral water to naked, sweaty old men. It was also his duty to hose down the tile floor, to clean the toilets, to time the customers under the sun lamp, to summon them for their massages and to guide them to their resting rooms after they had been steamed, sweated, dunked in the curative waters and slapped and pummelled by the masseurs.

The first day had been most uneventful, except that the head masseur had given him a bologna sandwich. The first night Randy slept on a pile of dirty sheets and towels. The second day had been *most* eventful, for on that day Mr. Bessamer favored the Roman Baths with his patronage.

"Watch out for that one, sonny," the masseur had muttered. "He's queer."

Randy hadn't the faintest idea what he was talking about. Mr. Bessamer had looked quite ordinary—short and bald with a flabby, white, hairless body. Randy was only conscious of being followed by Mr. Bessamer's watery blue eyes as he performed his duties around the baths. But when Mr. Bessamer had finished his massage and Randy shepherded him to a bedroom, Randy came to understand what the masseur meant. The second night Randy slept in Mr. Bessamer's hotel suite—and the third and the fourth and the fifth. He never returned to the Roman Baths, for Mr. Bessamer had offered him steady employment of a more specialized nature.

Life as Mr. Bessamer's companion—for that was the euphemistic title by which Mr. Bessamer called him—was, at least by Randy's none-too-stringent standards, easy, uncomplicated and almost

pleasant. Sixty and impotent, Mr. Bessamer derived his pleasure mainly from two things—looking at Randy's body and being gently slapped on the stomach with a tortoise shell comb, duties which Randy felt were not especially taxing and certainly adequately paid.

Mr. Bessamer was very rich. A bachelor, he derived his income from a Milwaukee brewery which his younger brother ran. Since Mr. Bessamer hated Milwaukee, his brother and his common sister-in-law, and since a lot of people were buying Bessamer Beer, he was quite content to spend his life elsewhere, happy traveling, collecting Fabergé cigarette boxes, sitting on the board of a community house for underprivileged boys, blowing Bach dismally into a recorder, admiring Randy's physique and gurgling ecstatically under the rhythmic thwack-thwack-thwack of the tortoise shell comb. Milwaukee and his brother were just as glad to have him elsewhere, so the arrangement worked out perfectly.

Randy spent five years in Mr. Bessamer's service; spent them in Europe and Palm Beach and Mexico City and in Mr. Bessamer's delicate apartment on Park Avenue. In that time Randy managed to acquire quite a lot of things. His accent vanished and a new, terribly refined one cropped up in its place. His eighth grade education was supplemented by a good deal of superficial knowledge of things fashionable—how to order dinner, what the better hotels were in London, what was being worn on the Côte d'Azure, how much to tip, important facts like that. His wardrobe expanded and grew, for Mr. Bessamer liked to see a well dressed man almost as much as a well undressed one. The only thing Randy did not manage to accumulate was money. Generous as he was, Mr. Bessamer was very close with a buck and the largest amount he ever gave Randy in cash was five dollars. So Randy's only recompense was excellent room and board, good clothes and stylish surroundings. That had seemed enough.

However, Randy had one failing, hazardous to his position; Randy preferred women. In his years with Mr. Bessamer Randy had been cautious, crafty, furtive in his affairs with females. There had been quick encounters with chambermaids and hurried trips to bordellos coincidental with Mr. Bessamer's visits to the barber, the tailor, the podiatrist and they had been almost satisfactory

to Randy until Mr. Bessamer placed true temptation in his way.

Randy's downfall occurred during his fifth year as Mr. Bessamer's companion, concurrent with the visit of Mr. Bessamer's niece. Mr. Bessamer's niece was named Besame, a name which made Mr. Bessamer shudder and rail at Besame's vulgar mother. But otherwise Mr. Bessamer adored the girl. She was sixteen, precocious, sophisticated and perfectly beautiful. Miss Bessamer had descended on her uncle's unusual ménage to spend her spring vacation from Miss Spaulding's School for Girls. Mr. Bessamer was delighted. Randy was delighted. The three of them spent a jolly week eating sumptuous meals, buying Besame pretty dresses, going to the theatre and attending night clubs appropriate to a subdebutante of sixteen, where Randy and Besame danced while Mr. Bessamer happily drummed a pudgy hand on the tablecloth in time to the music. Five idyllic evenings had been passed thus. But on the sixth night Mr. Bessamer really had to be excused. It was a board meeting of the boys' club and Mr. Bessamer was very interested in the boys.

"Behave yourselves, you young people," Mr. Bessamer had said with a kittenish wag of the finger as he departed. "I'll be back at eleven and perhaps we can all run over to La Rue." Gaily whistling "Sheep May Safely Graze," Mr. Bessamer stepped into the elevator.

Unfortunately, a severe twinge of heartburn overtook Mr. Bessamer during the meeting. At half-past-nine he stepped out of the elevator, quietly opened the apartment door to discover his niece and his protegé behaving themselves most carnally on *his* brocade bedspread.

Mr. Bessamer gasped. Mr. Bessamer shrieked. Mr. Bessamer *screamed*. Then Mr. Bessamer fell forward clutching at his heart. He writhed and wriggled and made terribly croaking, strangulated noises. By the time Randy and Besame had flung on their clothes and summoned the doctor, Mr. Bessamer was dead. Heart attack.

A codicil in Mr. Bessamer's will left five thousand dollars to "my faithful companion, Randolph Carter Lee." All the rest went to "my beloved niece, Besame Bessamer of Milwaukee, Wisconsin." Mr. Bessamer's brother flew on from Milwaukee and got

Randy out of the apartment so fast that Randy had hardly time to pack up his own belongings, let alone a few of his late patron's. Miss Besame Bessamer was hustled off to a school in Switzerland after a forced confession to her outraged father—and after making absolutely certain that she wasn't pregnant. The father had a number of home truths to deliver to Randy concerning his behavior with both his daughter and his late brother. Randy countered with a few home truths of his own and threatened to talk, but a tough family lawyer dissuaded him from any such action by describing, rather picturesquely, the penalty for blackmail. And so Randy went his own way with a measly five grand, Besame went to Switzerland with the swag and the surviving Bessamer brother started back for Milwaukee only to perish in an airplane crash over the Great Lakes. But Randy was so disgruntled that not even the headlines describing the Milwaukee brewer's tragic end managed to cheer him up.

At twenty-one with looks, clothes, manners and a five-thousand-dollar sinking fund, Randy might have begun a new way of life, but he had had no business experience, other than two days in a bath house, little formal education and even less ambition. Nor did the money last long. After five years of the high life, he was unable to economize. Within six months he was back in the companion business again, devoting his talents almost exclusively to women. There had been a Mrs. Gilchrist who had pink-dyed hair and a house in Sutton Place. But she also had two stuffy, muscular sons who sent Randy packing within a year.

His next stop was with a Mrs. Barrett, whom he picked up in the Barberry Room. She had brown-dyed hair and a penthouse and, it developed, a fearful temper when she caught him trying to seduce her married daughter. Then there was that attractive Mrs. Brewster for a whole summer, but her husband returned from duty at sea and that ended that.

Randy had spent a season in Mexico with a perfect virago known locally as Señora Mulcahey. Then he was named as co-respondent in a divorce case in Hollywood. Next came a very brief affair with a successful English dramatist whose play was packing them in at the Alvin Theatre, but the poor young man

was deported for moral turpitude and Randy was once again at loose ends. A Mrs. Miller brought surcease, and a trip to Bermuda, for a while, but she, too, dropped Randy when she discovered him in an infidelity. Then there had been three lean months of living in a cheap rooming house that was so grim that only a dalliance with the pretty file clerk next door made life possible. But the file clerk got pregnant and there was perfect hell to pay. Then came a time of cruising the Bird Circuit and then finally Grace.

Grace wasn't exactly what Randy was accustomed to. Grace was a broken-down actress of most minor sort, although she still considered herself somewhat greater than Eleanora Duse. Grace had given up acting—except around the apartment—and was married to a dolt named Herbert, who covered the New England territory for a hosiery manufacturer. They had extremely limited means. Randy was now living with them as a "boarder" and as Grace's "promising young actor protegé." But Herbert was getting less and less convinced that Randy was taking dramatic lessons from Grace. Every time Herbert came back from the road he was gruffer and gruffer with Randy and he had finally come right out and asked Randy to move on. And Randy was ready to move on, too. Grace was much too demanding. She was wearing him out. Randy had begun to long for dreary old Herbert to get back to town. And Grace was miserly, too. Ten bucks for a pair of shoes! *And* all of Grace's intellectual and artistic pretensions!

No, Randy would have to find something new and he'd have to find it right away. If Fran Hollister wasn't going to be his next hostess, he'd try for her little friend. Maybe this girl didn't have Fran's millions, but from her dress, her hat, her furs, her jewelry there was something there. Didn't she live at Riveredge? And she was a looker, too. Whatever she was, she was about twice as rich as Grace, about half as old and about a thousand times as attractive. She liked him, too. He could tell. No, she'd do until something big came along.

Running a hand over his hair, the Virginia gentleman unlocked the bathroom door and moved gracefully toward the living room to rejoin the party.

Sitting alone in the parlor of Fletcher Mackenzie's suite, she tried to orient herself, to decide just what had happened to her during the day. First of all, she had lost a husband. He was gone forever and she was just as glad. At least she supposed she was. If she had ever cared for him—and, oh yes, she *had* when she was younger and more naive than she was today—she didn't any longer. As of today she was her own free agent. She could come and go as she pleased and with whom she pleased. She could even take a lover. She wondered what that would be like. She'd never had a lover. But it certainly *sounded* romantic. Romantic *and* practical. When they got sick of each other then they could just go their own ways. No lawyers or property settlements or anything like that to worry about.

Yes, she'd get a quiet divorce; take nothing from him; lease a little flat here in town; do it up in turquoise blue, she guessed, and probably Biedermeyer furniture; get a job or maybe even open a shop of her own; and have lots and lots of different beaux and, maybe eventually, a lover. She thought about Randolph Carter Lee and wondered if he'd be interested in her.

There was a slight scuffling and a gasping sound from the pantry. Yes, now she was practically sure that Fran and Fletch were having an affair. Well, when *she* had *her* affair she certainly wasn't going to be groping around out in a pantry when there were guests in the house! Then she felt that she was being unbearably prim and laughed at herself.

She wished everybody would come back. She hated being alone. She wanted to be *with* people tonight and be very, very gay.

She looked around the room. There were three photographs on the desk in slightly tarnished silver frames. One, the largest, looked like Fletch wearing a frightful wig and a diamond tiara. His mother, undoubtedly. The second portrayed two little girls who looked disastrously like Fletch. They were the daughters by his first marriage. The third was a boxer bulldog that looked exactly like Fletch. That was the dog by his second marriage.

My, Mary thought, how lucky that my baby was never born. But she didn't really mean it. Now I'm getting morose, she thought. She took a sip of her brandy and let it trickle hotly and slowly down her throat. Then she felt a hand on her shoulder.

She looked up and there was the Virginia gentleman smiling down at her.

"Hello," she said, and she trembled very slightly.

"Hello," Randy said. "Mind if I sit down?"

"Please do," she said, moving over just enough so that he would have to sit very close to her.

He sat down next to her and without a word lighted two cigarettes and gave her one. She didn't much feel like smoking a cigarette but the gesture was so lovely—she halfway remembered having seen somebody do it in a movie years ago—that she took it. Wordlessly she smiled at him and he took her hand in his. She wondered what she should do next, if anything. She did nothing.

There was the sound of a glass crashing in the pantry. "Jesus, Fletch," Fran snapped, "don't *do* that when I've got my back turned!"

In a minute Fran and Fletch were back in the room. Fletch looked very red and very flustered. "Oh, ah, um, ahem," he said.

"Come on," Fran said. "I'm sick of sitting around this dump. Let's all drink up and get the hell over to the Chandelier."

"Oh, yes," she echoed, with a stab at gaiety. "Let's all do drink up and get the hell over to the Chandelier!"

seven

As nightclubs went, Chandelier was as firmly established as the Metropolitan Museum. Housed in a large, lofty old building which had once served as a showroom for tombstones and rather elaborate funerary statuary, it had been Chandelier for twenty-five years. Through long endurance and careful press agentry, the Chandelier had become synonymous with Elegance, Money and Taste, although the Chandelier management lacked all three attributes. The place had become an institution. (Happily the unfortunate shooting that took place there in 1936 had been largely forgotten). New York mothers would allow their subdebutante daughters to go to Chandelier, whereas they vetoed the Stork Club or El Morocco. Fairfield, Westchester and Suffolk Counties attended regularly. The place had developed such a reputation for catering to quiet New York Society, rather than free-spending out-of-town buyers, that Chandelier had been forced to develop its own quota system—one socialite (or someone who *looked* like a socialite) for every three butter and egg men admitted.

The place was named for a large central fixture of crystal and ormulu, said to have come from a Hapsburg palace, but actually purchased cheap from the wreckers of an old theatre in Schenectady. The exterior was painted an uncompromising black with a highly compromising white trim. The inside was done up with midnight blue walls, red plush divans and a carpet with an interesting all-over pattern of cigarette burns. It hadn't been painted, cleaned or properly aired since V-J day. Every year the room grew dingier, the chandelier dimmer until now a Seeing-Eye dog and a

Braille edition of the menu were almost essential. But that's the way the steady customers liked it. Chandelier was a home away from home.

Although management served food of sorts, trundled through an underground tunnel from the medium-priced restaurant next door and dished up at five-hundred-percent increase, few meals were ordered and the lazy waiters looked askance—and rather hurt—if anyone called for dinner or even supper. Deserted at seven, sparsely settled at eight, active at nine and teeming by ten, the Chandelier depended almost exclusively on the proceeds of its bar to pay the staff salaries and the overpriced, over-rated entertainers for which the place was famous.

It was just nine when Mr. and Mrs. Frederick Marshall entered with their party. Things were going perfectly according to the long-established Saturday night schedule. An unfashionable family from Jackson Heights were overspending their annual reunion at a table for twelve—and a very bad table it was, adorned with wilting ferns and silverware engraved with the names of defunct restaurants. An equally dowdy birthday party was going on at an equally undesirable table and a supercilious waiter had just carried in a large birthday cake, wincing at the half-hearted chorus of "Happy Birthday to You" sung *a cappella* by the embarrassed revellers. Two college kids, obviously watching their pennies, sat at a minuscule divan table making desultory conversation and trying to nurse their drinks until the floor show and a pair of honeymooners from Scranton, selfconscious of the newness of their clothes, were being served an inferior bottle of domestic champagne on the house.

The orchestra was playing gems from *The Boys from Syracuse* with the same, relentless beat-beat-beat they had used the season when *The Boys from Syracuse* opened. The waiters had just stopped examining their cuticles and gossiping in Greek and now began fluttering around their stations. Nine o'clock was the witching hour, the time when Chandelier came to life.

The headwaiter guided the Marshalls and their guests to three different tables before Alice found the one she liked. He privately considered them as frumpy looking a foursome as he'd seen in some years, yet he knew that it was on just solid, genteel people

that Chandelier built its reputation, if not its fortune. He also knew that Whitney and Beth Martin were sufficiently prominent to rate a ringside table, even if she looked like a sad, brown cow in her maternity evening dress and even if the overbearing woman with her looked like a comic valentine.

As Alice had an instinct for what was appropriate to the country, she also knew what was appropriate to town. Alice felt, perhaps incorrectly, that her height and weight, her large head and imperious beak of a nose were best set off by rich fabrics and long, sweeping skirts. One *dressed* for town, Alice said. No Theatre Guild Subscription Thursday, no trip to a mediocre French restaurant with Fred's clients, no little dinner in Gramercy Park with Dr. Needles and his mistress was complete without long gloves, long skirts, Granny's garnets and a towering structure which Alice called a Dinner Hat. Alice in brocade and osprey—shrouded in a mackintosh, with her glasses on the end of her nose and her fur cape on the seat beside her—racing to the New York-bound train in the Jeepster was a familiar twilight sight in Riveredge. At the same time, Fred would be furtively changing into dinner clothes behind the glass walls of his office, sick with apprehension at every distant rattle of the cleaning woman's pail, dropping his studs and twisting his suspensory. But the Marshalls made an awe-inspiring sight when they swept forth in full evening regalia.

Tonight Alice was resplendent in her old black maternity evening skirt with a new smocked jacket of electric blue satin and a feathered helmet to match. She sat down grandly and noted for the third time that Beth Martin looked rather dumpy and very pregnant in her brown silk. "How badly dressed most women in New York are," Alice said loudly, surveying the uniform black and pearls of the other women in the room. She positively sneered at a golden blonde in golden sable. "So few women really *know* how to wear furs nowadays," Alice said, patting the chain of crushed animals that lay across her shoulders. The gesture unsettled her furpiece and it slithered to the floor with a sad little plop.

"Oh, listen, Whit," Beth Martin said, "there's our song!" The orchestra was bouncing out "Night and Day" in its set of gems from *The Gay Divorce*. "Whit and I got engaged here. Didn't we, dear?" Beth asked with a sweet, shy smile.

"Yes, dear," Whitney Martin said with a dazzling array of teeth.

"How nice," Alice said and condemned them silently for mawkish sentimentality, even though Beth and Whit Martin *were* the right sort.

Alice was more than a little put out this evening. She had telephoned her sister time and time again, letting the phone jangle for ten, twenty, thirty rings. She'd called Central and complained and had learned—although she didn't quite believe it—that the telephone was in perfect order. Then she'd driven over to her sister's house and rung the bell for, it seemed, hours. There was no sign of life. She'd tried the back door with equal lack of success.

Then Alice had decided that the poor girl had Done Something Drastic. She'd put in a call to the gate keeper and forced him to force an entrance into the house. He'd put up a lot of resistance to this suggestion, but no one could hold out long against Alice—not if he knew what was good for him. So they had burst in through the cellar door. Alice had examined the house from the bottom up and then down again. There was no odor of gas, no limp body swinging from the rafters, no faint scent of bitter almonds.

Alice was, if anything, a little disappointed to have found that her sister was simply and undramatically not at home. In her embarrassment she gave the man a quarter for his pains and resolved to have words with her sister for causing so much trouble.

"Would you care to dance, Alice . . . dear?" Fred Marshall interrupted her thoughts. He didn't like dancing, but he knew that he'd have to ask her.

"Don't be infantile, Fred," she said. "Dr. Needles is right when he says that America is producing a race of boy-men. He feels that . . .

Well, you just couldn't win with Alice. Angry because he'd asked her to dance, she'd have been furious if he hadn't. Fred thought, rather miserably, that if he ever *had* liked dancing, which was doubtful, he had never liked dancing with Alice, who was taller than he was and inclined to do the leading. And he especially didn't like dancing with Alice when she was pregnant. It made him feel like a canoe towing the *Queen Mary* into port.

In fact, Fred decided, he didn't even like Alice and he probably never had. Yet they had been married for just fifteen years. Exactly fifteen years and two hours ago (Santa Barbara time) Alice, a jaundiced Amazon in the candle-lit chapel, had dragged her poor old father down the aisle, pronounced a few words in her stentorian whinny, and then dragged her poor young husband back up the aisle, secure forever in the belief that she was more intelligent, more intellectual, more desirable than any other woman in the world.

And for fifteen years—save for a blessed six months' respite at sea with the Navy, until Alice pulled enough strings to drag him back as a gunnery instructor at Columbia—Fred had been loving, honoring and obeying Alice. That was especially odd since Alice, always the modern bride, had issued instructions for "obey" to be stricken from the marriage service.

There had been fifteen years of commuting to Wall Street, of eating Alice's meals, paying Alice's bills, siring Alice's children, if and when Alice wanted children. Fifteen years of Planned Parenthood and the League of Women Voters and the Committee for Political Awareness and the American Association of University Women and the Mothers' Childhood Development Group and the Parent-Teachers' Association. Fifteen years of Alice's psychoanalytical claptrap, of Alice's never-ending, ever-changing theories. There had been fifteen years of the Mayo Diet, the Hauser Diet, the Salt-Free Diet, the Alexander Method, the Mensendieck System. And now Dr. Needles, who terrified him as an intellect, unnerved him as an informer and disgusted him as a charlatan, had been brought into Fred's life, at twenty-five dollars an hour.

Fred almost envied his sister-in-law's husband. There was a man who had just walked out on his wife, and his wife was a living saint—as well as a sweet little thing—compared to her sister, Alice. Fred wondered how it would be just to walk out on Alice. But terms like brute, cad, bounder, deserter and unnatural father crowded the wild notion out of his head. No, at forty-two it was too late to walk out. He should have done his walking out fifteen years and two hours ago. He should never have walked in.

Fred was startled from his musings by a dull thump on the table. There sat a magnum of champagne and four glasses.

"What's that?" Alice asked the waiter.

"Champagne, madame," the waiter said with the patience of the mother of a retarded child. "Mumm's."

"*I* didn't order it," Alice said indignantly.

"In fact, Alice," Fred said a little testily, "*nobody* has ordered anything. Not even *I*."

"It was sent to you by the party on the other side of the dance floor," the waiter said with a nod to the north. "They sent this card."

Scrawled on a card was:

Happy anniversary!
Jack and Adele Hennessey

"Oh, those awful climbers! I'm sure they trailed us here," Alice said, taking the trouble to lower her voice somewhat. "What shall I do?"

"I think you'd better thank them Alice," Fred said patiently.

"But we can't accept this, Fred," Alice fumed. "I mean, after all, the Hennesseys are simply not the kind of people we *go* with. They're very rude and vulgar."

"I think it would be very rude and vulgar *not* to accept it, Alice," Fred said. "They only meant to do something nice. Thank you," he said to the waiter, dismissing him.

"Well, *really* . . ." Alice fumed. She liked surprises even less than she liked the Hennesseys and being caught unawares like this unsettled her. "Where are they sitting, Fred?" she hissed. "You know I can't see that far in this light without my glasses."

"Directly opposite," Fred said.

Through a clearing on the dance floor, Alice bobbed her feathers majestically and cast a vague, myopic smile into space.

"Hi, neighbors!" Jack Hennessey shouted.

"You look as cute as a doll, Mrs. Marshall!" Adele shrieked. Alice shuddered and continued leering automatically at a couple from Nyack two tables to the left of Adele Hennessey. "An' I want you two—an' the Martins, too—to come over and meet two of my favorite people."

Then the dancers swirled in between them and Alice was bliss-

fully cut off from her benefactors. She wondered *what* Chandelier was coming to, admitting people like the Hennesseys.

"Ooooh!" Beth Martin cried, returning ponderously to the table. "Champagne."

"Ssssay!" her husband called out heartily, with a fine show of teeth, "and a whole magnum of it!"

"Oh! Oh, yes," Alice said grandly. "I thought—that is, *we* thought—a little celebration."

"Go on, Fletch," Fran groaned, "slip the bandit a fin so we don't have to sit out in Siberia. I want to see Bibi Bidet, or whatever the hell she calls herself."

"Chou-Chou la Grue, Fran," Mary said gently.

His face a study in sorrow, Fletcher tipped the headwaiter and they were led to a table on the edge of the dance floor.

"Dark as a nigger's pocket in here," Fran said, sweeping her mink coat around her. The gesture knocked over two drinks and completely enveloped the head and shoulders of a buyer from Marshall Fields.

"Say, listen, Madam," a man said rising and knocking his chair over.

"Drunks!" Fran boomed. "That's what I hate about these places: you never see anyone but a bunch of drunks!"

The party made its way to a table marked "Reserved."

They seated themselves decorously and Fletch murmured something about beer.

"Hell no," Fran said to the waiter, "just bring a bottle of Haig and Haig Pinch, some ice, four glasses and a pitcher of water and put 'em on the middle of the table. That'll save us having to call you every time we need something. Oh, and bring me a pack of Parliaments—I guess you'd better make it two—and a caviar sandwich on pumpernickel. That's all."

Fletcher turned pale.

"Would you like to dance?" Randy said to Mary.

"Yes. Yes, I'd love to," she said. She could always tell about a man—or thought she always could—by the way he danced. If he bumbled and stumbled he would undoubtedly be a bumbling

and stumbling person. If he pawed her, he'd probably be one of those pawing, groping men who felt that nothing pleased a woman quite so much as having her thigh pinched black and blue. If he danced too fancily, too slickly—well, that was a bad sign, too. She had adored dancing with her own husband before he was her husband and even during the years when he was. But recently all of his terpsichorean energies had been spent steering Mrs. Popescu around the floor in the sweet service of Mammon, while—and for the same reason—she had been pawed under the tablecloth by the president of Popescu Pulse-Beat Eternal Non-Magnetic Watches.

Now she was in Randy's arms on the dance floor and it was perfectly fine. He held her tightly, but not uncomfortably close—just close enough so that she could feel his muscular thighs against her own, his large hand supporting her back. His sense of rhythm was good and at one point she felt his lips brush against her ear. Not as though it were done on purpose, but almost as though it were an accident.

She closed her eyes and melted into his arms. It was just heavenly having a beau again—someone to help her forget the mistake of her marriage, and especially someone as heavenly as this heavenly Randolph Carter Lee.

He spun her gently at the edge of the floor and through the noise of the orchestra and the chatter of the crowd, she heard a familiar voice say something that sounded like "Awk!"

She opened her eyes and, seated at the table directly below her, she looked squarely into the equine face of her sister Alice, squinting nearsightedly through the darkness.

She closed her eyes—tight—and felt herself spinning away again. As they danced away she could hear Alice's strident voice saying "Fred, I could swear I saw . . ." Then the music swelled again.

As soon as she dared, she opened her eyes again. She was only vaguely conscious of the band's tried and true rendition of "Lover." Good Lord, she thought, either I've had too much to drink or that was Alice—*and* Fred—and of course Beth and Whitney Martin at the anniversary party we were supposed to come to tonight. I've simply *got* to get out of here.

"Hello, sweetie!" a voice shrilled. It was Adele Hennessey sitting at a table with Jack Hennessey and another couple. "Having fun at Alice's anniversary?"

Again Randy whirled her out of eye-and-earshot.

She closed her eyes and buried her head in Randy's shoulder. Oh, no, no, no! she thought. This is too dreadful! One innocent dance with a new man and it's like those stories about drowning people who see their whole lives go by in review. First Alice and Fred and then the Hennesseys. She halfway expected to see Mother and Daddy and Heavenly Rest and the headmistress at Baldwin School rise up to haunt her.

It's drink, she decided. I'll just keep my eyes closed good and tight and count to ten. Then when I open them, all these people will be gone. One. Two. Three. Still in waltz time, the Chandelier band bleated out with "My Foolish Heart" in its original 1943 arrangement. She spun deliriously in Randy's arms. Four. Five. Six. Seven. Eight. Nine. *Now*, everything will be perfectly fine. *Ten!*

She opened her eyes and stared squarely into the eyes of her husband.

eight

"FRAN," MARY GASPED, THRUSTING HER WAY BACK TO THE TABLE. "I've *got* to talk to you. Seriously. *Alone*," she added gazing into Fletch's glassy eyes. "Could you come up to the Powder Room with me?"

"Sure, why not?" Fran said thickly. "I've gotta go sooner or later anyhow." Fran groped for her shoes under the table and got up unsteadily. "Keep an eye on my coat, Fletch," Fran said. Then she announced to the room at large: "With the kind of people they let into this dump, you can never tell *who* might take it!" Casting a bloodshot, but scathing, eye upon the party at the next table—an elderly couple with two Catholic priests—Fran started off in the general direction of the kitchen.

"No, Fran," she said miserably. "*Please!* It's *this* way!"

"Okay, okay," Fran said. "Keep your pants on."

Randy sat down at the table with Fletch, quite mystified and unusually ill at ease. "Heh-heh, crowded here tonight, isn't it?"

"Wha' shay?" Fletch said, focusing stonily upon his guest.

Pepe la Pucha *y la Orquestra Sudamericana del Cafe Chandelier* had just taken over the bandstand with a vengeance. Five wizened old Mexicans, Pepe la Pucha's boys made up for their lack of size and youth by a sheer, exuberant volume that put the Vienna Philharmonic to shame. A flash of hair oil, a flutter of dusty ruffled sleeves, a shrill "*Ole!*" and the *Orquestra Sudamericana* was off with its deafening repertoire of mambos, merengues, baiaos, boleros and cha-cha-chas that nearly removed the top of Randy's head. With a long, loud run on the piano, the wailing blare of a muted trumpet, the clanging of a marimba and assorted thump-

ings, rattlings and scratchings of an artillery of unidentifiable instruments, Pepe and the boys shattered the comparative quiet of the room.

"I said," Randy began again, cupping his hands, "it's crowded . . ."

"*Mi acuesto pensando en ti* . . ." Pepe bleated into the microphone.

"Cha cha cha!" Pepe's boys bellowed from behind him, thumping, rattling and scratching with all their might.

"Goddam pack of greasers!" Fletch growled. Then very slowly his head sank down onto the ash-strewn tablecloth.

"Um, excuse me," Randy said rising and hastened toward the peace and quiet of the Men's Room downstairs.

The aisle was so crowded with last-minute customers and drinks coming in before the ten o'clock show—"Service is discontinued during the Mlle. la Grue's Chansons" the menus all read—that Randy cut across the dance floor, where only an intrepid few were braving the torrid rhythms of the *Orquestra Sudamericana* He collided with a couple wriggling across the floor.

"*Me llama la Habana!*" Pepe la Pucha shouted.

"Rrrrrrrrum-ba!" Pepe's boys shrieked.

Randy got off the floor in a hurry and decided that the easiest way to cross the room was by squeezing around past the undesirable tables for two along the side wall. His progress was better than fair. He had just slithered between the mink stole of an older woman who kept crooning, "Oh, Jimmy, I adore the way you cha-cha," and the back of a chair whose occupant was saying, "Aw, c'mawn, honey, let's go back to the room."

"Please *do*," Randy muttered, wedged firmly in the traffic.

"Oh, let's just stay to hear the French sing-ger. After all, it's our honeymoon!"

Free again, Randy inched past a table where two callow kids were sipping a Tom Collins and a beer very slowly. Another Tom Collins and another bottle of Budweiser also sat on the minuscule table. How do all those people *fit* at one table? Randy wondered.

The going was easier now. Still moving crabwise, Randy picked up speed. The next thing he knew, he had collided with an empty chair in the darkness. The chair toppled over and so did Randy.

"Excuse me," he said like the true Virginia gentleman. "I'm awfully sorry, I . . ."

Getting deftly up from the floor, all charming smiles and apologies, Randy found himself face to face with Besame Bessamer, seated alone at the table.

Neither was capable of speech.

Being up and faster on his feet, Randy was at an advantage. The field ahead was clear and Randy virtually shot towards the stairway leading to the Men's Room.

Mary half pushed, half pulled Fran up the creaking carpeted stairs to a tiny mezzanine decorated with peeling crimson and two Italianate doors. One marked "Powder Room," the other "No Admittance" in florid script.

"For God's sake don't tear the clothes off my back," Fran growled, yanking herself free. "I can walk!" With that, Fran walked through the door marked "No Admittance" to reveal the boys of Chandelier's *North* American band in undershirts and paper dickies, seated around a poker table, while one, more conscientious, pumped spit out of his trombone.

"Sorry, fellahs," Fran said and lurched out, bringing with her a pungent melange of odors made up of smoke, sweat, rye, beer and an odd scent like burning tea.

"In here, Fran," Mary cried, "and please hurry. I've *got* to talk to you."

"Okay, okay," Fran said, letting herself be propelled through the door marked "Powder Room."

The shrill gabble of female voices swirled and bellied around her. Listening to the cacophony, glancing with terror at the overupholstered furniture, the dusty tufted walls, she felt for just a second that she was in some kind of padded cell out of Poe or Kafka. The place was glutted with females, each one louder than the other, save for a fattish older woman who had passed out on the sofa and moaned with dulcet profanity at her daughter who was being alternately stern and solicitous. From the toilets in the room beyond came the sound of someone being very sick and a scolding voice that kept saying: "I *told* you what'd happen, Lucy—all those Manhattans and then frog's legs and wine!"

"Oh, pleeeeeze, just get out of here. Ohhhhh!"

"Listen, Fran," Mary began . . .

"If you ladies would kinely carry on your conversation somewheres elst except the only available doorway, I should like to rejoin my excort," a hard-eyed blonde said, wriggling past them in a visible aura of *Tabu*.

"Tramp!" Fran growled.

"Slob!" the blonde snapped and minced out, bosom and rear protruding.

"Fran, *listen* . . ."

"Jesus, let me sit down for a minute. This has been a rough night," Fran groaned.

"But, Fran, listen he's . . ."

Two older women from the South brushed by them. One was saying: "S'Ah told that sales cluck at Bug-doaf's, Ah said: 'Ah don't want a red mink oh a white mink oh a *blee-ew* mink. Jus' show me a play-yun old *mink* cull-lud mink . . .' 'Skyewze me."

"Fran sit here at the dressing table and let me tell you . . ."

"The light's too bright," Fran said, slumping to a stool.

"But, Fran, I tell you *he's* here!"

The woman on the couch moaned softly again.

"Mother," the girl said, "you've *got* to pull yourself together."

"Ahhh, go uff' yuhself . . . fat ole bish . . ."

"*Mother!*"

"Fran, what am I going to do?" she cried, grasping Fran's heavy upper arm.

"Ouch!" Fran said. "Leggo. *Who's* here?"

Down the long length of the dressing table two youngish women were cautiously touching up lips that didn't look quite like their own while a third, her tight skirt hoisted unbecomingly, was straightening her stockings. They did not typify the regular Chandelier customer. The three were overdressed in sleazy chemical satins and taffetas that fairly shouted Bargain Basement—dresses designed for pure dazzlement and a couple of wearings before their elaborate ornaments wilted and drooped, their skimpy seams burst, their cheap zippers jammed and their vivid colors faded from butterfly to moth.

"Just imagine! Six *dollars* for a little dabba sweetbreads!"

"I didn't think that wine was very good, dijoo?"

"Damn, I gotta run! I juss put these on tanight, too."

"Lissen, kids," one of the girls at the dressing table said, "*dontcha* think I outa comb it out? I know Walter doesn't like it this way—all stiff-like an' tight ta my head."

"Ohhh, Jesuz," the woman on the sofa moaned.

"You've only yourself to blame, Mother," her daughter said primly.

"Oh, Marge, leave it that way just fer tonight. That's the way Mr. Rudy set it. Din't he say all the stars were wearing their hair like that?"

"Y-yess, but if Walter doesn't like it—an' I can always tell if he doesn't . . ."

"Oh, Marge, don't comb it out. Leave it like that. It's yer birthday."

"Whyn't you just shave the whole Goddamned thing off, sister?" Fran snarled. She leaned heavily onto the dressing table, her long red hair swinging over one half-closed eye.

"Well, *reely!*" one of the young women snapped.

"I'd like to know what business it is of *hers!*" the head under discussion said.

"Exactly," the third said. "C'mon, Marge, we've gotta get back to the boys. The show's about ta start." The three of them marched out indignantly with audible sniffs and a haughty swishing of rayon.

"*Fran,*" Mary said intensely, shaking Fran slightly by the shoulder. "You've got to *listen* to me. I'm telling you, he's *here.* Right here. *Tonight.*"

"*Who's* here?" Fran roared, resting her head now on both hands.

"My *husband,*" she hissed. "Fran, *my husband is here!*"

"Damn attractive. Helluva fine piece of manflesh," Fran muttered. "Ask'm over have a drink with us. Helluva nice-lookin' guy."

"But, Fran, he's here with some other *woman!* I *saw* him!"

"You're out with another man, aren't you?" Fran said with a philosophical shrug.

"But Fran, she's someone—well, I don't know *who* she is. I *think* I've seen her before, but she's dark and—well—*ra-ther* attractive, but in an obvious sort of . . ."

She glanced nervously into the mirror and saw reflected behind her the very woman she had been discussing.

Vaguely she heard Fran saying something about tit for tat and life being a two-way street, but for the moment she was incapable of hearing or speaking. Instead, she gazed spellbound at the reflection of the tall dark girl whom she melodramatically labelled as The Other Woman. She had the disturbing feeling of having seen her somewhere before.

The Other Woman wasn't paying attention to her or to anyone else in the Powder Room. The Other Woman ran a comb nervously through her long, dark hair, gave it a pat and seemed satisfied with the results.

How vain, Mary thought. Long bobs went out years ago, she continued in her condemnation, forgetful that she had just recently found Fran's dirty red mane the quintessence of glamor.

Then The Other Woman bent closer to the mirror for a closer scrutiny.

Nearsighted? Now Mary could see the face clearly in the dressing-table lights and was almost wounded to observe the purity of the skin, the depth of the large dark eyes. If The Other Woman had to exist at all, couldn't she have been considerate enough to be pockmarked or badly made up?

Now The Other Woman fumbled in her bag for a lipstick. She applied it with a hand that trembled slightly and her mouth seemed to twitch once or twice. Nor was The Other Woman's breathing absolutely regular. Drink? Dope? Lust? For all her poise, The Other Woman was obviously an extreme neurotic and in a state about something. She knew quite a lot of neurotic people, besides her sister Alice, and she had never been able to surmount the sneaking envy of the well-adjusted for the disturbed. It was so dull to be normal, so interesting to be neurotic—unless you happened to be Alice.

So this was how John had been spending his time in New York. He had dismissed her as a dreary little housewife, exiled her to the remote acres of Riveredge and had taken up with this torrid

temptress undoubtedly versed in all the bedtime tricks that nicely brought-up American girls just wouldn't know. How pathetic and boring he must have found her prosaic lovemaking as compared—and of course he must have been comparing the suburban style unfavorably with the metropolitan technique every moment of the time—to the Continental fillips of The Other Woman's.

Now The Other Woman stood back and observed herself full length.

How *inordinately* vain! For the moment Mary forgot that she herself had a triple mirror arrangement in her dressing room at Riveredge and that there wasn't a pore, a curve or a bulge on her own body which she didn't know by first name.

The Other Woman bent to adjust her stockings. Her legs were distressingly good, long and slender. Then she drew herself up to full height and turned to get a quick sideways glimpse.

It's an awfully good figure, Mary thought miserably. And it was. Tall, slim and pleasingly full. "But it's probably not all hers," she said aloud.

"What are you talking about?" Fran muttered from the depths of her hair.

"Nothing, Fran," she sighed. No doubt about it, the figure was every bit of it genuinely The Other Woman's. She'd always wanted to be that tall, queenly type instead of what used to be called a Cute Trick.

Next The Other Woman plucked a hair from the shoulder of her suit.

Going bald? No, just *one* hair, Mary observed bitterly. She also saw that The Other Woman's suit was superb, beautifully made, perfectly fitted. It was as good as anything *she* had ever owned—better. Had *he* bought and paid for it, smiling his tender, half-cocked smile as The Other Woman preened herself before the grovelling fitters at some silken couturier's? No, she decided. He hadn't. She could account for practically every hour of his life until the day they moved to Riveredge. He'd simply found this rich and distressingly ladylike-looking goddess all ready and waiting with her trap baited.

"Now, Mother, *do* try to get up," the daughter said to the fat woman on the sofa.

"Old lush!" Fran mumbled.

The Other Woman tossed a scornful glance at the mother and daughter, gave a nervous look into the mirror and strode stylishly out, perfect in every detail. *Why* did she look so familiar?

"Oh," Mary said. "Oh!"

"Whatsamatter *now?*" Fran said.

Oh, if only The Other Woman could have seemed common or out of place, badly dressed or too wide in the hips or frigid or sluttish. But why did The Other Woman have to be so supremely flawless? Then, beyond her initial shock, she began to get good and boiling mad. The nerve of him!

"The *nerve* of him," she said aloud to her own pretty reflection, "to bring That Woman right out in the open to a place like this!" How beastly men could be.

"What are you *talking* about?" Fran said, looking up with blurred eyes.

"I'm talking about her, Fran—The Other Woman. The one he was dancing with tonight. She was right here."

"Who?" Fran said, swaying dangerously on the dressing-table stool. "That old frump who's out cold on the sofa? *Your* husband? Don't make me laugh!"

"No, Fran," she whispered. "Not *that* one. The tall brunette who was just in here a second ago. She's the one who . . ."

"Sweeeeeetie!"

"Oh, Christ!" Fran moaned.

Bearing down on them was Riveredge's own Adele Hennessey, locked arm in arm with her house guest.

"Doll," Adele said, "I want you to meet one of my favorite people in the whole wide world, Peggy Slattery. Jack and I met Dan and she on the *Lah Flon-derr* coming back from France last last summer. Peg, this is my friend Mrs. Fran Hollister an' this is . . ."

" 'Scuse me," Fran said, rising to her full height, "I may be sick." With a resonant hiccough, she tottered off in the direction of the toilet.

"Hahaha!" Adele laughed almost convincingly. "That Fran! What a doll! Such a sense of hu-merr! Gee, sweetie, we tried ta ring you two-three times this afternoon. I wanted to show Peg

an' Dan your lovely home. Peg, that's the place I told you about—it's all old Regent antiques. Cute as a doll's house!"

"Oh, it's de-vine," Peg Slattery said vivaciously. "Mr. Slattery—that's my husband—and I even went over an' peeked inta the windahs when Adele told us you weren't home . . ."

"Maybe tomorrah, sweetie," Adele began.

"Oh, we jus' loved it," Mrs. Slattery continued. "I said to Mr. Slattery, 'Dan,' I said, 'wunt you just love to buy it exactly like it is?' Dan's being transferred here from Dee-troit. And Dan—that's Mr. Slattery—said, Gee . . . if it was only for sale.' "

"H-how nice," Mary said weakly.

"Gosh, cutie," Adele Hennessey interrupted, "it looks like all of Riveredge is here tonight. The whole place has danced past our table—you an' yer cute husband . . ."

Mary shuddered.

". . . and darling Fran,"—Adele had obviously implied to the Slatterys, that she and Fran not only moved in but *formed* the same circle—"and Beth and Whit (that's the *Whit-teny* Martins, Peg) and the Marshalls. I guess you must all be celebrating Alice's anna-versary. Onnussly, Peg, you should meet her sister, Alice Marshall! Alice is . . ."

Adele Hennessey never had the opportunity to make clear just exactly what Alice Marshall was. The Powder Room door banged open with a force that set Adele's skirts to rippling and Alice herself burst into the room, as ever, the vengeful *dea ex machina.*

Mary had just time to catch her breath before Alice grabbed her by the arm and swept her off in the direction of the toilet.

"I want a *word* with *you!*" Alice boomed. "Good evening, *Missus* Hennessey!"

Before Mary knew quite what had happened, Alice had herded her into the pink-tiled room that housed the toilets and the wash basins. Four toilets and four wash basins, Mary noticed inanely. Toilets to the left, wash basins to the right.

By means of her surprise attack, superior size and main force, Alice had got her sister to the far end of the room, talking every second of the time. Now Mary found herself uncomfortably trapped between Alice and a small ineffectual radiator which

mercifully was not turned on. Above the radiator an opaque glass window was wide open. She wondered if she should jump and then decided that it wasn't high enough to be fatal—only most painful.

". . . very idea, out cavorting with another . . ." Alice was saying.

She saw Alice's large pink gums, her long pink tongue and then the pink-tiled walls, the four pink wash basins, the four pink toilet doors, the pink uniform of the toilet attendant—partly relieved by a ravelled gray cardigan with a hole in the elbow—the pink jars and lotions and cleansing tissues above the wash basins; the very rosiness of it all made her feel quite, quite faint.

In aimless misery she observed Alice's feathered hat and wondered fleetingly how even Alice could have bought such a thing.

". . . worried sick about you . . . tried to reach you all afternoon . . . Fred and I . . ."

Through the open window Mary could see the neon sign that proclaimed Chandelier. She watched the letters go on, one at a time, then all together, then flash three times, then singly again.

". . . immature conduct . . ."

C-H-A-N

". . . here I am with the children and another on the way . . ."

D-E-L

". . . that you, of all people, would act in this . . ."

I-E-R (darkness) CHANDELIER (darkness)

". . . degrading, juvenile manner . . ."

CHANDELIER (darkness) CHANDELIER (darkness) CHANDELIER

The sick woman named Lucy threw up again from behind one of the pink toilet doors.

"Lucy," her invisible friend said, "it isn't that you drank too *much*. It's simply the *combination* of so many Manhattans and then all those frogs legs . . ."

"Ohhhhhhhhh."

C-H-A-N

". . . position in the community where I happen to be a . . ."

D-E-L

She now noticed that the hot-water faucets in the second and fourth pink wash basins dripped, but out of unison. The second seemed to say "plip" and the fourth "plop."

I-E-R plip-plop-plip-plop (darkness) CHANDELIER

". . . years I've spent trying to make you a mature, well adjusted . . ."

CHANDELIER (darkness) plip-plop CHANDELIER (darkness) plip-plop CHANDELIER (darkness) plip-plop-plip-plop C-H-

". . . sneak off the minute my back is turned . . ."

plip-plop-plip A-N-D

". . . our fifteenth anniversary and Fred and I invite . . ."

plip-plop I-E-R (darkness) plip-plop-plip-plop CHANDELIER

There was the roar of a toilet flushing. The third pink door banged open and Fran clomped out, her skirt hiked up behind her.

"Fran . . ." Mary began, desperate for any kind of aid, no matter how inefficient, "*help* me!"

CHANDELIER (darkness) plip-plop

"*So!*" Alice thundered. "*This* is the sort of alcoholic, neurotic milieu you prefer to cultivate! *I* ask you out for a pleasant evening with the Martins—mature, intelligent, well-bred people—and *you* go prowling out with Mrs. *Holl*-iss-ter! Of all the notorious, wanton . . ."

"Aw, go blow it out your barracks bag!" Fran snapped and lurched out of the room.

Except for a plip and plop there was a moment of exquisite silence. Mary sensed the neon sign outside flashing CHANDELIER CHANDELIER CHANDELIER. Alice made a sound somewhere between a gasp and a whinny. "*What did that woman say?*" Alice breathed.

Mary had never heard the term—or a good many of Fran's other terms—before in her life, but its very succinct crispness gave her a simple faith.

She began very quietly. "Fran said, Alice, that you are a bossy, nosey, interfering old nag and that you are to leave me alone to bungle my own life just as you have bungled yours. Now get out of my way, please. I'm going."

Jaw hanging slack, Alice staggered back against the wall, colliding noisily with a sanitary-napkin dispenser.

"Thank you, Alice," Mary said. "Good night." Sheer shock carried her through the Powder Room and down the stairway.

Randolph Carter Lee came back up from the Men's Room and tried to regain his composure. It was next to hopeless. This evening that had started out so smoothly had taken a turn for the worst. Coming face to face with Besame Bessamer after all these years had been a terrible shock. He was both embarrassed and infuriated recalling the days of his youth, Besame's outraged father and those tough Wall Street lawyers—he'd learned later that he really had had them all in the palm of his hand, if he'd only realized it; such are the penalties of youth.

But downstairs in the Men's Room a man had damned near propositioned him. Not that he had ever minded that. In fact, this man had looked like a perfect gent—as tall as Randy was, about the same age and attractive. Randy was the veteran of numberless encounters in toilets ranging from the subway to the most expensive restaurants in town and "No" was a word which Randy found almost impossible to pronounce. But tonight Randy had just too many encumberances even to bother with giving his name and address when the good-looking man had asked for it.

He wondered now if he shouldn't have. After all, another man—one who could afford to wear English suits and who looked wholesome and normal and sort of innocent—might be a far surer bet than the pretty little Riveredge wren who was tagging along with Fran Hollister. But this evening, with Besame Bessamer within shooting distance, all Randy longed for was escape from Chandelier.

Randy looked into the main room and could see Fletcher McKenzie slumped over the table alone. The rumba band was still rattling and scratching away at a gay medley of Argentinian back-breakers. Should he go back to the table and run the risk of facing Besame Bessamer again or should he wait here and simply spirit this pretty young thing away? No, he decided, better to wait here. Then there couldn't possibly be any difficulty about dividing the check.

Randy took a deep breath, forced his facial muscles to relax and gazed upwards toward the staircase that led to the Powder Room. He saw a splendid pair of legs coming down. They looked familiar. Ah, at last she was on her way down. He smiled.

Besame did not smile. Instead, she came straight toward Randy, her eyes cold.

"Uh . . ." Randy began.

"Listen," Besame hissed. "If you're following me around looking for money, let me tell you that I don't have any—at least none for *you*. But if you want *trouble*, I can give you plenty. Now get out of here and leave me alone!"

"I only . . ." Randy sputtered.

It was too late. Besame was gone.

However, Randy saw that Miss Bessamer did have a point. Randy felt a little hurt to think that Besame Bessamer could have accused him so unjustly and *more* than a little hurt to think that she could think that he might think of putting the squeeze on her when he had never managed to think of it at all. As a matter of fact, he hadn't even known that Besame was around. Even so, Randy still had such a hearty respect for money that it bordered on fear and he was now twice as eager to get out of this place. Again he waited.

Would she *never* come down? All Randy asked for tonight was escape. He promised Mammon, the only God he had ever known, that if only he could get out of Chandelier alive this evening, he would never come back again. He even began to think of taking a business course, if Grace would just give him the tuition, and going straight. Maybe he could find a rich old woman who wanted a social secretary or . . .

An enomous pair of black suede pumps clumped unsteadily down the Powder Room stairs. Randy knew this was Fran. Again the boyish smile. It was wasted. Mrs. Hollister, unable to focus her eyes, was operating on radar. Mechanically she reached the bottom of the stairs, blinked owlishly to the left and the right, and then headed for the dining room.

"Uh, Fran," Randy said, advancing toward her, "I—um . . ."

"Not tonight, kid," Fran bellowed, "but give me a call next week. The number is RI-veredge 7-4324. Christ, but I feel rocky!"

With that aristocratic farewell, Fran swayed through the dusty portieres and made her way to the table. She was just able to check on the presence of her mink coat, then she sat down on it and kept on going. The resultant picture was as touching as it was dismembered—Fletch's face on the table from the top looking down; his forehead resting on the dirty damask cloth: Fran's face looming up from down under; her chin propped on the table's edge, surrounded by bottles and pitchers and the dregs of a caviar sandwich. Two miserable, misanthropic, middle-aged babes in the woods of their own planting.

Randy was now in a stew of impatience. Good God, what was Mary doing up there, having a baby? He cracked his knuckles twice and then stopped. He'd heard somewhere that cracking the knuckles makes them larger and he was inordinately proud of his long gentleman's hands. Would she *never* come downstairs?

A door opened somewhere above him and he heard the sound of someone being sick. That certainly couldn't be she? No. At last! He saw, with the fullest appreciation, two feet approaching. Could they be called tiny, small or little? Randy decided that they were about 5½ B. Then Randy saw superb ankles and calves and then the wool dress of a color that was not of this world, but from a dream. At last the face. Her face looked tense, but then so did Randy's. But anything to get out of here . . .

Randy turned on his boyish Southern smile.

"I thought you were never coming back," Randy said. "I thought you were only a beautiful dream."

Well, she'd never heard such beautiful words in her whole life.

"Uh, Fran had something she wanted to tell me," she said.

"Listen," Randy said with elegant shyness, "would you mind if we left here—I mean just *you* and *I?* I have this terrible kind of headache . . ."

"*Mind?*" she said. "I'd give my *soul* to get out of this place!"

"Well, then," Randy said, "let's go!"

"B-but Fran and F-fletch? The check?"

"I settled the check with—uh, with Fletch. And they want to be alone." Summoning more courage, Randy added, "And so do *I.*"

"W-well, all right," she said. She knew that whatever she was about to do, it wasn't right, but she wanted to disappear from

Chandelier—forever. Really! The nerve of John! He'd probably been dancing this mystery mistress around for . . . well, for a long time; making *her* the laughingstock of . . . "Yes," she said, "do let's get out of here!"

nine

"WELL," SHE SAID NERVOUSLY AS RANDY SWITCHED ON THE LIGHT in the dim little foyer, "here we are." The statement struck her as inane, but she was now faced with a problem of social usage that was entirely new to her. Just how does a young matron address a totally strange man who might or might not try to seduce her, who might or might not ask her to spend the night and who was even now propelling her into a pitch-dark living room? She rather doubted that Mrs. Post and Mrs. Vanderbilt could come up with any answer other than "Stop!" and she wasn't quite sure that she wanted to stop; at least not quite yet.

"Just a minute, I'll light the lamps," Randy said. He was feeling a little nervous, too. He had never before brought a woman up to the apartment where he had been living as Grace's protegé. He hadn't really wanted to tonight. In the first place, it was chancey. Of course he knew that Grace was safely away in New Jersey for the weekend and that Herbert was peddling his socks around Worcester, Massachusetts, so that there was no fear of a surprise attack. But he hated to think that the tabetic old elevator man might snitch on him or that the garrulous biddy across the hall would see them and blab to Grace. So far so good. But was it really so good? He felt that Grace and Herbert's dowdy three-room flat on West Eighty-first Street was hardly the correct setting for a young Virginia gentleman of aristocratic lineage. And he was right.

However, when he was down to his last sixteen bucks, he was damned if he was going to suggest a hotel. Nor had he looked forward to driving Mary all the way out to Riveredge and getting himself marooned fifty miles from town in case she didn't want

to play. This had been the only possible solution. They had left her car parked in the garage across from Chandelier and had taken a taxi direct to the Rock Cornish Arms—a dollar-fifty right there, including tip—and then the creaking old elevator up to Grace's eyrie, while the operator gave them the fish-eye. Here they were, indeed, and Randy would have to make the best of it.

"Please forgive the looks of this place," he said. "I'm only subletting it until my own apartment is ready."

"Oh?" she said.

"Yes," Randy went on hastily. "I've just bought a duplex over on Park Avenue—a tiny little place, but good enough. So I'm sort of camping out here until my things are sent up from down home. This is kind of tacky, but it's . . ." His speech faded away into silence.

Tacky hardly did the place justice, she thought, and then hated herself for thinking it. She had speculated briefly on the tweed and leather virility of Randy's bachelor apartment while riding west in the taxicab. She didn't know quite what she had expected it to be, but certainly not this. Helplessly her dismayed gaze travelled from one monstrosity to the next.

Randy sensed her surprise—almost shock—and felt his face go hot. True, he had been kept in more opulent quarters before, but he began now to see Grace's living room for almost the first time. Grace occasionally skimmed the more popular household magazines and talked a great deal about what was "in Good Taste" and what was "in Bad Taste." And Grace was *quite* critical of the tastes of others. But some of her own decorating experiments—either from lack of cash or judgment—hadn't quite come off. There were, for example, the very walls of the room which, after Grace's heated exchange of words with the landlord, had finally been unwillingly painted by Randy himself. Grace had been very professional about mixing the color. "Dusty rose," she had called it. "A soft, subtle pink the shade of a sweet pea." But between mixing and drying something had gone wrong with the color and the shade was more reminiscent of a set of cheap dentures than of anything in the floral world. Herbert had said "Jesus, it looks like a cat house!" There had been a scene. But Grace had

brazened it out and had finally sworn that it was the *exact* shade she had had in mind.

Somehow it just wasn't quite right with the burgundy slipcover on the studio couch, the red leatherette of Herbert's Heart-Ease Converto Club Chair, the coral formica top of the chrome dinette set or the gaudy hearts and flowers of the Pennsylvania Dutch-type prints Grace had picked up in that gift shop on Amsterdam Avenue. Yes Randy could see now that from the grimy ceiling with its harsh central fixture to the profusion of Mexican scatter rugs on the floor nothing in the room was right. The blackamoor lamps, the little copper skillet ashtrays, the brandy balloon goldfish bowl, Grace's chartreuse sling chairs, the early-American maple coffee table, the copies of *Silver Screen* and *Master Detective*, the artificial ivy in the planter lamp on the television set—none of these properties lent themselves convincingly either to aristocracy or seduction.

Mary sat down timidly on the studio couch which was Randy's bed when Herbert was in town, and regretted having done so. It was just slightly too wide for her to lean back. "It's very nice," she said lamely. Her attention was then riveted to a large photograph of a middle-aged brunette simpering out of a crimson plastic frame. "Your mother?" she asked, nodding toward the picture.

"Good God, no!" Randy said. He was really shocked. It was Grace's favorite study of herself—a picture taken by a Chicago theatrical photographer in 1937 when Grace had toured in a company of *Blossom Time*, her last professional engagement. Grace kept it around to remind herself that, beaded lashes and all, she was eternally irresistible and to remind Herbert that she had thrown away not only a brilliant career, but also the best years of her life by marrying him. "It just came with the apartment," he said quickly. "I have no idea who it is."

"It's probably just as well," she said. "There's one woman I'd hate to get on the wrong side of."

Randy shuddered involuntarily. Then he said, "Let me get you a drink."

She watched Randy make his way through the cluttered room

and disappear into the kitchen. She felt uncomfortable and was angry at herself for being uncomfortable. She just wished that she could let herself go, have the courage of her convictions, thumb her nose at convention and carry on madly, passionately, scandalously with this attractive young man. It had all seemed so simple coming over here in the taxi, but the sight of this dreary apartment house, its Moorish lobby, its threadbare renaissance chairs, its smirking old elevator man, the odors of cabbage and tomato sauce that wafted through its gloomy halls had rather depressed her. The erotic schemes that had seemed so gratifyingly disreputable in the dark cab, looked a good deal less appealing beneath the harsh lights of the Rock Cornish Arms.

She hadn't been exactly certain what her conduct would be tonight until she saw her husband spinning across the dance floor at Chandelier with the Other Woman. Then, when Randy had been just as anxious to leave early as she had—even more so, it seemed—she had made up her mind. "Two can play the game," she kept telling herself. "Life is for living!" It had all sounded more daring than trite at the moment and she had been about to ask Randy to come out to Riveredge for a nightcap. But Randy had beaten her to it. "Would you like to come up to my place for a drink?" he had said. Then he had added, "Do you have something for the doorman? I seem to be out of change."

Covered with confusion, she had started fishing in her purse for a tip. The next thing she knew she had been sitting in the taxi close to Randy, her hand in his. It was then that she had decided definitely in favor of an affair. Randy was handsome, charming, well bred and two *could*, after all, play the game. She just wished that the game could look a little more attractive than it did at the moment.

Randy just hoped that Grace hadn't locked up the liquor before she went off for the weekend. Not that it would have surprised him. Herbert was a terrible cheapskate, but Grace was even tighter and mean in the bargain. You could have a drink when *Grace* wanted a drink, but at no other time. And even then it meant that you had to sit in rapt and grateful attendance while Grace lapped up the Southern Comfort and No-Cal and keep

telling her that she was the most beautiful, the most talented, the most charming woman alive and that the theatre's loss had been Herbert's gain and that no producer in his right mind would dream of refusing her the title role in anything from *The Little Colonel* to *Medea* if only Herbert weren't holding her back from her brilliant career. And then about six Southern Comforts later you had to get into the hay with Grace. It was almost easier to buy your own drink.

But no, the old battleax had overlooked a half bottle of cheap rye and some syrupy domestic crème de menthe. He wished it were Scotch or something elegant, but the rye would have to do. There were no clean glasses in the cupboard, except for some tinted pink goblets which Grace called "my champagne glasses." There were plenty of glasses in the sink, however, along with a greasy frying pan, two egg-stained plates from breakfast and a dirty coffee cup stained with Grace's magenta lipstick. He rinsed out a couple of glasses, embellished with some Disney-esque fauns and which had once contained jelly. He dusted some crumbs off a fake tole tray, loaded it up and took it back to the living room.

"Rye is about all I could find," Randy said. "I told the liquor store to send around a case of Scotch today, but I guess they just don't want the business very much. I hope you don't mind."

"Rye will be fine, thank you," she said. "Not very strong, please."

"Here," he said, "let me have your hat and your furs. Might as well be comfortable."

She gave them to Randy with a smile and he carried them reverently to the dinette table, marvelling at their softness. Randy wondered what they must have cost and guessed fairly accurately. He was a captious connoisseur of expensive things and his approval amounted to something just short of the Nobel Prize. All of his life Randy had yearned to possess the rare, the beautiful, the costly trappings of people with money and breeding and, like someone that has always wanted to have—but never quite achieved—a beautiful voice, say, he was a biased and jealous judge, acerb in his criticism, quick to spot the false note, the offkey, the flat or the shrill. And, like the frustrated singer suddenly confronted with a flawless performance of *Norma*, Randy was slavish in his

admiration of harmonious perfection. True, Randy had seen more overpowering and more affluent women in his time, but for a production of exquisitively balanced tone and artistry, his hat was off to little Mrs. Riveredge.

"Now I'll fix us some drinks," he said coming back with a smile.

"Thank you, but not too strong."

The drink, she assumed, was the beginning of the seduction. Never having been seduced before, she wondered apprehensively if everything was going to be all right. Immediately she began to regret her underwear. Of course it was perfectly exquisite stuff—a seldom worn segment of the extensive trousseau her mother had supplied and all of it real silk. But she felt that it should be a wicked black or a virginal white and preferably transparent. Actually it was a shade known as "tea rose"—no longer in fashion and exuding an air of neither sin nor virtue. Well, it was too late in the game to worry about her underwear. She just hoped that when the time came—*if* the time came—she could sneak off to the bathroom and do her own disrobing. Or was the man really *supposed* to undress you? Her stomach stirred unpleasantly.

"Would you like a little, um, *background* music?" Randy said. It was a stab at levity and a stab that both of them regretted. Grace's record library was made up almost exclusively of light-operetta selections—*The Student Prince*, *Show Boat*, *My Maryland*, all good old stand-bys whose many touring companies had offered Grace saucy bit parts during the late twenties and early thirties. Grace enjoyed singing along with the recording artists, criticizing their diction and regaling whoever might be around with shrill anecdotes about her career in the theatre.

But it seemed to Randy that gems from *The New Moon* or *Naughty Marietta* would hardly serve as the backbone of a young aristocrat's collection, let alone suitable mood music for one of life's tenderest moments. Besides, Grace's record player was badly in need of an overhauling and a new needle.

Instead, Randy switched on Herbert's radio to a station known for its all-night program of soothing and/or high-type music. Long-hair stuff would make him look more cultivated. There was a slight crackling of static and then the restful strains of *Les Nuages* burst upon the room like a dum-dum shell. Mary cowered

on the edge of the studio couch. "Oh, my God!" Randy cried and rushed to turn down the volume. "There now," he said. The music was as at once subdued and caressing. "That's pretty," Randy said. He was about to ask what it was until he thought better of it.

He sat down on the lumpy studio couch and moved a little closer to her.

She looked deep into her jelly glass and took a sip of her drink. It was ghastly.

"Drink all right?" he asked.

"Mmmmmmm. Delicious," she said, struggling not to make a face. The ice cubes had already melted, making the drink tepid and imbuing it with an especially nasty taste.

"Are you fond of Debussy?" she asked, nodding toward the radio.

"Yes," Randy said, favoring her with a soft, slow smile. "But let's not talk about music, let's talk about you—about *us*."

This sounded dimly like one of the worst lines in one of the worst plays she had ever seen and she wondered if Randy could be really as bright as he had seemed. But she credited it to an attempt at small talk and thought, a little hopefully, that perhaps he was as uncertain and ill-at-ease as she was. That at least would be sweet. If their affair was not to be as scarlet as a tropical hibiscus (and she had rather hoped it would be), then it might be the soft, delicate pink of a dewy camellia. That might be easier for a starter in sin.

She wondered what her husband would think if he could see her here and the very notion made her angry. This is too ridiculous, she thought, when he's probably in a swan bed someplace over East with that brunette. Abruptly she lifted the horrid glass. Randy said, "Well, here's to *us!*"

"Shall we go into the other room?" he said at last.

"Oh, no!" she said. Then she remembered that her sole reason for coming here had been to embark upon a life of immorality. "Well, yes. I suppose we should," she added.

She wondered how long they had been here in the living room. Once she had been dimly conscious of a man's caramel voice on

the radio saying something about a brand of aspirin and tomorrow's weather, but she had no idea of the hour. Her own watch indicated ten minutes past nine. That was a Popescu watch for you—all diamonds and no time, even if you remembered to wind it.

She tried to recall just how this phase of their relationship had begun. It seemed to her that he had been sitting next to her and looking becomingly wistful when he had said, "I get so lonely up North here. New York's a nice place for a visit, but I wouldn't want to live here—that is, before I met a nice, understanding friend like you." It was a speech that had done yeoman service with Mr. Bessamer, with Mrs. Barrett, with Grace—with all of Randy's former protectors.

Tonight it had fallen flat. Mary had writhed with agony at such a tired old string of clichés. She detested prejudice and intellectual snobbery and she had always been able to resist the prevailing Northern notion that the I.Q. dropped several points at the Mason-Dixon Line. Hadn't she known girls from the really *deep* South who had got straight A's all through college? But if this Randy couldn't say something halfway original, why did he have to say anything at all?

"Tell me about your home," she had suggested lamely.

Nothing could have been more ill advised, because that was just what he did—the pillars, the shuffling darkies, the juleps, the hunt ball. He had described his birthplace, room by room, until she felt that Greenwood House was slightly larger than Versailles, Schloss Belvedere, Buckingham Palace and the Vatican combined. She had longed, then, to meet just *one* Southerner who hadn't left a glorious Greek-revival plantation behind. If this is seduction, she had thought, give me *Little Journeys Through Homes of the Great.*

"What happened to it?" she had said.

"Burned to the ground," Randy had replied sadly.

"By the Yankees?" she had murmured, stifling a cavernous yawn.

"What?" Randy had asked politely.

"I said that was a pity." Then he had drawn out his wallet and said, "If you'd like to see a picture . . ."

Not color slides? she had thought miserably.

Fortunately not. It had been a single snapshot of a cute little russet-haired boy wrapped in a sweater. Well enough behind him to be romantically blurred were some Ionic columns and a rakish old car.

Randy bent over her. "That was me—I mean *I*—a long time ago, and that was the West Portico and my sister's runabout and . . ."

"But what a darling little boy!" she had said. "You . . ."

Just then Randy had ceased being the darling little boy and Randy the man had asserted himself. Before she could finish her sentence, his arms were around her and he was hungrily seeking her lips with his.

And she certainly had to hand it to him. Except for her husband and her brother-in-law, no man had kissed her since she had been married. Before then she had escaped, aroused but unsullied, from the embraces of dozens of young men, for she had always been as popular as she had been chaste. But as soon as she had recovered from the initial shock, she realized that Randy was an artist in his own particular field. He was full of fits and starts, tricks and nuances when it came to making love and she had to admit that he was a persuasive and overwhelming adversary. It did her little good to protest his wandering hands, his far-too-intimate intimacies. He was a willful lover, so willful that once or twice she was almost afraid of him. They had lain there on the studio couch in the vicious light grappling and panting for—well, for she didn't know how long. Gasping, throbbing with desire, now the time had come to go to the bedroom and get down to the serious business of the evening. So *this* was seduction!

"J-just let me f-fix my face," she said uncertainly. She reached into her bag for her lipstick, but her hand shook so violently that she knew she'd be unable to manage a mouth just yet. Instead, she settled for a thorough powdering, spilling a good deal on her dress.

"W-would you give me a cigarette, please?" she asked.

Randy took two out of the box, put them in his mouth, lighted them and handed one to her. "Th-thank you," she said. "And why don't you pour us each a nice fresh drink?"

"Delighted," Randy said, springing to his feet.

This both irritated her and piqued her curiosity. At moments such as this her husband had always been too overwrought with emotion for such courtly gymnastics. Was this man simply a satyr or had he been that unmoved by her?

Randy mixed two drinks and handed her the stronger one. "Shall we take these in the other room?" he asked, sitting down next to her.

"No, let's just sit here for a moment," she said, relieved that her trembling had begun to subside enough so that she could repair her face and hair.

"To *us*," Randy said, raising his glass.

"Oh, shut up!"

"What?" Randy said.

"Nothing."

By the time she had finished the cigarette and her drink—this last had been done in a matter of six large and unrefreshing gulps—she guessed that there was nothing else to do except to go along quietly. He led her masterfully into the bower shared by Herbert and Grace.

If she had found Randy's living room depressing, the bedroom struck her as sordid. Not because it was, in its own way, any worse than the living room, but because of what she guessed she was expected to do in it.

It was a small room with a busy wallpaper, a window, three doors, four mirrors and a lot of pictures frantically vying for wall space. She had never seen so much furniture in her life—a double bed, two night tables, a dresser, a chest of drawers, a desk, a chair, a dressing table, a boudoir stool, a chaise longue all in a style known as Louis the Terrible. In addition there were two overstuffed chairs that seemed to have been relegated to this room from a local funeral parlor, a blond wood table much the worse for wear, two pairs of lamps, an old magazine rack, a smoking stand, a pasteboard lingerie chest, a full-length cheval glass, a plant stand filled with dusty artificial dahlias and an old wrought-iron bridge lamp. The place smelled overpoweringly of ashtrays, perfume and moth balls.

"Oh, listen, Randy," she began nervously, "I just can't . . ."

He took her in his arms and silenced her with a long kiss. "I'll turn down the bed," he said.

She couldn't quite look as he removed the long-legged French doll dressed in silver lace and rumpled orchid rayon and drew down the soiled chenille spread. Instead she went over to the window and tried to look at something more attractive.

But there was nothing any more beautiful to be seen outside the room. The window was open and the grimy glass curtains stirred with a stagnant little breeze coming off the airshaft. Outside she could hear the nocturnal noises of the other tenants of the Rock Cornish Arms. Below her a man was brushing his teeth, spitting and gagging. Someone else was having a severe coughing fit. One radio was playing a tinny rendition of "It Might As Well Be Spring" while another extolled the virtues of a cut-rate clothing company. A cat yowled from the courtyard and a harpie's voice called out "Would you kinely turn down that radio!" There was a staccato clatter of venetian blinds being rapidly raised or lowered.

The sounds of an argument wafted across the airshaft.

"G'wan, don't stan' there an' try to tell *me* you wasn't staring at Dolores all night!"

"Aw fer Chris sake, Della."

"Don't chew Della me. I suppose I haven' got eyes I can see yer practickly undressing every woman comes inta the room."

"Aw fer God's sake, Baby!"

"I suppose if I went around to evening potties practickly stark nakid, my bress hardly covered, you'd stare at me, too!"

"Aw, fer Pete's sake, Della!"

She closed the window and turned back toward the room. Randy was at the door.

"I'll just be in the bathroom for a minute," he said. "You can take off your things here." Then he was gone. She could hear the light go on and a door close. Then she heard the sound of water running.

Dismally she surveyed the bedroom once again. The bed, now turned down, had been very badly made. One of the pillow cases was stained with grease, with black and with red. She shuddered

and turned away, coming into sharp contact with the chest of drawers. (It was almost impossible to move in the room without bumping into some piece of furniture.) The top of the chest was empty except for a gritty dresser scarf, a thin film of dust and a large photograph in a rococo lucite frame. It was a sepia study of the same woman whose photograph dominated the living room. In this picture she was dressed as a shepherdess, all paniers and spit-curls with a pointed cupid's bow smirk. The photograph was signed in a florid scrawl with circular dots over the I's. It read "Always your girl—Grace des Lys—'The Goose Girl'—1929."

She turned away toward the dressing table and then the truth hit her like a bolt of lightning. But of course! Randy was living here with some woman. Why else would the dressing table be littered with jars of cleansing cream, with bobby pins, with lipsticks, and lotions and bottles of cheap scent? How perfectly obvious!

She knew now that she wanted none of this. That she had to get out of the place immediately. And what better time than now when he was shut away in the bathroom and unable to stop her? In her panic, she opened the first door she could find. It was a closet, crowded with dresses and a disorderly row of shoes.

She closed the closet door, snatched up her purse and tiptoed quietly from the room. Her furs, her gloves, her hat were someplace in the other room. Where had Randy put them? Out in the dark little hall she could see a crack of light from what she supposed was the bathroom door. She could hear the sound of a shoe being removed.

Yes, she'd just get her things and go. He'd never be able to find her again.

Through the living-room archway she saw her hat and furs sitting plumply on the dinette table. She hurried across to get them. Just as she reached them she heard the sound of a door opening and closing. She'd have to get out of here before he could stop her. She'd simply have to . . .

The stillness was shattered by a harsh female voice calling out, "Well, that's the *last* time *I* ever go all the way to New Jersey to be insulted by Elva!"

Randy called from the bathroom: "What did you say, darling?"

"Is that you, Lover Boy?" the woman called. "You know what that God-damn, snotty Elva said . . ."

Mary saw the woman before the woman saw her—she was a tall, broad-hipped creature. She was carrying a black patent leather hatbox, and wearing a balding fur cape.

"I'll be right out, darling," Randy called from the bathroom.

"Jesus, what a trip!" the woman said, dropping her hatbox with a clatter. "And then that stinking Elva acting so damned . . ." She turned toward the living room and the two women stared at one another for an eternal moment. Paralyzed, beyond speech, Mary recognized the stranger as the woman in the photograph. Grace Something. Yes! "Always your girl—Grace des Lys—'The Goose Girl'—1929."

Grace was the first to speak. She gaped into the living room. "What the . . . Who are you? What are you . . ."

The bathroom door opened behind her and Randy emerged in a dressing gown.

The woman wheeled around and caught a glimpse of Randy. Standing there as he was in a robe and sandals, his bare chest gleaming, there was only one conclusion to draw. Grace drew it.

"Grace!" Randy breathed.

"Yesssss," she hissed. "*Grace!* Grace is right, you two-timing son of a bitch!"

Ashen, Randy tried to speak. "Grace. I can explain . . ."

"Shut up!" she screamed. "Don't you try to explain *anything* to me, you dirty little moocher! Here I keep you, feed you, buy your clothes and the minute my back is turned you drag some floozie up to *my* apartment. Well I won't have it. Do you *hear?* I won't *have* it!" Her voice had now risen to a screech.

"Grace, sweetheart," Randy began, "I know this looks funny, but I can . . ."

"You know good an' damn well what you can do, you no-good sneak," Grace screamed. "You can get out of my house! *Tonight! Now!* I'm sick of paying your bills and then having you . . ."

"Please, Grace," Randy implored. "If you'd only . . ."

"*Shut up!*" Grace bellowed.

Randy shut up. There was little choice.

Then Grace turned slowly toward the living room, her finger

levelled theatrically. She began her tirade slowly, quietly. "As for *yeu-oo* . . ." Grace said haughtily.

Mary realized that this virago was denouncing her, that she was being called names she didn't even understand, that she was being roundly insulted and wrongly accused of all kinds of crimes. But she was too horrified, too terrified even to hear the words. Seeing this horrible fury standing at the threshold of the room, the terms "Dramatic Training" and "Stage Presence" came instantly to mind. It was all such bad theater. The torrent of words kept pouring forth shrilly and viciously, but she didn't even hear them. As with Alice earlier this evening, she could only think of inconsequentials. First she wondered why everything terrible seemed to happen to her in rooms that were painted pink. Numbly, she dismissed the problem of pink as too large to cope with at the moment.

She had concentrated on Alice's terrible hat earlier this evening, now she drank in the horror that was Grace: the swelling ankles above the scuffed pumps: the black crepe dress, too tight across the middle; the mended fabric gloves with a split seam at the accusatory index finger so that a long, reddened nail stuck out like the beak of a bird; the pathetic fur cape; the sagging throat above the myriads of fake pearls; the badly painted shrew's face; the skittish, but soiled white hat; and the hair.

Yes, it was the hair that fascinated her most. It was black, a solid, dull, unbelievable black. It was the lifeless black of a licorice stick, the black of an old station stove, the black of a battered man's umbrella. It hung in lank, dead curls and ringlets around the woman's heavy neck, in a flirtatious and presumably softening half-bang beneath her bobbing hat.

As the denunciation roared on Mary wondered whether Grace dyed it herself or if she made Randy dye it for her in a series of quarrelsome, pungent sessions bent over the washbasin. What on earth could they use to get human hair such a dreadful, deathly black? Shoe polish? Stove blacking? India ink? She was so curious, even in her anesthesia of misery, that she almost wanted to interrupt the great denunciation and ask. No, she thought deliriously, that would be rude. Now she really would have to collect her

wits and try to listen to what this madwoman was saying. Some sort of reply might be expected.

". . . I found him when he was down and out. No job. Locked out of his room. *Hungry* even! *I* took care of him. I . . ." Could it be some kind of coal product, she wondered. ". . . I even bought him his *shoes!* When he needed money, I . . ." Maybe it wasn't really hair at all, maybe it was patent leather just fitted onto her head. ". . . I gave him all the love, all the help I could. I . . ." Or could it be one of those wigs made out of synthetics like Nylon or mohair or something like that? ". . . and what did I ask in return? *Nothing!* Nothing except the affection and respect you'd give to a . . ." Or maybe this Grace had dipped her head, inadvertantly, into a bucket of tar. She supposed that such eccentric accidents *could* happen. ". . . but let me tell *you,* sister, I'm *finished* with him!" The tears began to run down Grace's face now and Mary wondered if they, too, would turn black. They did. "But *you* can have him. He's getting out of *my* place *tonight* and you can take him *with* you! Just *go!* Get out *now!* Go and leave me a-lo-o-o-one."

Grace burst into a fit of weeping. But it wasn't a good, honest, healthy cry. She just stood there in the middle of her horrible room racked and heaving with dry, strangulated sobs.

Oh, the poor thing, Mary thought. The poor old thing! She had originally placed Grace at around forty-five, now she felt that Grace was a good bit closer to sixty.

Except for the sobs, the room was still. Hypnotized by the horror of what she had been through, Mary gathered up her hat and her furs. She spoke automatically, almost as though what she was saying was a little speech of thanks learned by rote and delivered to the hostess at the end of some child's birthday party. "I'm awfully sorry to have stayed so late," she blurted. "I really must be going. Thank you for the drink." She tiptoed past the weeping figure of Grace. "I'm sorry," she said again.

"Listen," Randy said, reaching out and grasping her wrist, "wait till I get dressed. I'll drive you home. You shouldn't be out alone . . . I mean, I . . ."

She looked him up and down disinterestedly. In the relentless

light of the room Randy was a lot less attractive. Like Randy, his brocade dressing gown had undoubtedly seen better days. It was spotted and woefully frayed. *Just* like Randy.

"Wait," Randy said again. "I can send for my things tomorrow. We can go to . . ."

"How shabby you are," she said calmly. "How *pathetically* shabby."

In a trance, she opened the door, went out into the corridor and rang for the elevator. She heard Randy back in the apartment saying "Grace, sweetheart. Grace, listen to me. Grace . . ." The elevator door slid open. She stepped inside. The operator closed it with a bang and that was the last she heard of Randy.

ten

It wasn't until she reached the fresh air—until she found herself standing under the tattered canopy of the Rock Cornish Arms—that reality crowded in on her.

But when it struck it nearly knocked her flat. The terrible cheapness and slickness and glibness and phoniness of her fine Virginia gentleman. Randolph Carter Lee, pseudo Southern aristocrat, kept gentleman and professional tom cat. Inquiries invited. He was no better than a gigolo, and not honest enough to admit to being one. Greenwood House in old Virginny! That was rich! The sights, the smells, the squalor of that hideous apartment! The awful liquor. Even the thought of letting a man like that touch her made her stomach churn.

And then Grace! Poor, ludicrous, melodramatic old Grace! Grace, who looked like nothing so much as a down-and-out old doxie, ruining her hair and her health and her husband—whoever he might be—just to keep an utter stinker like Randy.

"But then," she said aloud, "am I any better than Grace?" Right then there appeared to be little difference save for the age, income and hair. Weren't they really cut of the same cloth—two restive married women hungry for adventure, for romance, for the flattery and cajolery that a heel like Randy—or any other young bounder so disposed—could supply.

Of course I meant to go, she reasoned with herself. I was on my way out when—when Grace arrived. Then she became relentlessly hard with herself. But was that because of virtue or fear or just plain snobbery? Would I have given in to him if the apartment had been halfway decent—or even clean? If I hadn't been certain,

all of a sudden, that it was another woman's apartment? If he'd had nice bachelor's quarters like Fletcher McKenzie?

Then the whole ghastly day revolved in her mind: the terrible fight with her husband this morning; Alice; Fran; Fran's frightening deaf-mute charwoman; the shopping center; the luncheon; Lisa's party; dinner in Fletch's apartment; the night club; her husband out dancing with the Other Woman, just as though nothing had ever happened; Adele Hennessey and her friend Mrs. Slattery in the ladies' room; Alice again; then that session with Randy; Grace; and finally the horrid old elevator man who had grinned at her with toothless gums and said, "Guess the old cat came back and caught you mice!"

Her stomach lurched once more and she swayed to the curb and considered getting sick between the bumpers of two cars. Embedded in the chromium were the names Oldsmobile and De Soto. Oldsmobile in front, De Soto behind. But she couldn't bring herself to it. She went back to the building and leaned against it.

"What's that, girlie?" a man's voice said.

She looked up and saw a man standing there. He was sinister and forbidding in the darkness.

"I didn't say anything," she quivered.

"Listen, honey," the man said genially, "I bet you an' me could have some fun together. How's about . . ." He touched her elbow.

"Get away from me!" she cried. "Leave me alone!" She broke away from him and ran wildly.

She pounded over the echoing pavements in her high heels, too frightened even to look back. She ran helplessly and hopelessly, across the wide avenue and right to the entrance of Central Park.

A policeman stopped her.

"I wouldn't go in there alone, lady," he said. "Not at this hour. Dangerous."

"Oh, if you'll only help me!" she sobbed. "I just want to get away from here. To go home!"

He looked her over casually, taking in the dress and the furs.

"Will a taxi do?" he asked. "Or do you need subway fare?"

"Oh, a taxi, please," she panted. "If you'd just help me to get one. I'd be so—I'd be so grateful."

"Surest thing you know, lady," the policeman said. "You got the fare?"

"Oh, yes. If you'd just . . ."

He stepped to the curb and waved his white-gloved hand. A taxicab, garishly yellow and green and violet, twinkling with colored lights, pulled up.

"Just take this little lady home, bud," the policeman said. He opened the door and helped her in.

"Thank you so very . . ."

"That's okay, lady," the officer said. "Take it easy." He slammed the door.

"Where to, lady?" the driver asked.

"Home, please," she sighed.

"Sure, sister, but where's home? Noo Yawk's a big city."

"Oh," she said. "Oh, yes. Why, it's one-two-three East Sixty-eighth Street."

"Okay by me, sister," the driver said, turning on the meter. "You just gotta tell me, that's all. I ain't psychic or anything like that. I bin drivin' a hack fer goin' on ten years now, I jus' gotta know the *add*-ress. All I ast was . . ."

She closed her eyes and her ears and remained in oblivion as he drove the cab through Central Park.

She had paid off the cab and watched it roll off before she realized her mistake. Of *course* this wasn't home! This had been home a year ago. This had been home in the pre-Popescu Pulse-Beat days, in the one-room-kitchenette-and-bath days, in the days when their income was limited and their happiness boundless. Home, now, was fifty miles up the Hudson River. Home was a fashionable Regency pavilion in fashionable Riveredge, and here she stood like a sentimental, romantic fool—and a fairly absent-minded one, at that—gaping at the place where once she had lived.

She knew that she had no business being here. That if she had any sense she'd hail a cab on the corner, go back to the garage across from Chandelier, pick up her car and drive out to Riveredge before it became too late. But she couldn't tear herself away from the spot.

She had always loved this building; not a building, really, but the turn-of-the-century conceit of a newly rich industrialist. He and his wife had felt that a limestone town house on a fashionable New York side street was essential to social advancement. The man had spared no effort in acquiring his tiny mansion. Thirty years later his son had spared no effort in ridding himself of it. The house had been converted into compact, inefficient little apartments, equipped with an iniquitous self-service elevator and a cantankerous superintendent, and rented out to the young, the frivolous and the undemanding.

Their apartment had been the old drawing room, one flight up at the front of the house, elegant with its French windows, its boiseries, its marble mantel and its scuffed parquet. In it she had reigned like a queen.

She looked longingly up at the windows of what had once been her domain. They were dark and curtainless. In the faint light cast by the street lamp she saw a sign that read APARTMENT TO LET.

"Oh no!" she said. "It just couldn't be vacant! Not *again!*"

Of course there were reasons for it to be vacant and on a permanent basis. The irregular supply of hot water, the two-burner stove, the minuscule refrigerator, the vicious indifference of the super. Oh, but the charm of the place! Its memories.

"I wonder if I could manage to swing it alone," she said.

Then she became conscious of someone watching her. She turned around and saw the figure of a man standing under one of the plane trees across the street, the collar of his jacket pulled up. Her heart began beating faster. She felt like running again. But then she summoned together the fragments of her courage. Why be afraid? After all, this was *her* old neighborhood. *Her block!* It was different from being molested in a strange section of the city. If the thug tried anything funny, she only had to dash across the street to the benevolent doorman. He had always hailed taxis for them and always refused to be tipped. Apparently he had liked her. Hadn't he said that she and John were the nicest young couple on the block? And hadn't she given him a lovely cashmere sweater to keep his old bones warm when they moved away?

No, she had nothing to fear. She took a deep breath, faced the

dim figure across the street squarely and said in a loud, imperious voice, "Sir, are you following me?"

"No, madam," the answer reverberated back, "I am not!"

"Oh! It's you!" she breathed.

It was the voice of her husband.

She watched him coming toward her from across the street with almost a feeling of relief. If only he hadn't followed her to the Rock Cornish Arms. If only he hadn't been spying on her. She didn't think that she could endure the humiliation of that.

"What are you doing out on the streets alone at night?" he asked in a tone of supreme unfriendliness.

"I don't see that it's any concern of yours," she said crisply. "Certainly not after this morning."

"Believe me," he said, "it's none of my affair *where* you go. But I shouldn't like to see *any* woman mugged or raped." That was certainly white of him!

"How thoughtful. I had no idea you cared so *very* deeply."

"I thought that you were probably safe at home until I saw you *cavorting* around Chandelier tonight."

How like a man. Of course *he* could be out all day and night doing God knows what, but he *expected* little Cinderella to be sitting out in Riveredge with her feet in the ashes!

"Oh, I could tell you were thinking about me every minute," she said elaborately. "I suppose that brunette snake was your marriage counselor."

"She happened to be Popescu's stepdaughter," he said. "So don't try to make anything out of that."

Of course! That's who the Other Woman had been. Besame Bessamer, the girl she had seen on that terrible *Pulse Beat* show last night. At least now she knew who the menace was. Well, he and Besame could just go and jump through the television tube together. "Who cares who she is or what she means to you," she said coldly. "I simply remarked that you didn't seem to be holed up in the exclusive male society of the Bacchus Club or some wholesome Y.M.C.A."

"The Bacchus Club is closed," he said.

"What a loss!" She had always detested the place, not that she'd ever been permitted past the front hall.

"And *you* seem to have picked up a prize package in Uncle Tom, or whoever that big economy-size helping of corn pone was."

"He's some friend of Fran Hollister's," she said levelly. "I don't even remember his name." There. That had been casual enough.

"Oh, Fran Hollister, eh?" he said unpleasantly. "You *are* running with a smart set."

Of course he was right. Fran Hollister actually had all the glamor of a sow. Fran was hardly worth the powder to blow her up. But she wasn't going to let *him* say so.

"After all," she said primly, "Fran and I were schoolmates at Baldwin and . . ." Then she gave up the pretense. "Oh, lay off please. Go away and leave me alone. I've spent the day with such awful people that I . . ."

"So have I," he said quietly.

Well, *that* was something of a confession, but she wasn't going to let it glide by quite so easily. "What?" she said. "With those charming Popescus and their gifted daughter? I should think you'd call it furthering your career. You'll get ahead."

He'd get ahead, all right. Even if Lillian Popescu danced his arches right through his shoes.

"Maybe," he said. "But not with Popescu. I'm quitting my job."

She didn't believe him for a second.

"*Quitting?*" she said. "Don't kid, please." But she wasn't entirely sure that he was kidding.

"If you're really still that interested, just try to call my office on Monday. You'll only get Toby."

What *was* he talking about? Certainly not about that infantile old school chum of his. That roommate from college who'd been his best man at their wedding, borrowed five hundred dollars from Mother and goosed Alice at the reception?

"Toby?" she said, incredulously. "Toby *Wentworth?* What does little Huckleberry Finn know about running a television show?"

"Nothing," he said delphically. "But he knows enough about Popescu to hang him. Or at least he will. It should be interesting to watch—like a fight to the finish between a ferret and a rat."

"What on earth are you talking about?" He was obviously just playing on her curiosity, and it was a mean trick.

"I didn't think you'd care," he said brutally.

"I don't," she said with delicately arched brows. "Really. Not in the least. I just love standing out in the middle of the street in the middle of the night making idiotic conversation with my ex-husband." She paused for just a second to let that sink in. Then she felt a little sorry for having said it. He looked cold and miserable standing there with his suit collar turned up around his ears. "Aren't you cold?"

"No, I am *not*," he answered indignantly. "Furthermore, I am not your *ex*-husband."

"You might as well be," she said calmly, just in case he was entertaining any illusions about a touching reconciliation.

"I suppose you're right," he said. Well, she liked that!

"However," she said hurriedly, "there's no reason why we can't act like civilized people. I hope you'll be very happy." And that was true, she felt. She wanted neither to act like a churl nor to have him suffer very much. "I just never want to see you again, that's all."

"That suits me fine," he said. "I would like to say, though, that I'm sorry about the coffee pot this morning." How generous of him! "That seemed to bring the whole thing to a . . ."

She decided that she could be magnanimous, too, but only within certain limits. "Oh, don't worry about that. It made lousy coffee anyhow. But of course you're right. It takes more than a broken coffee pot to ruin a marriage." She had planned to stop right there, but she felt impelled to go on. "It takes things like a husband who suddenly ends up married to his job and a Manfred Popescu pinching your rear and a year or so isolated in a stagnant backwater like Riveredge and . . ."

"Well," he said, interrupting her just as though she had never opened her mouth, "this *is* interesting. After you nearly drove me to bankruptcy moving out there with your sister Alice and a pack of snobs and squares to face on the commuters' train twice a day . . ."

Oh, the unfairness of a man! She wouldn't even listen to him any longer.

"Don't blame *me* for Riveredge," she said flatly. "I hate it. I always have."

"That's a pity. The house is in your name." And so it was.

"Well, it won't be for long," she said lifting her chin defiantly. "I'll sell it."

"Good," he said. "That'll give you a marriage settlement of some forty or fifty thousand dollars, provided you can find anyone who's fool enough to buy the place."

Oh, he thought he knew so much! So smug. So manly. Thinking he could just dump a wife and then pay her off with a chunk of cash. Well, if he tried to give her any money she'd throw it right back into his teeth. "Thank you, but I happen to be an independent, educated woman quite able to earn my own living without alimony *or* a settlement. And you may quote me in court." That covered that. And now to let him know that she wasn't entirely without business acumen. "But in case you should be interested, I do know of a couple of prize customers."

"Who?" he asked suspiciously.

"They're two of the Hennesseys' favorite people—Dan and Peggy Slattery from Dee-troit." Now it dawned on her that the Slatterys were just not what Riveredge called "the Riveredge Sort." Well, that was *his* lookout. "The only trouble is that you could never get them past the Membership Committee. That's too bad for *you*."

"Do you *really* know somebody who might want that house?" he asked.

"Yes indeed," she said archly. "Mrs. Slattery peeked through the windows and pronounced it de-vine. They want to buy it lock, stock and barrel. But as I say, they're even worse than the Hennesseys. That snobbish Membership Committee would never . . ."

"I think the Membership Committee could be handled," he said with maddening smugness. "A word or two with Whitney Martin and your friends would be in like Flynn."

Her friends. She liked that! And just when had he started getting so cosy with Whit Martin? He'd never been able to be more than civil to Whitney before. "That's your worry," she said with heroic indifference. "Not mine. You bought the house. You sell it. *I'm* going to try to get back into our old place."

"Here?" he said, moving a shoulder toward the general direction of their old apartment.

"You can see it's for rent," she said.

"Oh really?" he said. He was sounding awfully casual. "I just happened to be strolling past and kind of thought of moving back myself." Oh she could see it right now. The procession of blondes and redheads snaking their way up the stairs for a session of Sibelius with that attractive divorced man.

"You'll undoubtedly get it," she said with resignation. "You have all the money."

"That's a hot one!"

"What?"

"Nothing."

A querulous voice called down from above: "Would you two mind not standing directly below my window and talking at the tops of your lungs? It's one o'clock in the morning!"

He looked up smiling—that enchanting smile! "Sorry," he called.

"My God," she said laughing unhappily, "that's old Mrs. Larson who used to live above us and grow all the ivy." She had had words with Mrs. Larson before—especially the time when she had lopped off the ends of Mrs. Larson's ivy because it overhung their windows by a good two feet.

"I suppose she still bangs on the pipes every time the Condons upstairs pour a martini," he said good naturedly.

She began to relax a little. "Yes, those were awfully funny years living here at one-two-three. Well," she added primly, looking at her watch which was still stopped, "Mrs. Larson does have a point. I've got to be going anyhow."

"Where?" So, he really was concerned.

"I can't see how that's any of your business," she replied regally. "But as long as you ask, either back to the garage and then to Riveredge, or else to some hotel. I haven't decided which."

"You really oughtn't to be running around alone at night," he said. Still treating her as though she couldn't take care of herself. "No woman in her right mind . . ."

"Thank you for your vote of confidence," she said lifting her nose into the air. "But we're better off going our separate ways. I think you made that *quite* clear this morning."

Oh, please God, don't let me cry! she thought. Just let me get

through this interminable interview and off someplace by myself. Just let me bear up until he gets around the corner and then I can climb into a taxi and have a good old-fashioned weep.

She took a deep breath and plunged on. "I've managed beautifully by myself all day. So beautifully, in fact that . . ." Somehow she couldn't help herself. "That I'm just *miserable!*" The tears poured down her cheeks. She just stood there crying, too weak to stop and too strong to dissolve into his arms. "Oh, darling, I've been so lonely and frightened and unhappy. I've—I've . . ." This was too humiliating. She'd have to stop it. "Have you a hankie?"

"Here," he said, handing her the handkerchief from his breast pocket.

She blew her nose noisily, aware that the effect wasn't particularly attractive. She stood straighter and managed to get some sort of tenuous control over herself. "Thank you," she said more steadily. "I'll have it laundered and return it."

"Don't bother," he said, "I have dozens." Yes, he *was* born without a heart. Then she saw his whole face change. "Listen," he said suddenly, "you think *you've* suffered. I've never spent such a day in all my life." What was he talking about? I'd rather work all year in that Goddamned garden than spend another minute like the minutes I've put in today."

She looked up at him and noticed that at last the granite jaw had crumbled like chalk. "Do you honestly mean," she said slowly, "that the Other Woman—I mean the Bessamer girl—is nothing to you? That she isn't your mistress? That you only walked out this morning because of . . ."

He paused. Uh-huh. Inventing the Big Lie. "I swear that I've seen her just four times in my life," he said slowly. "First when she read for the part; again at dress rehearsal; last night over TV; and today for the last time." She realized that this was plausible. She wanted so much to believe him. "She means *less* than nothing to me. With both of us it was purely business." She decided that this could very easily be true, although she would have preferred a less dazzling business associate.

"You're telling the truth?" she said. It was almost as much a statement as a question.

"I'm telling the truth," he sighed. She decided that he was. "But Uncle Tom?"

Oh, Lord, she thought, I might have known that this was coming. "This friend of Fran's?" he asked pointedly.

"Who," she said, "Randy?"

"I thought you didn't even know his name!"

"I don't," she said. It was true. She had forced herself to forget as much about Randy as possible. "Randy's all I remember." That wasn't quite *all* she remembered but it was more than she wanted to remember. This was a moment for exact speech and exact truth. But within limits. Could she, for example, allow herself to tell him that she had almost been duped by a cardboard gentleman, a shabby little he-whore who lived on the bounty of lonely women? Not very well. That would be too humiliating. Nor would it be entirely necessary. But within the framework of fact, she could make it quite clear that it had been an ill-advised thing of the moment, wholly regretted and almost forgotten. "He's just someone I met with Fran five or six hours ago." True. "He's not a bit nice." Oh, so true! "None of Fran's friends could be called nice." True again. "Neither could Fran, in fact." There now. She had purged herself of even that last pretense. She just hoped that he believed her because it was the plain truth.

"God, but I'm sick of terrible people," he said. "After today, I . . ."

"So am I. And I'm so afraid that we've been turning into terrible people ourselves. Vicious, grasping, scheming, mean, withered people—just like the ones I've been with all afternoon and all night." Fran, Fletch, Randy, Mrs. Updike, Gerald, Ronny, Grace; yes, they all seemed to fit within that category. "And we're on our way, you know. I've even *admired* some of them." There again was an admission, and a discomforting one. "But their terribleness rubs off. I can *feel* it on me."

"Well," he said, "it won't any longer." Was this a bid to come back, and, if so, did he really *mean* it? "That is, it *wouldn't* any longer, if only we could get our feet back on the ground."

Eagerly she said, "You mean *off* the ground. Off the hallowed soil of Riveredge."

"And off the sandy soil of the Villa Manfrillian and off the

dance floor of El Morocco and off . . ." He really meant it! He *had* broken with the Popescus! Never again a night of gaiety, a trip to their garish home in Palm Beach on their vulgar yacht.

"We're too old for that sort of life, darling," she said recklessly. "I'm nearly thirty and . . . Well, I mean we should be grown up and . . ."

"And forget all this nonsense about who has the smartest house and the biggest car and the most progressive children. . ." he blurted. How wonderful! He meant it. He'd be willing to leave Riveredge and take her with him! "*Could* we, darling? Could we just chuck the whole thing and start right back where we were before. *Right here?*" Right here where they had been alone and happy and together!

"*Will* you?" he shouted. Would she indeed! "Remember," he said warningly. "I'm off the payroll. There won't be any Mr. Santa Claus with a fat check every week . . ."

As though she cared! "And no fat hand on my thigh every night," she said. "Of *course* you'll quit. You never should have gone there. It was all my fault. You should have refused. You should have finished your play. You've wasted a whole year with Popescu." She had never before admitted any blame for his connection with *Pulse Beat,* but she knew it was true. He had gone there in order to indulge her; to give her the things he thought would make her happy. She felt ten years younger already.

"Not wasted," he said. "I've learned a lot. I've met a lot of people who *know* I can write."

"You'll finish it then?" she said rapturously. "We'll sell the house and come back here. I'll get another job . . ."

"And a baby?" he asked.

"Certainly a baby. Several perhaps. But we'll worry about that when the time comes. And when that time *does* come, there won't be any overpriced little housing development, no interfering sister, no Dr. Needles. We'll raise our children where we're happy. Then they'll be happy." She was breathless with excitement.

"In one room?" he asked.

"Perhaps in two or three." Other people managed, why shouldn't they? "But only when the time comes and then not in Riveredge. I don't even want to go back there tonight."

"Where do you want to go?" he asked.

She threw her natural conservatism into the air and watched it explode. "Let's go to a hotel. They'll think we're lovers—no luggage, no reservation, no nightie . . ." She felt as wicked as she had earlier this evening. But wicked in a nice, moral way.

"No money," he said. "It's a . . ."

She didn't even listen. If fate had meant her to have a kept gentleman tonight, that gentleman would be her husband who was, after all, the most attractive man in the world. "I have some," she said. "We'll go nearby. The Margate's said to be sinful. Then we can get up first thing in the morning and beard the superintendent here. I know he'll let us come back. You tipped him when we left, didn't you?"

"I gave him millions, my beloved." The darling! The generous darling!

"Then come, darling," she was so impatient. "Come before some horrible thing or some terrible person happens along to ruin everything."

"Where to?" he asked. "The Margate?"

"*Any* place," she said wildly. "Just so we get there soon enough to save our lives—our *life*."

She saw a car turn slowly into East Sixty-eighth Street from Park Avenue. She was blinded, for a second, by its headlights.

"Stop the car, Fred," a voice shrieked. "*There* they are!"

She was petrified. She couldn't let the magic die.

"Wait, you two," the voice called. "I want a word with you!"

"My God," he groaned. "It's *Alice!*"

Her heart stopped beating. Then she tugged at his sleeve. "Run for it! It's our only chance!"

She felt him grab her hand and they dashed down the street together.

"Turn the car around, Fred," Alice called. "Follow them!"

She heard poor Fred's weary voice say, "I'm afraid we can't, dear. It's a one-way street."

Laughing and running down the sidewalk with her hand secure in his, she couldn't for the life of her remember just what their quarrel had been about.